SOFT LIKE
THUNDER
SAVAGE U
Special Edition

J. Wolf

This is for my mom who thought she wasted her money when I dropped out of college after just one year. Look at me putting my knowledge of dorms and classes and fraternities to good use!

Prologue

Helen

One Year Ago

I KNEW WHAT TROUBLE looked like.

It came in a lot of forms, some more easily recognizable than others. Today, it was brown-haired boys, rich and cocky with Daddy's money, basking in their first taste of real freedom.

College freshman boys. They descended on Savage River every year. Once their moms finished decorating their dorm rooms to look like their childhood bedroom take two, and their dads patted them on the back and slipped a few condoms in their pockets, they'd ditch the illustrious Savage University campus to explore the local terrain.

And these boys...these boys with perfect teeth, unblemished skin, bright eyes, and even brighter futures, *always* wandered in to Savage Wheelz. I'd been a skater since I could walk. One look at the three boys who sauntered in under the entrance's jingling bell was all I needed to tell they'd never touched a skateboard, much less ridden one.

They weren't here to buy skateboards. They were here to buy trouble.

I'd give them that for free.

I fingered the bat under the counter, narrowing my eyes on the three of them. One was legit, looking around at the T-shirts and decks on the walls. Wheelz was cool as hell, so I was offended the other two weren't even sparing our gear a glance. They were huddled together, probably discussing which of them was going to talk to me first.

I'd worked at Savage Wheelz since I was fourteen. This song and dance was more than familiar. Boys like them came in at the end of every summer looking to score in more ways than one. Even at fourteen, I never held back from breaking down the truth in tiny little words their smooth brains would understand: *this bitch does not like rich boys.*

That had not changed a single bit in the last four years, and these three boys reeked of money. There were probably some decent, rich people out there. Maybe I'd even met them and hadn't known. But like I said, I knew trouble, and this brand of rich boy wielded their money like a shield. From behind it, they could wreak havoc and never feel the bounce back.

I knew that all too well.

A decision made, one of the boys approached. He was what I thought of as medium. That bland, in-the-middle type, forgettable the second they were out of sight. Medium brown hair, medium attractive, medium height, medium, medium, medium. I'd feel sorry for his middling ass if he didn't look like he was one wild frat party away from roofying someone.

Bracing my hands on the counter, I gave him a big, fake smile. Customer service was my jam. "How can I help you, gentlemen?"

He stopped on the other side of the counter and rubbed his chin. Baby smooth, of course. One day, he'd probably have a medium amount of stubble.

"Hey. Are you from Savage River?"

I lowered my chin. "I am. Let me guess, you're new in town." I cocked a hip and bit the corner of my lip. Then, as if something dawned on me, I shook my finger at him. "Oh, I bet you're here for the furry convention. Honestly, I admire you guys for being true to yourselves. Some people say furries are sick, but what do they know?"

Medium guy stiffened. No sense of humor, that one. His friend over by the painted deck chuckled low, drawing my eye. He was looking at me now instead of the merchandise. Blue eyes twinkled right at me. I'd never seen eyes twinkle in my life. That must've been a rich boy thing.

The other guy, who was a bit too tall and lanky to be medium like his friend, approached the counter too. Sadly, he wasn't laughing.

"We go to Savage U," Lanky guy announced.

I let my mouth fall open like I was impressed. "You do? Wow. Was it hard to get in? That's just so impressive."

Lanky grinned. His teeth were big and white. I'd never seen any straighter. Did eighteen-year-olds get veneers? Not the ones I knew, but they weren't richie riches.

"We worked hard to get where we are," he explained like I was two. "Are you going to college?"

"Nope." I popped the P. "It's not part of my life plan. But good for you."

"Interesting choice. Do you plan on working at a skate shop all your life?" Lanky asked.

I folded my arms across my chest. "You have to pay my bills before you get to question my life choices. If you brought your debit card, then sure, I'm game to explain my five-year plan. If you want the ten-year plan, we're going to have to go a tad bigger."

Another laugh from Blue Eyes pulled my attention. His friends glanced back at him too. He had an elbow propped on a rack, his other hand tucked in the pocket of his shorts. Unbothered and casual, his wide grin said he was enjoying the hell out of the show. I raised a brow. His smile widened even more.

Medium cleared his throat, bringing my attention back to him. "Listen, we got off on the wrong foot."

"Did we? I'm not convinced we did," I answered. "I think we're on the exact right foot."

Medium huffed. "Are you allowed to speak to customers that way?"

I batted my lashes at him. "Are there any customers in here?"

He mimicked my stance, bracing his hands wide on the counter, bringing his face far too close to mine. I straightened, fingering the bat once more.

"We have money to spend, and we're more than willing to part with it. Now, you," his medium-brown eyes flicked over me, "look like the kind of girl who might need money."

"Really? What kind of girl is that?"

Ignoring my question, Medium went on. "We're new in town. Classes start next week, but parties are going strong all weekend," he thumbed in the direction of Blue Eyes, "and my boy could use a pick-me-up."

"Cool," I said dryly.

Lanky rolled his eyes. "Seriously, does your boss know how you deal with customers?"

"Yep."

My boss, Preston, felt comfortable leaving me alone in the store for a few hours at a time *because* of how I dealt with customers. I could be cool when they were cool, but I didn't take any shit, and I wasn't afraid to take care of what needed taking care of.

Blue Eyes finally had something to say. "Come on. Let's go. This was a stupid idea."

My chin lifted, and I addressed Lanky and Medium, studiously avoiding those twinkly blue eyes. "Your friend is obviously the brains of the bunch."

Medium's knuckles went white on the counter, and his jaw clenched. "We simply haven't come to an understanding yet. As I said, we got off on the wrong foot. I'm Deacon," he gestured to Lanky, "this is Daniel, and the kid lurking behind me is Theo."

I said nothing.

Deacon pressed on. "Do you give skating lessons?"

I canted my head. "Is that a real question?"

"Sure." He rocked back on his heels, smug in his richness.

"I do on occasion when I think someone really wants to learn. I'm too busy to waste my time with posers." My nail tapped on my bat. "I know that's not why you're in here. If you're not interested in the merchandise, I'll have to ask you to leave. Nothing else is for sale here."

Lanky had shifted while I spoke. Now, he was standing in the opening at the side of the counter, essentially blocking my path to the rest of the store. From the knowing expression on his face, this move had been purposeful. My fingers curled around the bat.

Deacon nodded and held his hands up, the picture of innocence. "You're right. You've caught me. We heard from sources there was a pretty girl with long brown hair and red lips who works in a skate shop and has the hookup for the finest weed. Since you're a pretty girl with long brown hair and red lips, I'm going to assume that's you."

My nostrils flared. It was true, I did have a weed hookup. What was also true was Deacon and Daniel were creeps. There was no way in hell I'd be doing business with them. Even if I was inclined to sell to them, I'd *never* cross that line at Savage Wheelz. I respected Preston far too much to put his business in jeopardy.

"Someone's been talking out of turn," I replied.

Daniel's hands went to his hips. "Maybe. Are you saying it's untrue? Or are you just being a bitch because we have money and you don't?"

I held up a finger. "First, I'm the only one allowed to call me a bitch. Second, what makes you think I don't have money?"

He burst out laughing. "Are you serious? Just...look at you."

"Jesus, Daniel," Blue Eyes groaned. "Let's get the fuck out of here. This is done."

I picked up my bat and rested it on the counter for all to see. "Listen to your pal. He's right."

Deacon clucked his tongue. "You're making a huge mistake. I could've brought you a lot of business." He leaned in, ignoring the bat. "You want to know how easy it is to tell you're poor?"

I lifted my chin high. "Educate me, big man."

He sneered. "You might be pretty, but it doesn't make up for the desperation dripping from your pores. You're saying no to us, but I can practically hear you panting at the thought of taking our money. The Target T-shirt and dollar lipstick don't help."

Blue Eyes moved swiftly, grabbing Deacon's shoulder. "Time to go."

I picked up the bat. "Listen to your friend. It's past time to make an exit and slip back into the primordial goo you crawled out of this morning."

Blue Eyes—Theo—snickered as he dragged Deacon backward. I met his gaze. He grinned at me. I snarled. That made him laugh again. It was deep and gritty, contradicting his blue-eyed sparkle.

Weirdo.

Movement at my side had me whipping my head to the left. Lanky had crowded into my space behind the counter while I'd been distracted.

"What the fuck do you think you're doing?" I pointed my bat at him, keeping him back from me. "You need to leave with your friends. This is over."

He smirked. "If you don't want to sell us weed, maybe you'll sell something else."

"You're kidding."

He shook his head slowly. "You look cheap, but I bet the head you give with those big red lips feels expensive. I can get it for free, but I'm curious how good it is when you pay for it."

My entire being was set aflame. I may have been poor. I may have lived in a trailer park with my drunk of a mother. I may have been going nowhere fast. But I definitely wasn't a rich boy's whore.

"Get out," I gritted through clenched teeth.

He laughed. "Come on, pretty. I've got a fifty burning a hole in my pocket. I'll even let you spit when you're done."

Seeing red, I shoved him in his bony chest with the end of the bat. "I'd never take the cash you earned from licking your daddy's boots. Now, get the fuck out before I put this beauty to use." I shoved his chest again, and he stumbled back a step, hitting the wall behind him.

Pure fury colored his face. "Who the hell do you think you are? Just a dumb bitch who'll be begging for my cock in a year or two after you're all stretched out from birthing a couple bastards from men who couldn't pay you child support, even if they wanted to."

As it had a tendency to do, my anger got the better of me. I lunged at him with the bat over my shoulder and took a swing. He jerked to the side at the last second, and the bat connected with the wall where his head had been.

"Fuck. You're not just a dumb bitch, you're a crazy bitch," he shouted.

His friends were at his back, tugging on his shoulders, and he was letting them.

"Don't ever come back here." I prowled toward them, the bat raised as they backed up. "You are not welcome to set foot in this store. Take your daddy's money and wipe your pasty white asses with it. It's no good here."

Deacon narrowed his medium eyes on me. "I don't know what happened. We just wanted some weed."

"Yeah...well, tell your friend not to be so rape-y and maybe lose the narc look."

They'd backed all the way up to the door. Daniel's face was bright red. Deacon's brows were set in waves of confusion. Theo...well, he looked pissed until our eyes met. Then he softened a fraction, and his perfect lips curved into a small smile.

I did not smile back.

"I'll make sure they don't come back," Theo vowed.

I said nothing.

They shoved out the door, and seconds later, the three of them disappeared down the sidewalk. I exhaled a long, heavy breath and pressed a hand to my chest, trying to manually calm my thrashing heart.

Wow. I didn't like that. Not one bit.

"That was quite an entertaining show."

My head jerked toward that quiet, quivering voice. A woman stood in the corner near the front window. She was bony and frail, her eyes dancing with amusement.

She giggled like a teenager even though she couldn't have been younger than thirty. It was a nice sound, especially after being subjected to the three boys I'd just tossed out.

"I'm sorry if I frightened you," she said.

"It's fine." She'd definitely startled me, but she also looked like a slight breeze would knock her over, so I wasn't going to give her a hard time. "Is there something I can help you with?"

"Maybe." She straightened and walked toward me. Her steps were slow, and something about the way she held herself told me they were also painful. From her clothing and the way she carried herself, this woman was clearly wealthy, but money didn't buy good health. "I'm hoping we can help each other."

"Oh?" I was wary of what she'd say next. If I had to chase this poor, frail lady out of the shop, I'd be done for the day.

"I'm Madeline McGarvey." She held out her hand, and I took it reluctantly, giving it the slightest shake so I didn't knock her over.

"Helen Ortega," I replied. "Everyone calls me Hells."

"Helen's a pretty name." When I didn't reply, her dry lips tipped at the corners. "Well, Hells, I really liked the way you handled those boys. I'd like to offer you a job."

My breath caught in my chest. I didn't know what I'd thought she'd say, but it wasn't that.

"A job."

She nodded, her expression a mix of pinched and placid. "A job, Hells. A very well-paying job that won't last more than a year."

My first instinct was to delicately eject her from Wheelz, but my gut was screaming for me to hear her out. So, I let my bat dangle from my side and took her by the elbow.

"Come sit down. I'll listen."

She finally gave me a real smile, and I realized she was much younger than I had originally estimated. Whatever was going on inside her body had aged her by a decade at least.

"You won't regret it, Hells. That, I promise you."

I'd listen because I wasn't stupid, but *I* wasn't making any promises.

"I don't have any regrets, Mads. That isn't my thing."

"I envy you." Her chin quivered, but her smile was brave.

We sat down behind the counter, and Madeline McGarvey told me the saddest story I'd ever heard. Then she made me an offer that changed the direction of my life forever.

One

Helen

MY DORM ROOM WAS bigger than my trailer. That wasn't saying much since my trailer was a rusted-out tin can, but still. I'd expected cinder block walls and barely any room to breathe—which, frankly, still would have been an improvement.

I should have known better. Savage U wasn't some overcrowded state school. Those endowments from the many, *many* one-percenter alumni paid for real walls, windows with views, and privacy. My dorm room wasn't really a room at all. It was a suite with a shared living area and three private bedrooms.

I'd slept on a couch for the last ten years, so having a room with a real bed all to myself was hard to wrap my head around.

I dropped my trash bags filled with my clothes and bedding. The contents of three large, black bags were all I had to my name, and the majority of it was hand-me-downs. The hand-me-downs were of much higher quality than anything I'd ever owned. That was because they were from Mads. She had only had the best of the best.

Rubbing the sudden pinch in my chest, I kicked a bag and decided I wasn't ready to unpack yet. I went back to the small living area and turned in a circle. The windows overlooked a sea of green, green grass where students were sunbathing and playing frisbee. There was a tiny kitchenette with a mini-fridge and microwave. Two loveseats and an armchair sat in the center of the room facing a TV mounted on the wall. Simple and plain, but to a girl like me, luxurious.

A girl in a sundress emerged from one of the bedrooms. Her eyes rounded when she saw me, then she waved.

"Hi," she said softly. "I'm Zadie."

"Helen." I looked her over. *Really* looked her over. "You're really fucking pretty. I'm not sure I've ever seen anyone prettier."

Zadie's apple cheeks were immediately engulfed in flames, and Jesus Christ, she got even prettier.

"I'm not," she almost whispered. "But thank you for saying so. You have the nicest hair I've ever seen."

"Thanks," I waved off her compliment, "but I'm going to need a minute to get over your face."

Honest to god, this girl looked like an angel. I wasn't the type to comment on other girls' appearances, but I was just so taken aback by her face. If soft was a person, Zadie would be her. Her brown hair flowed in ringlets around her shoulders and down her back. Her skin was fine and smooth, pure cream except at the cheeks where she was pink. Her eyes were big and blue, surrounded by the blackest, thickest lashes I'd ever seen. She was short and a little round, but in a perfectly proportionate way, with boobs and hips and, I suspected, an ass that didn't quit.

Yeah, Zadie was fucking stunning.

I blinked hard. "Sorry. I think I'll be okay now. Did I introduce myself?"

She giggled, but it was filled with nerves. "Yes. Helen. And I'm Zadie."

My nose scrunched. "I remember. You can call me Hells or Helen. Whatever. Do you know who our other roommate is?"

She shook her head. "No idea. There was a last-minute change and someone new was assigned to our suite, but her name wasn't online when I checked."

"Well," I plopped down on the couch, "I hope she's chill."

Zadie perched on the opposite couch. "I hope so too. My roommates last year were a disaster. They hated me instantly because I'm...you know, I guess chubby, and—"

"What the fuck?" I spit out.

She shrunk back. "They never said it out loud, but it was obvious. The girls at this school, well..."

"What about the girls at this school? I'm a transfer, so tell it to me straight. Are they bitches?"

Zadie gasped, then she giggled with less nerves. "Not all of them, of course. I guess I had some bad luck last year, rooming with two best friends who looked, spoke, and acted just alike. You don't seem anything like them, which is a relief."

"I've never met them, and I can guarantee I'm not like them." I slouched and spread my arms over the back of the couch. "So, what's your deal, Zadie? What are you into? Why did you choose Savage U out of all the universities in the land?"

Her cheeks went rosy again. It was cute, but since we were going to be living together, I hoped like hell she calmed down and got comfy with me. I didn't want to have to be concerned with making this pretty girl blush just by asking her a question.

And this was probably why I had so few girl friends. The ones I did have were the girlfriends of my guy besties. I mean, they were legit, but the friendship wouldn't have happened if they hadn't been attached to my boys.

"Well, my mom and stepdad went here, so that's most of it. Also, I'm majoring in accounting, and the business school is one of the best in the country."

My phone vibrated in my pocket. I slipped it out and read the screen.

StupidMotherfucker: *I haven't heard from you. You're late. Need you to deliver. No warnings. Don't fuck up, Helen.*

Tossing my phone on the couch with a groan, I crossed my legs and leaned an elbow on my knee. "Cool, cool. You want to take a walk?"

Zadie straightened. "Um...well, I was in the middle of setting up my room, so..."

"Is that on a strict timeline or can you walk with me? I need to go see someone about a thing, then maybe you can give me a campus tour."

I probably shouldn't have dragged Zadie into my business, but if she was there, I'd get in and out a lot faster. Hopefully.

"Okay." She blinked at me. "I'll go. My room will be there later, I guess."

"Pretty sure that's a definite, Z."

Savage U's campus was gorgeous. Very Southern California-chic, with lots of green space, palm trees, pristine white sidewalks, and blue, blue skies. The buildings were Art Deco era Spanish-style, some with ivy creeping up the sides, lending them an air of gravitas.

At least that's what the pamphlet had said.

I carried my skateboard under my arm, walking beside Zadie. A few people stopped in their tracks and stared at her, but she was completely oblivious, pointing out buildings where she took classes as we passed. I'd lived in Savage River my whole life and had been to more than a couple house parties off campus, but I couldn't say I'd spent any time exploring the university. So, this walk would legitimately kill two birds with one stone. I wasn't actually using my brand-new roommate, she was showing me around *and* she was my excuse.

Our destination was a frat house on the edge of campus. A place I only visited out of necessity. Five or six guys were out front on the porch in various states of lounging. Mostly shirtless. Mostly baby smooth and tan. And they were watching us closely.

"I'm not going in there," Zadie whispered.

"You want me to leave you out front with these fine gentlemen?" I asked.

She shook her head hard.

"Didn't think so. It'll be fine. We'll be in and out in a minute, then we can hit the dining hall or something. I just need to see a guy about a thing and he lives here."

I took her hand in mine. It was soft and trembled slightly. She sucked in a breath and flicked her eyes to mine, then back to the guys on the porch who were *still* watching us.

"Okay. But please don't leave me," she pleaded.

"I would never. It's always hos before bros."

She giggled again, and it was so mega cute.

One of the guys on the porch rose to his feet when we climbed the steps. I breezed past him through the open front door with Zadie in tow.

"Can I help you?" he called after us.

I lifted a hand, not bothering to turn around. "No thanks. We're good!"

Zadie scrambled to keep up with me as I strode through the house. "I think he wanted us to stop."

"Did he? I didn't notice."

I'd been to this house exactly once and had avoided it like the plague since. Me and frat boys did not mix. But sometimes evils were necessary. This one was. I wouldn't have been here otherwise.

At the top of the stairs, I stopped in front of the first room and pounded it with my fist. When no one answered, I kicked the door. My Vans barely made a thump, so I went back to my fist.

Then, Zadie reached around me and turned the knob. The door opened. I looked at her, and she shrugged.

"You seem like you really want in there," she said.

"Yeah." I shoved the door wide open. "I do."

There was a body on the bed, face down, barely moving, white, bare ass glistening in the sun streaming through the cracked curtains. It was four p.m. on move-in day. This fool was already toasted and buck naked.

"Deacon Forrester!" I slapped his left butt cheek as hard as I could.

That woke him up. He sprung from the bed, eyes bleary, his dick dangling like a worm on a hook, clutching his injured ass.

"Oh my god," Zadie uttered.

"Oh, Deacon, time to wake up and have a chat," I cooed.

He focused on me. Sort of. His body listed like he was on a ship during a storm, back and forth, back and forth.

"What're you doing in my room?" His words only came out slightly slurred, which was a relief. I needed his brain to be turned on, and I needed it to happen right now.

"You know why I'm here. Where's the grand you're supposed to have for me today?"

His eyes found mine, flitted away long enough for my stomach to take a nosedive, then came back. "Don't have it."

My stomach hit the floor. "Not an answer you're allowed to give. I'll ask again. Where's my money?"

He grabbed his junk, slowly pumping it as he licked his lips. Zadie whimpered behind me, which, unfortunately, drew his attention.

"Who's your friend? She's cute and looks like she eats cock like a pro." He took a step, just one, and I raised my skateboard. He stopped. Deacon had learned over the last year since he'd approached me at my old job at Savage Wheelz that I did not play.

"No one wants your dick. I can see the herpes from here. You might want to see a doctor soon because it's festering." I shuddered. Deacon scowled. "Just give me the grand you owe me and I'll be gone."

He walked over to his dresser and pulled out a pair of basketball shorts. "Can't." He dragged the shorts up his legs, then turned back to me. "I didn't sell the product."

Another wave of worry slapped at my belly. "Okay, then give me the product back. I'll take care of it myself."

"Can't." He grabbed a T-shirt from his drawer and tugged it over his head. "Flushed it."

I blinked long and hard. "Say that again. I know I didn't hear you correctly."

His hand went to his hips, and he got close to me. Not close enough for me to reach out and twist his balls off, but too close. "I flushed your weed, Helen. It's all gone. Down the tubes. History."

I blinked at him. My mouth fell open and closed. I couldn't quite believe what I was hearing. Zadie placed a hand on my back.

"Let's go," she whispered.

"Why the hell would you flush my weed?" Oh, I was angry. My blood roared in my ears. Deacon Forrester was lucky we weren't in a dark alley because he'd be kissing cement right about now. I didn't care that he was six inches taller and probably fifty pounds heavier, my fury would take him down in a heartbeat.

"Cops stopped by the party last night." He shrugged. "I panicked."

"You panicked?" I echoed.

He stared at me for a long beat, then tossed his head back, laughing. "Oh, fuck. Yeah, I panicked. The irony is, they didn't even come inside. They just checked IDs of the kids hanging out on the porch and left. I was in no danger of getting caught, but I guess I blazed a little too much because I was paranoid as hell."

"They didn't come inside."

He was still laughing. "I can't even tell you how sad it made me to see all that beautiful dope in the toilet. I took a sample of the merch, and it was top notch."

"But you flushed it."

Zadie rubbed my back again. "Hells, come on."

Deacon jerked his chin. "You should listen to your friend. I don't have anything for you. I'm not going to have anything for you. It's done, Helen. All gone. Bye-bye, ganja. Bye-bye, Helen."

I'd snapped out of my stupid, but I didn't say a word. Deacon started to turn away, and I drew back my skateboard. It whistled as it cut through the air, slamming into his bicep. His howl took half a second to rip from his throat.

"You fucking skanky-ass bitch!" His face flushed bright red, and when he screamed, his mouth frothed and spit flew out. "Get the fuck out. I don't have your money. I'm never going to have it. Get out!"

I flew at him, but I never made it. Strong arms wrapped around my middle from behind, and I was dragged backward. I slapped and clawed at the vise circling me. The owner of the arms grunted, but didn't slow, carrying me down the stairs.

"I'm not going to forget this, Deacon," I yelled.

He stood at the top of the stairs, smirking at me. "Have some class, Helen. No need to make a scene just because I won't let you suck my dick anymore, baby."

The man holding me put his mouth next to my ear. "Little Tiger, you're going to tear this house down." He shushed me like a baby. "Don't give him a reaction. It's what he wants."

The low, smooth timbre of his voice broke through my cloud of rage. I still struggled in his grasp, but I stopped yelling. It was pointless anyway. We were approaching the front door, and Deacon was probably back in his bed, doing unspeakable things to himself at the thought of screwing me over.

I was carried down the porch steps, which garnered most assholery from the loungers stationed there. I wasn't put down. He kept going, taking me around the side of the frat house. There, he finally set me on my feet.

Whipping around, I found Zadie first. She had my skateboard tucked under her arm, her cheeks tomato red. She moved to my side, and I took her hand, giving it a squeeze.

"Are you okay?" Deep velvet. Soft and rich. The owner of the most soothing, lovely voice was watching me. His voice matched his looks, including his twinkling blue eyes. Although, he wasn't smiling like he had been a year ago when he'd accompanied Deacon and Daniel to Savage Wheelz.

I rubbed my side. "I think I have a broken rib."

His brow dropped. "Shit. Did I hurt you?"

My eyes rolled. "As if you care."

His jaw hardened, carefully enunciating each word. "Did I hurt you?"

I leveled him with an unwavering gaze. "No, you did not. I don't love being dragged out of buildings by strangers, but I'm fine. It takes a lot more than some dude's spindly arms to hurt me."

"Stranger? Hmmm." His arms—which were taut with muscles, golden, and nowhere near spindly—folded across his chest. He looked me over, then he checked out Zadie. "You're both okay, Zadie?"

Zadie nodded. "Yeah, Theo."

I glared at him.

"Your friend is the hugest asshole I've ever met. I'm not anywhere near done with him. And just so you know, he deserves whatever I dish out."

"What'd Deacon do?" Blue Eyes asked.

"None of your business, Theodore."

His plush mouth broke into a wide, amused grin. "You do remember me."

"I remember the company you keep."

"It's just Theo, by the way."

I shrugged. "Well, this reunion has been real, but I have to go to work in, oh…" I tapped my imaginary watch on my wrist, "eighteen hours, so I have to dash. See you around, Theodore."

Spinning on my toes, I started walking back toward the dorms, pulling Zadie along with me. I didn't miss Theo's annoying, lovely laugh, unfortunately.

"How do you know that guy?" I asked.

"Theo? Oh, his girlfriend, Abby, was one of my roommates last year. I...um, saw him a lot. He was always nice to me, but she —"

"Was a bitch." I squeezed Zadie's wrist. "It figures he'd have a girlfriend like that."

When we were well away from the frat house, I dropped down on the grass, sprawling flat on my back, and groaned at the blue, blue sky. Zadie dropped down beside me, sitting near my shoulder.

"Are you okay?" she asked.

"No. I'm sorry I took you there, though. I shouldn't have done that."

Her lips twitched into a small smile. "Honestly, I should be freaked out, but it was kind of fun. Especially when you bashed him with your skateboard. I wish you'd gotten him in the dick."

I groaned again. "Me too, Z. Me too."

"So," she plucked a bunch of grass, "you deal drugs or...?"

I rolled to my side, propping myself on my elbow. "Not really, but it's sort of complicated and a long story. Can we just forget you saw all that happen?"

"Are you in danger?"

Right then and there, I decided Zadie was cool as hell. I'd been leaning that way, but that had sealed it for me. She had just seen some very real shit go down that was clearly outside her comfort zone and asked *me* if I was okay. She wasn't judging me or distancing herself from me.

Z was a real one for sure.

"No." I shook my head hard. "I'm not. I'm pissed off, but I'm not in danger."

The text message burning up my phone said otherwise, but Zadie didn't need to know that. This was my new life, my chance to rise above the shitty station I'd been born into. So there were a few bumps, it happened.

I'd figure this out.

I had no choice. I just didn't know how yet.

What I did know was Deacon Forrester was going to regret screwing me over just as much as I regretted ever laying eyes on him.

Two

THEO

DEACON'S DOOR HIT THE wall with a dull thud. He shot upright in his bed, all red and riled. When he saw who was barging into his room, he gave pause.

"What's up, man?" he grumbled.

"I'm here to ask you the same. I just got through carting a screaming, writhing girl from your room." I leaned a shoulder on the doorjamb. "An explanation would be nice."

He swung his legs over the side of his bed, rubbing his eye with the heel of his hand. "Bitch wanted more of this. I was through with her. She didn't like it. Went crazy." He shot me a cocky smirk. "What can I say? I'm irresistible, apparently."

I jerked, crossing my arms over my chest. "You're telling me you had that girl?"

He cocked his head. "Not much of a boon. Buy her a few drinks, and I'm pretty sure she's the kind of girl anyone can have."

I didn't believe a word Deacon was saying. Not because he couldn't pull. He absolutely could. He was smarmy as hell, but he came with a family name that meant something to a lot of people. He had connections, and he had ready cash.

Money wasn't hard to come by for most of the students at Savage U, but Deacon was on a different level. Even girls who had trust funds waiting for them when they graduated looked at Deacon as a ticket to the next echelon. Or they really wanted a ride on his sick-ass yacht—his words, not mine.

The reason I didn't believe Deacon was because I didn't want to. I'd be sorely disappointed if that wild little tiger I'd just held in my arms would stoop to Deacon's level. Surprised too. I didn't know anything about her, but the two times I'd encountered her gave me every indication she wouldn't touch Deacon even if her life depended on it.

"Yeah? I didn't catch that vibe from her." I shrugged. "I could be wrong."

Deacon's nostrils flared. "Yeah. While you were caught up with your little girlfriend all last year, I was getting to know our skater townie friend. I think I know her vibe a lot better than you, man."

My jaw instantly hardened. "Don't go there."

"I'm not going anywhere. You were busy doing your thing last year. Shit happened you don't know about."

"My *thing* was wrestling. My *thing* was waking up at five to train. My *thing* was tracking everything I ate down to the crumb. My *thing* was nightly runs even when I was exhausted. Don't act like I was off having fun. You know better."

He drew his knee up on the bed, facing me fully. "I'm not fighting with you, Theo. I remember all that shit. My point stands. You weren't around much freshman year, whether you were with Abby or training. So yeah, things changed, events occurred, don't be surprised you weren't kept apprised."

My gut twisted. He knew he was not allowed to say that name. She was not to be mentioned in this house or in my presence.

I charged on. There was no way on earth I'd let Deacon know how much hearing her name still bothered me. But fuck, I was here, in this frat house, because of her. Every damn day I spent here was a reminder.

"I don't know what you did to that girl but keep it out of the house. I don't need to be dragged into your mire, Deac."

He raised his chin. "You trying to tell me who I can fuck in my own house?"

"Nope. I'm telling you I don't want to have to haul a girl off you so she doesn't kick your ass. That's what I'm telling you."

He snorted a laugh. "That crazy bitch hit me with her skateboard. Shocked the shit out of me, no lie. That was the only way she got a swing in. She comes at me again, I'll swing back. I have no qualms hitting a chick if she asks for it."

I shook my head. "Don't say shit like that to me."

"Why?"

I threw my arms up. If it were up to me, I'd have nothing to do with Deacon Forrester. He'd call us friends. I wouldn't. The more time I spent around him, the deeper my disdain grew. That was the thing, though. I was stuck with him, at least until I graduated. Our fathers were friends, and as much as it pained me, my father held a good deal of control over my life. I'd pissed him off enough last year. Rocking the boat wasn't an option right now.

"Why? Why shouldn't you talk about hitting women in front of me?"

He laughed. "Not women. A specific crazy bitch who hit me first. What, am I supposed to stand there and take it?"

"No. You're supposed to not do shit that makes a woman whack you with her skateboard." I slapped the jamb, done with this conversation. "I gotta go get a workout in."

Deacon nodded, relaxing back into the pillows at his headboard. "Family dinner at the T tonight. You need to show."

He didn't mean either of our blood families. This was a frat dinner, unofficial, of course, since I wasn't an actual member. It'd just be some of the guys in Deac's inner circle, like Daniel.

Some of them were decent, some weren't. Like Daniel. The decent ones had me considering. Not spending the entire night locked in my room had me agreeing.

"All right. I'll be there."

"Close the door on your way out."

I gladly slammed it shut.

· · · ● · ● · ● · · ·

THE T WAS A diner in the heart of Savage River that had been there since the dawn of time. It was silver on the outside, sprawling and stuffed full of locals and university students on the inside. Our group took up two tables. Twelve guys got loud until they were fed. Our waitress brought our food out fast.

"So, Theo, what's it like not prepping for a wrestling season?" Daniel was sitting across from me at the end of the booth.

I nodded to the burger I was about to take a bite out of. "It's not bad." Then I dug in, savoring every single fucking bite.

"You miss it?" The guy beside Daniel, Rohan, was one of the decent ones. When he asked questions, he was genuinely curious. Daniel...well, he always had an angle.

I swallowed and wiped my mouth. "In some ways. I'm still adjusting to the life of a noncollegiate athlete, to be honest."

Daniel chuckled. "Are you getting soft?"

"Worried about my physique, Danny?" I bounced back. Rohan laughed. Daniel didn't. He wasn't much for humor.

"Just looking out for my pal, Theo." His eyes narrowed on me. I didn't let him bother me.

I'd known Daniel and Deacon since I moved from Las Vegas my senior year of high school to live with my dad in Malibu, California. I was shoved on them just as they were shoved on me, told we'd be friends—the "or else" heavily implied. Daniel had never liked me. I'd never liked him. Neither of us hid it back then, and nothing had changed now.

Taking another big bite of my burger, I leaned back in my seat and patted my stomach. I wasn't getting soft, only because working out and doing it hard had been ingrained in my mind since I'd started wrestling in middle school. Dropping the sport didn't mean I'd dropped the habit. I did eat now, though. Fuck, did I eat.

"I'm all good," I said. "All good."

A flash of red and then long, dark hair caught the corner of my eye. I turned in time to see the little tiger herself push through the diner exit into the night.

Helen. What a sweet name for a girl who seemed anything but. I wondered what her parents had been thinking naming her that. Maybe it was wishful thinking, name her a grandma name and she'll grow up to wear floral dresses and bake cookies.

Based on the two times I'd encountered her, I'd say they were disappointed if soft and sweet had been their goal.

Daniel kept talking, trying to dig at me, but I was through listening. I tossed the last of my burger on my plate and slid out of the booth.

"Left my phone in the car. I'll be back." I strode through the diner and into the parking lot. It was busy with people coming and going. Helen was nowhere in sight. I'd missed her, but if I had caught her, I wouldn't know what to do with her.

She'd probably claw my eyes out. *Tiger.* I chuckled to myself and headed toward my car. The brand-new BMW i8 my stepmom passed onto me over the summer when she decided she wanted something "more chic." Driving it made me feel like a conspicuous asshole, but I needed wheels, so I dealt.

And when Deacon asked to do the driving, I always let him, allowing him to be the conspicuous asshole, which he didn't mind. Plus, he gave a shit about keeping the car pristine, always parking on the far edge of lots so it didn't get dented, washing it down after a drive—the kind of things I should've been doing.

He'd parked in the very corner of the lot, far, far away from the lights and other cars. As I approached, I heard the telltale sign of glass breaking. Through the shadows, I spotted a figure standing on the hood, swinging something down on the windshield.

A skateboard.

My feet stopped moving, stupefied at the sight of Helen, on top of my car, her long hair flowing behind her in the breeze, looking like an angel of vengeance. She swung her skateboard high, bringing it down on the windshield with a crash.

It was so crazy, such a ridiculously glorious scene, I barked a loud laugh.

She whirled, eyes wide, but not panicked. Our gazes locked, and that got me moving toward her. Why, I didn't know yet. The second I moved, she did too, running to the edge of the hood. She was a step away from jumping off when I lunged, hooking my arms around her before she could escape.

"What's going on, Little Tiger? Are you getting into trouble again?"

She squirmed, batting at my arms and kicking at my legs. Helen was small, but I felt the power in her fight. Her muscles bunched and pumped, fighting me furiously.

"Get off me, you creepy fuck." She shoved hard at my arms, but I wasn't letting go. Not yet.

"I just caught you destroying a car. Don't you think I should be calling the cops?"

"This is Deacon's car," she gritted out. "If you knew what he owed me, you wouldn't even think of calling the cops."

"Wrong." Taking a chance with my life, I dipped my head to speak close to her ear. "This is *my* car. I let him drive sometimes."

"Oh." She went limp for a beat, then tipped her head back, showing me her face.

"Yeah, oh."

"The company you keep, Theodore."

"Theo. One day, you're going to tell me what Deacon did."

"No I'm not."

In the light of the moon and a few stars, I looked her over. It wasn't really bright enough to tell, but I knew her lips were crimson red. She painted them that way, and the red seemed to be a part of her.

Her thick, silky hair slid away from her face, down her back and over my arms. Even when she was snarling at me, Helen was strikingly beautiful. She had the kind of deep-set eyes, high cheekbones, sloped nose, and rounded chin that belonged in paintings from a different era. And holy Christ, was she sexy. Possibly unhinged, but sexy nonetheless.

"Why are you looking at me like that?" she whispered.

"I've never seen a criminal this close up before." I lowered my face so our noses were almost touching. "Didn't know they came this hideous."

She reached up, grazing her fingertips along my jaw. "You know, I've never seen a rich boy this close either. I didn't know the aristocracy still inbred, but I see they do. You're very ugly."

Her tits were flattened against my chest, and each panting breath she took shoved them deeper into me. My cock throbbed behind my zipper, harder than I'd been in a long time. It was disconcerting to be so fucking aroused by the little criminal I'd caught. That didn't stop me from pressing my dick against her.

Her red lips parted, and I felt her gasp and quick exhale across my mouth.

"Theodore," she breathed.

That mouth was as red as a stop sign, but it flipped the switch on my inner bull. All I saw was a red flag, and there was nothing that could've stopped me from charging. Not logic. Not reason. Nothing.

I leaned in, touching my mouth to hers.

And then...nothing.

The little shit had slipped right out of my arms. By the time I realized what was happening, she was booking it down the sidewalk, leaving me there with a hard dick and her skateboard on the ground.

What the hell had I been thinking?

The girl massacred my car, and I tried to kiss her like she was my girlfriend.

With my hand on my forehead, I checked out the damage. Cracked windshield, busted headlights, dented hood. My dad was going to be displeased, and he was already displeased as hell with me.

I was fucked. But if I went down, I wasn't going down alone. The next time I dealt with Helen, I'd remember exactly who she was. And who she wasn't.

Three

Helen

STUPIDMOTHERFUCKER: *I'm running out of patience, Helen.*
You're past due now.

My cereal curdled in my stomach. Destroying that Bimmer
had felt good in the moment, but it didn't solve my biggest
problem. I was short of funds at a time when being short of
funds was a danger to my health.

Zadie plopped down across from me at the table I'd claimed
for us in the dining hall. "Ready for our first day?"

I tossed my spoon in my bowl. "Yep. I think so. Although, I'm
not entirely sure online community college properly prepped me
for Savage U."

If Mads had had her way, I would have been enrolled at
Savage U last fall. But the thing was, my grades in high school
had been pretty shit. I'd done the bare minimum to graduate,
nothing more. It took me all year working my ass off in my CC
classes to have a sparkling three-point-eight GPA worthy of
admission at Savage U.

Besides the need to raise my GPA, going to in-person school
full time would have defeated the entire purpose of being her
companion. I actually had to be in her presence to do my job.

I rubbed the pinch in my chest I got every time I thought of my girl. My Mads.

"You'll do fine, Hells. If you can charge into a frat house and beat a guy up, you can handle classes here." She started peeling a banana. "I managed to get through an entire year here, you know."

"That's because you're smart."

Two days as Zadie's roommate had shown she was smart, chill, and funny when I got her going. Our third roommate still hadn't shown up, which was fine by me. The dynamic Z and I were developing was an easy one.

"True. But walking into a classroom where I don't know anyone isn't exactly easy."

"Too bad we don't have classes together."

Her nose wrinkled. "I know. Next semester, we'll have to plan it."

"Yeah." My stomach warmed. Two days, and this girl had my stomach warming. The bitches who had been her roommates last year had missed out on a treasure with this girl. What the hell had they been thinking?

When we were done with breakfast, we walked to the main quad together, then it was time to separate. I ran my hands down my sides.

"Do I look like a college girl?"

I had my holey Vans, a Hello Kitty Band-Aid on my knee, cut-offs two sizes too big hanging off my hips, a crop tie-dyed tee, and my hair tied back in a pony. Zadie looked me over from head to toe.

"You look beautiful, Helen," she said softly, like she really meant it.

"Well, you do too, Z. The boys are going to drool, and the girls are going to be jealous, catty bitches. Remember that."

Zadie was wearing a sweet little pink sundress and leather flip-flops. Not my style, but it fit her to a T. Two days, and I hadn't gotten over her soft beauty. I had also confirmed she did, indeed, have an ass that didn't quit. Z was completely oblivious to it, though.

She smoothed a hand over her middle. "See you, Hells. Have a good first day."

I tipped my chin to her. "You too, Z."

LAST CLASS OF THE day, and I was doing well. During my time with Mads, I'd learned a lot about myself. The biggest was that I liked taking care of people, and when I put in effort, I excelled at science and math. Losing Mads had affirmed my decision to go into nursing. My courses were focused mostly on those subjects, which I liked, but I still had to take an English class as part of my core requirements.

I wasn't so great with words, so I wasn't looking forward to dissecting Shakespeare. Now, if it had been Will's actual body I was dissecting...

Grumpy mood in full effect, I took a seat on the aisle in the third row of the lecture hall. This was my biggest class of the day, but it was nowhere near the giant auditorium-style classes I'd heard about from my friends who went to larger schools. Each row held two long tables with eight chairs spread apart from each other. There were five rows, and empty seats were quickly being filled. The spot beside me was taken by a massive guy with thick, dark hair falling in his face. He didn't say a word to me or seem interested in speaking to me, so I was fine with him being there.

A shift in the air brought my head up from my phone. Theo rushed into the room just as the professor was shutting the door and took the first empty seat in the front row, not noticing me.

Wonderful. Perfection. Stupendous.

I'd definitely broken his car two nights ago. That hadn't been my finest moment, but he probably deserved it, seeing as he was friends with Deacon and his girlfriend had been evil to Zadie. I was surprised the cops hadn't shown up at my door yet. Then again, Theo probably didn't know my full name, or that I was a student here.

I could only hope I'd fly under the radar in this class—and Theo would forget I'd bashed the shit out of his ride. I *definitely* didn't have the money to repair his car or the time to spend locked up for a crime I *absolutely* did commit.

The class went by quickly, and Professor Davis was mildly interesting, which was more than I'd been expecting. He went over the plays we'd be talking about and had us write out ten facts we knew about Shakespeare and his writing. I was really reaching by the time I got to eight, so I threw in some Leonardo DiCaprio references. Everyone knew his version of *Romeo and Juliet* was superior to all the rest, even though that story was utter bullshit.

Then he went over the syllabus and the breakdown of his grading system. That was when I began to panic. Not that the workload was too much, but because twenty-five percent of our grade would be coming from watching a modern interpretive performance of *Taming of the Shrew* on a night I'd be working.

I raised my hand. Professor Davis nodded to me.

"Excuse me, sir, but is there another time we can watch the play?"

He propped his butt on his desk and crossed his legs at the ankle, then he slanted his head. "Is that inconvenient for you?" I didn't know if I was imagining it, but he sounded amused.

"Actually, yes. I have to work that night."

He brought his hand up to his chin, stroking it in a way I figured was supposed to be thoughtful. "I don't know what to tell you. You'll have to take the night off. In this class, going to that play is a requirement. If you can't do that, I suggest you drop the class."

I swallowed. "There's no other time for the play? I work every night and I—"

His laugh boomed out of him. "Every night? I find that hard to believe. What's your name?"

"Helen Ortega, sir. And yes, I work every night. I'd have to ask for the night off to go to the play, and honestly, I can't afford it, but—"

He snapped his fingers. "There. You said 'but,' Ms. Ortega, which means you *can* ask for the night off, but you're unwilling to. So, I'm sticking to my original statement. Drop the class if you can't commit to the work."

An arm shot up in the front row. Professor Davis pointed to the student.

"Professor Davis, are you certain there aren't any exceptions?"

I knew that voice. That deep, low, lovely voice.

"Name?" the professor snapped.

"Theo Whitlock."

Professor Davis straightened, his eyes narrowing on Theo. "Do you have a conflict the evening of the play too, Theo?"

"I don't. However, it doesn't seem fair or at all ethical to pressure a student to drop a class because you choose to have a requirement on the syllabus to see a play that's only playing one night. To me, that speaks of poor planning on your part, and you shouldn't put the onus on your student. That's just my opinion, but I can't be the only one thinking it."

The huge guy next to me nodded along with Theo. A few other people in front of me did too. Professor Davis's face had flushed, and his arms were crossed in defiance.

"I hear your point, Mr. Whitlock." Jaw hardened, he focused on me again. "There's another showing in L.A. in two weeks. It's a matinee. I will add that information to the class portal so everyone can have it."

L.A. was an hour away. I didn't have a car. Still, I'd make it happen. If the professor hadn't been an asshole, I would have dropped the class. But now that he'd challenged me, no way was I backing down.

I gave him a jerk of my chin, averting my gaze to my laptop.

The guy beside me leaned over slightly but didn't turn his head. "What's fair is fair," he rumbled lowly.

"Um, true. Thanks."

He returned to his space like he'd never said a word. And that was fine. I was already thrown enough from Theo coming to my defense, I didn't know what to do with anything else.

The class went on for another ten minutes, and Professor Davis's face stayed flushed the entire time. I would have laughed if I didn't need this class. I was obviously on the professor's shitlist on my very first day—a place I did not want to be.

Naturally, when class ended, Theo was waiting at the door for me. I stalked past him without a word, and he followed me outside. I started to put my skateboard down on the sidewalk, but Theo snatched it out of my hands, tucking it firmly under his arm.

I rounded on him. "No."

He raised a brow. "Helen Ortega, huh?"

"Yes, Theodore. That's my name. Give me my skateboard back."

He chuckled under his breath. "I'm beginning to think it's cute when you call me that. Like a pet name."

"It's important to have dreams." I hitched my backpack higher on my shoulders. "You know what? Keep my skateboard. I don't need it."

I walked away, but Theo easily kept up, like he was out for a Sunday stroll. Long-legged asshole.

"I'm gaining a collection of your boards, Helen."

"It's interesting you want to keep mementos of our time together, Theodore."

He grabbed my arm and dragged me to the side of a building, boxing me in against the warm brick wall and dropping my board to brace his hands on either side of my head.

"Stop for two seconds," he gritted out.

"Why? I don't even know you."

"You fucked my car up like you know me."

"That was a mistake, but again, the company you keep."

His jaw tightened, and the muscles around his mouth pinched. "You don't know shit about me. You've made yourself judge and jury."

"I don't want to know anything about you."

He lowered his face a fraction. "Oh yeah? Is that why I can see the pulse in your neck fluttering?"

Raising my chin, I locked on his gaze. "Maybe I'm scared of you. Maybe it doesn't feel good to be cornered by a man who's a lot bigger than me, and basically a stranger."

He stilled, then he moved, grazing his nose along mine. "I don't believe you even for a second."

"You don't know me, Theo. You have no idea what makes me afraid." I braced my hands on his chest and shoved. "Back the hell off."

He took a step away, not because I pushed him, but because he chose to. I was strong, but not strong enough to move him on my own.

"Thank you," I mumbled.

"You're not escaping. You can, you know. I'm not holding you prisoner."

I let my head fall back on the wall, meeting his eyes. God, they even sparkled when he was angry. What *was* that?

"You obviously want to speak to me, so get on with it, then we can be done with this."

He backed up another step and turned his head away from me. The corner of his jaw ticced like he was grinding his teeth hard.

"I have your skateboard," he spit out.

"I know."

He faced me again. "I could fuck you over, Helen. You know that? You chose to fuck me over. I could return the favor."

I huffed. "Oh, please. Like Daddy'll even notice a bit of broken glass. I don't—"

His hand slammed on the brick beside my head. "You say I don't know what makes you afraid—you don't know the first thing about me either. You have no idea what my father can do."

"Is that a threat, Theodore?"

He hit the brick again, so hard, I wondered if he drew blood.

"You aren't listening. He'll want your name, which I now have, and I won't give it to him. There will be consequences for that, which I'll face."

I sucked in a breath, absorbing what he was saying. It didn't make sense. There was absolutely no reason for this guy to sacrifice himself for me. Unless he wanted something.

Now, I got it.

"What do you want in exchange? Because, honestly, I'm short on cash and out of favors."

His head dropped, and he groaned. "I don't want anything. I'm just talking to you, but you're making that really, really difficult."

I pushed his forehead, bringing his head up. "Then go. I'm not keeping you prisoner"

He jerked at me echoing his words. Then his eyes dropped to my mouth. "Not yet."

My breath hitched as he moved closer. He was going to kiss me, just like he'd started to outside the T. And I...I couldn't let that happen.

Raising a hand between us, I pressed my fingertips to his lips. "Don't kiss me, Theo."

His body went rigid, then he wrapped his fingers around my wrist and yanked my hand away. "Don't act like you don't want me to, Little Tiger."

"I don't." I shoved him again, and this time, I took the opportunity to stoop and grab my skateboard. "Even if I liked rich boys, I don't like cheaters. Your girlfriend probably *really* doesn't like cheaters. Poor thing."

My board clattered to the ground, and I pushed off, away from Theo's silence, back to my dorm. Hopefully it would be empty so I could stew over a plate of dining hall mozzarella sticks in peace.

• • • • ● • ● • • •

OUR SUITE SMELLED DIFFERENT. Like rare flowers and imported vanilla. I flung my backpack on the couch and placed my to-go box of mozzarella sticks on the coffee table.

Z emerged from her room with wide eyes. "Our roommate is here."

My eyes went round like hers. "Bad?"

She bit her lip, her eyes avoiding mine. "I'll let you be the judge. I don't want to color your opinion."

The door to the previously empty room suddenly opened. "Did I hear a new voice?" A blonde emerged, a big, white smile splitting her perfectly symmetrical face. "Hey, I'm Ele—"

"You're absolutely kidding me."

Elena Sanderson's fake smile wiped from her face faster than it had appeared.

"You're kidding me," I repeated.

Elena's manicured hands hit her hips. "Is this a joke?" She glanced at Zadie. "This is a joke, right? Are there cameras? Because this has to be a joke."

Zadie's eyes darted back and forth between us. "Do you know each other?"

I snorted. "Elena was the queen bitch in high school."

Elena smirked at my assessment. "I'll take that title gladly. It's far better than town whore. Isn't that what everyone called you?"

"Wow." Slowly nodding, I gave her a long once-over. "It's nice to know some things haven't changed. Even in college, in the throes of adulthood, you still remain a child. Go you, Elena."

Elena and I hadn't had many personal run-ins in high school. For one, our school had been massive, with over four-thousand students. For another, she'd been in classes aimed toward getting her into the best school while I'd been vying to make it out whole and alive.

I'd gotten it half right, at least.

But I knew who she was and the kind of things she had done. Elena was the type of girl who laughed at others' misery. She provoked for her own entertainment. She'd screwed with my friends and looked down on people who weren't born with a silver spoon up their asses.

Elena Sanderson was a monster in angel clothing.

"Is it possible to start over?" Zadie asked quietly.

Elena rounded on her, and I braced. If she was a bitch to Z, I wasn't sure I'd be able to hold myself back.

"I don't think I noticed when I came in, but wow, you're stunning." Elena dragged her knuckles down Zadie's cheek. "Your skin feels like you murdered a few virgins and bathed in their blood. Is that your secret? Do tell."

Zadie's blue eyes widened, and honestly, mine did too. Who the hell was this girl being all funny and nice to Z? I didn't trust it.

"I-I...no. I just use this lotion my mom bought me. It's Korean," Zadie answered.

Elena snapped her fingers. "First, I love that you took my question seriously and answered it. I'm totally relieved you don't bathe in virgin blood. Second, you're going to need to hook me up with the bottle, babe. Don't hold out on me."

"Well..." Z's eyes slid to me, then back to Elena. "Well, okay. My mom buys it by the case so I can give you one of my extras."

Elena pressed her hands together. "You're a doll baby. Has anyone ever told you that? Because you are." She draped her arm over Zadie's shoulder. "Now, tell me, has Helen been nice to you? She's not known for her couth."

Zadie didn't hesitate. "Helen's amazing."

Elena swung her gaze to me. It'd been over a year since I'd last seen her, and I could honestly say I hadn't thought of her once. Okay, maybe she'd flitted across my mind since she was my friend Penelope's cousin, but that was it. A passing idea. Nothing more.

"Is she?" Elena sounded like she didn't buy it. "I don't know about starting fresh, but I don't intend to be here a lot. When I am, I want my home to be peaceful. As long as Helen keeps up her end, I'll keep up mine, and we can coexist."

I measured my words. Peace was good, but coexisting with Elena Sanderson wasn't my idea of a good time. I was pretty sure I couldn't switch rooms, though, and I'd never leave Zadie in the clutches of Elena. She'd probably have all the cool sucked out of her.

"I'll coexist." My arms folded over my chest. "If you try any of your uppity bitch shit on me, I won't let it stand."

Elena snorted. "Lovely. And I'll have to lodge a protest if you turn my toothbrush into a shank."

"Your toothbrush? Come on, El. I make my shanks from sharpened spoons. The stainless steel is much more durable when I'm shivving my enemies."

Elena's brow rose. "I am disturbed, but I'm also filing that info away. You never know."

Zadie giggled. "Are we good? I hope we're good."

I eyed Elena. She let her eyes flit over me, bored and disinterested. I liked that. If she wasn't interested in me, she'd leave me alone. I sure as hell planned to leave her be too. If she stayed on her side of the suite, I could stick this out. It wasn't like I had any other choice anyway.

"I'm good," I assured Zadie.

Elena flicked her French-manicured nails. "Mmm. Everything's fine." She spun on her toes and marched back to her room, leaving Zadie and me in her wake of fire, brimstone, and imported vanilla.

Zadie sighed when Elena's door closed. "She wasn't so bad. Or...not as bad as my roommates last year."

I slumped on the couch, my box of mozzarella sticks in my lap. "That's a low bar." And of course, Theo's girlfriend was one of those evil wenches who had done my girl Z way, way wrong.

I held up the box to Z. "Come eat these with me or I'll feel guilty stuffing my face in front of you."

She perched on the cushion beside me and selected a mozzarella stick. "Thanks." She took a delicate bite, then elbowed my side. I cocked a brow. Her lips quirked. "Do you think you can teach me how to make a shank? It sounds handy."

A loud laugh burst out of me. Once I started, I couldn't stop. Days of stress and change poured out of me. Everything wasn't going to be okay, not if I didn't bust my ass to make it so. But for that single minute, Zadie giggling beside me, a container of mozzarella sticks in my lap, my first day of Savage U in the books, it *felt* like it was okay.

Only for a minute, though.

Four

THEO

I FINALLY GOT THE call. I'd been waiting for it ever since I'd filed a claim on my car's insurance policy. I shouldn't have been surprised my dad had let it fester. That was another way of exerting his control. He left me to wonder when he'd call, then he'd decide when it had been long enough.

"Sit down, Theo."

Andrew Whitlock was the father I never wanted. He wasn't a bad guy in an evil villain sense, but he wasn't a good man either. He'd been mostly disinterested my whole life but had flipped a switch a couple years ago. Now, I was in California, experiencing what it was like to be Andrew's pet project.

I took a seat opposite him, his grand, mahogany desk between us. The nameplate at the edge of his desk shined like it had been recently polished. *Dr. Whitlock, President.*

"Hey, Dad."

He clasped his hands together on top of a stack of papers. "Tell me about the car."

"Someone vandalized it while it was parked outside the T." I scrubbed at my jaw. "It's my fault for parking on the outer edge of the lot. Unfortunately, the cameras didn't reach that corner."

It wasn't a question of handing over Helen. My father, along with my stepmom, could more than afford to repair the car—a car I didn't give a shit about. And I got the feeling Helen could not.

But withholding her name wasn't about doing her a favor. No, this was entirely about a chance to stick it to my dad.

"Do you think I should foot the bill for that?" he asked.

I lifted a shoulder. "Do or don't. I didn't want the car in the first place."

His dark brows came down over his even darker eyes like thunder bolts. "Do you expect me to believe you want to go the next three years without a vehicle? More if you don't find an adequate-paying job post-graduation?" He leaned back in his chair, his clasped hands resting on his soft gut. "I don't get this car repaired, you'll be back in this office within a week telling me how right I was in the first place."

I turned my palms up. "Maybe, maybe not."

"Theo." He slapped his palm down on the leather arm of his chair. "I've put up with this lackadaisical attitude for months now. I'm done. I should have been done when you quit wrestling, but what can I do? I can't force you to go back. All I can do is sit back and watch you screw up and hope you'll see the error of your ways."

I shook my head hard. "There was no error when I quit wrestling."

It was laughable that he believed he'd sat back and done nothing when I told him I'd quit wrestling. He'd thrown a lamp across his pristine living room, then went on a ten-minute rant about work ethic, quitters, success, and how I was my mother's son, through and through.

There was no letting it slide, not when it affected Andrew Whitlock's reputation. As the president of Savage U, he enjoyed having a son who was a star athlete at his university. He'd never once been to a match, not a single one, but he took my accolades like they were his own.

His nostrils flared. His artificial tan became mottled with red. "I disagree. But beyond wrestling, you ended a relationship with a girl you should have been planning to marry. You've turned down multiple invitations from Miranda for dinner and brunch. And now this with the car. You're becoming someone I'm not proud to call my son, and I won't stand for it." He leaned forward in his chair, locking his gaze on mine. "You will not embarrass me on this campus."

My gaze on his never wavered. "That isn't my intention. Last semester, I maintained a three-point-five GPA and earned the respect of my teachers. I don't know...I'd think that would hold some weight." He didn't respond, but the rapid rise and fall of his chest was all I needed to see. My GPA wasn't big and flashy, like being one of the best collegiate wrestlers in California. A three point five didn't make up for the loss of bragging rights and status. Dear Father was disappointed.

I pushed my palm down my thigh. "I'll call Miranda and schedule a meal. It's been busy with the start of school. But I'll call her."

His nod was sharp. "You do that."

Miranda was my stepmom of three years. She was fine. Decent for someone who'd grown up in a mansion with servants and the finest of the fine. She'd married my dad for love, which blew my mind since I found him utterly unlovable. Seeing them together, I couldn't get a bead on if he returned the love to Miranda or her millions in the bank.

I'd turned down her invitations more as an excuse not to see my dad. Since she was more self-aware than Andrew Whitlock would ever be, I had a feeling she knew. But I could do a dinner to keep the peace.

"As for the car," Dad's fingertips turned white as they pressed down on his desk, "it will be repaired. This is your last chance, though, Theo. My patience is running thin. You will toe the line or I will cut it."

"I understand."

I fucking dreamed of cutting ties with this man. And I would, the minute my diploma was in my hand. Until then, I was stuck listening to his rants and throwing him a bone of cooperation every once in a while.

"I really hope you do. I don't want to have this type of conversation again. Keep your nose clean and in your books. No more bullshit."

Because I was done with *his* line of bullshit, I forgot myself for a split second and saluted him. "Aye, aye, captain."

His out-of-shape body went taut, and the fingers pressing into his desk went so white, I wondered if they would snap clean off.

"Get out, Theo," he groused. "This isn't the projects. Take that trashy attitude with you and don't let it out the next time I see you. I won't stand for it."

I rose, thunder reverberating off the walls of my chest. I could take a lot from him, but when he brought up where I grew up with my mother, violence filled my veins. He was lucky I had more self-control over my body than I did my mouth. Damn lucky.

Swiveling on my heel, I stalked to the door of his office. Hand on the knob, he called out, "Make sure to contact Miranda. I'll be checking with her."

I raised a hand, forcing my fingers to straighten from a fist. Then I walked the fuck out, asking myself for the thousandth time since I met Andrew Whitlock on my fifteenth birthday how I could be related to such a dumb fuck.

I still didn't have the answer.

With two hours to kill between classes on Thursdays, I wove through the stacks to claim the spot I'd discovered last year. It was the perfect location, out of the way and quieter than any other part of the library. A big part of the reason I'd maintained my decent grade point average was because of that spot. I'd gotten some intense studying done there since my freshman year.

After the meeting with my father, I needed the quiet to come down from the furious high he always brought on.

Except...my spot was occupied.

I couldn't stop the grin from taking over. The little tiger herself was sitting in the armchair tucked in the corner, her knees drawn up to her chest, a highlighter between her teeth, a pencil impaling the mass of shiny chocolate hair piled on top of her head. Not a shred of makeup on her face that I could tell except for her red, red lips. She held *The Taming of the Shrew*. Her brow was pinched as her eyes darted over the page.

She looked cute and cozy. She was probably getting some good studying done.

That didn't change the fact that this was my spot, and I needed it.

"Get up."

Helen's head jerked back. Her eyes landed on me, and the highlighter fell from her mouth when she scowled. "What did you say?" she hissed.

"I said, get up. This is my spot. For the last year, I'm the only one who's used it. Don't know how you found it, but it doesn't really matter. It's mine."

She snorted softly. "You're funny, Theodore." Then she went back to reading her play.

I'd had enough. Not even a week into the school year, and my patience was worn to scraps. So, I wasn't really thinking when I bent down, scooped Helen Ortega up, plopped her on the floor, and took over the chair. It was an act of pure impulse.

Helen was up from the floor as soon as I settled. I looked up at her, blinking. She fumed like a little raging bull. It was cute, but I was pretty well done with this interaction. I took out my phone and opened the reading app to my chem textbook. Helen was still standing over me, but I ignored her. It wasn't like she could move me out of this chair. She'd have to try harder next time.

"You fuck," she muttered.

From the corner of my eye, I watched her face away from me and toss her arms out to the side. It didn't register that she was backing up until she'd planted herself on my thighs and wiggled deep into the chair, her back pressed to my chest. It also meant her plush little ass was dangerously close to my dick.

"What do you think you're doing, Helen?" I whispered beside her ear.

She lifted her book in front of her face. "I'm reading, Theodore. Be quiet. We're in the library."

I dropped my phone on the arm of the chair and clamped my hands on her hips. "The thing is, Little Tiger, I have a girl on my lap, I'm going to think she likes being there and might get ideas."

"Well, your ideas would be wrong. I'm here to study. It's not my fault you placed yourself under me."

"Helen..." I rumbled, "you're on my dick, baby."

Her head tilted to the side, giving me a glimpse of the barest smirk ghosting her lips. "Oh, am I? What if your girlfriend sees? I've heard she's a bitch, but is she violent? To be honest, I'm not in the mood to fight."

I brushed a lock of hair off her face and tucked it behind her ear, and she stiffened all over. I dragged my fingers down to her jaw, and she jerked her head to the side.

"Don't," she whispered.

"I won't." My hand fell back to her hip. She returned her attention to her play. I sighed. I was done for. There was no way my brain was going to function with Helen on my lap, sending off waves of disdain directly to me.

I kept hold of her hips and watched her for a solid minute. She was stiff the entire time and didn't turn the page. Finally, she sighed.

"Stop looking at me."

I huffed a laugh. "*You're* on me. I don't know what you thought would happen."

"I thought you'd see how ridiculous you were to hijack the chair I'd rightfully claimed and find a different spot. I underestimated your level of asshole."

My hands slid down to the curve of her upper thighs. "I have to admit, I was taken aback when you first planted yourself on my dick, but I'm seeing the light. Now I'm not sure why I'd ever move."

She twisted so she could look at me. "Again, your bitch of a girlfriend. Or do you not care what she thinks?"

I shook my head. "I don't have a girlfriend. If you're referring to Abby, I'm wondering why you think she's a bitch. Do you know her?"

Abby Fitzgerald wasn't my favorite person anymore, but she had a good reputation. She wasn't overly kind, but she didn't go out of her way to be mean. At least, not that I'd ever seen. Then a-fucking-gain, she'd blindsided me near the end of our relationship, so I guess I could have missed it. It seemed I'd missed a lot with her.

Helen's teeth sank into the corner of her bottom lip, and her nose scrunched. "I've heard she's not very nice. I'm not going to throw my source under the bus, though."

I studied her big brown eyes and ruby lips. Up close, Helen was something else. God, she was fucking gorgeous. The last thing I needed was an attraction to this girl, but there was no denying it. Trouble was looking at me like I was dinner, and all I wanted to do was offer myself on a platter for feasting.

Then, my brain kicked into gear again, and it occurred to me what she was saying.

"Abby was a bitch to Zadie? Is that what you're telling me?" I asked.

From the lift of her chin and twitch of the corner of her mouth, I got my answer. Still, she denied it.

"I didn't say that."

"What'd she do to Zadie?" She tried to scoot forward, but I held her firm. "You broached this topic, throwing out strong accusations. Time to back it up, Tiger."

"I'm not scared of you, Theodore. And I'm not saying another word. If you had cared to see while you were still with her, I'm sure you would know exactly what I'm talking about."

My hand spread on her stomach. "I'm not trying to scare you. We're just talking."

"I'm reading. That's all I'm doing."

"Okay." The topic of Abby was dead, but I wasn't done with Helen. "Read to me then."

She sucked in a sharp breath. "What?"

"Yeah. Read to me. I haven't cracked that play yet. You want, we can take turns. Read it together. It might be more interesting that way."

For a long beat, she didn't say anything or move a muscle, then she gave a nod. "Keep your dick out of my ass and your hands to yourself and I'll read with you. Only because I was just thinking I'd understand Will's words better if I heard them out loud."

I chuckled. "Will? Are you close, personal friends with Shakespeare?"

She shifted so her bottom was sideways on one of my thighs, her mouth quirking. "You say that like you're surprised."

Laughing harder, I snatched the book from her hands and studied the page she was on.

"I'm not really surprised about anything when it comes to you, baby."

Her nose scrunched again. "None of that, Theodore. No cute nicknames. We're studying together. We're not friends, and your dick is never going to get closer to me than it is right now."

I could've pointed out that she kept calling me Theodore, which wasn't my name, so it was technically a nickname, but since I didn't want her to stop, I did not.

"As fun as it is, I'm done arguing now." I tapped the page the book was opened to. "You want to begin, or should I?"

"You."

"All right. Let's read some Will."

The fuck of it was, an hour later, when we unfolded ourselves from the chair and went our separate ways without another word, I had absorbed more of what I'd read than I ever had on my own. That was when I knew, without a doubt, if Helen was in my chair the next time I sought out my spot, I'd plop her on my lap instead of the floor.

As for Helen...well, I was pretty fucking certain she'd stay right where I put her.

Five

HELEN

STUPIDMOTHERFUCKER: *I'm done, Helen. I'm gonna need the money today or I visit your trailer. Don't make me do it.*

Swallowing down bile, I turned my phone off and walked into class. Few things scared me—not because I was especially brave, but because I'd experienced the worst of the worst and survived it—but this...this freaked me out.

I shut it all down when I slid into my seat in the third row of my Shakespeare class. The seat beside me was still empty when Theo walked into the room. Dread pitted my gut when he headed for the steps instead of sitting in the front row like he had previously. I couldn't deal with him after receiving that text. I needed to get my head straight, not get distracted by rich boys with sparkling blue eyes who smelled like cool, fresh air.

A huge form sank down in the chair next to me, and I smirked at Theo. He scowled and shook his head. The big, silent guy was back, having come from the other end of the aisle, forcing Theo back to where he belonged in the front row.

I turned to the guy beside me. "Hey."

He barely cocked his head in my direction. "Hey."

"I'm Helen. I thought, if you're going to be sitting beside me this semester, I should know your name instead of calling you the big, silent guy in my head."

He huffed what sounded like a laugh and turned in my direction. "Lachlan. Mostly go by Lock, though." He held his hand out to me. When I slipped mine into his grip, it basically disappeared. This was one big boulder of a man. Wowza.

"Nice to meet you, Lock."

He nodded to Theo. "That guy bothering you?"

"Sometimes." I wished I felt more bothered by Theo. He was a stone-cold asshole, but holy hell, spending over an hour in his lap at the library, his lovely voice in my ear, had weakened me. I hated being weak, so naturally, when I walked out of the library, I was pissed off at his existence while wishing I could tuck myself back in his lap again.

I was the stupid motherfucker, it turned out.

A rumble sounded from his massive chest. "Let me know if you need me to step in."

"Really?"

He turned to me again. "Really."

I lifted a shoulder. "That's a nice offer. I'll keep you posted."

That was the end of our interaction, but it gave me the warm fuzzies. Lock reminded me of my best guy friends from high school, Bash and Gabe. They were off at different colleges, living their best lives with their girls, but if push came to shove, they'd have my back.

Professor Davis started class, keeping my attention the whole way through. After the first day, I'd been concerned he was going to be the thorn in my side all semester, but so far, he'd been proving me wrong. Then again, Savage U was known for only hiring the best of the best, so it made sense he was a passionate and knowledgeable instructor, despite his classism and latent misogyny.

At the end of class, Lock waited for me, and we walked out together. Theo was by the door, his eyes homed in on Lock at my side. My mouth curved into a satisfied grin. Maybe having an enormous man with massive hands and a looming presence as a friend would keep the wolves at bay.

Except, Theo fell into step on my other side as soon as we were outside, sandwiching me between the two of them—and not in a good way.

"You want a ride?" Lock asked.

"She's good," Theo replied for me.

I rolled my eyes. "I've got my board, but thanks."

Lock peered down at me from his place in the clouds. "You're good?"

I craned my neck back to look at him. "I'm just swell, Lachlan."

He nodded decisively, gave Theo a hard look, then veered off in a different direction, leaving just the two of us—which wasn't what I wanted.

"New boyfriend?" His tone was light, teasing, but I heard the edge.

"Yep. We consummated our relationship during Davis's analysis of the use of hunting as a metaphor throughout the play. That was a first for me, but having my brain stimulated at the same time as my pus—"

Theo jerked me into his chest, knocking the wind out of me. "Don't say it, Helen. Shut up right now."

"Pussy," I finished with a smile. "Now do you regret asking me a stupid question?"

His mouth tightened. "I regret ever setting eyes on you."

That knocked the wind out of me in a different way. "I have a solution, Theodore: stop looking at me. And maybe take your hands off me while you're at it."

Theo dropped his hand from my arm, and I didn't hesitate to take off on my skateboard, rolling away from him as fast as my legs would take me. There was no relief in my escape, though. Classes were over, and I had to face my situation head-on. No more denial.

Even if I wanted to deny it, my situation was waiting for me outside my dorm. He saw me before I saw him. Otherwise, I might have kept going.

Amir stepped in my path. "Helen."

I kicked up my board into my hand. "Amir."

Amir Vasquez would be hot if he wasn't scary, but scary he was. Tall, lean, and powerful, he could snap me in half if he wanted. The thing was, he wouldn't. He had people who did that for him. Amir didn't peddle violence, he thrived off fear.

And I'd stupidly gotten tangled up with him.

He stepped toward me until I had no choice but to back up. He kept coming, walking me right into the brick side of the dorm, where we were partially hidden by the thick trunk of an old tree. Once he had me where he wanted me, he backed up a step.

"You know why I'm here." His face was impassive. I had no idea if he was angry, annoyed, or something else entirely. He never showed his hand.

I swallowed down the ball of barbed wire in my throat. "I'm working tonight. I'll have your money after my shift."

His head cocked, dark eyes sweeping over me. Amir had been my hookup for weed since high school. A year older, he used to prowl the halls of Savage River High like an untouchable specter. Kids knew who he was, but they stayed away. Except me, because I was dumb and desperate and I'd had a really hopeless crush on him. I sold for him at parties for extra funds, and I'd never had a problem.

Until now.

I got cocky and flew too close to the sun.

"Why don't you have it now?" He stepped into my space, peering down his nose at me. "You're a week late, and now your loan payment is coming due to Reno too."

I swallowed again. This time, it was even more difficult. That loan payment was an albatross around my neck. My mother, the impetuous genius she was, went to Amir's older brother, Reno, and borrowed ten *K* with absolutely zero plan of how to pay it back. Reno wasn't the kind of man you borrowed money from without a plan to pay him back. He *did* peddle violence, and he most certainly would take a pound of flesh for every day—hell, every hour—payment went past due. And because I was the oldest daughter and a sucker, I'd taken the loan on myself. My mother had made sure Reno knew this, extricating herself from Reno's bloody hook.

That was a concern for another day. The one in front of me required all my attention.

"I promise, Amir. If you want me to come to your place after my shift tonight, I will. It'll be two or two thirty, but if you want me to—"

He gripped my jaw, squishing my cheeks and lips into a grotesque shape. "I asked you why you don't have my money, Helen. I want an answer, then we'll talk about your payment."

"I had this kid selling for me at his frat and—"

Amir's palm slammed into the brick next to my head. "What the fuck did you just say?" he growled. "A frat kid was distributing *my* product?"

If he hadn't sent me the threat of visiting my trailer, I would have kneed him in the dick for getting in my face. But Amir held the power in this situation—and we both knew it.

"I needed more money. The frat boy was my way in to deep pockets. Our arrangement had been working for months, but then he fucked me over, so I'm—"

He slapped the brick again, cutting me off. "This isn't a pyramid scheme, Helen. We're not selling fucking leggings or magic oil. You are my employee. You don't subcontract. That's not how this shit works, and this is exactly why. You got fucked, and in turn, I got fucked. This kid, I didn't vet him. I never gave permission for my product or my money to pass through his hands. Now, we're here, a week late on your payment to me, coming up due to Reno. I'm gonna guess you don't have his money either."

"No, I've got most of it. I'll have it when it's due."

His nose twitched. "You didn't borrow from your Reno fund to pay me?"

"I would have, but I knew I'd be able to earn the money tonight at work."

He leaned so close to me, his nose almost brushed mine. "That's the problem, Helen. You obviously don't respect me. If you did, you would have borrowed from your Reno fund right away. Leaving me hanging for a week sends me a message. A message I don't like. A message I'm not gonna stand for. You hear me?"

Even though I wanted to knee him in the dick, I *really* didn't want him to visit the trailer. Nodding, I lowered my eyes like I was ashamed. In reality, I was pissed at myself and Deacon fucking Forrester.

"I hear you, Amir. It won't happen again."

"I know it won't. You're done. No more handouts from me."

My eyes flicked up to his. He was still studying me in his Amir way. Silent. Curious. Tucking details away for later use. Ticking off vulnerabilities. I had no doubt Amir Vasquez's brain was like a war manual. He had a profile to take down each of his enemies and possible compatriots if he needed to.

He knew exactly where to press to get me to fold. My little sister, Luciana. The trailer could go to hell, but not when she was living in it. Unfortunately, she currently was.

"Amir—"

"No, Helen." He straightened, running his hand along his hardened jaw. "What are you doing anyway? Taking money from Reno, working for me—where do you think it's gonna lead? You're here, getting your degree. You need to get out of this life."

I lifted my chin. "What are you, the pious drug dealer?"

His entire body stilled, except his eyes. They bounded over me, keeping me in his snare.

"Make no mistake. If you go down, it'll barely be a blip in my timeline. I do not care what happens to you. That isn't who I am. But when I see someone being stupid, I call it out. You, little girl, are being really, *really* stupid."

My chin shot up even more, and my hackles rose. "I owe you money, so I'm not going to say everything I want to say."

He folded his arms, his mouth curving into something that would have resembled a smile on anyone else. On Amir, it only looked like a threat. "Say it."

I sucked in a breath. "All right. You say I'm being stupid, but here you are, hanging out on campus, pushing dope to college kids. You grew up with criminals, and you're wallowing in the life, even though everyone knows you're way too smart to be a low-level drug dealer. So, if I'm being stupid, so are you."

He clucked his tongue. "Yeah, it turns out, I don't give a damn what you think. Save your concern for one of your friends." He pointed a finger gun at me and squeezed an eye shut like he was aiming. "Bring me the cash in the morning. Any later than ten, I'll take a trip out to The Palisades with a gas can." He pulled the finger trigger. "You feel me, Hells Belles?"

The barbed wire in my throat wrapped around my lungs. The Palisades was the ironic name for the broke-down trailer park I grew up in. I didn't want to believe Amir would burn it down, but I was smart enough not to test him.

"I feel you, Amir."

I slipped away from the wall, hurrying back to the sidewalk in front of my dorm. Amir caught me by the arm and swung me back around, his face slashed with quiet fury.

"That's not how this works. You don't walk away from me until I'm done with you," he gritted out.

I yanked at my arm, but his hand was clamped down tight. Panic stirred in my gut. It was irrational. It was broad daylight and plenty of people were milling around. But I hated being grabbed and held. It brought back bad memories I kept carefully stored away.

Someone came to a stop beside us. "Excuse me."

Amir and I both turned our attention to the frowning blonde. Elena Sanderson had her hands on her cocked hips, her attention shifting from Amir's grip on my arm to my eyes.

"Go away, Elena." I didn't like the girl, but no way was I getting her mixed up with Amir.

She rolled her eyes. "I just wanted to say there are no psycho boyfriends allowed in the suite. Clearly, the person currently manhandling you has severe mental health issues that drive him to commit violence against a girl half his size. While you may be into being battered and bruised by the male variety, it's my personal inclination to call the authorities when I witness such things." She drew her phone from her pocket and tapped out 9-1-1. "Since you don't seem willing to help yourself, I'll be happy to take matters into my own hands. I'll also add, you have terrible taste in men, Helen, if this guy is your idea of a good time. He *is* hot, but no doubt he'd look hotter in handcuffs."

Amir's grip on me had loosened during Elena's whacked-out speech. I tugged my arm free and moved a foot away from him. This brought me beside Elena. I wasn't sure she was a better choice, but I'd take my chances—especially since I was pretty sure she was helping me in her weird, evil Elena Sanderson way.

Amir tipped his chin at me, then turned and sauntered in the other direction without another word. Inside, I was sighing with relief, but I kept myself upright, covered in armor, unaffected.

Elena gave me a long once-over. "I'd ask if you're okay, but if you say no, I might feel inclined to comfort you, and no one wants that."

I snorted. "Thanks for not asking then."

She hesitated. "I'm assuming that man won't be around again."

I couldn't promise that. He was Amir, and he did what he wanted. "Probably not."

"Well," she held up her phone, "I'll keep the police on speed dial. It seems like the wisest course with a roommate with your type of...connections."

Needing an out, I tossed my skateboard on the ground. "You do that, Elena." I pushed off, leaving her and my dorm behind.

If only I could skate away from the wildfire that was my life. Every time I got a handle on it, another spark spread it wider. One day, hopefully soon, I'd be able to breathe without constantly putting out fires. Today just wasn't that day.

Six

HELEN

ON THE FLOOR OF the dressing room at work, I counted out a thick stack of bills. It looked like a lot, but it was mostly ones. The sight of the cash filled me with relief and sickness. But I kept counting. It was what I did: moved on, did what needed to be done to survive, no dwelling.

Carina sat down across from me, kicking off her platform heels. "How much, girlie?"

"I'm not done, but it looks like a little less than nine hundred," I answered.

She whistled. "Girl, you know you'd make bank in the private rooms."

I shook my head. "I know, but I can't. If a dude got handsy—which we both know they do, don't try to tell me otherwise—I'd be carted out of here in cuffs. I don't have the disposition to let that shit slide."

I worked at a strip club and had since the beginning of summer. Ninety-five percent of the time, I served drinks in booty shorts and a crop top. Tonight had been part of the five percent I tried not to think about.

The first time, I'd promised myself it was a one-time thing. I hated every second of taking my clothes off on stage. The jeers, the sweaty, frothing men staring at me...I felt disgusting the whole time. But I made a lot of money doing it—money I needed because of my poor excuse for a mother.

"I get that, babe. I guess I'm too good at detaching my brain from my body. It's like it's not even me they're touching, you know?"

Carina was one of the few dancers I liked at Savage Beauties. The rest were catty bitches, but she was real and sweet for a tough girl. She had a kid she was raising on her own, and like me, she did what she had to do to survive. She was a bomb-ass dancer, with a fat ass and gorgeous tits, so she was rolling in green every night she worked. I liked serving in her section because her customers tended to be in happy, spendy moods.

"Tonight was desperation, C. I make enough to get by serving." I tucked the cash in my purse and stretched my legs out in front of me. They were shiny with oil, and my toes were red from being stuffed into borrowed platforms a full size too small. "And maybe I don't want to get to the point where I can detach from my body."

She gave me a sad smile. "Yeah, I get that." Then she nudged my leg. "No more blues tonight. You made some good money. You'll be square with the scary dude. Take a victory lap."

That made me laugh. Carina had lived through a lot of darkness and didn't blink when I shared mine. She knew about Reno, Amir, my little sister, and my wretched mother. She'd even offered to front me the money I owed, but I couldn't take it. Not when it was going toward building a life for her and her kid.

Besides, showing my tits and ass to a bunch of pervs didn't kill me. It made me feel gross, but I was alive and mostly intact. I hoped like hell I could avoid a repeat performance, but I'd ride the pole again if I needed to. It was a strange comfort to know I always had that as backup.

I climbed to my sore feet and reached down to help Carina up. She took my hand, and we almost both went down when she wobbled on her sky-high heels.

"Thanks, boo." She smacked a kiss on my cheek. "See you tomorrow night?"

"Yep." I squeezed her bicep. "I'm out. Have a good night, love."

It was a long bus ride home. In my suite, I scoured the oil and memories off my skin until I was raw, then climbed into Madeline's old sheets, tucked them around me, and fell into an exhausted, dead-to-the-world sleep.

**

The Palisades never changed. It had been in the same state of decay for as long as I could remember. And for the most part, it was like the Hotel California—people never checked out.

I guess I should've said they rarely checked out. My best friend, Gabe, used to live in the trailer behind mine. He moved up and out after graduating high school, using his soccer skills to land him a full ride to college. I was happy he had no more ties to this place, even if I felt somewhat left behind. Not that I blamed him. I'd turn my back on this place in a heartbeat if Luciana weren't here.

After dropping off the cash I owed Amir, I skated to my old neighborhood to pick up my sister. She was waiting for me outside the trailer, her own skateboard in her hands. Since she'd moved back in with our mom last summer, she'd become my mini-me. I got her a board and taught her how to skate. She stole my Supreme hat and saved her pennies for a pair of checkered Vans. I bought her a pair of black high-tops, because I liked having a mini-me a little too much.

"Luc!" I called.

Her smile was bright and wide. "Hells!"

"Come on, girlie. I'm starving."

She ran down the two steps leading to our trailer, rushing toward me. The front door opened, and my mom stuck her head out. Once upon a time, people would smile at us and tell her I could be her twin. That was before the pills and heavy drinking

had demolished her beauty. Now, she was rail thin with a
bloated face, mottled skin, and sunken eyes. Victoria Ortega
was a shell of her former self. Looking at her would've made me
sad if she didn't make me so very angry.

"Not gonna say hi to your mom, Helen Maria?" She lit a
cigarette and took a long drag.

"Hi, Mom." Luciana reached me and tucked herself into my
side. "I'm taking Luc to breakfast. Want to join us?"

Luc stiffened at my invitation. Our Saturday mornings were
her escape from our mom. Luc definitely didn't want her
company. But I knew our mother better than that. If Luciana
wasn't home, Mom could take a pill, shoot up, invite a guy over,
and get laid in exchange for some cash or drugs…or whatever
the hell she did.

"Not hungry this morning," she answered. "Do you have the
money for Reno, baby?"

I rolled my eyes. "What if I didn't?"

She shook her cig in my direction. "Make sure you do. You
don't want him coming around here when your sister's home, do
you?"

As if she cared about Luciana's safety. "I've got it, Mom. Don't
even worry about it."

If she had something else to say, I didn't stay and listen. I
turned Luc around, and we walked down the cracked and
crumbling path through the gravel parking lot to the sidewalk
that led to Main Street, where the T was.

We put down our boards and skated together. For the first
time in a week, I felt the tension releasing from my shoulders. I
basked in the wind whipping through my hair and my sister's
random giggles. I loved that she still giggled at twelve. Luciana
had maintained a childlike sweetness even though her life had
been pretty tumultuous from the start. Now, it was my job to
ensure she didn't have it squeezed out of her, living where she
did, seeing what she was bound to see.

The T was crowded when we walked through the door. I stood on my toes, scanning for an empty booth. Luc grabbed my free hand, so we didn't get separated when a big group slid by us to get to the exit.

I spotted a loner taking up a whole booth when he *should* have been occupying a single stool at the counter, considering how busy it was. When I realized who the loner was, I tugged Luciana along with me straight to his table. When we arrived, I pushed her into the empty side and slid my ass in next to her.

"Good morning, Theodore."

Theo had a cup of coffee and a textbook spread out in front of him, and he was grinning at me like he wasn't surprised at all I was suddenly across from him.

"Good morning, Little Tiger. I didn't know we had plans, but I can't say I'm disappointed you're here." He was practically cooing at me in his lovely, low voice. I wanted to cover Luc's ears so she wouldn't succumb to it. And since the last thing he'd said to me was he regretted ever setting eyes on me, I was surprised at the coo.

"None of that." I wagged a finger.

His grin widened, no sign of regret anywhere. "None of that? Okay, Helen. Whatever you say. What brings you to my table?"

"We're sitting here since you're taking up more than your fair share of the restaurant."

He looked at me for a long time. Way too long to be socially acceptable. His stare weighed a hundred pounds, and I felt it as it slid along my skin. Then he closed his textbook and pushed it aside.

"I was under the impression you were avoiding me."

I shrugged. His impression was correct, but I didn't need to confirm it. "If Freddy Krueger had been sitting here, I would have joined him. It's not personal, I'm just really hungry and didn't want to wait for a table."

After a long beat where he did some more staring, his attention shifted to Luc. "I know you're not her daughter because the age difference is too close, but you look like a shrunken version of Helen. I'm going to guess you're her sister."

Luc bit her bottom lip and nodded. "I am. I'm Luciana. Helen calls me Luc."

He tipped his head at her. "I'm Theo. Helen calls me Theodore. No idea why, since it's not my name."

She giggled. "Do you mind?"

"Not in the least. Do you mind when she calls you Luc?"

"Nope. I like it because it means she cares about me."

Theo's blue eyes had the audacity to twinkle at me. "Think that's why she calls me Theodore?"

"No," I answered for her. "Don't get it twisted, dude."

He guffawed. "Oh, I've been downgraded to dude now?"

Luc nodded. "That's what Hells calls all her guy friends. They're all dude or bro. She's got a lot of guy friends. They're all skaters. They call me Little Hells when I go to the skate park with her."

Theo raised his eyebrows at me. "I don't think Helen considers me her friend."

Luc, being the sweet, innocent girl she was, tilted her head. "You're not her friend? Then why did she want to sit with you?"

He shook his head. "Your sister is a mystery to me."

She took her hat off and placed it on the seat next to her. "She's not so mysterious. Helen likes skating and me. She doesn't like bullcrap or fake people. Don't be fake or feed her bullcrap, and she'll like you eventually."

Theo tapped his forehead. "I'm committing that to memory."

The waitress stopped by and took our orders, then Theo and Luc fell into an easy conversation about her school and skateboarding. I'd made a mistake sitting here. First, she'd never let me hear the end of Theo from this point forward. But more importantly, Saturday breakfasts were a way for me to touch base and find out what our mom had been pulling during the week. So far, nothing alarming had gone down, but I spent a lot of time waiting for the other shoe to drop. It had definitely dropped on me a few times growing up, and it had always been filled with lead, leaving me bloody and broken. But Mom knew I was watching. I hadn't had anyone watching out for me—Luc always would.

Our food arrived, and Luc tucked in. Her omelet was as big as her head, and she'd devour every last bite. I cut into my stack of pancakes. Right as I stuffed a huge bite in my mouth, two blonde girls stopped at our table, and Theo stiffened.

"Hi, The." Blondie One reached out and squeezed his hand.

"Hey, Theo." Blondie Two tossed her hair behind her shoulder, giving me and Luciana her back, and since I was sitting, her ass.

Nice.

He nodded at them, but no eye twinkle. "Hey."

Luciana elbowed me, but I was too interested in the show to look at her. Blondie One was still touching Theo's hand. Interesting.

"How are you, The?" she asked.

"Good. Fine. You?" Theo was polite but curt.

"I'm okay. I was hoping we could talk. Don't you think we should?"

His eyes didn't sparkle. Instead, they hardened like stone. "I don't think we have anything to say. But you can text me, and I'll see if I have time. Right now, I'm having breakfast with my friends."

"Oh." She dragged her index finger from his wrist to his fingertip, then twisted her head to glance back at Luciana and me. "I didn't even notice you had company."

He exhaled heavily through his nose, his cheeks tinting pink. "I'm gonna guess my company is the only reason you walked into this restaurant, Abby."

She sucked in a breath, the sound covering my own gasp. This bitch. I'd bet my hat Blondie Two was Zadie's other roommate from last year.

"That isn't true. Kayleigh saw you through the window when we were on our way to the café for coffee. We had to come in and say hi," Abby explained.

Kayleigh nodded hard enough for her hair to swish around her shoulders. "She's right, Theo. We were just walking by. I haven't seen you in ages, so I made Abs come in with me." Even though I could only see her ass, I imagined she was poking her lip out in a pout. "I miss you."

Theo moved his hand from under Abby's to grip the edge of the table. "You've said hello. I'll text you when I'm not having breakfast with friends."

That was a dismissal if I ever heard one. These bitches had to be dense because they didn't leave, so I was done. They could stay or go, I didn't care. I just wanted to eat my food. I looked at Luciana. She was staring at me with wide eyes.

"Eat, boo," I whispered. "Don't let it get cold."

"You too," she said softly.

I stabbed my fork into my pancakes, holding up the bite I was about to take. "Down the hatch."

Giggling, she followed suit, digging into her omelet. The blondes lingered, but my ears were closed to them, and I had lifted my leg onto the seat to face Luciana, giving them my back. Abby was still murmuring to Theo, but I decided not to give a damn.

"I'm sorry." Theo tapped the table in front of my plate to get my attention. "They're gone."

Luciana scrunched her nose. "Those girls were so rude. One of them stuck her butt in Helen's face, and the other one was all smoochy touchy with you, then pretended like she hadn't even seen us sitting here. God, who were those girls?"

I snorted a laugh, peeking at Theo from under my lashes. His shoulders were shaking with silent laughter.

"Theodore has unfortunate taste in girls. The smoochy-touchy one is his ex. Although, I'm not sure she's gotten the message that they're broken up."

Luciana's gaze whipped to Theo. "*That* rude girl was your girlfriend? Ugh."

He wiped his hand over his mouth, somewhat sobering. "I don't have any idea what was up with her. Never seen her do anything like that." His eyes flicked to me. "Considering she did the breaking, pretty sure she knows we're through."

Something about the knowledge that that beautiful, rude girl dumped Theo lodged in the pit of my stomach. I couldn't really explain it, except now I knew he'd still be with her if he'd had a choice.

"Didn't look like it," I muttered, giving my attention to my pancakes again.

"Yeah," Luc agreed. "She was being all flirty. But that's probably because she saw you sitting here with Helen, who's ten times hotter than she is, and got jealous. Honestly, no one can compete with Helen, so why even try?"

"You have a point, little hell-raiser," Theo told her.

"You just agreed Helen's hot." She elbowed me hard under the table, and from his huff of breath, Theo didn't miss it.

He picked up his coffee, staring at me over the brim. "I can't argue with facts."

She fell back against her seat and sighed. "Wow. Just wow."

I groaned. "Don't fall for it, boo. Yesterday, a guy with no teeth and extremely questionable personal hygiene practices told me I was hot. It's not the compliment you might think it is." Not to mention the slimy assholes who'd thrown money at me while I shook my tits for them last night. But I'd really rather not think about them. Really, really.

He winced at that but didn't argue. A man calling his girl hot was a compliment. A man calling a woman he barely knew and who'd never belong to him hot wasn't.

When our plates were empty and we were waiting for the check, Theo checked his phone, then asked, "What's the plan for today?"

Luc answered before I could spit out 'None of your business.' "Hells always takes me grocery shopping for the week because our mom is a loser and would let me starve if it was up to her. She'd let herself starve too, so it's not like personal or anything."

I squeezed her leg, digging my fingers into the hollow beside her knee. "You don't need to tell Theodore our business, kid."

She frowned at me. "It's my business. I can tell it to whoever I want."

Theo mimed zipping his lips. "I won't tell anyone. I can't say I'll forget what you just said, because damn, little hell-raiser, I don't think I ever will. But your business is yours, and I'm really glad you have Helen watching out for you."

I squared my shoulders, not appreciating his rich-boy sympathy in the least. "We don't need your pity, dude." I slapped a twenty on the table. "This should cover us plus tip. We're out. It's been real."

Grabbing my board off the floor, I slid from the booth and gestured for Luc to follow me. She was slower, more reluctant, moving at a snail's pace. That gave Theo the opportunity to slap down another twenty on top of mine and rise to his feet. His mouth was pinched with displeasure. When he eyed our boards tucked under our arms, it became even tighter.

Outside the diner, Theo rounded on me. "You're going to the store on your skateboards?"

"Yeah. We're fine."

Luc got between us. "Helen carries the bags herself. She's so good at balancing, you wouldn't believe it. Mom has a car, but it doesn't run anymore. But Helen skateboards everywhere, and she can carry a lot when she's doing it. I mean, it'd be easier if we had a car, but she's the GOAT, I'm telling you. She doesn't let anything stop her."

I grabbed Luciana's arm. "Enough telling tales. We've got places to go."

Theo jerked his head toward the parking lot. "I've got a car and no plans. I'll drive."

Luc started toward him, but I held on. "No, we're good."

He stared me down, his features pulling into a sharp line. "I'll drive, Helen. Don't be obstinate."

Luc kept tugging in my hold. "I'm going with Theo."

Two against one, I wasn't going to win. As stubborn as I could be, I didn't hold a candle to my sister when she got stuck on an idea—and she was very clearly stuck on the idea of Theo being a nice guy.

"Fine." I stomped by him, my arm going around Luciana's shoulders. "But if you kidnap and murder us, I'm going to be pissed, Theodore."

He laughed, not denying his homicidal intentions.

Even if he didn't murder us, I had a feeling I was still going to walk away pissed.

Seven

THEO

HELEN HAD GROWN UP in a shithole. Even though she hadn't allowed me to follow her and her little sister to their trailer, the second I pulled into the gravel parking lot, I came to that conclusion. As I waited for Helen to come back, I got out of my loaner car and wandered down the path that wound between trailers.

Rust. Trash. Broken windows. Hanging doors.

There were decent, even nice, trailer parks, and then there was The Palisades. It was so far from being nice or decent, those words didn't exist in the same universe.

Once they unloaded their groceries in the trailer, I drove Hells and Luc to an apartment complex a few minutes away. I waited again while Helen walked her sister up to her friend's apartment to hang out for the afternoon.

Ten minutes later, Helen reappeared, stopping in front of where I leaned against the car.

"Good deed done for the day. Let me get my board out of your trunk and you can go on your way."

I tipped my head to the side. "Get in the car, Helen."

"Give me my board, Theodore."

"Nope." Striking fast, I circled my arms under her ass, lifting her off the ground. She squealed and kicked, but not hard enough for me to believe she meant it. "I'm driving you to campus like a fucking gentleman."

"Like a fucking psycho."

I tossed her in the passenger seat and leaned over her to strap her in. Little pants escaped her parted lips, hitting my ear. I turned my head, bringing our noses an inch apart.

Jesus, she was pretty. There was not a spot of blemish on her masterpiece of a face. Her lips were as red as they'd been when she'd sat down for breakfast, leading me to believe there was witchcraft in her lipstick. All I could think about was how much effort it would take to make it disappear. And how enjoyable it would be finding out.

I pinched her chin between two fingers. "Stay here, Tiger."

She swatted my hand away, and I laughed and locked her inside the car while I rounded it to the driver's side. As I slid into my seat and hit the ignition, it hit me that I was always laughing with this girl. After an unbelievably shitty few months, it was a relief to know I still had it in me.

I turned to her. "Do you need to stop anywhere else before we hit campus?"

"No." Her focus was anywhere but me. "Straight back to the dorm is good."

"All right." Nodding to the apartment building, I asked, "Think she's good here?"

Her head twisted my way. "Yeah. I've met her friend and the family a few times. They're solid. They let her hang out as much as she wants, which is a lot."

"Is she going to be okay when she goes home?"

Helen's breath hitched. "My mother knows the consequences if anything happens to Luc. She's neglectful, but she won't hurt her."

"I could've used a sister like you growing up."

"Me too," she murmured, her head falling back on her seat. "Can we go? I need a nap."

"Yeah." I threw her a glance as I pulled out of the lot. "Late night?"

"Mmm."

That was it. Stonewall Helen was back in full force, arms crossed over her chest, jaw set. So far, I'd seen her soft twice. The first, when she'd relaxed in my lap in the library. The second was with her sister. After seeing where she grew up, I got it. I carried the same hardness in me. It had taken me a solid year of living with my father and stepmom to let my guard down and feel physically safe. Helen wasn't there. The part of me that loved to rise to a challenge really wanted to get her there.

But shit, I was no white knight. My head was barely above water as it was. I couldn't carry her too. If I tried, she'd probably shove me under anyway.

Taking the long route, I cruised down Main Street, passing Savage Wheelz. "Last year, whenever I was down here, I peeked in the windows. Never saw you inside."

I shouldn't have been looking at all, not when I'd had Abby, but that one encounter with Helen had left me curious. I was *still* curious.

Helen glanced at the skate shop as we passed. "Yeah, I don't work there anymore. I haven't for over a year."

I took that in. "Where do you work now?"

"Are you going to peek in the windows there too?"

"Don't need to do that. I see you all the time now."

"You needed to last year?"

I bit the inside of my cheek. I had no answer for that. Helen sighed, slumping lower in her seat. I drove through campus in silence and pulled into a spot outside Helen's dorm. She didn't get out right away, and I was in no rush for her to be gone.

"Thanks for being cool to Luciana." She unbuckled her seat belt but stayed put.

My brow pinched. "That's not something you need to thank me for. She's a kid. A good kid at that."

She nodded, peering out the windshield. "Yeah...well, that doesn't mean shit to a lot of people. She's sweet, and I try to show her the good so she'll keep it as long as she can, you know? I lost my sweet way too young. I'm not letting that be her."

"I'm glad she has you, but I don't think all your sweet is gone, Tiger. I saw it when you were with your sister. And maybe I felt it a little when you were curled up in my lap reading Shakespeare."

Twisting in my seat, I studied her profile. The straight slope of her nose. The pout of her red lips. The stubborn jut of her chin. Every one of her features was so purely Helen.

The face that launched a thousand ships. *Jesus.*

She turned suddenly, her gaze whipping over my face in a way that seemed accusatory. Of what, I had no idea. I never got to ask, because the next second, she lunged across the console, and her mouth landed on mine. Hard. Fierce. Her fingers balled my T-shirt while she licked at my lips until they opened from pure instinct and my tongue pushed hers back into her own mouth, twisting around it.

This wasn't sweet. I didn't know what it was. My mind was two steps behind, and her warm, soft lips on mine refused to let me catch up. But I wasn't one to let things happen to me without having a say—and that included a sneak attack kiss by a girl I never saw coming.

I held her face in my hands, tipped it back, and took her deeper. She moaned, high and tremulous, and I licked the inside of her mouth, tasting that moan, swallowing it down my throat, letting it heat my chest and belly. It was pure Helen.

As suddenly as she came, she ripped away, covering her mouth with her hand. Her eyes flicked to mine for one beat of my thrashing heart, then she threw open the car door and jumped out.

"Helen." I climbed out my side, no plan other than not letting her leave it like this. I rounded to the rear of my car and caught her arm. "Stop."

She looked from my grip on her to the trunk. "Pop the trunk. I need my board."

Tugging her into me, I narrowed my eyes. "I don't get you, baby."

Her shoulder lifted, and it infuriated me. She was not going to shrug off that fire she'd just sparked—not when it was still smoldering and my dick was about to punch a hole through my shorts.

"Nothing to get, dude. You're cute, you were being nice, I felt like kissing you, it's done. Now, I want my board so I can go into my dorm and take a really long nap."

"That's it?" Her breasts pressed flush to my chest with each heaving breath she took. No way I believed a word coming from her pretty red mouth. "That's all it was?"

"That's it." She tapped on my car. "Trunk, Theo. I work tonight, so I need that nap right now."

"Where do you work?" I volleyed back.

"Somewhere you can't peek through the windows." She tapped the car harder. "Trunk. Now."

I studied her, but it did no good. That warm, soft woman who'd been sprawled across my chest only minutes ago, clinging to me like I was her favorite thing ever, had disappeared so completely, it was like it had never happened. Her lips were still red when she rubbed them together. I didn't even manage to kiss that damn lipstick off her.

I let go of her and opened the trunk. She snatched up her board before I could reach for it, and I grabbed her arm, stopping her from sprinting away.

"You don't have a car."

Her eyes rolled sideways. "No kidding."

"Then how are you getting to L.A. to see the performance next weekend?"

"Bus."

Nope. Never happening.

"I'll drive you."

"I can take the bus."

I slid my hand from her arm to the center of her back. "You can, but you won't, because I'll be driving you. You can keep arguing, but it's a waste of time. As pragmatic as you are, I don't think you're a girl who *likes* wasting time. Agree to ride with me here and now so we don't argue for a week just to come to a conclusion that's already foregone. You're coming in my car, not riding the bus."

"You know," her toe kicked mine, "I existed before you knew me. I have ridden the bus my whole life. It's no big deal."

My hand traveled under her hair to squeeze her nape. "Like you said, that was before I knew you. I'm here now. No more bus, Helen."

Her head cocked. "Will you have the Bimmer back?"

"I should."

Her eyes flitted over me, then she gave a sharp nod. "Fine. You're right. I don't want to argue. You can give me a ride."

I huffed a short laugh. "Thanks for allowing me the privilege."

Her mouth quirked. "I *really* like your car."

That laugh went on longer. "Asshole."

Her lips curved a bit higher. "Dick." She shoved my chest. "Go away now. I need sleep."

"All right." I dropped my hand. "Have a good rest of your weekend, Hells."

She gave me a mocking salute, ducked out from under my hold on her neck, and ran up the steps to her front door. Just before she disappeared inside, she turned back, gave me a long look, then let the door close behind her.

SWEAT DRIPPED INTO MY eyes as I climbed the steps to the frat house. A couple beer cans littered the porch, but the guys chipped in for a cleaning service on top of the one provided by the university, so the place stayed pretty clean despite the filth stirred up in these walls. That was the one thing I really liked about living here.

But then, I was a non-frat guy living in a frat house. One of these things didn't look like the others—and that thing was me. It was out of necessity. If I'd stayed on track, I'd be in the athlete's dorm, but since I'd quit wrestling over the summer, that was out of the question. Even if I'd been allowed to live there, most of the guys from the team were pissed at me for abandoning them without warning, so it would have been untenable. My dad, being who he was, pulled some strings and got me a single room in the frat. As much as I didn't love it, the other option was moving back home, and that really fucking wasn't an option.

I'd put up with this living arrangement for a year. Anything was doable for a year.

"Wait up, man."

I paused at the front door, turning back to see Daniel jogging up the steps. He clapped my shoulder. "Hey."

He shook his head and followed me inside. "Look at you, already up and working out. Meanwhile, some of us are just getting in from last night."

"Oh yeah?" He stayed on my heels to the kitchen where I filled a cup of water. A few other guys were in there, scrounging for food, but Daniel had been right, it was early, so the house was still pretty quiet.

"Good night?" I wasn't really interested, but he clearly wanted me to ask.

"Fucking fantastic." He fished the OJ out of the fridge and poured himself a glass. "Got a new dime piece I'm tagging. Sophomore transfer, fine as hell."

Deacon staggered in, rubbing his eyes. He jabbed a finger at me. "Fuck you. You were supposed to wake me up so I could run with you."

"I tried. You were dead to the world." I'd knocked on his door once. Working out was my time. Deacon sometimes horned in on it when he got his ass out of bed, but I wasn't about to put much effort into waking him since I didn't want him there in the first place.

"*Unf.*" He swung around to Daniel. "I caught the tail end of your conversation. Who's fine as hell?"

"New girl. Elena. Blonde, mouthy, fire in bed. What was it John Mayer called Jessica Simpson? 'Sexual napalm'? That's my girl too." He bit his bottom lip. "Cannot get enough."

Deacon groaned, and my stomach churned. I could've gone the rest of my life without witnessing Daniel bite his lip like that. Jesus.

"Does your girl have a friend?" Deacon asked.

Daniel wagged a finger. "Funny you say that. I was just getting around to that topic with my boy Theo here. Elena does have a friend or two, one of them being Miss Abigail Fitzgerald."

I said nothing. What was there to say about Abby? We went to the same school. Our paths would cross. Friends would see her. Sightings would be reported. I didn't want to hear it. Seeing her still didn't feel natural or easy. And honestly, I was still pissed off enough to avoid her when I could.

I hadn't returned her texts after our run-in at the diner. For one, she'd acted like a cunt, which I wasn't down for. But also, I wasn't sure there was anything to say, or if I wanted to hear anything else from her ever again. In my opinion, she'd said quite e-fucking-nough when I'd failed her ultimatum and she'd unceremoniously broken us after two years together.

So, yeah, I didn't need to hear about Abby sightings. When I didn't rise to Daniel's bait, he and Deacon continued right along.

I drank my water.

Daniel slammed down his glass a couple minutes later. "Excellent weekend. Now, I have to shower the pussy off my dick and get myself to class. Jesus, I'm so behind, and it's only week two."

He pushed off the counter, leaving his dirty glass behind. In a move that was surprisingly responsible, Deacon placed it in the sink.

"How far did you run this morning?" he asked.

"Seven miles."

His brows popped. "How early did you go out?"

"Six thirty. Like I said, you were dead to the world."

He shook his head. "You know, you don't have to keep going so hard now that you're not wrestling."

"My body needs it. I can't tell it no."

A long stare. Cluck of his tongue. Tragic headshake. Deacon judged where he had no room to be judging. "Pretty sure your body sent you a very loud and clear message in May, man. I heard it when I sat in the ER with you. No idea how you missed it."

I froze. "We're not talking about that."

His head bowed. "Just giving you a reminder. You don't need to push yourself so hard anymore."

The scoff that came out of me was bitter. "Seven miles isn't pushing myself. I think you know that. Don't need a reminder anyway." I swiped at my mouth, then my forehead. "I need to shower. I stink."

It would probably take me a lifetime to forget the feeling of sitting in the ER with Deacon, thinking my heart was going to explode in my chest. Stress, they said. Arrhythmia, they said.

Take it easy, they said. All I heard was a body I'd treated like a fucking temple had failed me.

In the shower, I felt it. The pressure mounting, tight in my chest. It still pissed me off, especially that Deacon had been there to see me like that. Scared and weak and vulnerable—and he would not let me forget it.

I still pushed myself because I was not scared or weak or vulnerable. I'd rid myself of some of the major stressors in my life. Now, my body needed to understand it wasn't going to fail me again. That wasn't an option.

Dry from my shower, awake from the seven miles I put in this morning, I grabbed my laptop, shoved it in my backpack, and set off to my first class.

Shit start to the week, with Deacon and Daniel getting in my face and my ex being thrust to the front of my mind. It was only Monday, though. Plenty of time to get better.

Eight

HELEN

LACHLAN TOOK THE SEAT beside me, giving me a chin tip. I tipped right back.

He went about his business, like he did at the start of every class, setting up his laptop, stretching out his long-ass legs, ignoring me and everyone else while he waited for Professor Davis to commence his lecture.

"You know, you could have stayed with me on Monday, but you just left me with *him*."

His head swiveled my way. "You get hurt?"

"No."

"He say something you didn't like?"

"No." *Yes. Always.*

His big shoulder lifted. "You're all right, girl."

"He *could've* said something I didn't like."

His eyes held mine. "Didn't, though. I think you can take care of yourself against that guy anyway."

"Not all of us are seven feet tall, Lock."

"You don't need to be. That guy *could* hurt you, but I get the impression he'd saw off his arms before hurting a woman."

"I don't know about that," I mumbled.

He chuckled, low and velvety. "Yeah, you do."

Lachlan had taken the title of my seat neighbor for one hour, Monday, Wednesday, and Friday. At first, I liked him because he was silent. Then because he occupied the chair Theo might have otherwise taken. And last, because he'd stuck by my side on the way out of class both Friday and Monday. Until he'd essentially handed me off to Theo, which was bullshit.

Lock knew less about Theo than I did. He'd used some bro-code instinct to declare him non-threatening. When you were a six foot six, iron teddy bear, I guess not too many people were threatening, so perhaps his impression was slightly skewed.

All that to say, Theo had walked me to my dorm on Monday. And annoyingly, he'd pinned me to yet another wall, as was his way, it seemed.

"*Bad start to my day. Why's it looking better now that I'm seeing you?*"

"*That sounds like something you should be asking yourself.*"

Forget that those words did things to me. I wasn't interested in the things the words were doing or the man who'd said them.

"*I keep thinking about you lunging at me, Tiger.*"

My nose crinkled. "*I didn't lunge. Wrong girl, dude.*"

He lowered his face, bringing it close to mine. "*Don't call me dude.*"

"*I'm a skater. Everyone's dude.*"

He slowly shook his head, never looking away from me, not even for a second. "*I know why you're doing it. I don't like it, and it will not stand.*"

My breath came faster as desire and panic swirled in my chest. But my mouth ignored the panic, and as always, got me in trouble when I was trying to avoid it.

"*Oh yeah? What will you do if I say it again...dude?*"

In a flash, I was whirled around, cheek flattened to the brick wall, Theo, warm and dominant, at my back. One arm braced next to my head, the other moved his palm along my ribs and hip, skating over the outside curve of my ass.

"Why do you drive me crazy, Helen? Why are you in my head?"

His mouth spoke hot, frustrated words against my neck.

"Again, Theodore, that's a question you really need to ask yourself." I would have been more convincing without the quiver in my voice.

Or maybe I was convincing enough. One long, wet touch of his lips on my nape, and he backed up, turned me around, nodded, then walked away.

I did not like Theo, and I was still beating myself up for kissing him, because yeah, there was no denying I'd lunged at him. The only excuse I had was I'd been emotionally depleted from school and Luciana and Amir's visit and stripping and all the stress and bad of the week. I wasn't in the market for a boyfriend—definitely not one like Theo. No-strings fucking wasn't my thing anymore either. So, yeah, I shouldn't have been kissing random rich boys in their luxury cars—especially not ones with bitchy ex-girlfriends who clearly hadn't retracted their hooks.

· · ● **●** · **●** ● · ·

NEAR THE END OF class, I leaned into Lock. "You're not going to protect me when we walk out of here today, are you?"

His attention remained on his laptop. "You don't need it."

"And if I want it?"

His head moved back and forth. "Not getting tangled in your drama, girl."

"It's Helen, not girl."

"I know."

"You're annoying, Lock."

"I'm not."

"You are." I leaned closer so Professor Davis didn't beam me with his laser eyes for talking during his class. "You know I don't want his attention."

"If I knew that, I'd walk with you, keep him away."

"Annoying," I muttered.

His lips curved into a smirk as he shut down his laptop and clicked the lid shut. This was why my best friends growing up had been boys. They were easy to get, emotions didn't run high, and yeah, they'd protect me if I picked a fight with someone I shouldn't have. Or if one of my mom's boyfriends got a little too handsy. Not that I couldn't hold my own when shit went down, but my size put serious limitations on the pack of my punch.

I shouldn't have worried anyway. At the end of class, Theo tore out of the room without a backward glance. Which was good. It was what I wanted. The game we'd been playing was getting old. It was high time it was over.

That was why I did my studying in my room on Thursday. Shakespeare didn't have the same feeling when it was inside my head and not read aloud while cradled in the lap of a guy who smelled delicious and felt even better. But it was safer for everyone. I was at Savage U for a purpose—and it didn't include wasting time and energy on things and people that didn't matter.

By Friday, I was dragging. I'd worked three nights in an attempt to recoup the money I'd lost from trusting asshole Deacon, not to mention the boost of income I got through selling for Amir. I'd never been a big dealer or anything, but that extra couple hundred every week or two had sometimes meant whether I had food on the table, especially back in high school.

Since I was dragging, my patience was thin, which meant when I saw Theo lurking around the door at the end of Davis's class, he took the brunt when I snapped.

"I'm not sucking your dick, Theodore. Why won't you take a hint?" My voice...wasn't quiet. Classmates behind me released a collective gasp. Beside me, Lock clucked his tongue. But I was done, you know? Ignoring their judgment, Lock's "not cool, girl," and Theo's expression of pure shock, I strode from the building, *needing* my bed more than anything.

Theo fell into step beside me. Hands tucked in his pockets, fury emanated from his taut muscles. Any second, I expected to be shoved into a brick wall and shown that yeah, I *was* going to be sucking his dick.

"I don't know what the fuck happened to you that led you to believe a guy paying you some attention and kindness is only out for getting his cock sucked, but that's not me."

His hard, furious tone had me stumbling more than his words. And when I stumbled, he reached out and caught me, steadying me. Theo stepped backward, off the path cutting through a courtyard between buildings, pulling me into the grass and under the shade of an ancient tree.

"Life happened," I said simply, even though it was anything but simple. "Don't pretend you wouldn't take it if I offered. Or take it if you thought you could get away with it."

The tendons at the side of his neck swelled. His face flushed. "Tell me you don't believe that about me, Hells. Tell me you don't believe I'd take something from you you didn't freely give me. Tell me you know I wouldn't do that."

I met his eyes. His angry, sparking with rage, blue eyes. "Any man is capable of getting to the place where he'll take what he isn't given."

He released me to drag his fingers through the sides of his black hair. "Helen...no."

I lifted a shoulder. My guts were a writhing mess, but I didn't let it play out on the surface.

"Was there a reason you were waiting for me?"

Exhaling heavily, Theo paced like a caged lion right in front of me. I waited him out when I could have been escaping because maybe guilt was seeping in a little. I didn't know Theo, but from what he'd shown me, he wasn't deserving of my wrath. Not yet, at least.

"Theo—"

He stopped abruptly, swinging his fury onto me. Even then, barely more than strangers, I could read him, and I knew that fury wasn't mine. If the men who'd shaped me, turned me wary and skittish, were standing here with us, Theo would've unleashed on them. It was only us, though. There was nowhere for it to go. So he paced, tugged his hair, grunted for me to go on.

"I shouldn't have said that." I dragged my teeth along my lip. "I don't know if it makes you feel better, but I think what I said reflects more poorly on me than you. I made myself look like a crazy bitch, and you, my poor, hapless victim."

"Is that an apology?" he groused.

"Yeah." I wasn't much for saying sorry, but right was right, and I wasn't that. "Sorry, Theodore."

Theo stopped pacing and stared at me. He did it for so long, he made me twitchy. My fingers brushed over my hair, under my bottom lip, smoothed my shirt, and finally tucked away in my pockets when I couldn't keep still.

Then he burst out laughing and grabbed me by the nape, pulling me into him. "I didn't expect that, Little Tiger. Not in a million years."

My hands were trapped in my pockets, otherwise, I definitely would have pushed him away. "Don't kiss me."

His head lowered. "Why do you think I'm going to kiss you?"

My eyes narrowed. "You're getting closer and your eyes are twinkling at me."

He chuckled, his warm breath ghosting over my lips. "You were just a complete dick to me. What makes you think I'd even *want* to kiss you?"

"Because you're obviously obsessed with—"

His mouth came down hard on mine, his playful mood vanishing. Wet, deep, he kissed me like we were naked in bed, not the middle of campus where anyone and everyone could see. And I participated, because along with his playful mood, my brain function ceased. My hands magically came untucked from my pockets and wound up beneath the back of his T-shirt, exploring the smooth, hard planes of his back and hips.

We were so close, pressed together so tight, when Theo's phone vibrated in his front pocket, I felt it too. It might as well have been a strike with a Taser zapping me back to reality. Except Theo didn't let me jump back from him when I tore my mouth away. He kept his hand buried in my hair, the other claiming the small of my back.

"Don't run," he warned.

"You're a liar. You said you didn't want to kiss me."

"Never said that."

Maybe he hadn't. I couldn't think straight—and that was a problem. I needed my wits around this man.

His phone vibrated again.

"Someone wants to talk to you."

He lowered his chin. "I'm talking to the only person I want to talk to right now. Whoever is texting can wait."

I couldn't handle the underlying sweetness of that. Not in a million years could I take that in and make it mine.

"So talk, Theodore."

His kiss-swollen lips twitched. "I need your phone number."

"Why?"

"So I can text when I'm out front of your dorm tomorrow."

My forehead fell into his chin. "Oh. I forgot."

He chuckled. "Yeah."

"I'm an asshole."

"You are an asshole, no argument."

I raised my face, laughing in spite of myself. "Give me your phone."

He let me go to dig his phone from his pocket, swiped his thumb on the screen to turn it on, then handed it over. At the top was a notification for a text.

Abby: *It was so good to see you on Wed.*

Okay. That didn't feel great to see, but it wasn't my business. I went to his contacts and typed in my name. Another text came in.

Abby: *I miss you too, you know.*

Too? Mmhmm. She probably wouldn't miss him if she knew where his tongue had just been.

Abby: *Come over tonight. We should talk. Or not. We don't have to talk. My bed is cold, baby.*

I tossed his phone at him, making him scramble to catch it. "My number's in there. You should check your texts, dude. Your girlfriend's all kinds of thirsty."

He caught my arm before I could leave, holding me while he read his texts. I tapped my foot impatiently in the grass, wishing I was the size of my attitude. I would have busted free with just my little pinkie as a weapon.

Tucking his phone away, he slipped his hand around mine and began walking. Since I was attached to him, I had to go with him.

"Um—"

"I'm taking you to the dorm," he gritted out.

"I know where it is."

"Stop fighting me. I had you soft for a minute, Helen. You were kissing me back, wanting it like I did. Then it was gone. All that soft covered by spikes and metal."

I tried to pull my hand away, even though it was futile. "You have a girlfriend."

"I don't."

"Then you have a complication I'm not interested in being part of. I'll take a ride from you if it's still on the table, but I'm not going any deeper than that. If the ride's off the table, tell me now so I can look up the bus schedule."

His hand tightened around mine. "You know I wouldn't do that."

He didn't deny he had a complication. But honestly, it was there in black and white. What was there to deny?

"Fine. I'll accept the ride and be grateful for it. But I don't want to walk through campus holding hands, I don't want to be pressed up against buildings, and most importantly, I don't want to be kissed. I made the mistake of opening that door last weekend. Now, I'm rectifying it. I've got way too much going on in my life to deal with your complications too. *Way* too much, Theodore."

"Okay." He didn't let go of my hand.

"Okay what?" I wiggled my fingers, but it was a no go.

"Okay. I heard what you said. We'll see."

"What will we see?"

"We'll see where this goes. Right now, I don't agree. You can close the door all you want, but I have the fucking key, so expect me to open it right back up."

I sighed, long and ragged. "Oh my fuck, you're demented. You are, aren't you? Did a screw get knocked loose when you were performing homoerotic acts disguised as a sport or have you always been this way?"

That made him snort. "You're calling wrestling homoerotic?"

Turning my head to look at him, I raised my brows. "Come on, dude. I saw the video where the guy had his face right in the other guy's boner. It was hot, and if you try to convince me, that's not the point of wrestling, I'll laugh. Plus, the outfits? Spandex, two young, fit guys grabbing each other? I'm not buying it."

Any other guy would have been pissed, but Theo laughed harder, letting go of my hand to wrap his arm around my shoulders and pull me deep into his side. And I liked it. Jesus, I liked hearing him laugh and having his arm around me like that.

Which meant I had to push him away. I couldn't like it. I had no room for twinkly eyes or kissing under ancient trees or complications. Theo was all those and more—and I. Just. Could. Not. Do. It.

Even though a small, sparkly heart-shaped part of me wished I could.

I slipped from beneath his arm. He let me do it, probably because we were at my dorm. Most likely also because he knew he'd have me for hours tomorrow, and I'd have to be nice to him or he could leave me in L.A.

"Bye, Tiger," he called after me.

Scrambling up the steps, I waved over my shoulder. I could still hear his low, lovely chuckle as I swiped my card to enter the dorm.

The faint buzz my interaction with Theo had given me evaporated when I entered my suite to find Elena lounging on the couch. Zadie was there too, a book in her lap in the armchair.

Elena's eagle eyes landed on me immediately. "My, my, our little Helen is blushing. Were you having a rendezvous with your criminal boyfriend in the bushes again?"

I scoffed and tossed my skateboard next to the door. "Hi, Zadie. There's no way you're doing homework on a Friday."

She was chewing on the corner of her lip. "I am. But only because if I get it all done tonight, I won't have to think about school until Monday."

"Genius," Elena supplied. "If I didn't have plans in an hour, I'd join you. Maybe next weekend."

"Really?" Zadie asked.

"Mmhmm." Elena nodded. "Lazy Sundays are my favorite, but I can get on board with lazy Saturdays too."

"Well, I do other things, so—"

Elena sliced her perfectly manicured nails through the air. "Shhh...shhh. I know you probably volunteer to sew blankets for orphans or plant trees or something, but that's not me. And you know, they say laziness is next to godliness."

Zadie's mouth fell open, but I shook my head. If Elena wanted to believe that was the saying, we should let her have it.

I went to the kitchenette, grabbed a soda from the mini-fridge, cracked it open, then started for my room. As much as I liked Zadie, I needed a nap before I faced another night at Savage Beauties. Plus...well, Elena.

"I'm taking a nap." I hit the frame of my door.

"Getting ready for a long night at the strip club?" Elena asked.

I stopped, froze, my eyes darting to Zadie. Her cheeks bloomed with color. She had told our third, unwanted roommate where I worked. I was none too pleased. And disappointed. She'd always given me the impression of being real and loyal.

"Wow, Z."

Zadie's eyes went round, her pretty face the picture of innocence.

Elena untucked her legs and rose from the couch. "Oh, come off it. Zadie didn't say shit. I used context clues to figure you out, girl. Skanky outfit, stack of one-dollar bills on your nightstand. You smell like perfume and desperation when you leave, and you come back with the scent of blue balls and old-man sweat clinging to you like a cloud. That reads strip club to me. You just confirmed it."

"I waitress," I said flatly. "But I think it's interesting you so closely study me. Consider discussing that with your therapist."

Elena pursed her lips. "Oooh, joking about mental health is such a sick burn."

"And putting down sex work when you were born with a silver spoon crammed up your lily-white ass is about as privileged and narrow minded as it comes."

I closed my door more gently than I thought myself capable and leaned heavy against it, tired down to my bones, and not from lack of sleep. Every day was a fight. It had been that way my whole life. Yeah, I brought some of it on myself. I knew that. I just didn't know how to lower my fists. I'd give a lot for a peaceful living situation, but simply looking at Elena's perfect, bitchtastic face made me pissy.

I could try. Maybe.

Throwing myself on my bed, I put my soda on my nightstand and took out my phone. If I was going to do some deep introspection, I needed company for that. I sent a text to my girl Penelope, who happened to be Elena's much nicer cousin and my best friend Gabe's girlfriend.

Me: *How do I live with Elena without murdering her?*

Pen: *Hi, babe.*

Me: *Hey, girlie. Now, advice.*

Pen: *Elena isn't so different from you.*

Me: *What did I do to you to make you hate me this way?*

Pen: *I'm serious! She's fiercely loyal, tough as nails, kinda scary, and wicked smart. Like you, Hells.*

Me: *Ugh.*

Pen: *Love you, babe, but she's the other side of your coin.*

Me: *All right. Done with that line of convo. I need help.*

Pen: *Anything. BTW, Gabe's here reading over my shoulder. He's still dying that you and El are roommates.*

Me: *Tell Gabe to go fuck himself.*

Pen: *I would never! (he says to tell you he loves you endlessly)*

Me: *Ugh, same. Anyway, the help I need is how do I stop fighting?*

Pen: *Explain.*

Me: *There's a guy. Our lips keep touching. And every fucking time, I push him away. I don't even know if I want to push him away, but I can't stop doing it.*

Pen: *This is Gabe. You kissed a boy?!?!?*

Me: *Give Pen the phone back. Adults are speaking!*

Gabe: *Nope. You don't need to be nice, boo. If the dude is a real man, he wants you, he'll keep coming back. He gets scared by a little bitchy attitude, he's a pencil dick. My Pen was a bitchy angel to me, but she let me touch her legs, so it didn't deter me. I liked the abuse.*

Laughing, I dropped my phone on my stomach. No one was like Gabriel fucking Fuller. Just then, I was homesick for the days we skinned our knees in the skate park, stole money from our parents to buy popsicles from the ice cream man, and generally wreaked havoc around Savage River together. I was glad he and Pen had gotten out and were living the good life, but I missed the hell out of my boy.

Me: *There's wisdom somewhere in that insanity. I know there is.*

Gabe: *Damn straight, Hells. Am I gonna meet this boy next weekend?*

Me: *Next weekend? What?!?*

Gabe: *Wouldn't miss my girl's birthday. Me and Pen, Bash and Grace, Bex and Ash—we're all coming to SR. Gonna flip the bird to your teen years, boo. Now, I repeat, will I be meeting pencil dick?*

Me: *Ahhh! What?? I'm so excited. Also, no. No meeting the boy, dick size yet to be determined. I don't even know how I feel about him. He's got complications.*

Gabe: *Aw, you're no fun.*

Pen: *I got my phone back. Ignore Gabe. If you think the guy is safe, maybe try to have one conversation without fighting and see how it feels. If he doesn't make you feel safe, then ditch him, Hells. You're too rad to waste time with unworthy boys.*

Me: *K. Sound advice. I'll try. Thanks for being a real one, Penelope. Kick Gabe's shins for me.*

Pen: *Never. Love you, girlie.*

Me: *Love you too.*

I tossed my phone aside and sipped my soda. A whole conversation without fighting? Theo and I hadn't had one of those. I shouldn't have been contemplating it. He had a girl who clearly wasn't over him. A girl who matched his golden-god status.

Complicated.

But I hadn't kissed anyone in a year and a half. There was something about Theo that had made me break my fast.

Something beyond his hotness. It was still up in the air what it was.

Tomorrow, I'd be nice to Theo, then we'd see.

Nine

THEO

HELEN HAD HER BARE feet on my dash, sipping coffee, singing softly to the music filling my car. She had a red string tied around her ankle with a tiny bell that made a faint jingle when she moved. Not something I would have noticed normally, but we were a half hour into the drive to L.A. and Helen's shorts stopped at the tops of her thighs. Tan legs and small, almost dainty feet filled my vision.

Because I kept looking.

Her head turned, catching me looking at her, and I didn't care.

"What?" Her lips curved. She knew what.

"Your legs, Tiger. Nice."

Her palm smoothed from her knee to her ankle. "They're covered in scars, Theodore. Not nice by a stretch, but they get the job done."

"Scars don't detract." Helen's legs were undeniably sexy. Not long, but long enough. Tan with lean, taut muscles. The kind of legs a man imagined wrapped around him. Hard to look away from. Hard to think about anything else when they were on display.

"Mmm."

Yeah, time for another topic.

"Did you see Luciana this morning?"

"Mmhmm. No time for breakfast at the T, so we grabbed a donut at the grocery store. She's easy, so she adapted."

I clicked my tongue. "I would've given you a ride. Next weekend, I'm there."

"It's cool, Theodore. We've got a system down to get the groceries back to the trailer on our boards. Better to do it that way than rely on help that won't always be there."

I didn't know how to answer that. All I knew was now that I was aware Helen and her little sister rode their skateboards with groceries in their hands every week, it was going to be impossible for me to stand by and do nothing. I felt like a dick for not being there for them this morning.

"You're probably going to tell me it's none of my business, but I have to ask: where's your dad and why isn't he helping you two?"

She dropped her legs from the dash and tucked them to the side on her seat. "My dad's in prison for dealing and assault. Probably more, but he's been in and out of jail so many times, I mix up the charges. If he weren't in prison, he still wouldn't be helping. He takes, he doesn't give. Luc's dad died last summer. Accident, but can you call it an accident when you're so high out of your mind, you drive your truck into a tree going full speed?"

Shocked at both her answer and the fact that she'd given me all that of her own free will, it took me a minute to formulate a response. In that time, the heavy silence only filled with an old Sublime song filtering through the speakers. Helen had closed up shop. She twisted her body toward her window, her head on the glass.

She sucked in a shaky, ragged breath.

"Sorry you asked?"

"No. Sorry you were born into that. Luciana too. She's just a kid, and that, knowing how her dad went out, god, that must've been—"

"A relief," Helena supplied.

"Relief?"

"It was a relief for her. He had custody, but if you can believe it, her living situation with him was worse than our mom. He had money, though, so he got the kid. When her dad died, I got to have her."

Reaching out, I dug my fingers into the side of her hair, letting that silk slide along my skin. Her head tipped my way a little.

"She's lucky to have a big sister like you, Tiger. So fucking lucky."

I kept stroking her hair until I needed my hand on the wheel again. She stayed quiet, leaning into me, letting me soothe her, and that was enough, because with Helen, it was huge.

She sank into her seat and yawned, big and noisy.

"Tired?"

"Mmm. I worked late last night, and when I got home, my roommate had a guy over who was banging her like a jackhammer. From the fake-ass noises she was making, she enjoyed it as much as I did. She had him over last weekend too, same story. Don't know why she wanted a repeat performance."

That made me laugh. "Not touching the roommate thing, except to say I'll buy you earplugs. No one should have to be an innocent bystander to bad sex."

She snorted. "It's no big deal. You grow up in a tiny trailer with a skanky mom, you learn to tune it out. I was just ready to crash when I got home last night but it took me a while to shut down with all the jackhammering."

"Where do you work?"

"I told you I don't want you peering in the windows, Theodore."

I glanced at her. "Really? You're not going to tell me?"

"Nope."

"Your dad being in prison isn't a secret, but your job is?"

"I'm not my dad."

I nodded. "True. Glad you don't take his shit on."

"Let me guess what your dad does. Hmmm...real estate? No, I bet he's in money management. Rich people like to manage other rich people's money. Or wait, is he—?"

"President Whitlock. My father is the president of Savage U."

Helen whistled. "Your dad's the head bitch in charge? Damn, Theodore, I did not expect that. I guess that explains why Davis's knees were knocking when you told him your full name on the first day of class."

"Yeah. I don't like my father very much, but I'm not afraid to throw his name out if I need to." I chuckled under my breath. "I would really like to see his face if he heard you calling him head bitch in charge."

"Let me get my diploma first, then it's on."

I turned, finding her ruby lips upturned, relaxed in her seat, pretty as hell and comfortable with me. Fucking finally.

"I get my diploma, *I* might do the honors," I replied.

She went quiet again, humming to a White Stripes song, tapping along with the drum section on her thigh. We were only ten or fifteen minutes out from the performance site.

"Did you work things out with your girlfriend?"

Damn. I'd been feeling smug for drawing Helen out, and now we were right back to this. She hadn't been wrong yesterday. My breakup with Abby had been complicated. Humiliating. Heartbreaking. I'd loved her for two years. Treated her right, gave her all I was able to give. Everyone thought we had a future, the real kind. She ripped that out from under me like it was nothing. Because I didn't fall in line—the line she created well after we'd established who we were together. Because I'd loved her, it had been tempting to give in for her. But the fact that she could end us so easily, without a discussion, only an ultimatum, had given me the will to say no—the answer that broke us.

It had also happened months ago. My head was straight now.

"Not my girlfriend, Helen. I've told you that. I wouldn't be touching you if I thought there was a microscopic chance for that relationship to be revived."

"But she misses you *too*, and she had such a good time with you Wednesday."

"Sounds a lot like jealousy, Tiger."

"I'd have to want you to be jealous another girl has you."

I shook my head. "No one has me. Abby and her parents were at my dad and stepmom's house Wednesday for dinner. It was awkward, we barely spoke, and I sure as shit didn't tell her I missed her."

Out the corner of my eye, I saw her cross her arms. "I don't care. Your messy personal life is none of my business."

"Nothing messy about it. Our break was swift and clean."

"Yet her parents and yours are buddy-buddy, having dinner together. Might've been swift, but it doesn't sound clean."

"Jealous, baby," I murmured.

"I would smack you if you weren't driving." She shook her head. "You're so damn smug. I do not play these kinds of games, Theodore."

"I'm not playing any games. I'm driving you to a show an hour out of town. A show I didn't need to go to because I could have easily hit the performance during the week. I can't control what other people do or the texts that show up on my phone. You don't know me well, I get that. But I'm straightforward, baby. Games are not in my wheelhouse. I think you're gorgeous, interesting, sexy, and when you don't have a massive wall of spikes around you, the kind of soft I could sink into. Maybe I get a kick out of you being jealous, but that's only because it lets me know you might be interested too. That's not a game—that's me getting a read on you. Do you get me?"

A breath whooshed out of her. "You can't just say shit like that. No one says shit like that."

"Like what?"

Her hands flailed in the air in front of her. "All that you just said. People don't just lay it on the line. It's not—"

"I don't know what other people do. I don't really care."

I could feel her aiming eye daggers at me. "I hope you don't expect anything like that from me."

I grinned. "Nope. I don't have any expectations."

"Good. Because people don't talk like that," she muttered.

"It's obvious you've never been treated the way you deserve."

"Or is it possible I've been treated exactly how I deserve and you are grossly overestimating who I am?"

My hands tightened on the wheel. "Don't say shit like that about yourself."

She inhaled sharply, then reached out and traced her fingertip over my tight knuckles. "Okay. I won't. But don't break your steering wheel. I need a good grade in this class. In order to get that, I have to attend this performance. If you break your car, I'll have to hitchhike and—"

Grabbing her hand, I brought it to my mouth and bit down on her knuckles. "Stop talking." I rubbed my lips along the smooth skin on the top of her hand.

"'Kay. But do you think I can have my hand back?"

"Nope."

"'Kay."

• • • ● • ● • • •

HELEN WANTED BLUEBERRIES. SHE'D never say it, but I saw her eyeing people around us eating them. I rose from the blanket I'd brought for us to share, and she looked up at me.

"Stay here."

She rolled her eyes and gestured to the stage. "Where would I go?"

I picked up a piece of her hair, rubbing it between my fingers. "Stay, Tiger."

There was a stand at the opening of the park selling blueberries in small baskets. The price was astronomical, but I didn't blink. I wanted to see her reaction when I gave them to her.

Helen wasn't alone when I got back. Seated beside her on his own blanket was the big motherfucker from class who'd taken it upon himself to be her bodyguard. Lachlan. And he was holding out his own basket of blueberries, which Helen helped herself to.

I thought he was cool, but I was reconsidering.

I sat down beside her. She turned, grinning. "Look who's here."

Lachlan jerked his chin at me. I stared at him, unblinking. He chuckled as he turned away.

I shoved the blueberries at Helen. "Now you have all the berries in the world."

Something small and cold hit my forehead. I picked it up, my eyes flicking to Helen's. Her red lips were spread wide. She'd thrown a blueberry at me.

"Now you have one. Let me know when you want another one."

I threw it back at her. "Brat."

She leaned in, bringing her lips close to my ear. "Jealous, baby."

"What's he doing here?"

Her face turned up to mine. "He works during the week too. I bet he's not the only classmate of ours here."

"He's the only one sitting beside you."

Her hand fell on my upper thigh and squeezed. "You're sitting beside me, aren't you?"

I stared at her, thinking about what she'd do if I pushed her on her back and shoved my hand down her tiny shorts. Her fingers touched my lips.

"Don't kiss me, dude."

"I wasn't planning on it."

"You were."

I took a blueberry from her basket and slipped it between her lips. She smiled, giving me a taste of her softness.

"Thanks for the berries. I never buy them because they're way too expensive for my blood." She put another one in her mouth. "Thank you." Soft, low, quiet, just for me.

"You're welcome."

The show started, and from the parts I paid attention to, it was good. Helen sat up, cross-legged, spine straight, rapt. I might've watched her more than the people on stage. And kept my eye on Lachlan, who was more laid back and relaxed on his blanket than a motherfucker that size had any room to be.

Intermission came, and Helen stretched out on her back. "Okay, I like this. Is this how rich people live? Shakespeare in the park with berries?"

"The tickets were ten dollars each, Tiger."

Her lids lowered. "Some of us don't have ten dollars to spare. Or the time to watch a play in a park."

Lachlan shifted, so he was leaning back on his hands. "Had to take the day off work for this."

Helen shook her finger at him. "See? Luckily, I work nights, otherwise I would have been screwed."

"Where do you work?" I asked Lachlan.

"Maintenance and mechanics on campus. I take care of the vehicles and machinery," he answered.

I peered down at Helen. "See how easy that was? I asked where he worked, he told me."

Lachlan cocked his head, eyes on Helen. "Where do you work, girl?"

She tucked her hands behind her head, drawing her shirt up to just below her tits. Her stomach was as sexy as her legs, defined muscles and a tiny, round belly button.

"Sorry, Lock. I don't want you peering in the windows either."

He raised a brow. "I don't peer."

A laugh burst out of her. "No, I don't suppose you do."

I stretched out on my side next to her, laying my hand in the center of her stomach. Her head turned my way, but she didn't protest my touch.

"I'm still deciding if I like you," she murmured.

"Oh yeah?"

"Yeah. So, if I decide I do, I'll tell you where I work. It's not a state secret or anything. It's just, you know, I'm still thinking on you. Okay?"

She might not have decided if she liked me, but she let me skim my fingers over her abdomen in broad daylight. Her breath caught when I broached her waistband, which was loose enough to see her little black panties underneath. I traced the ridge of her hip bone, dipping my finger into her shorts, then back out. When I dipped in again, she caught my hand, and my eyes flicked to hers. They were wide, and maybe a little worried.

"No."

"Okay," I agreed.

She sighed in relief.

"Shit, Helen," I rasped.

"Show's starting."

She sat up, but I stayed, the breath kicked out of me. Then she reached for me, catching my hand and giving it a tug. I sat up behind her, and she leaned back against my chest, her head beneath my chin.

I had my work cut out for me with this girl. We both had some decisions to make. She had to decide if she wanted me. I had to decide if she was worth all the trouble she was going to bring me.

But I knew without thinking.

My pops used to pat my head and say, "If there's trouble, you'll find it, then you'll take it home and keep it."

Yeah, I knew.

Ten

Helen

LOCK KNEW A RESTAURANT off the beaten path near Santa Monica. Theo grumbled, but he followed behind Lock's truck to the divey biker bar slash restaurant because I'd asked him to. As delicious as the blueberries were, by the time the play ended, my stomach was audibly growling. I was past hungry, verging on hangry. The only thing stopping me from being pissy was Theo.

"*No.*"

"*Okay.*"

God, he had no idea what that had done to me. Throughout my life, I'd heard a lot of different responses to the word "no," but none had been so easy.

Come on, don't be a tease.

I'll make it good for you.

Just another minute.

You want it.

Shut up, bitch.

You little slut.

Theo had said okay. Like it was natural. Like it didn't mean the entire world.

And then he'd said okay again to having dinner with Lock because I asked, even though I could tell he was jealous. He didn't enjoy me splitting my attention with another man. He'd said okay anyway.

Now, the three of us were seated in a gritty bar, drinks in hand, waiting for our burgers. The other tables were filled too, mostly with bikers. We stuck out, but no one was paying us any attention. Probably because Lock could crush heads with his bare hands.

"How'd you find this place?" Theo asked.

Lock lifted one of his massive shoulders. "I drive. Wander. Found it on one of my drives. Looked interesting, so I stopped in. Best burger of my life, so I come back whenever I'm around."

"Looking forward to it," Theo replied. "The good thing about no longer wrestling is I can actually eat burgers and not worry about making weight."

I wrinkled my nose. "What a stupid sport. You have to wear a silly outfit, rub your faces on other guys' dicks, and you can't eat hamburgers. I'm glad you wised up, Theodore."

Lock snorted. Theo's mouth curved into a slow grin. He really didn't give a shit when I messed with him.

"Again, I've never rubbed my face against a guy's dick."

My eyes leveled with his. "I notice you didn't deny the other things I said."

He canted his head. "I didn't. Although, you missed out, baby. I looked fly as hell in my singlet, and now, you'll never get the privilege of seeing it."

Lock passed his phone to me, and I burst out laughing when I looked at the screen. He'd Googled and pulled up a picture of Theodore in his uniform. There wasn't much funnier than a grown man in a spandex onesie, even when he was as hot as Theo.

Theo snatched the phone from me, saw what I was laughing at, and slid it back to Lock, face down. His brow pinched, but I couldn't read him. I didn't think he was mad, but it was impossible to tell.

"I bet it's better in person," I teased.

"You're damn right it is," he replied. "I might have it hanging in my closet."

I tapped my chin. "I wonder what I'll have to do for you to let me see you in it."

His eyes locked on mine, the humor melting from both of us. Our waitress approached with our food, but he kept his gaze on me. Then his mouth tipped at the corners and his lips moved.

"*Be soft.*"

He wanted me to be soft. The crazy thing was, I imagined maybe I could be with him.

"*Maybe,*" I mouthed back.

I wasn't soft. That wasn't me. Not because I wasn't capable, but because it had never been safe for me to be that way.

But I could try.

"*No.*"

"*Okay.*"

I could try.

· · ● ● ● ● ● ● · ·

I GAVE LOCK A hug by his truck. He was stiff, and so was I, but I was trying this being soft thing, and that seemed to be something people did. They hugged their friends hello and goodbye.

"Best burger ever," I said.

Theo tugged me back to his side. "I agree. Fucking delicious."

Lock nodded once. "Don't spread it around. Some greedy asshole will swoop in and try to make some green off it."

"Maybe the owners want to make some green," I replied.

"Maybe." Lock put his hand on the door of his truck. "And they might. I just don't want any part in destroying the good that's already there."

Theo patted his heart. "Secret's safe, man."

My eyes bugged. "Who am I going to tell?"

Lock climbed into his truck without another word.

"I like him," I said.

Theo grunted.

"You like him too."

He could deny it, but Lock was quietly likable. He told us about his job, his major, the piece-of-shit house he lived in off campus, the small town he was from in Northern Cali. He did this all in as few words as possible, which I appreciated. I also liked watching him eat. He packed away the food, tucking it in the small, soft gut he carried—which only made him more of a teddy bear—but he looked like he truly enjoyed everything he put in his mouth. I could've seen him starring on one of those Food Network shows where they went around to divey restaurants to taste test massive portions of local fare. His groans of pleasure would get all the housewives in a tizzy.

So, maybe I had a tiny crush on Lock. Not *that* kind of crush, but yeah. Lock was a *whole* thing.

"He's fine, but he was in my way. Now, he's out of my way, I don't need to spend time talking about him."

Theo took my hand, and we walked across the parking lot to his car, which he pinned me against. My breath stuttered at the intense sweep of his gaze over me, and I forgot Lock ever existed. It was just me and Theo now.

I tipped my head back, giving him the permission he was seeking. He wasted no time in taking my mouth, slipping his tongue between my lips to give me a deep, wet kiss.

My fingers fisted his T-shirt. He took handfuls of my ass, flattening me against him. He kept kissing me, groaning into my mouth, and I kissed him back. He tasted like mint and icy water. I licked the inside of his mouth, taking his flavor with me, mewling for more.

Theo could kiss. He kissed the hard out of me and found my soft. He lapped at it until I felt like I was going to fall apart and shatter into a thousand pieces in his arms. It wasn't quite dark, we were in a public parking lot, but when his hand slid inside my shorts, I didn't stop him. Then he pushed my underwear to the side, and I opened my legs a little wider, inviting him in.

"Tell me to stop, Tiger," he murmured against my lips. "Tell me you don't want me touching you."

I grabbed his arm and held it tight to my belly. "If we get arrested, I expect you to bail me out."

I felt his smile even as his fingers drew a line along my slit. "No one's gonna see you. This is just for me, baby."

My back was pressed against the car. His body shielded mine. I was clothed. So was he. And in that moment, I didn't care about any of it. I could have been naked and on fire so long as Theo continued what he was doing to my clit. My hips rolled with the movement of his hand, chasing his retreat until he came back to me again and again.

Theo's breath was hot on my lips. His eyes were on mine. My palms skated down his back to the slope of his muscular ass. I dug my hands into his back pockets, holding him against me.

My head fell back into the car, lips parting on a moan. Our gazes locked as he brought me over so quickly, I might have been embarrassed if I'd cared about anything but what we were doing. Because I was coming hard on the hand of a guy who drove me to see Shakespeare, had twinkly blue eyes, and kissed me like the sky was falling and I was his only shelter.

Theo leaned deeper into me, panting on my lips, watchful eyes keeping me in place almost as much as his body. His dick prodded my hip, but he didn't thrust or rub it on me. It was just there, and it felt perfect.

"Gorgeous," he murmured. "You're so incredibly hot, Tiger. You make me crazy."

I hooked my arm around his neck, steadying myself on him. "You just made me come in a parking lot, Theodore. I think I'm the one who's out of my mind."

His forehead dropped to mine. "Just made you come. Still have my fingers in your hot pussy. Think you can call me my name for a minute?"

"Yeah." I nodded. "I can do that, Theo."

"Shit." He shifted his hips, but only slightly. "I need to back up a couple steps, baby. Then I'm going to need you to get in the car and give me a minute to get a handle on things."

He didn't move, and I laughed, rubbing the side of his neck. "Back up. We need to get on the road after you deal with your dick. I've got work tonight."

That did it. He let me go, then walked around the hood of the car after he adjusted himself. I slipped inside, drawing in wobbly breaths. That wasn't how I'd expected the day to go, but I couldn't say I was mad about it.

I shifted in my seat to watch Theo circle the car, the ache between my thighs pulsing with aftershocks. No, I wasn't mad about it at all.

Theo finally climbed in, and when he did, he leaned over the console, gripped my chin, and laid a long, hard kiss on my lips. Then he left me with a softer one.

"Did you get a handle on it?" I asked.

"Yeah." He shoved a hand through his hair. "That was not expected."

"I know. That's why it's okay it happened."

His gaze narrowed as he inspected me. "You're sure?"

"Mmhmm. I think you know me well enough to know I'd tell you if I was displeased."

That brought out a sardonic grin. "I do know that." He put the car in reverse, backing out of the parking spot, and pulled onto the road. "What time do you have to be at work?"

"Nine. We have time."

Two hours. It would be close, but he could drop me at the dorm, I'd grab my skank clothes, change fast, and take the bus to the club. Almost not enough time, but I'd make it.

"That's late, so I'm thinking you must work in a club."

I tucked my foot under my leg so I could turn to him. "Why is that your guess? I could be a cleaner or a factory worker. Lots of night-shift jobs."

He tapped the steering wheel. "Because you're smart and know you're beautiful. If I was an old married guy and you served me a drink, I'd give you a massive tip for existing and allowing me to breathe the same air."

"Sweet." I ran my fingers along his arm. "You're saying *you*, Theodosius Longbottom Whitlock, wouldn't give me a massive tip for existing?"

He sputtered. "Theodosius now? Honestly, baby, I think you should be giving *me* a tip for not complaining about you calling me by the wrong name."

"You didn't answer the question."

His mouth tipped at the corners. "If you came at me, I didn't know you at all, pouting those red lips, undoubtedly wearing something sexy as fuck, I would get your attention any way I could. Paying you for it? No, baby. I want your attention because you're interested in what we can have with each other."

His profile was a study in proportion. Strong jaw, jutting to just the right degree. Lips full, but still masculine. Straight, distinguished nose with the smallest bump that made it interesting. Even from the side, his eyes twinkled. Theo was so ridiculously beautiful, it was hard to comprehend.

"You have my attention, Theo."

His head fell back on his seat while his eyes remained on the road in front of him. "Thank Christ for that."

Laughing, I propped my feet up on the dashboard and turned on the radio. Now that we'd established we were into each other, it was music time.

We hit traffic, and I was pissed. Not at Theo, although he was feeling it. No, I was pissed at myself for basking in the day like I'd had any room to bask. That wasn't my life. I needed to be on time for my job so I could make enough money to support my sister and pay back the loan my mother owed a violent criminal so he didn't murder my family.

A year of working for Mads had made me soft. Before Madeline McGarvey came into my life, I never once would have allowed myself to be in a situation that would've threatened what little I had. She'd given me room to breathe, and I'd let myself get used to what it felt like not being squeezed all the time.

She was gone, and so was my breathing room. Now, when life squeezed me hard, I cracked.

"Shit, shit, shit." My fingers dug into my legs. "I never should have agreed to dinner."

"It's okay, Helen. We'll get there. If you're a couple minutes late—"

"I'll be fired, Theo. I know in your world, getting fired is no big deal, but I don't live in that world. This job means a roof over my sister's head. I don't think Zadie and Elena would appreciate me bringing Luciana to live with me in our dorm."

"Okay." He took my hand in his, threading our fingers tight. "I'm gonna get you there."

As soon as we passed the accident that had been slowing us down, Theo drove like a bat out of hell. The damage had already been done to our timeline, though. I had no time to go back to the dorm first—or ride the bus after.

"I need you to take me directly to work. I have clothes there I can change into." And makeup in my purse I could apply while Theo drove.

"Anything. Give me the address."

I spouted off the address to Savage Beauties while digging in my purse for mascara and my lipstick. Fortunately, the lights were low in the club, so I could get away with car makeup.

Theo kept glancing at me from the corner of his eye, silent, though his questions were screaming. He could keep screaming.

I wasn't up for giving out answers. Not when I was hanging on by the skin of my teeth.

"We're making it. I'll get you there." His low, lovely voice was like an hour of meditation. If I was capable of being calmed at this point, that would have done it. At least my simmering anger fell away. It wasn't Theo's fault there was traffic, and I'd been all for having dinner with Lock. This was just bad luck, and yeah, maybe poor planning.

Theo skidded into the lot of Savage Beauties with ten minutes to spare. He didn't say a word about where we were, but he didn't have to. His body language said everything. The tightness of his shoulders told me he was judging me. The frown pulling at his mouth broadcasted his disappointment. His white knuckles around the steering wheel said he was *pissed*.

I scrambled out of the car, and Theo followed, snagging my waist before I could make a dash across the parking lot.

"Thank you for getting me here. I need to run in and change at the speed of light." I pressed on his chest. "You can't come in, Theodore."

"Why not?"

I swiped at my lashes, performing nonchalance. "I won't be able to get my job done if you're glaring at all my customers."

He stared me down, nostrils flaring. "I'm not driving away and leaving you here."

"You don't have a choice." My pulse quickened in my throat. "I need to go."

"How are you getting home?"

"Bus."

He practically shook. Savage Beauties wasn't in the best neighborhood, but the bus stop was only a block away, and if I needed, one of the bouncers would wait with me. It wasn't a huge deal.

"What time do you get off?"

"Two, but I'll be fine." I glanced over my shoulder at the door, then back to Theo. "I really have to get inside."

He took my jaw in his hand and tipped my head back. "I'll be here at two. Then we're going to talk."

I nodded, all out of time for arguments. "You don't have to be here, but okay. I'll see you if you are." I blew him a kiss, then swiveled on my toes and ran.

He'd either be here at the end of my shift or he wouldn't. I'd be disappointed if this was the thing that scared him off, but I also might be relieved if he didn't come back for me.

I didn't have the time to think about what my contradicting feelings meant. I shut my brain off, pushed my tits up, and plastered a smile on my face.

It was time to get the job done.

Eleven

THEO

HELEN EXITED THE BUILDING in a baggy hoodie and fishnets. Her silky hair was pulled in a high ponytail, red lipstick firmly in place. Her head swiveled side to side before she locked on my car. Hitching her bag on her shoulder, she took her time making her way across the parking lot. I was holding open the passenger door by the time she got to me. She slipped into my car without a word.

I pulled out of the lot and drove toward campus. Helen tucked herself by the door, turned away from me.

"You strip, Tiger?"

She dragged a finger down the glass. "I'm a waitress. I serve drinks in a skanky outfit to horny dudes."

The exhale that shot from my lungs was filled with relief. I didn't know what I would have done if her answer had been yes, but I'd have been more than disappointed. She was too fucking good to give that part of herself up for a few bucks. Way too good.

I couldn't stop myself from pressing it.

"Do they touch you?"

In my periphery, she shrugged. "It's not a big deal, dude. Can you just drive me home? I'm really tired and not in the mood for a play-by-play."

"I'll drive you home."

"Thanks," she mumbled, her head knocking into the glass.

My grip on the steering wheel tightened. I couldn't let this lay between us. "I'm not trying to encroach on your independence, this is me showing you concern."

She knocked her head twice more. "It feels like judgment."

"I promise you it's not. I saw your and Luciana's situation. This is what you feel you need to do and—"

She twisted in her seat. "Theo, I make bank working there. Triple what I made at Wheelz. I keep my sister in nice clothes and food that's not made entirely of chemicals. One day, this place will be in my rearview, but today isn't that day. It's a necessity."

"I get it, baby." Reaching across the console, I grasped her leg, squeezing to reassure me as much as her. She covered my hand with hers in an attempt to push me off, but I stayed, and she relented with a heavy sigh. "What happened to the job you had last year? You said you worked somewhere els—"

"Can we listen to music? I don't really want to talk right now."

Helen was quiet and still the rest of the drive. I almost thought she'd fallen asleep, except as soon as her dorm came into view, she grabbed her things, ready to bolt.

I parked. She hopped out, and I followed. At the door to her building, she turned to me.

"I'm good. I can take it from here."

Reaching around her, I took her key card, scanned it to unlock the door, and pulled it open. Laying a palm on her belly, I walked her backward until we were both inside, the door falling shut behind us. She frowned at me, her brow crinkling. My mouth twitching, I wrapped my arm around her waist to grip her hip and guided her to the elevator. She scowled at me in silence all the way up to her floor, down her hall, and into her room.

There, I kissed the fucking frown right off her face, pressing my tongue inside to restake the ground I'd claimed that she was trying to take back. Helen shoved at my chest, not hard, but enough for me to pull back.

"I'm tired, Theodore. Go home."

"No. I'm not leaving. We had a spectacular day. I'm not letting you take tonight to build up your walls because you showed me something you didn't mean to."

Her head dropped onto my shoulder, and she sighed. "I don't do this."

"What?" Hooking my knuckle under her chin, I dragged her gaze up to mine. "What, baby?"

"I don't, you know, fuck around. I mean, I used to, but I don't now. You need to know that and not expect it from me because you're not going to get it. I shouldn't have let you touch me today, but I was caught up, because you're right, we did have a spectacular day. But now we're back, and this is reality. I'm not having sex with you, so you can just go now."

I couldn't stop my flinch. "Fuck, baby. What happened to you?"

Helen's face went hard. She backed out of my arms, walking straight to her dresser. "I'm putting on my pajamas, washing my face, and climbing into bed to go to sleep. That's all I'm doing for the short time I remain conscious. You decide what to do with that." She disappeared into her en suite bathroom, pajamas in her arms.

I did the only thing I *could* do. Shirt and shoes off, I shoved a pillow against the headboard of Helen's bed and reclined against it while I waited for her to come out. It took her a couple minutes, but when she emerged, I stopped breathing.

"Your mouth."

She blinked. "You're still here...in my bed. Why are you in my bed, Theodore?"

"Your mouth, Helen."

Her hand shot to cover her mouth. "What? Why are you looking at me like that?"

I patted the bed beside me. "Come here."

She shook her head slowly. "No."

Jackknifing upright, I hit the bed with more force. "Get over here."

Helen wasn't happy with me, but she came, one knee on the bed. "I'm here."

"No." I wrapped my arms around the backs of her legs, sweeping her off balance. She fell forward, landing on my chest. "Now you're here."

She jerked her head back, and my thumb swiped across her bottom lip. No lipstick, all Helen.

"Your mouth."

"Yeah, I don't wear lipstick to bed," she stated flatly. "Can you let me go now?"

Back and forth, I rubbed her lips, bottom, then top. "Love the red, but this..."

"It's just my lips," she whispered.

"I'm seeing something you don't show anyone."

She stayed perfectly still, eyes on me while I touched her. "Except I wasn't trying to show you. I thought you'd listen and leave."

I shook my head. "Nope. You knew I'd still be here."

Slowly, her gaze on mine, she lowered her head until her lips touched mine. "I kind of hoped, but I didn't know."

Something squeezed deep inside my chest, knowing what that had to cost her to admit. Moving fast, I wrapped my arms around her and rolled her to her back, hovering over her. Her hands came up to my neck, cupping the sides. She lifted her face, touching her mouth to mine again. The kiss I gave her back was a lot more than a touch, pushing her head down to her pillow. Her lips were smooth and warm under mine, her movement languid. It killed me to pull back, but I did.

"You should know I'm relentless," I murmured. "But you're tired, and to be honest, so am I. We need to talk, but we need to sleep more."

"Are you asking to stay?"

I shook my head. "I'm not asking." Rolling off her, I pulled back the covers, then pulled them over both of us. "I'm not going to take anything you don't want to give, and I will keep telling you that until you believe it."

Her lids were heavy as she looked me over. "You're in my bed without permission."

Arm around her, I slid her into my side. Her head settled on my shoulder. Her arm draped across my middle. "I saw the bat you keep next to the bed. If you really minded, I have no doubt you'd let me know." My mouth pressed to the top of her head. "Go to sleep, Tiger."

She shifted and flung a leg over mine. "This doesn't mean anything."

I pulled her deeper into me. "Nothing."

• • • ● • ● • • •

WARM AND WET. OVER me. Everywhere. Silk sheets on my skin. Soft hands touching me. Too good to be a dream.

Fuck.

My eyes opened. Helen was in front of me, her body aligned with mine, head tucked against my chest. But she wasn't asleep. She was exploring, and I was her terrain. Her fingertips traced down the length of my spine. Tipping her head, she pressed her mouth to the base of my throat, sucking gently. My cock responded to her in an instant, swelling behind my zipper.

"Helen," I rasped. "What are you doing, baby?"

"Mmm." Her sucks turned to light kisses, and her hand splayed on my back, pressing me closer.

"Are you dreaming?"

"Mmm."

My hand shot up, fisting the side of her hair to tug her back. In the dawn light, her eyes were wide and startled, but fully awake.

"You know what you're doing, Tiger?" I gruffed.

She lunged at my mouth, taking my bottom lip between hers for a long suck. "I know what I'm doing, Theodore."

"You keep touching me like that, I'm going to need to touch you back."

Helen sat up part way and yanked her shirt off her head. She stayed like that, letting me see her, watching me while I drank in her pretty tits, the tight, brown nipples, the perfectly round swell of them. Then she cupped one, thumbing her nipple, sighing.

I licked my top lip, hungry for her. "Give it to me."

She dropped forward, bringing her breast to my mouth, and that was it. I was done, gone, fully lost in everything that was Helen. Latching on, I sucked deep, bringing more mewls from her. Her legs shifted and tangled with mine under the sheets. We grappled with each other, touching, kissing, licking.

Helen felt as good as I thought she would. God, she felt even better. Hot and solid, silky and soft, her skin was like nothing I'd ever had in my hands. I rolled her to her back, and she spread her legs, welcoming me between them. But if my cock came anywhere close to her heat, I'd need to be inside. Helen was on fire, but I wasn't sure we were going there. Not now.

More importantly, I needed my mouth on her before I did anything else.

Rearing back on my knees, I took her in. Swollen lips. Silky hair spread over her white sheets. Puckered nipples. Taut belly. Perfection. The beauty ideal I hadn't realized I'd carried with me my whole life until I found her.

She hooked her fingers on my waistband. "Stop wasting time, Theodore," she panted. "Get back here."

Cuffing her wrists, I tucked them to her sides. "Shut up and let me look at you. After I do that, I'm going to eat you until I'm satisfied."

Her belly rippled with a breathy laugh. "Until *you're* satisfied?"

"Yeah, baby. You woke me up, pulled me out of a peaceful sleep, so I need compensation. Eating your pussy is what I'm taking." I patted her hip. "Lift up."

She raised her butt from the bed so I could slide her shorts off. When I got a look at her, I nearly came in my underwear. From *looking*. She wasn't even touching me. Jesus, she was pretty *everywhere*. Smooth skin, bare pussy, low, low tan lines, fucking gorgeous.

I traced the line where her skin went from tan to pale, only inches from her slit. "I need to see the bikini that gave you these tan lines. Then I need to burn it so no one else ever sees it."

Her hips rolled. "Stop talking."

Cupping her between her legs, I grazed her little clit with my thumb. "You want this? You want my mouth on you?"

Nodding, she wrapped her legs around my waist. "I'm beginning to think you're all talk. Do you even know how to eat a puss—?"

Hands around her calves, I flipped her to her belly and slid my arm under her to raise her hips. Then I was on her, spreading her thighs and burying my face between them. She moaned at the first lash of my tongue, from clit to ass. I grunted in response, diving deeper, sucking, licking, tasting every inch of her. Holding on to her hips, my thumbs kept her lips parted, displaying all of her to me. Dark pink, glistening with my spit and her desire, she was a work of art. A gorgeous, naughty masterpiece.

Helen reached behind her to thread her fingers through my hair and curl them around a fistful of it. Using her grip on me, she shoved me closer, rocking her hips to ride my face.

"So good, Theo," she cooed. "I'm going to come for you. I've never, Theo, I've never—" A long moan cut off whatever she'd been about to say.

"Theo, *please*, don't stop. Don't stop," she begged.

If I could have spoken, I would have assured her I'd never stop. Never leave her alone until she got hers. And even then, I might not stop, not with her tasting the way she did, smelling and looking so perfect. I was already addicted.

Helen's thighs started to shake. She reached forward, then outward, nails scrambling for purchase on the sheets. Neck arching, she tossed her head back, her long hair spilling all the way down her back to the base of her spine. My name fell from her lips on a drawn-out moan of soul-rending pleasure.

I flipped her to her back again and kept at her, licking her, sucking her, filling myself to the brim with her sweetness. Legs over my shoulders, heels digging into my back, Helen writhed on the bed, just as lost as I was. My cock was aching, pressing into the mattress, so close to losing it, I was shocked I hadn't. My control was tenuous, but I held it so fucking tight, it was close to strangling. Because I could not lose it with this girl. Not all of it. I had to remember who she was, what she'd shown me, what she carried.

Helen came again, and again after that. I would have kept going, but she grabbed my hair and dragged me up her body. For a second, she held my face and stared, frozen except for her feet on the backs of my legs. Then she raised her head to suck on my lips, taking her flavor into her mouth and moaning.

"Theodore," her legs banded around my waist, trapping me against her, "why aren't you inside me?"

"Got busy for a while." I nibbled her bottom lip. "I need you to tell me that's what you want."

She tucked her face in my throat, nodding while she kissed me. "That's what I want. Right now. Give it to me. *Please*."

There was my soft. What I needed to hear. My shorts were lost somewhere in the sheets, then Helen's hand was on me, stroking so well, all I could do was stay still and let it happen.

"Come on," she said against my lips. "Come inside and let me have this. I'll give you me. Come on."

"Shit, fuck." I peered down at the beauty under me. "Condom."

"Nightstand. Our RA gave all of us a strip when we moved in."

I found them in her drawer and ripped open the packet. "Remind me to thank them later."

"This is just ours, Theodore. Only for us."

"I know." Condom on, I fell over her, holding myself up on my forearms. "I get what you're giving me. I get it."

Biting her bottom lip, she raised her hips, my tip nudging her entrance. "Take it then."

Her wet heat surrounded me as I pushed in. Jesus, I tried to go slow, to savor my first feel of her, but it was impossible, not with her fingertips gripping my shoulders tight, her thighs spread wide and welcoming. Not with her lids lowered to half-mast, watching me join our bodies.

I drove into her to the hilt, and I did not stop. Retreating as far as I could without leaving her, I returned to her in another hard thrust. Helen was with me, meeting me, sighing when I slid away, moaning when I came back.

God, I didn't want to think about anyone else, not when I was inside Helen for the first time, but it took one thrust for me to know I'd never had better. Helen was so there, so incredibly present and part of what we were doing. It wasn't just me fucking her. We were fucking each other, and god*damn*, that made all the difference.

My mouth covered hers, kissing her hard and fierce. She answered with her own brand of fierce, nipping my lips, sucking my tongue.

I tore my lips off when I couldn't take it anymore. "You're too damn hot, baby." My nose grazed hers. "Pussy so tight, so wet, I can't fuck you as long as I want to."

Shifting back to my knees, I held her hips in my hands, digging my fingers into her ass. Helen let out a gasp, hands flying forward so she could brace herself on my arms.

"Theo, please, please, don't stop." Nails scratched at my forearms.

"You think I'll stop?" My eyes went to where I entered her, her pretty pussy taking me again and again. Clinging to me, sucking me in deeper with every pass. "Look at that. Look how you take me."

She watched too, her pants coming a little faster. "I'm close. I didn't think I could, but I need it. I need to come, Theo. Fuck me harder."

"I'll give it to you. I have you." Rising on my knees, her back half off the mattress, I slammed into her. Long, deep strokes, slapping her pelvis with mine, making her moan and claw at my arms. I thought she was gorgeous before, but nothing compared to Helen writhing on the sheets, wholly giving herself over to me.

It took everything out of me not to follow her over when she came apart on my cock. Her swollen lips parted, breathing her pleasure into the air. It was a show in itself, and I wouldn't allow myself to miss any of it.

"Theo," she sighed, sweet and soft.

Shifting again, I fell over her, hiking her knees back so I could drive into her. Her breath came in stuttering pants each time I seated myself. I took her tit in my hand, the other cupped her jaw, and I fucked her until there was no more holding back. It was savage and rough, but I wouldn't have gone there with her if she hadn't been right there with me. The fact that she was, that she was mewling like a kitten in my arms, sent me over the edge, draining every last ounce of pleasure until I had nothing left.

"*Fuck*," I gritted out, collapsing on top of her.

Helen shoved her face into my neck, heating my skin with her uneven pants. I stayed there, out of strength and energy, until I had to move to take care of the condom. Then I flopped on my back with a deep groan.

Something light landed on my chest. I laughed when I saw it was a tissue. "Thanks, baby."

Helen's grin was as lazy as the flick of her fingers. "Any time, Theodore."

I got rid of the condom, wrapped it in the tissue, and tossed it on the floor. Then I tucked Helen into my side, closing my eyes.

"What time is it?" I asked.

"I don't know. My phone's behind me on the nightstand." Her nail traced the outline of the muscles on my chest. "Before I woke you, it was four."

I threw my hand up. "No. Four? Jesus, why?"

She smacked me. "You're complaining that I woke you up?"

My eyes opened, and I dipped my chin to look at her. "Nope. I'd give up sleep forever for another shot at sinking inside you. Best I ever had."

She smacked me again. "Don't play me."

"Was that not the best you ever had?"

Instead of answering, she rolled away from me onto her other side. I followed, bringing her back to my chest. She squirmed, but she didn't put up much of a fight.

Brushing her hair from her face, I kissed her ear. "Was that a hard question?"

"No. Maybe." She crammed her face into her pillow so it muffled her voice, but I heard her anyway. "That was the first time I've had sex sober."

I stilled. "First time ever?"

She nodded, still buried in the pillow.

"I have to say I'm honored. I don't know what I did to deserve being woken up by your mouth, but I want to know so I can keep doing it."

She waved me off, keeping her face hidden. "I thought sleepy sex might be like drunk or high sex. It wasn't."

I touched my lips to her shoulder. "You were wide awake."

She nodded. "Yeah. Now I'm tripping."

"No need to trip. That was incredibly hot. I want a repeat as soon as possible, but we're not getting married. Let's just let this ride, okay?"

When I'd picked Helen up to take her to see Shakespeare, I hadn't envisioned us ending up here. I liked her, I was attracted to her, but I really wasn't in a place to pursue anything serious. Not that I wouldn't treat Helen right now that we were here. I didn't have it in me to mistreat this girl who'd been mistreated all her life.

She blindly swatted at me. "Go back to sleep."

"You too." I settled behind her. After a minute or two, she relaxed against me, so I kissed her shoulder. "Cute little spoon."

The giggle she let out hit me square in the chest. "Shut up, Theodore."

I grinned against the back of her neck and pulled her tighter to me.

"Night, Helen."

Twelve

Helen

UP UNTIL THEO, LUCIANA was the only person I'd ever shared a bed with. I had to say, sleeping with a big, warm man who'd spent a considerable amount of time making me come was infinitely better than fighting for space and being elbowed all night by my little sister.

Which was why, as soon as I regained consciousness, I was out of bed and away from his too-comfy arms. *That* was not something I was going to allow myself to get used to.

The sex part, I could do that. At my bathroom door, I glanced back at Theo's long, muscular body, taking up more than his fair share of my bed, and bit my lip. Yeah, I could definitely deal with a little more of that.

I did my thing in the bathroom, scrubbing the sleep from my face and brushing the slime from my teeth. Not awake enough to shower, I slapped on some deodorant, wove my hair into a loose braid, and I was done.

The sleeping boy in my bed was awake and sitting up when I came out. As soon as I opened the bathroom door, Theo was up, crossing the room in a few steps and swooping me into his arms. He shoved his face into my neck, pressing his lips firmly under my ear.

"I need to head out," he murmured against my skin. "Want to feed me breakfast before I go?"

"You're going to take up my entire bed all night, then mooch breakfast off me?"

He brought his head up, blue eyes already twinkling at full force. "Yeah, I am."

I tilted my head, sweeping a look over all his Theo hotness. "That's fair." I smacked his butt, which I happened to know was deliciously round and rock hard, because I'd spent a good amount of time with my legs wrapped around it. "Come on, Theodore. It's time for a gourmet dining hall meal."

He kissed my forehead. "Give me a couple minutes, then it's on."

He disappeared into the bathroom. I threw a hoodie on over my pajamas, slipped my feet into a pair of rainbow-checkered Vans, then I went into the living room to wait.

Elena lounged on the couch reading a newspaper.

Yeah. She did that. Apparently, it was her Sunday ritual.

"Is Zadie still sleeping?" I asked.

She slowly lowered the paper. "I haven't seen her this morning."

"Cool. I just wanted to see if she'd like to get breakfast with me."

Brow arched, lips pursed, bitch face activated. "With you and the random ass you brought back to your room in the middle of the night?"

"Wow, you're really interested in my life. Are you miffed I didn't invite you to breakfast?"

Her eyes rolled. "I've been up since seven, Helen. Actually, that was the second time I woke up. The first time was to the sounds of what I assumed was either you being murdered or taken to pound town. I see it was the latter."

My eyes boggled in my head. "You thought I was being murdered, and you didn't check on me?"

Her nose scrunched. "Clearly you weren't being murdered because there you stand, but honestly, I didn't want to chance it. If I'd seen that horror show, I'd need to bleach both my brain and my eyeballs, and I just don't have time for that."

I had nothing to say to that. Except if Theo came calling again, I'd be sure to throw a pillow over my face. The idea of Elena hearing what went down between us gave me the heebie-jeebies.

"Hey." Theo came up behind me and slid his arm around my middle. His hand splayed on my stomach like he owned me, and I liked it. It wasn't real, but I liked it. "Ready?"

I twisted my head to peer up at him. "Yes. Let's go."

The rustle of the newspaper attracted both our attention. "I know you," Elena drawled. "Theo, right? You're Abby's."

Theo stiffened behind me and pulled me even tighter against him. "Right and wrong. I am Theo, but I'm not Abby's."

Elena's wicked mouth curled into a smirk, and she waved the facts Theo gave her away like a pesky fly. "Oh, I guess my info is outdated. This meeting would be crazy awkward if you were still with Abby, especially since I know what it sounds like when you're coming."

I had to laugh, because what the fuck? "You did not just say that."

Theo's chuckle vibrated my back. "She did. Jesus, am I that loud?"

Elena nodded with wide eyes. "Honestly, it was like you were in competition with each other. I had to hold my teddy bear, I was so frightened."

I snorted again. This girl was out of her mind. "Okay, now I'm totally weirded out."

"Holy fuck," Theo mumbled against my hair.

With that, I grabbed his hand and tugged him out of the room. He laughed the entire way to the dining hall, repeating the line about Elena's teddy bear and cracking himself up again.

Thankfully, he'd settled by the time we were seated with plates of pancakes and bacon. Theo had unapologetically mooched off my dining plan, but it was cool. I wasn't rich, but my dining plan was rolling in it.

I tipped my chin to Theo's rapidly emptying plate. "There's more where that came from."

"Oh yeah?" He grinned. "You're saying you want to buy me dinner sometime?"

"If that dinner happens in this swanky as hell dining hall, then yep. My dining plan is the deluxe, baby."

He waggled his brows at me. "You're gonna be my sugar mama?"

"I'll buy you mozzarella sticks for services rendered."

Theo's grin slowly faded, but he didn't take his eyes off me. Then he reached for my hand, taking it in his. "This is good, right? I want to keep doing this, but I can't make any kind of promises."

I swallowed, fighting the urge to take my hand back. "Which part is good? The free breakfast or the fucking?"

He didn't even flinch. "Both, Tiger. I can pay for breakfast, but I like sharing it with you because you make me laugh and you're incredibly gorgeous to look at. The fucking...if you want that to happen again, I'm all in. Told you this morning that was the best I've ever had."

Sliding my hand away from his, I propped my chin on it. "So, you want to fuck me, share a couple meals with me, but not be responsible for my feelings? Or is that not it? You could tell me what you *don't* want with me. That might make it easier."

Sighing, he swiped his hand over his mouth. "I don't want to be a jackass to you."

"Got it. That's an admirable goal."

"Helen...I like you, but I was just with a girl for two years and I haven't been with anyone else since. I'm not looking for something serious. That's not where my head is right now." He steepled his hands under his chin, pausing like he was waiting for me to speak. I wasn't letting him off that easy. Not until he told me what I'd asked.

"I guess, yeah, I don't want to be responsible for your feelings, even though I will always go out of my way to make sure I don't screw you over. I don't want complicated. The other thing I'm dealing with, beyond Abby and all that shit, is my father and his severe disappointment in me for quitting wrestling and losing Abby. The thought of introducing him to someone new and all that comes with it—" He shook his head hard. "No, I'm not there right now. If you need me to say what I don't want, it's this: a relationship with a future. Expectations to take certain steps. Promises."

His words hit me harder than I thought they would, and that was no good. I wasn't having feelings for this rich boy with twinkly eyes. No matter how hard he made me come, or how sweet he had been to my sister. He didn't get to draw a line between us, because I'd drawn it before I'd ever met him, and no man, no matter how lovely his voice was, got beyond it.

Theo needed to understand who I was. He clearly had some fantasy of Helen Ortega being the marrying kind. Nope. Not gonna happen.

"I've never had a boyfriend, Theo. I've never wanted one, and I'm not looking for one. The sex was good, great even, but I don't want to meet your dad. I don't want to love you or for you to fall in love with me. My future involves me and Luciana getting out of this town. A man is not part of that. Maybe in a decade or two, but definitely not right now."

His nostrils flared, and the hinge of his jaw worked as he gritted his teeth. Call me crazy, but I didn't think Theo Whitlock seemed too pleased about me telling him I didn't want him for more than his dick, even though he'd just told me basically the same.

"No boyfriend? And you've never had sex sober? Why hasn't anyone treated you right?" He sounded like he was asking the universe instead of me, but I had an answer.

"I just told you I've never wanted a boyfriend. My best friends growing up were guys. They protected me from the big bads when I couldn't fight my own battles. They skated with me, learned tricks with me, laughed at our wounds while we wrapped them up. My boys would drive me places when we got older, or fix shit in my house that absolutely needed to be fixed. And sometimes, when we partied, we fooled around. I got everything I needed and nothing I didn't want."

Theo reached forward, grabbed my chair, and jerked it so I was right beside him. Then he took my jaw in his hand. "Where are these boys now? Because I seem to be the only fucking one taking care of you, baby."

"If I needed them, I'd call, and they'd come." I pushed his hand from my face. He cupped the side of my neck instead. "My two closest guy friends are away at school. With their girlfriends. So, the sex part of our relationship is finished—and honestly, it was a small part anyway—but they're still my boys. Ride or die. They *always* treated me right."

Gabe and Sebastian did, at least. Other boys, periphery friends, hadn't been as good to me. They were history now.

"I'm glad you have that." Theo tugged me close, his forehead resting on mine. "I feel like I'm messing this up with you, Helen. You're cool, you've always been cool. I'm the one being stupid."

"You are being stupid. We had sex one time and you think I want to meet your dad. Get a grip, dude."

I did not want to meet Theo's dad. Ever. But I also really hated everything about this conversation.

Theo exhaled heavily against my lips. "I've had one girlfriend. I don't know how to do anything but be a boyfriend. So excuse me for being a jackass. That's all I know."

"You were doing fine up until about five minutes ago. I mean, the stalking was kind of heavy handed, but you're cute, and you eat pussy like a champ, so I can look past that."

His smiling lips touched mine. "Thanks for being such a goddamn awesome girl. There's no one like you, baby."

"I know that, dude. Count yourself lucky I'm allowing you in my presence."

I didn't really understand why there was a knot wrapped in barbed wire in my throat, but damn, it did not feel great to swallow.

Theo kissed me again, and I let him go deep, because that felt better than listening to the words that kept coming from his torturous mouth. It went on too long and got too hot for a Sunday morning in the dining hall, but we didn't stop until someone, somewhere, dragged a chair across the tile floor, creating a long, loud screech.

He pulled back, but not far. "I have so much to do today."

"Me too."

"Are you working tonight?"

"No, not tonight. I'm going to hang out with Luc and take her to dinner."

"Tell me when you're working. I don't want you on the bus. I'll drive you."

I sighed and slumped away from him. "That sounds like a boyfriend thing."

He leveled a hard stare at me. "You're telling me the guys, the ones you call your ride or dies, would let you take the bus at two in the morning?"

I chewed on the corner of my lip. It had never come up while they'd lived in town, so I wasn't completely sure. Chances were, I'd do what I needed to do without letting them know.

"If they found out, they'd probably be pissed, but I do my own thing and don't answer to anyone. That's how I like it."

"Our friendship is going to work a little differently, baby. I won't allow you to do shit that endangers you. And before you get pissed at me using 'allow,' let me tell you what I mean." He tucked a stray lock of hair behind my ear and ran his hand down my braid. "I like this."

I rolled my eyes even though that little gesture sent a mini arrow straight through my chest.

"What I mean is I'm going to be there for you, so endangering yourself is not a choice. I don't have anything going on at two in the morning, so you tell me the days you work, I'll drive you home."

"And end up in my bed?"

The look he gave me could have burned down the ocean. "That's not why I'm doing it, but if you're offering that sweet, tight little pussy, I'm never going to turn it down."

"You know how to charm a girl, Theodore."

He didn't grin like I expected. His thumb stroked the center of my throat while his eyes swept over me, from lips to forehead.

"It's not about charming you, Helen. I'm telling you like it is. This works between us because we don't play games. We're straight with each other. It's a relief to have that with someone —with you. I think we get one another."

I nodded. "I think you're right, which is strange. You're the last person I should get."

His mouth tightened. "There's a lot you don't know about me, but you will. Then I think you'll see."

"Cryptic."

"Yeah," he breathed out. "I don't mean to be. I really do have to run."

"All right. Let's hit it."

We dumped our trays, then Theo took my hand. For a guy who didn't want to be a boyfriend, he really had a bad habit of acting like one. But I guess that was his point. This in-between kind of thing was brand new to him. It was new to me too. I sure as hell had never held hands with Bash or Gabe. The idea made me shudder, and those boys would have probably died of laughter if I suggested it.

Not that I ever would. Ew.

Back at my dorm, Theo walked me backward into the same wall Amir had trapped me against just over a week ago. Hidden by a tree, Theo went at me, wrecking my mouth, grabbing my ass, my belly, my tits—everywhere he could get his hands. I attacked back, shoving my hands under his shirt, biting his lips, sucking his tongue, grinding my pussy against his dick.

Just two pals saying goodbye. Nothing special.

He groaned with my breast in his hand. "Gotta stop. I need to go. I don't have time to take you upstairs."

"'Kay. Then you're going to have to get your hand out of my pants." Yeah, his other hand was currently down the back of my pants, gripping a handful of my ass.

"You're going to have to get *your* hand out of my pants, Helen."

Oh yeah. I was totally feeling up his butt too, but it was such a nice one, all bubbly and muscular.

We stepped away from each other, me zipping up my hoodie, Theo adjusting his dick. Watching him do that, I wanted to jump him again, so I stuffed my hands in my pockets and hurried out from behind the tree to the sidewalk.

It took Theo a minute, then he joined me. "I'm gonna go."

I smirked. "You should."

He stared me down. I stared right back. With a pained groan, he grabbed me by the back of my head and pulled me into his chest, kissing me hard and fast. Then he dropped his hands and walked away, shaking his head the entire way to his car. I had to clamp down on my bottom lip to keep the smile at bay.

Theo Whitlock wasn't going to be my boyfriend. That was a fact. But whatever this was, it was nothing like my friendships from high school.

I swiveled on my toes, heading back to my dorm for a shower and study session. No need to analyze the hell out of anything. I'd let this ride while it was fun and hot. When it changed—which it inevitably would—I'd end it.

• • • ◆ • ◆ • • •

THEO HAD ME ON all fours. He was behind me, driving into me relentlessly.

"You can't be loud," I panted.

"That's you being loud."

"But you're making me loud."

He smacked my ass. "Shut up. No one's home."

I arched my back, and he went impossibly deeper. "They might come home. They'll hear us."

He smacked me again. "I don't care," he said, punctuating each word with a thrust.

"Oh god," my neck arched when he hit something raw inside me, "who knew you'd be a bad influence?"

One more slap, then his arms banded around me, pulling me upright and onto his lap. My knees were on the outside of his, but he controlled my movements, bouncing me on his cock. Every time my butt slapped his thighs, breath knocked out of my lungs in frantic pants.

"No more talking unless you're telling me what you need, baby."

My head fell back on his shoulder. I turned to lick a line along his throat. "Need you to make me come." He'd already done that with his tongue, but the fire in my core was burning so hot, if I didn't find release, I'd combust.

He dipped down to cover my mouth at the same time he started working my clit with his fingers. Theo ate my moans, swallowed down my cries while he pounded into me from below.

I came hard, my entire body quaking. He rode me through it, never letting up on his savage rhythm. He was rough with me, gripping my flesh with a firmness just short of painful. He fucked me like he knew I wasn't going to break but kissed me like I was a treasure. The sweetest dichotomy kept me coming and moaning until Theo emptied himself inside me with one more wild thrust, then he stilled, pulsing deep, holding me in place.

We fell sideways in a sweaty lump. My head hit my textbook, making me groan. Theo grunted and pushed the book off my bed, then he curled around my back and nuzzled my nape.

"That hurt," I whined.

"Sorry, baby." He rubbed the side of my head, making it better.

A paper crinkled under my boob. It was the syllabus from my art history class. The class I was supposed to be studying for. Instead, I was well fucked and ready for a nap.

"You really are a bad influence." I patted Theo's face, which was resting beside mine, and felt his grin. "You're proud of yourself?"

"It was your idea to study in your dorm."

"Study, Theodore."

He cupped my tit. "We'll study, but I'm not going to be on a bed with you and not need to be inside you. That's just not possible. You need to know that now."

"The time to tell me that was when I suggested studying here instead of the library."

His teeth scraped my shoulder. "You don't have to fight me. You were with me the whole way."

I sighed. "I was. You're hot and your dick is nice, so yeah, I was with you. That doesn't mean it was a good choice. I still have to study, and now all I want to do is nap or sit on your face."

His laughter shook me. "You're telling me I didn't take good enough care of you?" His hand drifted from my tit to cup between my thighs. "This pussy isn't satisfied?"

"Satisfied? Yes. A greedy bitch? Also yes." I rolled to my other side, so we were facing each other. "I'm ninety-seven percent joking. Not about the studying—about the face sitting."

Because it was Thursday, we should have been in the library in Theo's hidey spot. My intentions had been mostly pure, inviting him back to my room to study instead. After his big speech about not committing and not wanting a relationship or complications, I was the only one actually putting distance between us. Theo kept holding my hand after class, making out with me against walls and under trees, picking me up from work at two in the morning. So, I figured if he was going to go all in on this...thing, then it was time I relaxed and gave in to the pull that made me want to hang out with him all the time.

I'd been stupid to think we'd actually get any studying done with an empty dorm and a bed at our disposal. Because, like I said, Theo was hot and his dick was nice.

Theo patted my hip. "Get dressed. You study like a good girl, I'll take care of your pussy again. You can sit on my face any time you want."

I palmed his face. "Shush. Don't call me a good girl in that voice when I'm trying to get my shit together. That's not fair in any way."

"What voice?" His expression was bemused. My entire face and chest heated.

"You know your voice. It's all lovely and low and sounds like you're about to recite sonnets about the way my hair catches the sun or my eyes glimmer in the moonlight." I snarled. "You know the voice."

He slowly shook his head. "No one's ever said anything about my voice. I think that's a you thing, Tiger."

Needing out of this conversation, I sat up and swung my legs over the side of the bed. My T-shirt was on the other side of the room, but my underwear was on the ground. I slipped them on, then stalked to where my shirt had been flung. I felt Theo's eyes on me—my ass—but I kept my back to him, tugging on my shirt, then disappeared into the bathroom.

I shouldn't have said anything about his voice. What had I even been thinking? I wasn't. He'd dicked me so well, part of my brain had fallen out. Obviously, I wasn't in my right mind, waxing poetic about Theo's voice.

I washed my hands, brushed my hair, and swiped on a thick coat of lipstick. The red brought me back to myself. I shook the orgasm haze out of my limbs, sucked in a breath, and opened the door.

My room was empty, my shorts folded neatly on the bed. I tugged them on, then I found Theo on the couch in the living room, his computer open in his lap, feet kicked up on the coffee table.

He looked me over with a slight quirk of his mouth but he didn't say a peep. I fell down on the armchair with my textbook, opening it to a random page, knowing I wasn't going to be able to study with him here.

A text on my phone saved me from having to pretend.

Bash: *Hey. What do you want for your birthday?*

Sebastian Vega never wasted words. He'd been like that since we met our freshman year of high school. His girlie, Grace, had cracked him open, but she was the only one who got to see inside. We got along because he was solid, he skated, he put up with my attitude, and these days, he had a kick-ass girlfriend.

Me: *Did Grace make you text?*

Bash: *Yeah. Question still stands.*

Me: *I really don't need anything.*

Bash: *You know that's not gonna fly with Grace.*

Me: *Fine. If you or Gracie have a piece of art lying around, that's just wasting away, I'll take it.*

Sebastian was a graffiti artist while Grace sculpted metal. They were both incredible at what they did. I didn't actually expect a piece of their art, but it was the first thing that had popped into my head. I hated asking for anything, even for my own birthday.

Bash: *Covered. Javi's throwing a party. You cool going there?*

Me: *I'm cool. I haven't been to a Javi party in too long.*

Bash: *Looking forward to it, Hells.*

Me: *Me too. Say hi to Gracie for me.*

Bash: *Yeah.*

Tossing my phone aside, I lifted my eyes to find Theo's on me. His brow was furrowed, the corners of his mouth turned down.

"Who's making you smile like that?" he gritted out.

"A friend. Sebastian. A few of my high school friends are coming to town Saturday. We were making plans."

His head cocked, that frown still in place. "You're not working Saturday?"

"No. I took the night off."

"Were you going to tell me?"

Leaning forward to rest my elbows on my knees, I leveled a hard gaze on him. "I definitely would have told you I didn't need a ride because I'm not inconsiderate. Was I going to tell you my plans? I don't know. Maybe. Maybe not."

His laptop closed with a loud snap. "Maybe not?"

"Do I owe you my Saturday nights, Theodore? That sounds like a boyfriend thing."

In a flash, he was in front of me, scooping me out of my chair, taking my place with me on his lap. His hands threaded in the sides of my hair, tugging me into him, then his mouth covered mine in a deep, wet, possessive kiss. I tried to pull back, but not that hard. When he held my head and licked my mouth, I forgot everything but the feel of him.

Forehead to mine, his inhales were jagged. "I know I messed up with you and I have to pay for it. But we're not playing games with each other. I don't claim your Saturday nights, but if I ask you where you're going, I expect a modicum of respect and for you to answer me. If you're doing something you don't want me to know about, then we need to have a whole other conversation."

"You don't have to pay for anything." My fingers curled around his wrists. "No games. I'm hanging out with a group of high school friends Saturday night. We're gonna go to a party at this guy Javi's. If you want to come, I'll text you the addy."

His chin bumped mine. "You want me there?"

"If you want to be there. Warning, though, you'll have to meet my boys, and you'll have to be okay with that."

"Boys you've fucked." He said it flatly, but his displeasure was obvious.

"Yeah. And the girlfriends they're gonna put a ring on as soon as possible."

He stroked my bottom lip with his thumb, his eyes tracing the same line. "I'll come."

"And be decent?"

"And be decent," he echoed.

This should be interesting.

Thirteen

HELEN

IN MY HAND, I held the most beautiful, intricate metal flower I'd ever seen. And it was mine. Slipping it over my head on a metal chain, I pressed it against my chest.

"Gracie." I had to blink hard not to cry. I was not a crier. It just wasn't me. But my girl, my boo, my tall drink of stunningly beautiful water of a friend, Grace Patel, had given me art. And not just any art, but art she'd created at the last minute when Bash had told her my request.

Grace wrapped me in her arms, giving me a hard squeeze. "If you'd given me more notice, I would have made you something better."

"No, girlie. I can't even. There's nothing better."

She pulled back and gave me a hard kiss on my cheek. "Happy birthday, Hells Belles."

Sebastian took hold of his girl, nuzzling the side of her head. "Happy birthday, Hells."

I touched my necklace with the tip of my finger, swallowing a big ball of emotion. "You're the realest, you two."

I liked Zadie. Lock was cool. And Theo...yeah, he was a little more than all right. But there was nothing like being surrounded by my people. The ones I grew up with and who shared my history. Being back at Javi's with them was even better. Javi was a mysterious being who opened his legit lake house on the weekends for relaxed kickbacks. There was a pool, a big yard, sick patio, and an unending supply of alcohol and weed.

An arm slung around my shoulders, a blunt waving in my face. "You need this, boo." Gabe squeezed me into his side, bringing the blunt to my lips. "This is my present to you. Pen got you a gift card for some fancy salon, and that's cool, but this strain is top notch. You're gonna thank me when your head is floating on your neck."

Penelope, my angel friend, elbowed her boyfriend. "I haven't given Hells her gift yet. You can't just tell her what I got her!"

He grinned wide and let go of me to take her in his arms. "Can and did, Lucky-luck. Accept it."

Pinching the *J* between my fingers, I took a long inhale. "I'll smoke this in your honor."

Poor Gabe couldn't partake since he played college soccer, but he'd smoked enough weed in high school to make up for the time off now.

"Mine too." Asher Beck, football star and golden god, had become absorbed in our group of miscreants when he hooked his little goth girl, Bex Lim. He'd come straight to Savage River after a day game just to celebrate little ol' me.

Bex was sprawled on a lounge chair next to the pool, puffing away. "I thought that's what I was doing."

Gabe flung himself down beside her, practically knocking her off the chair. "No, you're smoking for me. Everyone's smoking for me."

Asher hauled him off the chair, and Gabe went flying into Penelope, spinning her in a circle so they both didn't end up in the grass. Penelope giggled, her blonde hair flowing in the wind while Gabe spun her silly.

Asher and Bex were curled up in one lounge chair, and I pulled one up beside them, watching the stars and enjoying my smoke. The party would get a little crazier later, but not much. That wasn't why we went to Javi's. We came for laughs and to kick back—exactly what I needed tonight. Theo wasn't here. He had the address. Maybe he was coming, maybe not. I'd be disappointed if he didn't show, but it wasn't a huge deal. Not when I had all this.

Eventually, everyone pulled up chairs or loungers so we were in a circle. The athletes had drinks, the rest of us had drinks and smokes.

Grace kicked my chair. "How's tricks?"

"Good, good." I nodded. My head was definitely starting to float. "School, Shakespeare, boys. All the things."

Bex sputtered. "That does sound like all the things."

Gabe held up a hand. "Okay, no one wants to hear about you kissing a boy. That's like seeing your sister boning and shit. Gross. You know what everyone wants to know."

Bex muttered something about Gabe having boned his "sister," but Asher smothered her with his mouth to keep her quiet. She didn't object. Those two were gonna have so many sporty-goth babies, it was ridiculous.

"What does everyone want to know?" I asked.

Grace kicked my seat again. "Elena."

I groaned. "The only reason I haven't punched her is because she has Pen's face. Chick is a terror." I looked at Penelope Shade, tall, ultra curvy and deliciously plump, blonde and angelic Pen, and puffed a breath. "How do you share a gene pool with that hell beast?"

Pen's full mouth spread wide. "She has all good things to say about you. I heard about your near-death experience last weekend." Her brows popped.

I had no idea what she was talking about. Then again, I was high as fuck, so life was good and Elena was a distant memory.

Grace gasped. "What happened? You didn't tell me."

Pen snorted and shook her head. "Not my place to tell. I just think our Hells had a really good time. That's all I'm saying."

Gabe put his face in hers. "Are you keeping something from me, love of my fucking life?"

She pressed a hand to his scruffy cheek. "This is one of those things you don't want to know about Helen."

I finally caught on to what Pen was talking about. "Oh my god, no one is talking about my sex life. And Elena needs to mind her damn business."

Bash grunted. "Change of subject."

I tipped my Solo cup in his direction. "Yes. Smart man. I'm the least interesting person here. I want to know what all my people are doing."

They talked. I toked and drank, happy as a little clam. Bex and Asher were hitting the books hard, he was killing it on the field, and she'd just had her second art show of her college career where two of her photographs had sold for a chunk of change. They were so cute and golden, and you wouldn't think they'd fit, but they were so gone for each other.

Bash and Grace were living together in psycho-obsessive bliss —his, but a little bit hers too. He'd been in community college, but the demand for his graffiti murals had grown so much, he'd dropped his classes to do that full time—and my friend was making *bank*. Gracie was happy in college, working on her art on the side, supporting her man. They were so cute, I could gag, but I didn't because I loved them.

Gabe and Pen were my constants. I was equally close to them both, and we were always texting and calling, so I knew what they were up to. Gabe was a soccer star. Pen was a science nerd. They were a power couple, set to dominate the world.

All up to date, I went for a walk to the kitchen in search of something else to drink. My Solo cup was woefully empty. A few people were hanging there, but the area in front of the rows of alcohol was empty. I picked up a bottle, then another, contemplating which combination would keep me in this floaty, happy state.

I was not thinking about Theo's absence. Or that he hadn't responded to my text telling him the address. That wouldn't keep me floaty—and definitely not happy.

It was no big deal if he didn't show. Six people had traveled to town just for me. They'd dropped their responsibilities to celebrate my birthday. I had that, so I didn't need a single other thing. Or person.

Our group migrated to the den where Bex and Ash were playing pool. I squeezed between Bash and Grace and Gabe and Pen on a big couch, my boys at my sides. Gabe procured another blunt for me because he was the absolute shit. I laid my head on his shoulder while I smoked and reached across his legs to hold Penelope's hand. My sweet angel girl, letting me borrow her boyfriend's shoulder and holding my hand. Never been a realer one than Penelope Shade.

"Helen?"

From nowhere, Theo appeared in front of me. He didn't look happy, with slanted brows, his mouth in a tight line.

I waved. "Dude, you're here."

"I'm here." His head cocked as he scanned the scene. Me between two hot boys, one with his arm around me, my head on the other's shoulder. I was pretty certain he was missing the girls on their other sides. The ones they were devoted to down to their bones. The ones I was devoted to in the same way.

"Who's that?" Gabe barked.

"That's Theo," I answered.

Gabe shot off the couch, making me tumble into Penelope's side. She caught me with a giggle, pushing me back toward Bash, who was rising slower, but with purpose.

Gabe stuck his hand out. "Gabe Fuller. Who are you?"

Theo shook his hand, an even deeper frown marring his face. "Helen told you. I'm Theo Whitlock."

"Sounds fancy as shit." Gabe twisted around to look at me. "You hook up with a fancy boy?"

"Shut up." Yeah, it was dawning on me that inviting Theo here had been a very bad idea. I'd obviously been dick drunk when I'd issued the invitation.

"You're here for Helen?" Bash asked lowly.

Theo didn't flinch. "Yeah. I'm here for Helen."

With a chin jerk, Bash shook his hand. "Don't be an asshole to her. She's had enough of that in her life. Doesn't need more of it."

Asher and Bex had come over too. Ash had his arms crossed over his wide football player chest. I knew him, and I found him intimidating.

"This is dumb." I hopped up as fast as I could with a floaty head and got in front of Theo. "Stop being dumb. This is Theo. He's my friend. He's not going to hurt me because there's nothing to hurt. I'm safe. I don't need three daddies chasing him away with a shotgun."

Theo clamped a hand on my hip and pulled my back to his chest. Gabe zeroed in on where I was being held. Asher shrugged. Bash's nostrils flared.

"You're our girl," Gabe pouted. "It's our job to look out for you."

"Nothing you can say will convince me. Time will tell." Bash glowered at Theo. Then again, Bash glowered at almost everyone.

"It's not like that," I insisted.

Theo lowered his mouth to my ear. "It is."

"Dude," I hissed.

It so wasn't like that. Otherwise, I'd be pissed he hadn't texted me for hours and showed up late to the party. Since we were just friends with bennies, it was cool. All was cool. No big deal. I wasn't mad, and I definitely hadn't been disappointed before he got here. Cool, cool.

Grace and Penelope, who were much nicer than their boyfriends, introduced themselves to Theo. Bex did too, though she was kind of snarly about it, which I appreciated, since I shared the same trait.

I twisted in Theo's hold. "You need a drink. Or a smoke. Do you smoke?"

He stared at me, sweeping me with his gaze, then nodded once. "Show me where the drinks are?"

"Yeah."

Theo wove his fingers with mine, but I led the way back to the kitchen. I showed him the rows of liquor, but he ignored them and backed me into the counter, bracketing my hips with his hands on either side of me.

"Helen," he growled.

I raised my chin. "Theodore."

"You're high."

"A little. Is that a problem?"

"Nope. You're cute."

"You were late." Oh shit, I hadn't meant to say that.

He bowed his head so his forehead landed on mine. "Your text didn't come through until about forty-five minutes ago. I was getting pissed, thinking you had changed your mind, and then it was there. You said you were getting here at nine in the text, and it was already eleven. I immediately felt like shit for being pissed and hauled ass to get here."

I swallowed. "That explains it."

"Did you think I wasn't coming?"

"Yes."

He brushed his lips against mine. "I'm sorry."

That made me wobbly. I wasn't used to anyone being sorry they'd let me down. But here Theo stood, owning and apologizing for something he couldn't control, because he was that guy. The one who was too good to be true.

"It's not your fault."

"Still sorry." He kissed me a little harder. "I didn't like the scene I walked in on, if I'm being honest."

Oh yeah, there was reality. I knew it had been around here somewhere. Theo was good, but he definitely wasn't perfect. He could be a judgy asshole, just like the rest of them.

"Me hanging out with my friends? And their girlfriends?"

"It took me a while to notice the other girls."

I laughed softly. "I was holding Penelope's hand, dude."

"And had your head on that guy's shoulder." He cupped my jaw. "Don't dude me. I'm not your bro."

"Who are you then?"

"You know." He was getting growly, and I was just drunk enough not to buck against his possessive streak. If I'd been sober, it would have annoyed me, but right now, my clit was throbbing.

"Tell me, Theodore. I'm confused."

His lips ghosted over mine. "I'm the guy whose dick you're going to take tonight—and for the foreseeable future. My mouth is the one you're going to come on. My hands are the only hands that get to touch you like this. You're mine, Tiger."

Okay, maybe I wasn't drunk enough not to buck against him. "I'm not yours, dude. We established that."

"Nope. You're not calling me dude and turning me into one of your little pals." His fingers flexed on my jaw. "You're mine until we're done with this thing."

I shook my head back and forth. "I'm mine. I let you into my body because I want to. If I want to let someone else into me, I will."

"Yeah?" He got in my face, his nose touching mine.

"Yeah." I shoved at his chest, giving myself an inch of space to turn away from him. He didn't allow it. His arms banded around my middle, and then I was off my feet, being carried from the kitchen. I writhed and kicked, but Theo was sober, and he had that wrestler strength. I wasn't going anywhere until he decided I could.

He wrenched open a door and carried me inside, kicking it closed behind us. We were in a powder room, with only a small vanity and toilet. My feet hit the ground in front of the vanity. I met Theo's wild eyes in the mirror. He shoved my hair to the side and attacked my neck, scraping his teeth down the length of it, then latching on. His arms circled my chest, and his hands were on my tits, kneading and thumbing my nipples through my thin shirt.

"What are you doing?" I breathed.

He rocked against me, grinding his thick erection into me. Unable to help myself, I arched my back and pushed back. He shoved my tank and bra down to get his hands on my bare skin. Fingers both abused and worshiped my nipples, rolling and plucking, driving me out of my mind.

"Proving a point." He sucked on my neck again. I knew he was doing it to mark me, and I should have hated it, but it made my knees turn to jelly.

"What point?"

He snapped open my shorts and shoved them down in one swift move. Then his hand was in my underwear, fingers sliding easily between my soaked folds. Our reflection let me watch everything he was doing to me, touching me, destroying my neck, thoroughly proving his point.

Then my panties went along with my shorts, and Theo pressed on my lower back, bending me forward. And I went, because it was my birthday, and suddenly, all I wanted were some birthday orgasms Theo was more than capable of giving me.

He sank two fingers deep inside me without warning. My head reared back. Our gazes clashed in the mirror. His was both smug and heated.

"This point." He worked me hard, thrusting his fingers with brutal force that made me soak his hand. "You're not going to let anyone else inside because I'm the only one who can do this to you. You can be pissed at me and flooding my hand at the same time. You know it, I know it. Let go, baby. You don't have to fight."

His lovely voice, the things he was saying, his heated, muscular body pressing into mine, the precision with which he touched me—it all sent me spinning into a climax that would have knocked me off my feet if he hadn't been *right there*, holding me up, crowding my space, leaving no room for argument or escape.

Then he turned and lifted me onto the vanity, held my legs wide open, and drove into me. His cock wedged so deep, he hit a raw part of me that would have had me screaming, except Theo's mouth crashed into mine and he swallowed it down.

We were wild like we always were when we came together, but it was magnified tonight. So needy I could burst, I ripped his shirt from his body to get my hands on him. I was addicted to the way his muscles rippled under his skin when he moved inside me. It was powerful and intimate at the same time.

Theo didn't let up on me, fucking me breathless, making me come with his thumb on my clit, whispering filthy things about my tight little pussy and how I was his. I soaked it all up, letting it go to my head just like the blunts I'd smoked tonight.

I was loud, and he let me be, never muffling me after the first scream. His grunts were carnal, and they only spurred me on to moan and scratch and suck on his throat to make a matching claim on him.

"I'm going to come all over you. But first, I need to make you come one more time. I need it to happen soon. Can you get there?"

"Get me there," I panted.

"Yeah," he grunted, driving in deeper. "I'll get you there, my good girl. My precious, sexy, good girl."

"Tell me how good I am."

He cupped my ass to angle my hips so when he thrust, his pelvis hit my clit, and I nearly spiraled into ecstasy.

"The most beautiful woman I've ever seen with the sweetest little pussy. It gets wet for me because this pussy knows I'm going to take care of it." He added a finger to my clit, and my thighs started to quiver. "When you open your legs for me like I ask and take me deep, I know you're *my* good girl. Aren't you, Helen? Tell me."

"I'm your good girl." The last word was cut off by a soul-deep moan. My belly tightened into knots, then burst into a thousand pieces. Theo pulled out fast, replacing his cock with his fingers, pumping them into me while I came.

With his other hand, he fisted his cock. We both watched him finger fucking me while his dick throbbed in his hand until jets of cum shot onto my belly, my slit, my thighs. I was an utter mess, and I kept coming and coming while he did.

"Fuck," he murmured, bringing his forehead to mind. "That is beautiful, Tiger. I like that more than you'll ever know."

Those words shattered something internal. A wall made of glass Theo had been knocking against since day one. Maybe I was too high and sated to be thinking clearly, but it felt like he'd cracked an integral part of me open.

Then someone knocked on the bathroom door, and our little cloud of bliss went up like smoke.

We looked at each other. Theo was a hot mess with a dark hickey blossoming on his neck, his dick glistening, his hair wild. I probably looked similar. I had to laugh, so I did.

Theo kissed the tip of my nose and grinned at me. "Phenomenal, baby. Let's get you cleaned up before whoever's out there pisses themselves."

Theo took care of me, and we righted ourselves. I draped my hair over the shoulder he'd devoured, leaving behind several hickeys. I didn't mind that they were there, but they were for Theo and me. I didn't need to show them off to everyone to feel their claim.

Besides, Gabe might throw an actual fit if he had to lay eyes on evidence of me being a sexual human being. It was ironic considering our past, but I was glad that chapter was so far in the rearview, he'd swung the complete opposite way with me.

"Are we good?" Theo asked.

I nodded. "We're really good."

"I didn't wear a condom."

"I know. I'm covered, as long as you're—" I raised my brows. It had been a long, long time since I'd let anyone inside me, and never without a rubber, so I was square. And yeah, I should've made Theo suit up, but I didn't. I just didn't.

"Yeah, I did the whole testing thing at my last checkup."

"Good." I touched the mark I'd left on his neck. "Then no worries."

"No worries," he rumbled in agreement.

I opened the powder room door, Theo behind me, but only took one step before I stopped. Amir was slouched against the opposite wall, his foot kicked up against it.

Shit. Fuck. I did not want to do this with him in front of Theo.

He slowly clapped his hands. "Nice show. I didn't know you had it in you, Hells."

I shook my head. "Not doing this tonight."

He straightened, his attention over my shoulder, a smirk on his lips. To my surprise, he bowed his head. "Whitlock."

Theo didn't say a word. His fingers dug into my hips as he quickly steered me down the hall, leaving a laughing Amir behind.

"Do you know him?" I asked.

"Not really. Do you?"

"He went to my high school." Not a lie. Not the entire truth, but not a lie.

"Mmm. I've seen him around at parties."

I had a feeling Theo was answering me the same way I'd answered him. Half-truths were cousins to lies, but they weren't lies.

I dropped it since I didn't want him pressing me on my relationship with Amir. Theo didn't need to know every single dirty, ugly thing about me—not when he had me feeling like I was his good girl and I wanted to keep that for a while.

We got drinks and found my crew outside by the pool again, kicked back on loungers. Theo and I grabbed the last available one, pulling it over to join the group.

"We thought you left," Grace said.

Bash crossed his arms. "She sent me looking for you."

Pen's eyes rounded. "Then we...uh, heard you."

Gabe fell into her chest face-first. "Don't make me say what I heard."

"We stayed here," Bex added.

"Wisely, apparently," Asher said.

"Go Helen." Grace twirled her finger in the air.

"We weren't that loud." I crinkled my nose, refusing to be embarrassed.

"You were," Gabe wheezed. "You very much were."

Theo curled his arms around me, holding me tight while he shook with laughter. I settled into it, his arms, his hold, his nature that swept away all the bad to make room for the good. In the dark, I met Pen's gaze. She was smiling at me in Theo's embrace. I couldn't explain to her we weren't together, we were only...well, whatever we were, that this didn't mean anything. I'd tell her later. For tonight, I sank into what I had at my fingertips.

It was my birthday, and one night with Theo as mine was the present I was giving myself.

• • • ● • ● • • •

THEO PARKED OUTSIDE MY dorm and walked up the stairs with me. Then he followed me inside the elevator.

"What are you doing?" I leaned against his chest, giving him most of my weight. I wasn't hammered, but I was more than a little toasty, and Theo felt mighty fine.

"Taking you home." He gripped my ass like he had every right to. And I guess he did, because I wasn't arguing. I liked his hands there.

"Door-to-door service. Way to make a girl feel special."

He practically carried me to my suite because the thought of walking bummed me out. Once we were inside, he kept me in his arms all the way to my bedroom. There, he set me on the bed and kicked off his shoes.

"What are you doing?" I asked.

His shirt went next. "Getting ready for bed. You should too, unless you want me to help you."

I blinked. "But why are you getting ready for bed here? In my room?"

He continued stripping his clothes, like this was an everyday occurrence. "I'm sleeping here." Hands on his hips, he stood in front of me in just his boxer briefs. My mouth salivated at the ridges of muscles at his hips. I would have leaned forward to trace them with my tongue if my head hadn't been so spinny.

"God, you're hot." Oh shit. My hands flew up to cover my mouth, but it was too late. Theo knew my weakness—him.

He dragged his thumb down my cheek. "Arms up."

My arms went up automatically, then my shirt was on the floor with his. "This doesn't feel like sexy-time stuff."

He chuckled under his breath. "Fuck, you're cute when you're wasted."

"Not wasted," I muttered. "Happily toasted. There's a difference."

Theo was digging through my dresser, and I didn't question it. I also didn't question the way he'd easily found my pajamas without asking me. That was just Theo, with his twinkly eyes and too-good-to-be-true nature.

I stood up to take off my shorts and pull on my boxers and tee. That was when I remembered my new necklace. Slipping it over my head, I handed it to Theo.

"Can you put it somewhere safe? It's important."

He held it in his palm, brow furrowed. "I haven't seen this before. It's beautiful."

"Mmm...Grace made it. She gave it to me tonight for my birthday. Can you believe someone that pretty is also talented and sweet? I doubted her at first, but that bitch is legit."

I started for the bathroom, but only got two steps before I was launched backward onto the bed, Theo landing on top of me.

"Hi," I breathed.

"It's your birthday." Oh, he sounded displeased.

"Yeah."

"It's your *birthday*."

I nodded. "I'm twenty, weee."

I could practically feel the thunder booming in his skull. "It's your birthday, Helen."

"Yeah, it is. Why does that make you angry?"

His elbows bracketing my head, he shoved his fingers in the sides of my hair. "You didn't think to tell me? Like an asshole, I show up late as hell to that party and don't even wish my girl a happy birthday?"

I rubbed my feet on the backs of his calves. "It's no big deal. I never make my birthday a thing."

"Helen..." He growled my name like a warning, but since I was me, I didn't heed it.

"If you're worried about my friends thinking you're shitty for not wishing me a happy birthday, don't worry. They were more traumatized by the sounds they hear—"

"No." His fingers fisted, tilting my head back. "I give a shit what they think because they're your friends. But I'm not thinking about them. I'm thinking I would've liked to make an effort for you. I'm thinking I would've taken you to dinner, gotten you a present, *something*." He rolled off me, rubbing the heel of his hand into his eye.

"Boyfriend things," I whispered.

"Shit."

I turned over, tucking myself into his side. His arm came around me, pulling me even closer. I was sleepy, and Theo was warm, so even though we were in the middle of something, I was close to drifting off. My fingers traced the ridges of his abs and hips, and for once, I didn't want to climb on his dick. I liked this, being close, touching his warm skin, hearing him breathe. It wasn't something I'd experienced before. I'd consider it a birthday treat.

"I'm good with how my birthday turned out."

His arm tightened. "Good." His lips touched my temple. "Your friends care about you."

"They do. Pretty sure Bash and Gabe would happily hide a dozen dead bodies for me."

"Not surprised. You've got a way about you."

I laughed into his chest. "A way that you think I'd have a dozen dead bodies to hide?"

That made him huff a short laugh. "No. I meant you'd inspire that kind of loyalty."

"Mmm." I didn't know how to answer that, but it made my chest feel like there were hot coals piled inside.

After a beat of silence, Theo spoke again, his voice rough and deep. Still lovely, though. "It was incredibly hard not to think about them knowing what you feel like from the inside."

I tapped on his chest, needing his attention so he really heard me. "Ancient history. Besides, no one *really* knows except you."

His breath stopped. He got it. He was the only one who'd taken me raw. What he didn't get was he had me in a way no one ever had. I couldn't put a name to it, but I knew it was the truth. And realizing that made me all kinds of uncomfortable.

"Tiger," he murmured, his lips to my crown.

This was too much for me to handle. His soft voice, my feelings, just no. Not now. Maybe not ever.

"I'm tired as hell, Theodosius. Time for me to turn in." I extracted myself from his arms and nearly leaped from the bed. "I call the bathroom first."

Then I was safe behind the door of my bathroom, staring at myself hard in the mirror.

"We do not catch feelings for twinkly-eyed rich boys. Stop being dumb." I shook my toothbrush at my reflection. "You're a hard-ass bitch. You give boys a baseball bat to the balls, not your heart. Shut it down, Helen."

My Mads wouldn't be happy I was putting myself through this. She'd had a lot to say in the ten months I knew her. Her most pervasive advice was to never shut out experiences and to live life like it was supposed to be lived: to the goddamn fullest.

But she wasn't here anymore, and my reflection agreed with me. I didn't like Theo Whitlock. I had no room for that. Sex, yes. Friendship, sure. Beyond that was out of the question for us both.

Fourteen

Helen

I THREW MY HEAD back, biting on my bottom lip to stifle my moans. We were in an empty classroom. I didn't even know who it belonged to—or the desk Theo had spread me out on. Theo had pulled me inside, yanked off my shorts and panties, dropped to his knees, and started devouring me. Not a single word passed between us. His tongue on my clit spoke a thousand words by itself.

If someone heard us or walked in, it would be more than embarrassing. At least for me. The threat of being caught didn't stop me from opening my legs wider, shoving Theo's face deeper, and coming on his lips, though.

Then he was on his feet, pushing his shorts down to free his cock, palms on my inner thighs, keeping me in place so he could drive inside me. I locked my ankles around his back, held on to his shoulders, and let him ride me.

He wasn't kidding around, slamming into me like if he didn't get as deep inside me as he could, the world would collapse. Since my birthday a week ago, Theo had come unleashed, spending his spare time either making me come or getting us both off. This was the only way I could completely let myself go with him. My walls crashed the second he put his mouth on me. Every. Single. Time. He was *that* good.

"Look at you, baby." His head dropped to watch where we were joined. "Taking me so beautifully. I can't go a minute without thinking of what this looks like and how you feel wrapped around me."

"I think about it too," I breathed back.

"You think about me?" He belted my waist with his hands and captured my gaze with his sharp eyes.

"I do think about you. All the time. Too much."

With a groan, he shoved his face into my neck and pistoned impossibly deeper inside me.

"That's my beautiful girl, honest and real." His lips found my pulse, sucking my skin into his mouth. "Perfect, Helen. Can't get enough of you."

I believed him, the way he kissed me, sucked me, fucked me. He'd nabbed me while I'd been walking down the hallway after my last class. We weren't supposed to see each other today. But here I was, coming all over his cock so hard, I saw stars on the backs of my eyelids.

"Theo," I cried.

He cupped the back of my head and pushed my face into his chest, muffling my moans with his body. I couldn't help it, I had to make noise, show him what he did to me. It was biological, instinctual, something that couldn't be stopped.

"That's it, Tiger, that's it," he cooed in a deep, velvety tone that prolonged my climax until I was wrung out and all I could do was hold on.

Theo tipped me back on the desk, allowing him to go deeper. I felt him swell, stretching my walls until he rutted into me in earnest. Fucking hard and fast, holding my legs like reins, he rode me until finally he gritted out my name and coated my insides with wet heat.

He stilled, staying joined with me even as he set me upright and kissed me wet, hard, and with a passion that took me by surprise, even after the way we'd just gone at each other. I answered him back with the same fervor, nipping, biting, licking until we were both breathless.

Theo's forehead knocked against mine. "I'm sorry. I was running late for sociology, saw you walking toward me down the hall, and something came over me. I had to have you."

"Your apology is wasted." I rubbed my heels down the bubble of his butt to his thighs. "I enjoyed every second of that. You need to pull out, though so I can get dressed. I *really* don't want to be expelled for being naked with President Whitlock's beloved son."

He cupped my cheeks, staying wedged inside me. "I'd never let anything happen to you."

"Okay," I whispered. I didn't believe him, but it was nice that he made that promise.

We got dressed and Theo left the class first, checking if the hall was clear. When he signaled it was, I met him in the hall.

"Where are you going now?" he asked.

"I'm gonna go skate in the courtyard by my dorm, then I need to write a paper."

"Schoolgirl." He slid his fingers through his hair. "I'm supposed to be in sociology right now."

"What? Theodore, get your ass to class!"

He grabbed me, holding me against him. "I'd rather skip it."

"Hey." I held his jaw in my hand. "Go to class. Do not take this place for granted."

His lips touched my nose. "You're right." He started to let me go, but he yanked me right back, then he dipped his head to bite my throat. "Too fucking delicious."

With my neck stinging from his teeth, my mouth thoroughly kissed, and a smile on my face, Theo sent me on my way.

• • • • • • • • • •

IT WAS DARK, AND the night held just a tiny bit of chill. Not much, but since my legs were bare, I felt it.

Theo was parked in his usual spot. Normally when he caught sight of me, he would hop out to open my door, because he was a gentleman like that. Tonight, there was no movement coming from inside his car.

He'd left it unlocked, so I climbed in the passenger side. That was when I saw him. Eyes closed, chin to chest, breathing deeply. Theo had fallen asleep waiting for me.

I worked four or five nights a week, and Theo had been here to pick me up each of those nights for weeks. I guess I'd been so caught up in school, work, Luc, and Theo, I hadn't taken a step back to understand what that really meant. But here it was, right in front of my eyes.

Lashes brushing his cheeks. His mouth slack. Lips looking so soft, I had to quell the urge to kiss them. His arms hanging limp at his sides. Body slumped in his seat. Theo was exhausted, but he was here. He was always here. I didn't want that to ping around my chest, touching raw nerves and filling black chasms, but it did.

I couldn't do this. If Theo filled my empty places, I'd get used to it and crave it. That wasn't what this was, and I didn't want it to be that.

I poked his shoulder. "Wakey-wakey, Theodosius."

He startled, jumping in his seat, hand flying up in defense. "What?"

"Time to go home, dude."

Clearing his throat and wiping the sleep from his eyes, he straightened and turned to me. He took a long moment to look me over, his brow pinched in concentration.

"God, you're gorgeous." He sounded like he was coming out of a dream, and that rocked me.

"And you're tired." I couldn't help myself. Reaching across the console, I snagged the back of his neck and brought him toward me. His mouth hit mine in a sleepy kiss that was so tender, I regretted it instantly. "Theo..."

"Tiger," he murmured, kissing me again. His tongue slipped in my mouth, and his arm circled around me, pulling me halfway out of my seat. I clung to him, easily giving in and meeting his kiss with the same slow, sensual caress of my lips and tongue.

"You need to go to bed," I whispered. "Come on."

He released me, but he didn't move to put the car in drive. In fact, he stayed looking at me while he gripped the steering wheel with one hand, the other catching mine.

"I hate that you work here." His confession came out hard and fast, and kind of pissy.

"You don't have to keep picking me up, you know." Oh, I was definitely pissy.

"You don't get me, baby. Picking you up is not the problem. I'd give you a ride out of hell if you needed it." He nodded toward Savage Beauties. "I don't want you working at this club, serving the kind of men who go in there."

"I need the money. You know that."

His fingers flexed around mine. "So, work at a regular bar where half your ass doesn't have to hang out."

If he had any clue there'd been a few times I'd let a lot more than half my ass hang out behind those Savage walls, he'd never look at me the same. No more tender kisses. No more sleepy smiles and calling me gorgeous. I read the judgment all over him.

"I wouldn't make half the money at a regular bar, and I hate to break it to you, but dudes at regular bars are the same ones who go to strip clubs. It's just that at regular bars, they can get away with being gropey because the bouncers don't watch the floor like hawks the same way they do at strip clubs. Any time I have a customer even *think* they have a right to my body in there, Ronaldo, Hakim, or Xavier set them straight." I yanked my hand away and crossed my arms over my chest. "If you have a problem with it, that's on you. It's not on me."

His hand shot out to grip my nape, tugging me toward him so fast he took my breath away. Then his mouth was on mine, crashing, tongue fucking, plundering. I answered back with my teeth, nipping at his lips, scraping his tongue. It was hard, fast, a little painful, and it seared my chest like a brand. Then he gently shoved me back in my seat and pulled out of his spot, driving away from Savage Beauties at a careful pace.

"I do have a problem with it, but you're right, it's on me." His lovely voice was low and tired, with an edge of bitterness, but he wasn't angry. "I don't want anyone thinking they get to have any part of you."

"Dudes think that when I walk down the street, Theo."

"Theodore," he gritted out, his hands twisting around the steering wheel like he was trying to strangle it.

"Theodore." I gave it to him soft, the way he liked it, and his shoulders almost instantly fell from around his ears. "You can't control people's thoughts."

His jaw remained hard. "No one gets to think they can have you. That is not acceptable."

I really didn't know where this was coming from or how to handle it. No one had ever been this...I guess, possessive over me. I'd been a friend, a convenient lay, a hookup, but that had always been where it began and ended because that was how I'd always wanted it.

He parked outside my dorm, eyes on the windshield. I should have gotten out and made a run for it. Almost everything inside me screamed to run from this, from him. But the soft part of me Theo kept uncovering wanted him to understand me.

"I get to have Luciana when I graduate."

Theo's head whipped sideways, his expression fierce. "What?" he breathed.

"My mom and I have a deal. I support Luc while I'm in school, pay my mom's debts, and I get my girl when I graduate. My mom'll sign over custody to me and Luc will be mine. I'm going to take summer classes so I can graduate in two years because three years is way too long for her to live there."

"You're taking on your sister?"

I nodded hard. "Yeah. She's mine. I'm hers. There's no choice. I have to get her out of there as soon as I can. I refuse to let her live like that."

He was so still, I had no idea what he was thinking, but I braced myself. I hadn't told anyone my plans for Luciana, except Mads. She'd been the one to help me formulate my plan and pushed me—pushed me *hard*—to fulfill it.

"Jesus...tell me to fuck off." He took my face in his hand, and even in the dark, I could make out his pleading expression. "Please, baby. I have no idea what I'm talking about. Do what you need to do for Luc and tell me to fuck off."

Leaning into his palm, my mouth curved. "Fuck off, Theodore."

"That's right." He leaned over and kissed my cheek, then, when I turned, my mouth. "You're a good girl, Helen. You know that?"

Those words trapped me in a velvet web. Theo could come along, eat my heart out, and I'd just lie there and take it because he'd called me a good girl.

"I know nothing of the sort." I unbuckled my belt and grabbed my bag, intent on making a run for it. But like always with him, I couldn't quite tear myself away. "Don't fall asleep at the wheel. I'd be sad if you died."

His shoulders shook with laughter. "Sweetest thing you ever said to me."

I ran then, taking his lovely laugh and sweet words with me. I just didn't know how to escape them.

Fucking Theodore. He was really going to mess me up if I wasn't careful.

• • • ●• ● • ●• ••

LAST YEAR, I'D TAKEN online courses at Savage River Community College. Once, Madeline had looked at my syllabus and started hysterically laughing. At the time, I'd wanted to be offended, but I couldn't really get it up, because my Mads hadn't had very much cause to laugh anymore. Once she'd calmed herself, she told me I was in for a surprise when I enrolled at Savage U. Like always, Mads had been right. My classes were no joke. The work was backbreaking, and it started right out of the gate. If I hadn't spent a year with Mads, learning how to take notes, study, and write—things I'd never done in high school—I would have been screwed.

Thursdays in the library with Theo were an indulgence. The hour we read Shakespeare could have been shaved down by half if I'd been on my own. I wasn't giving them up.

After staying behind to speak with my professor, I was running a few minutes late. Theo was going to claim the chair first, and that wouldn't do. I liked our battle for the seat far too much.

When I rushed down the aisle to our hidden spot, low voices pulled me to a stop. Theo's, I recognized. I thought I knew who the other voice belonged to, especially when she called him "The," which was honestly the worst nickname ever.

Slowly, I stuck my head around the end of the aisle, and yeah, I should have backed away instead. Theo was in our chair, and his pretty, blonde ex had her little ass perched on the arm, her legs nestled against his. I was nosy, so I stayed to watch the horror show before me.

"I don't understand, The."

He dug his fingers into the sides of his hair. "There's nothing to understand. I don't want to talk to you."

Frustration poured from him. I had a feeling this wasn't their first time around this circle.

Bitch sniffled. "But, baby, I still love you, you know? I made a mistake, but so did you. If we talk, I know we can get past it. We can get back to how we were. Remember Sarah and Thomas? Remember?"

Theo's hands dropped, and for a moment, his eyes went hazy. Whoever Abby was talking about, he obviously remembered, and it affected him. His head jerked in my direction, so I fell back a few steps, behind the cover of the bookshelf.

"Yeah, I remember." He sounded gritty and tired. I was relieved not to be looking at him. If he'd been wistful or pining, I would have punched someone. Maybe both of them. "I also remember you telling me I had to give up the sport I was deeply committed to in order to keep you. And when I didn't jump, you walked out on two years of me giving you my everything. That's why this is done, Abby. That's why there's nothing more to talk about."

"You didn't give me everything. You didn't. You had more." She sniffled again, and this time, a choked sob followed. If she hadn't been an absolute bitch to me and Luc at the T, I would have felt sorry for her. Now, she was just in my way.

"I need you to do what you do and walk away. Right now."

"Theo...no..."

"Then I will."

There was shuffling, books slamming, Abby whining, then footsteps coming my way. Fast. Too fast for me to hide, so I didn't. Theo charged toward me, and he didn't look the least bit surprised to find me there. Without a word or pause, he grabbed my arm, dragging me with him.

He shoved me into the unisex bathroom, locked the door behind him, and pushed me into the wall. His mouth was on mine, his hands were tearing at my clothes, his steely length prodding my belly.

"Theo—"

"No," he barked. "I have to have this with you."

Fisting my hair, he tugged my head back sharply and took my mouth, kissing me deep and hard. His tongue lashed mine, licking my taste, stealing my protests. And then my shorts were unbuttoned and his hand was between my legs, and I forgot to protest when the pad of his finger met my clit.

"Wet, baby," he mumbled. "So wet, just how I need you."

Then my shorts were gone. Theo pinned me to the wall with his hips, the tip of him nudging my entrance. A single heartbeat was all it took for us to go from two to one. He speared his cock deep into me. Once he had me where he wanted me, he took control of my body, how I moved on him, bouncing me up and down his length while driving into me with brutal force. My nails grappled on his shoulders. All I could do was hold on and let him take me.

He covered me with his body, his raging emotions, his mouth, his hands, all of him. I took all he gave, holding on, shutting my brain off, solely focusing on the pleasure between my thighs. If I focused on anything else, like *why* this was happening, I wouldn't be able to handle it. So I pushed it all aside, keeping only Theo.

And he gave it to me. Even though he was out of his mind, barely there, he took care of me, rubbing my clit in a perfect rhythm that made my legs tremble and my belly quiver. He shoved my shirt under my chin, took my nipple between his lips, and sucked deep, groaning around my flesh. My head fell against the tile. Anguished moans escaped my throat, echoing around the small room.

My climax spurred Theo on even more. He pounded into me so rough, I couldn't take a full breath. I knew I'd feel where he'd been and what he'd done tomorrow. He gripped my ass with bruising strength, digging his fingertips in.

I hated and loved the way he handled me in equal measures. I wanted him to stop and for this to never end. This was wrong. And so right. When he buried himself all the way to the deepest part of me, the twin tears trailing down my cheeks were mourning the end and crying out that this ever began.

Theo was breathing heavily. He shoved his face into my neck, kissing my throat like feathers.

And that was when I woke up from my sex-addled stupor. That dose of sweet pissed me off. I slapped him on the chest, then I shoved him hard. Of course, the only movement that got me was him lifting his head to give me a confused look.

"Put me down right fucking now, Theo," I growled.

He walked me to the counter next to the sink and plopped me on it, but he did not back away, nor did he disengage our bodies. His cock was still sunk deep inside me. He held me tight, so I had no hope of kicking him out of my body.

"What just changed?" he demanded. "One second, we're both here, breathing hard after what was honestly the hottest experience of my life—and maybe yours too, based on how tight your pussy was strangling me. The next, you're pissy and telling me to let you go. So, tell me, what changed?"

"Get out of me immediately. I don't want you inside me anymore."

He froze, glaring at me. Then he slowly backed away until we were no longer joined.

"*No.*"

"*Okay.*"

I winced at the sting he left behind. But he didn't let me move. He still stood between my open legs, rubbing his palms along my upper thighs.

"Talk, Helen. I need you to give me your words."

"Oh, so you do know it's me? I wasn't sure if you were fucking me or Abby. Or maybe it didn't really matter who you fucked, as long as you had a warm hole to dump your rage into." I slapped his chest with enough force to make him wince. "I don't need you to be my boyfriend, but my pussy is not a receptacle for your feelings for another woman. You owe me a lot more respect than that. So fuck you. And get the hell out of my way so I can put my underwear on before I catch hepatitis from this counter."

"Helen—"

"No." I hopped down, and he allowed me to slide by to grab my clothes. I shoved my legs in my shorts and glared at him. "You told me when we started this you don't want to be responsible for my emotions—and you hammered that home just now. This is my line in the sand I will not let you cross again. We can be done. We don't have to have a conversation. I'm out, Theo."

"Theodore," he murmured.

"Fuck you, Theo," I hissed.

I got a step toward the door before Theo was on me, whipping me around to face him.

"I knew it was you," he shot out. "How can you think I didn't know exactly who I was with? I've never been this way with anyone else. What we have is only ours."

"I saw you and Abby."

He nodded. "I know you did, baby. I saw you too."

"Who are Sarah and Thomas?"

He jerked back, clearly surprised by my question. He answered anyway, and I wished he hadn't. "They're the names we thought of for our future kids. In *high school*, Helen."

I winced like he'd struck me. "Cute. Very Waspy and perfect. You're obviously still torn up about your breakup. You're so devastated and angry at her, you had to wreck my pussy and—"

He came at me, cupping my face with both hands. All the anger and roughness from earlier was gone, replaced with the gentle Theo I knew.

"Did I hurt you, baby?"

"Yeah, you did."

His eyes flared. His hands went to the top of his head. "I hurt you, Helen? You're telling me I hurt you?"

I nodded, but my fight had evaporated at his devastation. Because that's what I was seeing. Theo was beside himself right now, pacing the small bathroom like a feral cat.

"Theo, I didn't mean it like that. Yeah, you were rougher than you've ever been, and I will definitely feel it tomorrow, but that would have been okay if you were with me the whole time." I pressed my hand to my forehead. "You made me feel used and cheap—and you've *never* made me feel that way before. That's what hurt—getting that from you."

He dropped his hands, sweeping me with his gaze. And then he was on me, pulling me in his arms, not to ravage me, but to hold me against him.

"I don't think that of you. I will never think that of you. Ever, Helen." His lips touched the top of my head again and again. "I *was* out of my mind, but there was never a second I didn't know who I was with. And that was about you and me. Because the whole time she was there, I was thinking about how badly I wanted you in my lap reading Shakespeare with me."

"You were angry."

"Yeah, I was. I was angry at her for getting in my face, finding our spot, bringing up shit we've settled. I was pissed you had to see it and would think I had invited that to our spot. I shouldn't have taken you when I was mad, but I need you to believe when I'm inside you, it's only you and me. I will never bring anyone else between us."

In my head, Mads was telling me to listen to what he was saying. To feel his arms around me and take it all in. But I didn't want this, these emotions, this attachment. We agreed from the beginning what we were and what we weren't, but we hadn't agreed on this. And I just couldn't.

I blinked up at him. "This is too much."

"What?" he breathed.

"This, what's happening here. We said sex, friendship, but not this. I'm not your girlfriend."

He studied me with eyes that were duller than they'd ever been. Then he nodded. "You're right. I'm bad at keeping to my own rules."

I removed myself from his arms, grinning as I did, even though I didn't like it.

"Do better, Theodore." I tapped his chest. "You have it easy with me. Lots of sex, no responsibilities except not being an asshole. Don't screw it up."

I shoved every ounce of light I had left into my words to convince us both we weren't more than just sex.

He cocked his head, studying me some more, now from a distance. Then he grinned, and I knew his smiles enough to recognize it was forced.

"I'll work on that." Then he shook his head. "I don't want to screw up a *really* good thing."

"Then don't."

Our gazes locked, and the heaviness in them betrayed the lightness of our words. But neither of us were ready nor willing to take on the weight of what could be, that much was obvious.

Maybe one day, though. For Mads and all she'd lost, all she'd never have, I'd keep my one day open.

Fifteen

THEO

"STILL CAN'T BELIEVE YOU were trying to shut me out."

Helen scratched the back of my neck and leaned into me. "Lock is smarter than you. Obviously I'm going to pair up with the smartest dude in our class. That's just good thinking. You can't blame me for that."

I took her leg and slung it over mine. "I can, and I absolutely will. You need a partner in class, it's me. We'll rub our two dumb brains together and come up with something smart."

She snorted an adorable laugh, but I wasn't about to tell her that. "That's not how it works. And we both know if we were alone, working on this project, we would not be rubbing brains."

Considering we were in the library and my hand was creeping up her inner thigh, she had a point. A terrible fucking point, but still a point.

It'd been a couple weeks since our post-Abby bathroom encounter. Things were smooth. I wouldn't say easy, because Helen wasn't an easy kind of girl. But that was fine. I'd take her difficult any day. And I did. Bent over the side of her bed. In the back of my car. Pinned to her wall. On top of her. Behind her. Every way we could have each other. Except sleeping. The one time I'd wanted to crash at her place, she'd shoved me out the door.

I got it. I'd been tired as hell from fucking the living shit out of her, but I still got it. We functioned within parameters I'd set for us. If Helen was sticking to them, all the better. As long as I got to be inside her, I could deal, because I was well and truly addicted to having her raw and unencumbered. I could deal for now, at least.

That was why, when Professor Davis announced we had to pick a partner for our midterm project, Helen choosing to work with Lock sent me sideways. Luck was on my side, though. We had an uneven number of students in the class, so after some cajoling, Davis allowed me to wedge myself between Lock and Helen.

Her reasoning for the partnership was sound. Lock's brain was in proportion to the rest of him—big, meaty, and able to crush lesser mortals. She was also right that if it had just been Helen and me, we'd spend our work time fucking and flunk the assignment. The difference between us was I didn't care. I should have. My dad would dance on my metaphorical grave if I fucked my academics the way I'd done my athletics. Maybe spending so much time with Helen, I'd found a streak of rebellion deep in me, and I was thinking about leaning into it. Luck found me again that I had a girl who was far wiser than me and took her grades seriously.

She swatted my hand off her when the door pushed open, Lock ducking his head inside. We were in a private study room to work out the breakdown of the project.

"Yo." Lock lumbered into the room, threw his backpack down on the table, and folded himself into a chair. "I have a half hour before I have to head to work."

Helen straightened, crossing her legs and opening her laptop. My dick twitched at her being a serious schoolgirl. Those smooth, muscular, tan legs pressed together. Her straight spine leading to plump little hips and a ridiculous round ass. Long, shiny hair flowing down her back in tumbling waves. Red, red lips pursed in concentration, then moving to shape words as she and Lock bounced ideas back and forth.

"What do you think, Theodore?" Helen slapped my arm. "Do you have any ideas?"

"No. What you guys were saying works for me."

God, I was sick in the head. What the hell was wrong with me? I was sitting there with an erection, no idea what was going on around me, while my girl and Lock were both looking at me like the weak link.

"Are we boring you?" Helen teased.

I cleared my throat. "No, I'm here."

Lock glanced up from his laptop, giving me a long look that said he didn't find any fucking thing about me spacing in the middle of our first group meeting amusing.

"I have twenty minutes now," he said lowly. "Can we get the preliminary planning done?"

"Yeah. I apologize. My weight, from here on out, will be pulled by me." My laptop open, eyes turned away from Helen, I shifted my mind to Shakespeare and the project that was going to take up twenty-five percent of my grade.

Lock cracked his knuckles. "Let's get started."

• • • ● • ● • • ••

AFTER THE STUDY SESSION, I trapped Helen in a quiet stairwell so I could kiss the Shakespeare out of both our brains. She was the one to push me away, but she did it laughing.

"What was going on with you in there?" she asked.

I raked my hand through the side of my hair. "God, nothing. My mind just wasn't there in the beginning. I'm square now. I know what I need to be doing for the project."

She nibbled my chin. "Good, because Lock will squash you like a bug if you even think about being a deadbeat." Then she bit my chin a little harder. "I need to get my ass in gear. I have homework and I want to take a nap before work."

Pulling her closer, I took two handfuls of her ass. "This isn't an invitation, is it?"

She shook her head. "Nope. I have shit to do, Theodore, and you do too."

I gave her ass a squeeze. "Who knew you'd be the responsible one of us?"

The change in her was swift and complete. Her mouth turned down. The light in her deep brown eyes fluttered out. Her expression shuttered. The muscles in her body tensed, bracing to fight or run. "Just because I'm poor doesn't mean I'm not responsible. I haven't had anything handed to me. I work for everything I have, including being here at this university. So yeah, I'm forsaking a couple orgasms for good grades so I can stay here."

My hands flexed. I could have said a lot. A whole lot. But I chose to say one thing. "I haven't had anything handed to me."

That was most of the truth. As much as I was willing to get into.

Her eyes rolled, sensing the bullshit in my statement. It wasn't what she thought, but I *was* full of shit. I may have grown up rough, but I'd lived on easy street for years now. Still, my memory of the hunger might have dulled, but I hadn't forgotten it.

"Okay." She pushed off me, and I let her go. "Text me if you're going to pick me up tonight. It's cool if you're not. I'll take the bus."

She trotted down the steps like I wasn't going to follow her. It was crazy how we could go from making out to being miles and miles apart. But that was my decision. I could give Helen my history so she'd understand me, but she'd already taken the majority of my headspace. I couldn't give up anything else to her and walk away whole.

We were outside when I was through chasing her. Taking her shoulder in hand, I spun her around to face me. "I pick you up every night."

"I don't take anything for granted." She reached up to cup my face. "I like you, I'm not going to take advantage of you, and I don't want to fight. We're really different people and we think differently."

"We're not that different."

"We are, and that's cool. I still like you. But a lot of the time, I'm in survival mode. I get that it's hard for you to understand, but I need you to try. Because I really would like you to be someone I can just be chill with, you know? I don't want to feel like I'm fighting when I'm with you."

"I can do that for you, Tiger." Dipping down, I touched my mouth to hers. "I actually have to go see my father anyway. I think I was hoping you'd offer me an out. But you're right, your grades are important, and I'm not going to mess with that for you."

She poked at my chest. "Your grades are important too."

I waggled a brow. "Sure they are. Now, leave before I forget everything I just said and drag you back to the stairwell."

Helen pulled away easily, tossed her board on the sidewalk, and skated off. I stood there, hands on my head, reeling. The messy, crazy, wild, reckless girl I'd caught smashing my car had herself more together than I did. I didn't quite know how to wrap my head around that, so I didn't. Turning in the opposite direction, I dragged myself to President Whitlock's office.

My father had lost his mind. He was absolutely bananas. Needed to be committed. The cuckoo's nest had been flown over.

"I'm not an escort service." My fingertips dug into my knees. "This isn't happening. You can't pimp me out."

He exhaled heavily through his flared nostrils. "This isn't a discussion."

I'd been summoned to President Whitlock's office. It was never a good sign when my dad wanted to see me, but I knew I was in for pure delight when he requested my presence in his office.

Today was no different. My father, the exalted president of Savage University, was now my pimp. That he was trying to force me on my ex-girlfriend made no difference. He wanted Abby's father to make a donation to the university's art program, so the Fitzgerald family had been invited to the art and design school's annual fundraiser banquet. Daddy Fitzgerald accepted, the caveat being me acting as Abby's date.

"Abby and I aren't together anymore."

I'd successfully avoided seeing her face since the library. What she didn't seem to understand was that she may have been the one to end us, but I wanted nothing to do with her. I'd *loved* her. Two years, I'd been fully committed, and she'd ended it like what I had to give wasn't enough. I was done with her. There was no going back for me, and whatever she wanted to say now was months too late. Rehashing something that was in the past held no interest for me.

My father clasped his hands on his desk, his fingers turning white from pressure. "Be that as it may, Abby wants you to be there with her, and since I'm unaware of any valid reason that can't happen, it will."

"And if I say no?"

He leaned forward, leveling me with a gaze that brooked no argument. "I played golf with Dr. Marino over the weekend. Imagine my utter shame when he mentioned my son got a D on a paper worth ten percent of his grade."

My muscles locked as my brain rattled around in my head. "That doesn't sound ethical. I'm an adult. Can professors legally divulge grades to parents?"

He slammed his hand down on his desk, then immediately smoothed out the scattered papers. "Toe the line, Theo! I take care of your tuition. Every one of your teachers is aware of who your father is. If Marino gave you a D, then know this, you earned an F. He was being generous with that D because of who you are. I don't even want to think of what kind of drivel you must have turned in to get a goddamn D, but it's unacceptable."

Squeezing my eyes shut, I knocked my fist against my forehead. I'd fucked up on that paper, completely forgotten it was due until the night before. Then I'd scrambled to write it, pick Helen up, fuck Helen, then go back home to finish it and catch a couple hours of sleep. I'd known it was drivel when I handed it in, but there was nothing I could do at that point.

"Okay. I screwed up. I have time to turn that grade around, and I will."

His brows raised expectantly. "And your other courses?"

"You don't know?" I countered.

"Answer me."

"They're fine." As fine as they could be when I couldn't get it up to care. The only one I was pulling an A in was my Shakespeare class, and that was all down to Helen.

His eyes narrowed to slits, and something that felt like disgust poured out of him. Andrew Whitlock was an academic, through and through. He'd moved up into administration over time, but he'd always be an educator and an intellect. His one indulgence while earning his PhD had been a weekend away to Vegas for a friend's bachelor party. That weekend resulted in my existence, which to him, was his ultimate screwup—one he expected me to right by being his well-heeled son and representing him the only way a Whitlock should: being talented, and if not talented, then hardworking and intelligent. Always, *always* exceptional.

I'd been born an athlete, not a natural academic. Since I'd been exceptional at what I did, my father had accepted that as my path. When I dropped wrestling, he'd expected me to shift my focus to my education and excel there. So far, being only slightly above average—when I worked my ass off—made me a severe disappointment.

"You asked a question a minute ago." My father's jaw ticced while he steadied himself. "If you decline to escort Abby to the banquet, I won't waste my resources in keeping you here."

Fear licked at my gut, but I pushed it down. I was used to Andrew Whitlock's rants, but this was a new direction. "What exactly do you mean?"

"I mean exactly that. I'm asking you for a favor, one that's not difficult, which will likely result in a boon to the university. If that doesn't mean enough to you to give me one evening of your time, that will tell me this university doesn't mean anything to you. If that's the case, then I can't see why you'd continue to attend."

That rocked me back in my chair. "You'd kick me out of school? Can you even do that?"

He opened his hands. "I can do whatever I like. Your tuition is free so long as I'm president. If I don't think this school is a good fit, then I will rescind your enrollment. It's pretty simple."

"And you'd do that?" I had a hard time believing what I was hearing. My dad was a hard-ass, but this was beyond the pale, even for him. He knew I didn't have anywhere to go if he took this away. I *needed* my degree.

He looked me square in the eye. "I'd do that without hesitation."

"Because I won't date the girl who dumped me months ago?"

My father wasn't a man who rolled his eyes, but if he was, he would have then. Looking at him, I knew I was fucked before he even started speaking.

"This is the culmination of months of screwups. I've been watching you throw your future down the drain, bit by bit. First Abby, then wrestling, and now your grades. Your attitude has been flagrantly disrespectful, you've ignored Miranda for weeks, and god only knows what you got up to over the summer since you disappeared on us. I'm done, Theo. I brought you to California with the expectation you'd apply yourself. Otherwise, I could have left you rotting in the projects in Las Vegas. I need to see you're here to excel, not waste the resources another student would kill to have access to."

"And me taking Abby would prove that to you?"

He sighed, leaning back in his throne-like chair. "I'm looking for a sign of life from you, Theo. Show me you care about this institution. Give a damn what I think. Taking Abby would be a good start. Getting your grades up is imperative."

The knowledge that I wasn't getting out of this settled over me like a blanket woven with thorns. If he took away school, I had nothing. As much as I would have liked to shoot up my middle finger and stalk out of here, I couldn't. I'd played my entire hand when I quit wrestling without warning or explanation. Now, my dad was playing his.

"All right." It was a sharp kick to the gut to acquiesce, but in that moment, I saw no way out. "I'll take her to the banquet and my grades will be a priority."

He nodded. "That's right. And you'll stop ignoring your stepmom. I want you at the house once a week, minimum."

"Okay." My gut was on fire, urging me to rage against his unbearably heavy hand. I reminded myself this was temporary. One night with Abby in a public space wouldn't kill me. Putting in the much-needed work in my classes was necessary anyway. And I liked Miranda, so that wasn't even a chore. I just really didn't fucking enjoy being threatened by my own father to bow to his demands.

"Okay." He flicked his hand toward the door. "You can go now. I'm certain you have studying you should be doing instead of wasting my time."

My father didn't expect formalities when it was just the two of us, so that was my cue to exit. I grabbed my backpack and walked out, feeling yoked with my hands tied behind my back.

He owned me for the next three years. It wasn't forever, but Jesus, it felt like it.

· · · ● · ● · · ·

DEACON FLICKED THE BACK of my head as he walked by me. "Is that Theo Whitlock reading a book? In this house?" He swung himself over the back of the couch to plop down a cushion over from me.

"I was."

"On a Friday night? It's like I don't even know you anymore."

I closed my sociology book and dropped my head back on the cushion. "It's not even midterm and my sociology grade is almost toast."

Exaggeration, but I needed to dig into the material in a big way to fix what I'd fucked up. Coasting wasn't an option at this point. I'd been taking more time to read and study since my visit to my father's office earlier in the week. Helen had been all for it since my little schoolgirl was serious as hell about her grades, and my constant presence all up in her business—her words, obviously—was distracting.

He groaned. "You have Marino?"

"Yep." I scrubbed my face with both hands. "He's golf buddies with good ol' Andrew."

He groaned even louder. "Shit. Let me guess, Marino narc'd."

"Mmhmm. I got my ass handed to me. A whole shape-up-or-ship-out speech."

He kicked my backpack on the floor. "So, this is you shaping up? Studying when you should be getting ready to go out?"

"Not in the mood to go out."

I'd never had a thing for sitting at parties with a bunch of bros trying to pull the first semi-hot, semi-willing chick. Abby had always dragged me out when I wasn't away wrestling, and I'd gone because I wanted to be with her, but those days were over. Now, I was sitting in the study den—the small room reserved for homework and, as the name implied, studying—

waiting for Helen to get off work at a job I hated her doing. I hated it mostly because it was at a strip club, but also because it took her from me and cut into the time I had to be inside her, and with her, and looking at her beautiful fucking face.

"You know, I thought when you quit wrestling, you'd be more fun. This was supposed to be our year. No girl. No responsibilities. Just pure, unadulterated bacchanalia. Instead, you're Mr. Schoolwork all of a sudden. And you disappear every fucking night. I'm beginning to think you're keeping secrets, Theo."

I felt his stare, but I kept my eyes on the ceiling. I didn't have answers for the fantasies he'd come up with on his own. He assumed a lot because he'd been the one with me at the ER and then had let me stay at his family's unused beach house for most of the summer to get my head on straight. While I was grateful for both, I didn't feel suddenly close to him, nor beholden to hold his dick every Saturday night. Neither was ever going to happen.

"I'm Mr. Schoolwork because Andrew threatened to pull my enrollment if I didn't *apply* myself."

"I notice you didn't answer where you're disappearing to."

"Nope." I sucked in a breath, ready for this interaction to be done.

"Fine. Be a little bitch." He slapped my arm. "Hey, do you have that dealer's number? The one you bought from last year?"

My head jerked up in a rush. "No."

"No? You're telling me you lost his number?"

"No, I'm telling you I'm not giving you his number."

Deacon pressed his palms together in prayer. "Come on, Theo. My regular dealer won't talk to me since I kinda screwed her over. I need your guy."

Deacon only knew Amir existed because I'd been far too honest at the ER and he'd overheard it all. He hadn't mentioned it until now, but clearly, he'd socked away the info for a rainy day.

"He's not my guy, and I'm not giving you his number. He'd wind up slitting your throat. I've got too much going on to live with that guilt for the rest of my life."

Deacon grinned and waggled his eyebrows. "Sweet that you care, man. Give me the number."

"No. Full stop. Never happening." I grabbed my shit, heading for the exit. Deacon bit at my heels.

"That's shit, man. I'd do anything for you."

I kept walking toward the stairs. "You don't need to do anything for me. I'm square. I promise you, it's a favor I don't give you his number."

From my left, Deacon grumbled, "It's just weed."

"I don't care if you smoke out of your ass. What I don't want is you being anywhere near that guy. If you knew better, you wouldn't want it either." I stopped at the base of the stairs and twisted my head to look over my shoulder. "Have fun tonight. And remember, 'no' is a full sentence."

I took the steps two at a time, Deacon mumbling, "Fuck off" behind me. When I got to my room, I shut myself in, locking it down tight, then I took out my phone.

Me: *Are you at work, baby?*

Helen: *Yeah. I'm doing my makeup, then I'm out on the floor.*

Me: *Send me a picture.*

Helen: *No please?*

Me: *Please, Tiger. I just had to lock myself in my room to get away from Deacon. I need to see your face.*

Within a minute, a picture came through. Taken from a high angle, I saw red lips, stunning face, tits pushed up high, smooth belly, legs crossed, and spiked platform heels. Helen's waitressing uniform was uncalled-for sexy, and it made me irrationally angry. Or maybe it *was* rational not to want to share my girl's body with every perv who wandered into her job.

Me: *You're so beautiful.*

Helen: *And you hate it?*

Me: *Hate what you're wearing at work, but I'm not saying anything because I get why you do.*

Helen: *You don't have to say anything for me to hear it, even in your texts. I'm glad you get it. That makes me like you.*

Me: *You like me anyway.*

Helen: *You have your moments, Theodore. What are you doing?*

Me: *I was trying to cram sociology into my unwilling head. Now I'm waiting for you to get off work so I can cram my cock in your pretty pussy.*

Helen: *Bahahahahahaha...dude. You just screwed up my mascara, I laughed so hard. Please never cram your cock anywhere near me.*

Laughing, I fell back on the bed. This girl got to me. She knew how to flip the switch and turn my mood around. That worked in the other direction too, but tonight, she was using her powers for good instead of evil.

Me: *Cram is bad?*

Helen: *Absolutely. Thrust, drive, grind, slide, all good words. Cram = no.*

Me: *Then what if I say I can't wait to put your pretty, soaking pussy on my dick tonight? Does that work for you?*

Helen: *Yeah, that works for me. I can't wait for that too. But I need you to do me a favor, Theodore.*

Me: *Tell me.*

Helen: *If you want this pussy, I need you to study hard. So hard, it hurts. Fill that big brain with facts, then you can fill my pussy with cum. Stuff it, baby. And while I'm riding you, you can whisper dirty, sociology words in my ear...*

Me: *Ethnomethodology.*

Helen: *Oh yeah, keep going, I'm going to be ready for you.*

Me: *Groupthink.*

Helen: *My favorite kind of think. So kinky. More, Theodore!*

Me: *Matrilocality.*

Helen: *Yes!*

Me: *Neocolonialism.*

Helen: *I'm close...omg...*

Me: *Patrilocality.*

Helen: *Yes, give it to me.*

Me: *Conflict theory.*

Helen: *Oooh, yeah, you filthy, dirty man.*

Me: *How does everything you do make me hard? Care to explain it?*

Helen: *I'm sure there's some sociological term for it. I hate to end our study/sexting session, but I need to get out on the floor before my boss's head explodes. See you later. xoxo*

Me: *I'll be there, baby. xxx.*

Tossing my phone aside, I picked up my textbook, grinning to myself as I read through the passages that had been putting me to sleep earlier. I'd never look at sociology the same. And if I got to fuck Helen every time I studied, I was going to ace this class.

My levity slowly crashed as the hours ticked by, waiting for Helen. The thorny blanket of reality that Andrew Whitlock had created for me once again settled over me. This was only the beginning. I wouldn't have a choice the next time he made demands of me. Not until I was out of school.

I had to grab hold of what I had for as long as I could. Because when Dear Father decided to pull the rug out from under me again, I'd have no option but to let go.

Sixteen

Helen

LUCIANA BARRELED DOWN THE cracked path toward me. Her smile, bright, optimistic, and brave, contrasted so starkly with her surroundings, the sight of her drove a knife through my gut. We were on borrowed time. This place would dim her light every day she spent here. I'd do everything I could for her to keep it. Everything.

She hit me hard, knocking me back a step. Theo caught me and steadied us both.

"Watch it, wild woman. You're like a little cannonball." I stroked her waves and bent over her to inhale everything Luciana.

She let go of me to jump up and down. "I can't believe I get to spend the night in your dorm. Every single one of my friends is jealous." She smiled at Theo. "Do you think the boys will think I'm a college girl? Like a freshman, of course."

He winced, the same way I did on the inside. "Nope. You look your age, little hell-raiser, and that's a good thing. If an eighteen-year-old guy tries to hit on you, run for the hills." He rubbed his chin. "Actually, *any* guy tries to hit on you, even if he's twelve like you, book it."

She rolled her eyes. "Terrible advice, Theo."

I slipped my arm around his waist. "I don't know, I think he's right. When you're about twenty, like me, then you can consider having a boyfriend."

Luc's eyes bounced from my face to where I was holding on to Theo, then to his arm around my shoulders. I realized then this was the first time we'd been tactile with each other in front of her, and she'd noticed.

"So, are you guys boyfriend and girlfriend?" Her finger waggled back and forth between us.

I pushed away from Theo. "Oh god, no, gross."

He held his hands up. "Yeah, she's not into me. She says I'm far too handsome for her."

Luc's hands went to her hips. "I don't think that's a valid reason not to date someone. You shouldn't judge a book by its cover, Hells."

I hugged her again, then kept my arm around her to steer her toward Theo's car. "I know, babe. You're right."

Theo cuffed under her chin, which was cute. From Luc's wrinkled nose, she probably thought it was better reserved for a younger kid.

"Helen and I are just friends. Neither of us are into having a boyfriend or girlfriend right now. Friends are good, though, right?"

He opened the car door for her. She stopped right before she slid in, holding on to the side. "But if either of you started to be into having a girlfriend or boyfriend, you'd choose each other, right?"

Theo froze. I was behind him, so I couldn't see his face, but I did see the tension hit his spine and squeeze his muscles taut. Yeah, that was awkward.

"Why don't you hop in the car, kid?" Theo gave her a gentle shove. "I'm starving. If I don't find some pizza to demolish, I'm going to eat your face off."

Luciana accepted his dodge of her question easily, because she was Luciana. I told myself I hadn't been waiting for his answer with even more interest than my little sister.

I wasn't a robot. Theo and I had been doing this friends with benefits thing for well over a month. And when we weren't fighting, it worked. God, did it work. But as hard as I raged against it, I had to admit I had feelings. Soft ones. Sweet ones. Heart-swelling ones.

I did not know what to do with feelings like that. I'd never had them before or wanted *more* with a guy.

Did I even want more? Theo gave me a lot. To be honest, I couldn't picture what *more* would even look like since he was generous with me in every way.

Even as I thought that, I knew it wasn't true. Theo gave a lot, but he didn't give himself. I'd slipped out details, important details, like my plans for Luc and me, my dad, things about my mom and my past, and Theo had been such a keen listener, it wasn't until later that I'd realize he hadn't reciprocated. That wasn't to say I'd been fully open, but Theo hadn't even cracked a sliver.

I guess that was answer enough. There were limits here, I had mine, and Theo had his. So, I'd tuck away my little tender feelings because there was no way I'd be getting my heart broken by a richie rich. Never gonna happen, no matter how twinkly his eyes were.

Theo reached across the console and squeezed my knee before backing out of his spot and heading toward the pizza shop. Yeah, we worked. My lips were sealed. My heart was behind a padlocked door.

• • • ● • ● • • ·

BETWEEN LUC, ZADIE, THEO, and me, we nearly demolished two pizzas. We FaceTimed with Gabe and Pen and watched *Parasite* with them. Elena stopped by, sneered at Gabe and waved at Pen, stole a piece of pizza, then left like she'd never been there.

Luc was passed out in my bed and had been for an hour or so. Zadie left soon after to crash in her room. Elena was still blissfully absent. Theo and I were slumped low on the couch, our legs woven and feet resting on the coffee table. It was late, well past midnight. He should have gone home, but we were cozy, and I wasn't quite ready to go to sleep yet.

The movie *Gladiator* was playing on the TV, the volume barely a whisper. Other than that, the lights were off, so all we had was the glow to push back the dark.

"I like this movie," I mumbled.

"It's sad."

"Yeah. When I was a kid, we had a cat named Maximus. My mom named it after Russell Crowe's character. He was really cute—the cat, I mean. Russell Crowe isn't really my type."

Theo snorted a laugh and picked up my hand from where it'd been resting on his thigh to toy with my fingers. He ran his thumb back and forth along the tips, sending goose bumps blooming on my arms.

"Your mom has a way with names," he said.

I snatched my hand away, but he took it right back, trapping it between both of his.

"Are you making fun of my name?"

He shook his head. "I used to think it didn't fit you, but it does. *A face that launched a thousand ships.* That's you."

He meant to be sweet, but I cringed at his Helen of Troy reference. "That's the Helen my mom named me for, but not because she thought or hoped I'd be some great beauty." He brought my hand to his mouth, brushing his lips back and forth. "When I was old enough to sort of understand, she told me Helen of Troy was a ruiner of men. She said some people saw her as a victim, but she was really a seductress. Her beauty and wiles had set off a full-blown war. My mom wanted a daughter who'd be like that, to have men so worshipful of her, they would destroy the world to right the wrongs done to her."

"Shit," he breathed.

"It was a lot for a kid to hear and take in, and she kept telling me that as I got older. *'Make them love you, Helen, and they'll do anything you want them to.'* I don't want to launch a thousand ships. I don't want to cause a war, and I sure as shit don't want a man fighting *for* me or *over* me."

"You had me until the last part. If you ever decide to give yourself to a man, he'd better be willing to fight for you and over you. Only way he'd be worthy of having you as his woman."

I huffed. "Okay, whatever. I won't hold my breath."

He rubbed his mouth back and forth on my hand, then he brought it to his forehead. His silence told me he was thinking. His sigh said it was about something heavy.

"I speak from experience, Helen. I didn't fight for Abby. That's how I knew it was really over. Two years together, she dumps me, and I let it lie. I didn't have the urge to chase her down and fight. I knew, and I accepted it."

Since he was being open and I was curious, I asked. "Why'd she break up with you?"

He lifted a shoulder. "She said it was wrestling. It took too much of me from her, and that was true. The training was grueling. But she knew that's who I was. She signed up for it, and she liked being the girlfriend of a champion. So, I don't know. It might've been that the *more* she was looking for wasn't my time, but me. I wasn't giving her all of me."

"Why not?" I tried not to move, so I didn't draw his attention and end his sharing.

He sighed, and it was so heavy, it weighed down the air in the room.

"I know you think I was born into this life, but I wasn't. I grew up in government housing where you *did not* go out at night unless you were wearing gang colors and prepared to defend yourself. I lived there with my pops until Andrew Whitlock swooped in and brought me here so he could trot me around like a prized pony."

"Theo...what?" This was...not expected. At all. That was how closed off he was. He'd given me no inkling he hadn't grown up here, living with his esteemed dad, in a big house, with no worries or cares except making weight for wrestling.

He turned his head, the light from the TV making his eyes practically glow. "It doesn't matter. I grew up rough, and I had no choice but to be hard. I had to fight to survive that world, and when I got pulled into this one, the fight didn't end, it just got better dressed, you know?"

I nodded. I knew that intimately. Being in a rich, fancy, private institution didn't keep out the ugly. The ugly just wore designer clothes and could shoot you down with a flick of their powerful connections instead of a Glock.

"I know," I whispered.

He moved his foot over mine, rubbing it rhythmically. "Abby fit my new life—pretty, popular, rich, Andrew Whitlock approved—and I did love her. But I didn't fight for her because I was never going to give her all of me. I don't even know if I know how, but if I ever figured it out, it never would have been with her." His foot scooped mine up, pulling it toward him so my leg draped over his. "You should have a man who'll burn down the world and rebuild it for you, Helen. Nothing less for you. *Nothing.*"

My heart twitched painfully in its binds. I heard the implications behind his words. He wouldn't be that man. He wouldn't burn down the world for me. Not now. Not ever. He thought I should walk away because I deserved more than he would ever give. I heard all that, took it in, and hated it. I hated it, not because I believed I deserved it, but because Theo did, and he knew he wasn't going to be that for me.

"You should have a woman who'll make it easy for you to light the match, Theodore." I took my feet back and tucked them to my side, ending our physical connection.

Theo rounded on me, and in the dim light, his glare was slightly menacing. Not that I was afraid of him. I wasn't. Except I didn't know what that glare meant.

A second later, I did. Theo shifted his body, and then mine, so I was flat on my back and he lay half on me, half on the cushions. His head was on my chest, arm firmly wrapped around my middle. I was trapped beneath his weight, but it was the most dangerous type of trap, the kind that felt so good, I didn't even attempt to escape.

"Don't pull away from me the second I get real with you," he groused.

"Maybe I don't want to get real." But even as I said it, I stroked his hair, feeling myself sinking into this very real moment.

"Yeah, you do. But you're like me. Hard because you had to be. I'm telling you right now, you don't have to be hard with me. When you give me soft Helen, I feel like I've uncovered a treasure. I want to huddle around it like Gollum."

"My precious," I murmured, fighting a grin.

"Mmhmm." He lifted his head to peer at me. "This thing between you and me didn't go where I thought it would."

"Where'd you think it would go? Did you think we'd be having Bible study?"

His mouth curled at the corners. "Oh, I had no doubt we'd be fucking a lot. I think I thought it'd burn hot and fast and we'd be done with each other."

"And now?"

"Now, I'm spilling my secrets and inner thoughts after having a pizza and movie night with your little sister and roommate."

I scratched at his scalp, allowing myself a smug grin. "And snuggling."

"Yeah." He cocked his head, leaning into my palm. "What's up with that? Helen Ortega snuggles?"

I yanked his head down, and he fitted it under my chin, resting his cheek on my breast. I knew better than to bask in this, but I did. People didn't hug girls like me. They sure as hell didn't lie with me, fully clothed, and wrap themselves around me. So, I closed my eyes, took in Theo's heat, his scent, the feel of him, and committed it to memory for when he went away—which he'd just finished telling me he would. It would have been easier to let him walk if I hadn't known what this felt like, but that ship had sailed. This was all I had.

"I didn't. You've ruined me."

His hand came up to cup my cheek. "I really fucking hope not. I like you exactly like this."

I stiffened all over. "Don't say things like that to me."

He raised his head again, glowing eyes darting back and forth between mine in the dark. "Do you have any idea how stunningly beautiful you are? I find it hard to believe no one has gotten past your spikes to give you what you deserve."

My nose tingled, and something deep inside me twisted in knots. "The only men who've gotten past did it by force."

"Tiger," he breathed. "Fuck."

I found myself stroking his tight jaw, comforting him from the ugliness of my admission. I hadn't really meant to say it, but there was something about being in the dark with Theo that had let it slip past my lips far too easily.

"You knew." My fingers trailed down his throat. "If you grew up the way I did, you can't be surprised."

"I had an idea. An idea and the truth are two separate things." He stilled, looking down at me. "Give me names."

"No." I would have never sent him to fight my battles, but why did it feel so good that he might've wanted to? "It's over and done with. The last guy who touched me wrong got the shit beat out of him by my boys and then he died in a car accident last fall. But if you're wondering why I am the way I am, why I have a bat next to my bed and chase boys out of my shop when they corner me, now you know. No one's getting past my spikes unless I invite them. Not ever again."

He stayed like that, watching me, jaw tight, shoulders bunched, for several long moments. I didn't know what he'd say, or how he'd react, but when he exhaled a ragged breath and lay back down on me, pulling me tight into his body, I was taken by surprise. I guess I half expected him to brush me off and tell me I was too much for a casual fuck buddy.

"I know you can fight your own battles, Tiger. I've seen you in all your warrior glory, taking vengeance on my car. What I hope for you, is when you let someone past those spikes, they're the kind of man who'll be shoulder to shoulder with you in battle, and when push comes to shove, they'll step in front of you and take the brunt of it." I started to protest, but he covered my mouth with his fingertips. "Don't argue with me, baby. That's what I want for you. You don't need to say anything back."

We quieted then, turning on another movie to fill the dead air. Theo fell asleep like that, and I was close to following when a sudden thought jerked me away from unconsciousness.

I'd spilled my guts yet again, while Theo had only given the smallest piece of himself. Pretty soon, he'd own all of me, and I'd still be right here, empty-handed.

My thoughts were still coalescing when the door swung open and Elena stumbled into the room, followed by a tall, lanky guy draped all over her. She flicked the light on, momentarily blinding me. Theo didn't even stir.

"Oh no, my roommate is here with her little bubble-butt boyfriend," Elena slurred, knocking her head back on her man's chest. My horrified gaze jerked to his face, and when I recognized him, my stomach churned.

"Theo?" Daniel hissed. "He's with *her*?"

"Mmhmm," Elena confirmed. "Those two have been boning like bunnies for weeks. It's so disgusting."

"Turn off the light," I barked.

"Get a room, bitch," Elena responded. "And stop faking it so loud. Some of us don't want to hear your fake 'I'm coming' cry." Then she flipped off the light and dragged dirty Daniel to her room, shutting the door tight behind them.

That didn't stop me from hearing *her* fake moans a few minutes later. Fortunately, after years of living in a tiny space with paper-thin walls with a mother who went looking for love in all the wrong places, I'd become adept at tuning out sounds I really didn't want to hear.

I should have woken Theo up and sent him home, especially with Luc sleeping in my bed. But I really didn't want to. Not with how good it felt to be held by him and how sweet the rise and fall of his chest was against mine. So, I let him stay, and I did what I'd been doing with him all along:

I fell.

Seventeen

THEO

MY EYES WERE CLOSED. The words were blurring. I jerked myself awake and tried to focus on the page, but it was no use. I was tired from Helen kicking me out of her dorm before the sun rose so Luc wouldn't know I had slept over, and my sociology textbook wasn't even close to interesting enough to keep me awake.

Daniel strolled into the study room just as I was contemplating whether I had enough time to take a nap before I picked Helen up from work.

"Hey," I greeted.

He took a seat on the couch opposite mine, something brewing behind his sharp features. "What's up, man? Have a good night last night?"

My head cocked. "Yeah. You?"

"Oh yeah. Spent some quality time with my girl. I told you about her. Elena..."

I rubbed my forehead, trying to jog that memory back around. "Oh, yeah. I think I remember."

He leveled me with a serious stare that made me uneasy. "I saw you last night."

"I don't think so. I wasn't out."

"I know." He chuckled. "I saw you when I went back to Elena's suite."

I pounded my forehead with the side of my fist. That was it. Elena was Helen's roommate—the one who had called me Abby's boyfriend. Jesus, I had completely forgotten, and I definitely hadn't connected her to Daniel.

"I didn't see you."

"That's because you were passed out. You had to be so wasted." He raised his eyebrows, like he was waiting for a good story.

I shook my head. "No. Just tired." I closed up my textbook and started gathering my stuff. "Speaking of, I'm still tired as hell. I'm going up to my room."

"Wait, wait, wait. Are you actually with that girl?"

I shot him a glare. "What's with the tone?"

He lifted his hands, palms up, like he was the picture of innocence. "I mean, if you're with her, cool. She's pretty. It's just...I know how your dad is. I didn't think he'd like you dating a stripper. Obviously, you know him better than—"

"Helen isn't a stripper."

Daniel chuckled again, this time giving me a look that was something akin to pity. "Hate to be the one to break it to you, but she is. She works at Savage Beauties."

My eyes sharpened. "I know where she works. She serves drinks, not her tits."

"Maybe some nights, that's true. But I saw those pretty tits and that very fine ass with my own eyes, man. A bunch of the guys from the house were with me and can vouch if you ask. I get why you're into her. She's fine as hell. Very fine. That little heart-shaped birthmark on her right butt cheek is all kinds of sexy—"

My ears were ringing. I hadn't wanted to believe him, then he mentioned Helen's birthmark, and I didn't hear another word that came from his mouth.

My girl had lied to me. She'd explicitly said she didn't strip. I remembered being relieved I wouldn't have to walk since that would have been a deal breaker. I'd wanted to believe her because I'd been so hard up for her. I'd *liked* her so much, I hadn't wanted to be disappointed in her. But this...I was in too deep to call this disappointment. Finding out Helen had betrayed my trust, had been betraying my trust all this time...this was gutting.

Fuck.

The assholes I lived with all knew what Helen looked like naked. They'd probably jerked it to the thought of her. Hell, I would have if I'd been there with them. All that hair, those red lips, perfect face, immaculate tits, tear-worthy ass. Helen was a walking wet dream. No doubt she made a pretty penny taking her clothes off on stage.

God, had they touched her? Had she taken money from the guys I lived with and let them put their hands all over her? My stomach roiled violently, sickness swelling in my throat.

Every single night, I picked her up from that place. Had she spent hours teasing other men and grinding on their hard dicks? Most of those nights, I let her grind on *my* dick. No, I more than let her, I put her there because I'd been so desperate to have her.

Before I lost my shit, I strode from the room with a calmness I in no way felt, telling Daniel I needed to take a nap. He was still talking, but I was already gone. The last thing I'd ever give Daniel was a peek at the riot raging within me. He already knew more than enough.

Somewhere in my chaotic thoughts, I latched on to something I'd pushed aside because it had been easier that way. Deacon's door was open, so I went in without knocking. He was on his bed, laptop in his lap. He looked up, a smile beginning to form, failing halfway there when he got a look at me.

"What's up?" he asked warily.

"How do you know Helen?"

"Who?" That ass was such a liar.

"Helen? The girl I had to haul out of your room so she didn't beat your ass."

"Ahhh." He nodded as if it was just coming to him. "Helen, the little firecracker townie. She was my weed hookup for a while."

That jolted me. I hadn't known what to expect, but it wasn't that. "What do you mean?"

"I mean what you think. She sold me weed."

I had to tuck my hand in my pockets so Deacon didn't see how tight I'd balled them into fists. "She told you no. I was there when you went into Savage Wheelz. She chased you out with a bat."

He chuckled. "Yeah, bitch is wild. I approached her all wrong that day. I ran into her at a party last fall. We talked and made a deal. She gave me weed, I sold it to dudes in the house, we split the profit. It went swimmingly until the cops showed up at a kickback right before school started and I had to flush all that beautiful ganja. I didn't have the money for her, of course. That's what you walked in on. The little wildcat was quite pissed at me." His face turned bright red as he laughed at the memory.

I interrupted his laughter with another question about the woman I thought I knew but was clearly a stranger. "Is she still selling you weed?"

He rubbed his mouth. "Are you kidding? If I see her on campus, I walk the other way. Bitch is crazy. She'd probably brain me with her skateboard. No fucking way she'd hook me up again. That's why I need your dealer's number."

Amir, the dealer Helen happened to know. From high school, she'd said. I now saw what a load of bullshit she'd been serving.

"Not happening." I slapped the doorjamb. "Good night."

Deacon called after me, probably with questions, but I was in no mood to answer. Not when I had a thousand questions of my own. No one in this house could put my mind at ease. Nothing could.

• • • ● • ● • • •

BY THE TIME HELEN came jogging out of Savage Beauties, a sweet smile on her painted red lips, my decision was made. It hadn't been hard to come to it. If I had been less of a man, I wouldn't have been here to pick her up. But I wasn't a liar, and I didn't go back on my word. I said I'd be here, so I was.

She slid into the car and leaned over the console. I always kissed her when she got in. That was done. I pulled out of the parking lot without looking at her.

"Okay, what's up?" She turned sideways in her seat, her eyes boring into the side of my head. "I can feel you simmering. Just say it. Tell me now, Theo."

"When we get to the dorm. I'm not talking while I'm driving."

"So, there's something to say? You know you can't dump me when we're not really together, right?"

Stonewall Helen was back, and just in time, reminding me this was who we were. Two strangers who fucked. We weren't the people who fell asleep together on her couch. Not when she had this whole secret life—a life I'd never sign up to be a part of.

"Right."

She rotated to face the window, leaning as far from me as possible. From my periphery, I could see her ready to flee. Hand on the door, body tense, focused on the outside. It was a long drive, the silence between us so thick it was suffocating. When I pulled up in front of her dorm, I idled at the curb instead of parking in a spot like I normally did. This wouldn't take long.

"Say it, Theo." She refused to face me.

"This is done."

"Okay." Just like that, her fingers wrapped around the door handle. "Thanks for the ride."

I could have let her go, but I was too angry to end it that easily. I needed her to understand exactly why I couldn't be with her anymore. And maybe I needed to drill it in my own head, because lurking on the other side of my anger was a world of regret that this had to end.

"You lied to me, Helen."

She looked at me over her shoulder. "Did I? And I suppose instead of just dumping me, which again, is unnecessary since we're not together, you feel it necessary to lay out my shortcomings?" She twisted around to fully face me again. "Have at it. I'm all ears, Theo."

The full force of Helen's stunning face tripped me up. She was seething. Her cheeks were aflame, eyes flared and coal black. That only served to enrage me further. She had no room to be angry.

"I point blank asked you if you strip. You said no. You lied." Her flinch was subtle, but I didn't miss it. I should have stopped there, but that flinch only pissed me off more. "Tonight, I had to hear one of my housemates describe your tits to me. And he's not the only one who's seen you. A lot of them watched you take your clothes off. You really think I want to be with a girl like that? Who *every*-fucking-one of my friends could close their eyes and picture naked?"

A long stretch of silence settled between us. I focused on her black nails picking at her fishnet stocking. She was unraveling them, making a wider hole with each pick.

"Is that it?" I lifted my eyes to her. She barely blinked. "Or is there more?"

"Nothing, Helen? You have nothing to say?"

She rubbed her lips together, and all I wanted to do was reach out and smear that lipstick all over her face with my fingers. I didn't.

"No." She flipped her pretty hair behind her back. "We're done, so no. You don't owe me anything, I don't owe you anything."

"Deacon."

She nodded once. "Yeah. Deacon. Is that all?"

"Hel—"

Reaching behind her, she threw the door open. And then she was gone, racing up the stairs and disappearing inside her dorm before I could get her full name to leave my throat.

I knew I was in the right, but I didn't feel righteous. Not after last night. Not after we'd opened up to each other, fell asleep together, tore apart regretfully at sunrise. I'd been thinking maybe this could be real. Maybe I was ready to start something deeper. If I did with anyone, it would have been her.

A bitter laugh clawed up from my chest when I imagined Andrew finding out my girlfriend was a stripper. He'd have a field day with that, revoke my tuition, disown me. Whitlocks didn't lower themselves that way—barring the time he'd screwed my eighteen-year-old stripper mom in the champagne room without protection. But we didn't talk about the circumstances surrounding my conception because, like I said, Whitlocks didn't *do* that.

Even if I was in a position to tell my dad to fuck off, I wouldn't. Not for Helen. Not when she'd lied, omitted, made a fool out of me. I would never knowingly be with a woman who sold her body to other men. I saw what that did to my mom. I wasn't interested in a replay.

Helen wasn't who I thought she was in the beginning. I figured that was why my chest felt like it was being pounded in one spot with a hammer and chisel—disappointment that the woman I knew didn't really exist.

It couldn't have been anything other than that.

Eighteen

Helen

HE'D STAGGERED ME, BOTH literally and figuratively. The way he'd looked at me. The cold that had rolled off him the second I'd climbed into his passenger seat. He'd never once looked at me that way. Not even when I was beating the shit out of his car.

I had to hold on to the rail in the elevator and then support myself on the wall in order to make it to my suite without collapsing to my knees. They were so weak, they would have shattered if I had.

It was late. So late. I'd wished, I'd hope for, I'd needed the living room to be empty. But like everything in my life, I didn't get what I wanted.

Zadie and Elena both jerked their heads toward the door when I flung myself inside. They were side by side on one couch, a bowl of popcorn between them, something playing on TV. But they were watching me now, eyes wide and attentive.

I touched my chest, which I swore had caved in, but there it was. Solid and whole.

"I can't do this," I rasped. "How do I keep doing this?"

It was a question that couldn't be answered. Besides that, they had no idea what I was talking about.

"Helen, are you okay?" Zadie rose from the couch as I trudged past into my bedroom. "Helen?" She followed me, hovering over me as I collapsed onto my side on my bed and curled into a ball.

A hand on my shoulder, another in my hair. Soft, so soft. I wasn't crying, but the tenderness of those touches sent me as close to tears as I'd been since I lost my Mads.

A weight depressed the bed in front of me. Another behind me. I opened my eyes to find Zadie in front of me, which meant the gentle strokes on my hair were coming from Elena. That alone would have sent me off the deep end if I wasn't already there.

"Honey, what happened? Are you hurt?" Zadie asked in her sweet Zadie voice.

Elena brushed my hair from my face, peering over my shoulder to look at me. "Do I need to call Penelope? Do you need her?"

"I don't know." I scrubbed at my cheeks and forehead, but there was no removing the cloying film of shame that coated me. "I don't know how to keep going when there's so much hurt, you know? I thought...I thought I could have one good thing after so much bad, but not me."

"You can have every good thing, honey," Zadie promised.

Elena rubbed up and down my arm. "Tell me who I have to bitch slap."

"I'm filth." I threw my hands out blindly. "I'm at this beautiful school, in this lovely room, but I'm still filth. I don't know what Mads was thinking sending me here. Sometimes I hate her for doing it."

I hated myself for saying that out loud. How could I hate Madeline when she'd given me the world? But I did. Because she wasn't here and I was. She'd shown me *more*, made me want to strive for it, even though sometimes it was so hard, all I wanted to do was curl into a ball until I faded away.

Elena's hand paused. "Who's Mads? What did she do? Is she your girlfriend? I don't mind cutting a bitch if I need to."

I almost laughed, but I was too far past humor. I was...I was sad. So fucking sad. I had been for a long time. I just never admitted it, not even to myself. I didn't have time to be sad. I had a job, a sister, a loan, gangsters, strip clubs, school, studying, a boy...

"Madeline. I took care of her last year while she was dying." Something ripped inside me. Netting that had been holding back a flood. Tears, two by two, marched down my cheeks like good little soldiers. "She passed away in May. I had ten months with her, and we spent every moment together. She was only thirty years old, but she'd been dying her whole life. And I miss her. I miss her so deeply, I don't like to think about her, because when I do, I sink, and I don't know how to swim back up. But I can't help thinking about her because she gave me everything."

Elena settled behind me, wrapping her arm around my middle. Zadie followed suit, lying in front of me, holding my hands in hers.

"You're not filth, Helen. I live with you, so I should know. You're so kind." Zadie squeezed my hands. "Madeline sounds like she was very important to you."

"She was. She is," I rasped. "Mads left me money to go to school, but I had to come here, to Savage U. I don't fit here. I don't know what she was thinking, I just—"

"You fit." Elena rested her chin on my shoulder. "If any of the bitches here try to tell you otherwise, it's because they're jealous."

I let out something between a sob and a scoff. "No one's jealous. I'm a filthy stripper from a trailer park."

"No." Zadie cupped my cheeks. "You're Helen."

Nodding, I tucked my chin into my chest and let myself feel the stabbing in my gut. It wasn't all Mads. This was for Theo too. He'd seen me as Helen, but now, he saw me as nothing more than a desperate body. And I was that, I couldn't deny it. I hadn't been born with much, except I had this shell that appealed to men, so I used it. I used it and hoped Theo would never find out because I knew a boy like him would never be with a girl like me. Not if he had all the information.

I'd be angry at Theo later. For now, I was staggered. The way he'd looked at me from the shadows of his car...

"What happened tonight?" Elena asked.

Another sobbed ripped through me, so deep and gut wrenching, it nearly rendered me in two. It wasn't for Theo. He hadn't torn me apart. But his blow was the last in a line of vicious pummels that just kept coming. Worse, because when he punched, I hadn't been prepared, so it hurt on a deeper level than all the others.

"Theo. He found out."

Elena pushed herself up behind me and peered down at me. "He found out what? That you stripped?"

I nodded. "He couldn't even look at me."

"Are you telling me you're crying over a boy?" She sounded incredulous, like the very idea was preposterous.

"I'm crying over everything. Not just him." But the tears were already turning to salt on my cheeks.

"Wow, okay." Elena leaned down so her face was inches from mine. "Here's the first rule of bad bitches: we don't cry over unworthy boys. Theo is hot, I'll give you that. But worthy of tears? No, bitch. Not even close."

"He's too good for me," I whispered, the words burning in my throat like acid.

Zadie gasped. "He's not. You're too good for a guy who would leave you in this state."

Elena's clear blue eyes turned to fire. "Are you kidding me? Did you literally just say that?"

"Elena," Zadie admonished. "Be nice to her."

Elena stared down at me, fury pinching her pale brows. "Theo is a pussy-whipped little boy. His ex told me all about him. His dad controls him, and he lets it happen. He seems like a nice guy, but that's only to get what he wants. If you think that kind of dick is better than you, then you're not the girl I thought you were back in high school when you intimidated the hell out of every soft boy you passed in the halls."

"She's sad, El. Let her be sad," Zadie said.

"I'm letting her be sad over her dead friend. I refuse to allow her to cry over Theo fucking Whitlock. He's hot, but he's proven himself unworthy. Helen is a warrior. Theo is bullshit."

They bickered back and forth while I sank into my heartache. I knew it wasn't for Theo. Well, not just for him. These tears belonged to Mads and stress and the cruelty that was life. The fight in me ran deep, but some days, it was too much, even for me.

"Let me be sad tonight. When I wake up, I'll be over him." I swiped at the mostly dried tears on my cheeks. "Just give me tonight."

Elena lay back down behind me and curled around me. It was all kinds of disconcerting, but Penelope had told me more than once there was a different side of her cousin she rarely showed other people. I had a feeling this was the side Pen had been talking about.

"Fine. Tonight is yours to wallow. Even bad bitches deserve to pity themselves for a few hours." Her fingers combed through the back of my hair. "But if I catch you crying over this kid again, I will sneak into your room while you're sleeping and chop off all your pretty hair."

Zadie's hands flew to her mouth. "Elena! You can't say that."

"I can and I did. Helen knows me well enough not to test me." She kept finger-combing my hair even as she threatened to chop it all off. "Do you have any idea how much I could get for pristine hair like this if I sold it?"

"Oh my god," Zadie mumbled.

A bubble of laughter swelled into the aching places in my chest, pushing the hurt aside so it could fall from my lips. I barked a loud laugh, and then smaller ones, until my shoulders were shaking and Zadie let out a tentative giggle.

"You're not selling my hair, Sanderson," I said between laughs.

Elena gave it a light tug. "Try me, Ortega."

Lying there between my two roommates, I still hurt, but I didn't feel like I was seconds from walking into the ocean with stones in my pockets. This sad girl wasn't me. I'd never get over losing Mads, but Theo was a different story. By tomorrow, I'd forget he ever existed.

· · ● ● ● · ● ● · · ·

FORGETTING SOMEONE EXISTED WASN'T as easy as it sounded. Staring at the back of Theo's stupid head for an hour on Monday during class hammered that point home. He was still alive and breathing the same air as me. Whether he deserved that privilege was debatable.

Lock tipped his chin toward me. "Are you okay?"

I jerked from where I'd been hunched over my notebook, digging my pen into the paper. "I'm...fine. But do you think you could walk with me today?"

His nostrils flared as his eyes traveled toward Theo, then back to me. "No problem."

At the end of class, I took my time gathering my things, giving Theo a chance to be long gone by the time I headed for the door. Except, as Lock and I walked down the steps, Theo was talking with Davis, and it was impossible not to overhear what he was saying.

"I'm sorry, Mr. Whitlock. You asked me to put you into that group. Unless you have a valid reason to be removed, you're not moving."

Theo hitched his bag higher on his shoulder. "I work better on my own."

I felt Lock tense beside me, then he cupped my nape, steering me around Theo and Davis toward the door. Their voices followed us.

"Except this is a group project," Davis replied. "Is there something you need to tell me about your chosen group?"

A short pause. My ears perked up, even as Lock steered me away. "No. Nothing to tell you," Theo gritted out.

Lock practically shoved me out the door and down the hall until we were outside. He kept me walking, even though I would have liked to turn around and explain to Theo how little I was going to enjoy working with him too. But I wasn't a little pussy, running to the teacher just because my feelings were hurt.

"Don't let him see it," Lock grumbled.

"I'm not. He's the biggest asshole I've ever met—and that says a lot."

Lock kept hold of me, ensuring I couldn't turn around and let my anger loose, which was a good thing, even though I *really* wanted to rebel against it. He walked me all the way to my dorm, stopped me at the base of the stairs, and gave me a long once-over. His scrutinizing gaze made me squirm, but I stayed still, allowing him to check me out, to see what he needed to see. I didn't know what that was, but after a solid minute, he seemed satisfied.

He nodded once. "You'll be all right."

Then he dropped his hand, swiveled on his heel, and lumbered off in the direction from which we came.

And for some reason, when he said it like that, decisively and like it was fact, I believed him. I *would* be all right.

Lock beat me to our group work session on Friday, which was relieving. He kicked the chair beside him out from under the table, and I took a seat. I'd been dreading this all week. Three classes worth of boring holes in the back of Theo's head had taken a lot out of me.

"I'll handle him," he said.

"Okay."

His head cocked. I met his gaze. He did the same assessing sweep he'd been doing all week, and I stayed still so he could. I was tired, slightly melancholy, but other than that, I was fine, and he must have seen that, since he nodded and let it go without saying a word.

We both set up our computers and the research and work we'd done for our project, and then discussed what we'd completed, all while waiting for Theo to show. He was fifteen minutes late by the time he pushed through the door and tossed his bag on the table. I kept my gaze trained on my computer, but from the corner of my eye, I saw Lock staring him down.

Theo took a seat across from Lock, set up his computer, and pulled out a notebook, all without offering an explanation or apology for his tardiness. When he had it all set up, he released a heavy breath.

"Do you have the historical comparison prepared?" Lock asked.

"Uh..." Theo shifted, "no. I haven't had the chance to get to it."

Lock's head dipped, and his eyes met mine for a fleeting moment. "Okay. Have you started?"

"Not yet," Theo admitted. "My nights have been freed up, though, so I'll have the time this weekend to pound it out."

The truth behind those words made me flinch, even though giving Theo a reaction was the last thing I wanted to do. His absence at the end of my nights had been the worst part of this week. Knowing he'd been waiting for me with a smile and a kiss at the end of my shift had made it so much more bearable. Now that I'd lost that, I wished I'd never had it in the first place.

"What were you doing?" Lock asked without intonation.

"What?" Theo came up short with an answer.

"I'm asking what you were doing instead of working on our group project. If your nights have been free, then you had extra time to do your part. You didn't, so I want to know what you were doing instead." Lock kept his voice level, but there was no missing what he was saying and exactly how he felt about it. I happily stayed silent behind my computer screen, allowing Theo to dig his own grave.

"I'll have it ready the next time we meet." Theo's jaw twitched.

Lock clasped his hands on the table and leaned forward. "We all know you asked Davis to leave this group, which is fair. Helen and I would have done fine without you, since you've barely pulled your weight from the beginning. I let it go then, but I'm less inclined now."

"I said I have it handled," Theo gritted out.

"You didn't answer my question," Lock said lowly.

"I didn't. Because it isn't your business."

He leaned farther across the table, his massive shoulders bunching into boulders. "It is if it affects me. You not doing your part on our *group* project certainly affects me. Helen and I both work full-time hours along with going to school, but we were here today, on time and prepared. As far as I can tell, you're jobless and living off your dad's dime. You don't have wrestling or a girlfriend to use as an excuse for not getting shit done. So, from where I'm sitting, you spent all week holding your dick instead of doing what you were supposed to be doing."

I chanced a glance from my screen to find Theo's glare trained on me, filled with accusation. "Are you fucking him now?"

I didn't know that I would have answered that ludicrous and insulting question, but I never had the chance. Lock slammed his palms on the table with a resounding bang.

"You can leave, Whitlock. You show up to a group session like this again, I'll report you to Davis. And I *will* have valid reasons not to want you in this group." Lock's tone was low and unmistakably serious. He brooked no argument because he was so right. Theo was behaving like a tool, and with all the work Lock and I were putting into this project, he didn't deserve a free ride from us.

Theo took in a long breath, then his gaze skimmed from me to Lock. "I was out of line. I apologize for being late, unprepared, and bringing personal issues into the group. It won't happen again."

Lock stared him down. There was nothing teddy bear about him then. He was unyielding in his demeanor. Quite honestly, if I were on his bad side, I'd be shitting my pants. But Theo managed to hold eye contact until they both nodded, like something was settled.

Lock patted my arm. "Do you want to continue with what you were telling me about the plague and quarantine?"

"Yeah." I slid my eyes to Theo, who was watching me carefully. "I don't know if you remember I researched—"

"I remember," he cut me off, but he did it gently, and I hated it. Especially because he'd accused me of fucking Lock only a couple minutes ago.

"Great. Then I won't have to backtrack for you." There was nothing gentle about the way I addressed him. I'd given him my soft, and he'd trampled all over it. He could take my spikes and fuck himself with them.

We stayed in that room for another hour. The tension had eased minute by minute, but it was still thick by the time we were packing up. My stomach ached from it, and my chest throbbed from the stabbing sensation being in proximity to Theo caused. But it was good. I'd remember this feeling the next time a handsome guy with twinkly eyes tried to get too close. It wouldn't happen again.

The three of us left the library at the same time. I gave Lock a punch on his tree trunk arm. "Have a good weekend, dude."

He tapped my shoulder with his huge fist. "Be good, Hells."

"I always am."

We split off, Lock heading toward the campus maintenance building, me in the direction of my dorm. It took me a second to determine I was not alone.

"Do you and Luc need a ride tomorrow? With your groceries?"

I stopped walking and stared at Theo Whitlock, my mouth hanging open. Because what the fuck?

"You're kidding me."

He crossed his arms over his chest. "No. I'm not."

"You are *kidding me*. There's no way that's a real question."

"I'm completely real."

I shook my head. "What if someone saw me with you, Theo? They might tell your dad you're riding around with a stripper." I spread my arms out at my sides and started to walk backward. "No thank you. If I need a ride, I'll ask one of the many, *many* men I'm currently spreading my legs for, because apparently that's what I'm doing."

"What do you expect from me, Helen? You lied to me. That makes me wonder what else you've been lying about. But Luciana shouldn't be riding her skateboard on the side of the road, loaded down with groceries. I'd like to give you both a ride to keep—"

"Shut up, Theo. I don't want to hear what you'd like. You said enough to me Sunday night. I heard you. You and I never started, but we're *really* through now. That includes my sister. I don't care what you'd like. It doesn't mean anything to me."

His jaw worked, and I wondered how much vitriol he was biting back. "Don't you think you owe me an explanation?"

My stomach was on fire, and his question was kerosene to my flames. I walked up to him, clutching my middle.

"No, I don't. Besides, you never asked for one."

He bowed his head. "I'm asking for one now."

He was too close. Too soft. The fury that had been wrapped around him and pounding into me in his car had melted away. He was almost my Theo, except my Theo wasn't real. He never would have accused me of fucking Lock or told me I wasn't good enough for him. This man in front of me was a stranger, and I'd learned a long time ago to never talk to strangers.

"I've been explaining to you since we met. You took and took my story, my history, my *life*. You know things about me only my closest friends do. I'm sorry I never sat you down and laid out for you that I've stripped four times when I came up short on my mom's loan repayment and it was either do that or hope to god the gangster she owed money to wouldn't *really* burn down our trailer with my sister inside."

His inhale was harsh. "Why didn't you *say* that?"

I lifted a shoulder. "What's the point? You made up your mind about me. I'm not going to beg you to see me as a human when one decision—that I would make again if I had to—turned me into nothing but trash in your eyes."

"You're not trash. I don't think that, and I didn't say it. I was pissed and betrayed—"

"Nope." My arms went tighter around me. "You weren't betrayed. You were embarrassed, and your overinflated male ego took a hit. I didn't betray you, Theo, and I'm not going to let you lay that on me. You can keep saying it for a thousand years, and I will never take it on."

His jaw worked, and again, I wondered what he was biting back. "We're never going to agree on that."

I jutted my chin out. "We don't need to agree. This is over."

He stared at me. A lot of his bitterness had fallen away, leaving behind an expression I didn't know, but recognized all the same: longing.

I felt it. God, did I feel it. I longed for us to go back to the night he'd spent sleeping with his head in my chest, covering me with his body, holding me tight. I also wished we'd never had that night so I didn't know what I'd lost a day later.

"It never started, isn't that right?" He rocked back on his heels, still staring at me the same way.

"That's right. Can't break a thing that never existed."

Now, we were both liars. And in the broad light of day, there was no hiding it. But Theo and I, we'd perfected our facades so well, we could look in each other's eyes and lie without flinching. I was scraped raw on the inside, but I'd never show him that.

"I gotta go." I saluted him and started backing away. "Do your work, Theo. I won't stop Lock from kicking your ass if you don't."

He said something, but I was already gone. I walked faster than I should have, but I couldn't try to play it cool another second longer. Boys didn't hurt me like this. I'd never let them. I'd been stupid to allow Theo inside the cracks losing Mads had left behind.

I'd learned, though, and I'd learned well.

Nineteen

Helen

HAKIM GAVE ME A wave. I nodded as I set down drinks at my table, giving my ass a little sway and dodging grabby hands faux playfully, then made my way across the floor to see what was up with the big man.

"Hey." Hakim was nearly seven feet tall of pure muscle and very little brain. He was also sweet as sugar and took his job as bouncer at Savage Beauties seriously. No one touched his girls without their permission, and when they did, all his sweetness was left at the door. Hakim did not play when it came to his girls.

He jerked his big, bald head to the side. "Group in the Blue Room requested you."

"I'm not stripping tonight."

He glared at me with his deep black eyes, looking offended. "Who do you think I am, baby girl? I know all. I see all. They want you to serve them."

I laid my hand on his sinewy forearm. "Sorry, dude. I'm cranky tonight."

He wrapped an arm around my shoulders. "I got you, boo. The boys in there are throwing green around like candy. Carina's bag is filled. Get in there and take them for all they're worth."

I tossed my hair behind my shoulders and gave Hakim a bright smile. "Okay. I can be perky for cash."

His laughter was a roll of thunder in my ears. "That's my girl."

The Blue Room was for private VIP parties. I'd never worked it as a stripper, but I had served drinks in there before and always came out with twice as much cash as a regular night. As soon as I stepped inside tonight, I wished I hadn't. Seven or eight men were scattered around on chairs and benches, five girls mingling between them. I knew most of these men, if not by name, then by sight, and all of them filled me with dread.

Reno spotted me before I could back out and run for the hills. He beckoned me with a wave of his hand. My footsteps were leaden, and I kept my tray in front of me like a shield. Amir raised a brow at me as I passed him, Carina perched on his lap. He had a handful of her ass in his palm, but he was watching me walk to his brother, paying her no attention.

"Careful," Amir murmured.

I stopped in front of Reno, who was flanked by two guys I knew to be his muscle. Reno had inherited blood money and corrupt power from his uncle, and he'd taken to the gangster life like a fish to water. He was all fine tailoring, sleek lines, diamonds in his ears, manspreading like he owned the world.

"Helen, baby," he cooed.

"Hey. Can I get you something to drink?"

He turned to his goon and laughed. "I told you how cute she is, right?"

The goon appeared to have less brains than Hakim, but he laughed along with Reno as if there was something funny about a cocktail waitress asking for his drink order.

Reno tipped his head back to scan me long and slow. He bit his bottom lip, his eyelids growing heavy. Reno was hot, and in his nice clothes, he was sexy. He made my stomach turn.

"Vodka soda, baby. But first, we need to talk." He patted his thigh, and I went, because I understood I didn't have a choice.

When I perched on his knee, he laughed again, but he let me stay there instead of plopping me on his dick, which was what I had expected.

"What's up?" I peered at him from under my fake lashes, aiming for demure instead of flirty. God, I hoped I pulled it off.

"Your moms, baby. She came around, asking for another loan." He didn't pull me closer, but he *did* cup my ass and give it a squeeze. "Because I care about you, I told her I'd have to think about it."

"She can't pay you back," I blurted out fast.

"This I know." His fingers dug into my flesh hard enough to bruise. "What I wonder is, I give her the cash, can *you* pay me back?"

I shook my head hard. "I'm strapped. I can barely make the payments she owes now. I can't take on more."

"You could work just three nights a week, make double what you do now. You know that, Helen."

"I'm not stripping, Reno. It's not my thing."

He stroked the flesh he'd just been pinching. "You've done it before, baby. Too bad I wasn't here those nights. I would've enjoyed getting an up close and personal look at those pretty tits."

I kept my lips pressed tight. There was no right answer to that.

Reno released a long exhale, then he smacked my ass hard. "All right. Get your ass up and get my drink. Send me a girl who looks like you but doesn't think she's too good to shove her tits in my face."

With an aching butt cheek, I walked away from Reno. I was furious at my mother and relieved the asshole gangster who'd just been groping me hadn't allowed her to turn my hole into a grave. Then I was pissed all over again that my mom had made me feel gratitude toward Reno.

As I passed him on the way to the bar, Amir grabbed my wrist, bringing me to a stop. Carina was grinding her ass on his crotch, swiveling her hips like the absolute pro she was.

"Yo, Helen." Amir sounded casual, like he wasn't a few scraps of fabric away from fucking the pretty girl in his lap. "You still with that guy?"

"Why?" There was only one guy he could be talking about, and I wasn't about to give anything up to Amir before he gave something up to me.

His mouth curved into a smirk. "Does he ever go off on a roid rage? You have to be careful. I wouldn't want to see you hurt."

I canted my head, letting my hair tumble over my shoulder. "What does that mean, dude?"

His thumb stroked the inside of my wrist. The gentleness of the gesture contrasted so starkly with our surroundings and the debauchery going on around us, I nearly laughed. But there wasn't really anything funny, so I didn't.

"Your boy's a juicer, Hells."

"What are you talking about?"

Amir tapped Carina's hips, getting her to move off him, then he rose from his seat, adjusting the bulge in his pants while he held my gaze.

"Walk with me." He took me by the waist, stroking my bare belly with his fingertips. We left the Blue Room like that, making our way across the floor to the bar in tandem. He waited for me to place my drink orders with the bartender, all while holding on to me and pressing into my side.

"You know I've always liked you," he said close to my ear.

I turned my head, but that was a mistake, since it brought my cheek to his lips. "You have?"

"Mmm. Shoulda made my move in high school."

"I didn't think you knew I existed."

He bit his bottom lip. "Oh, I knew."

"Oh," I breathed.

Amir cocked a sexy, amused smile. "Yeah, oh. And I hate to see you getting mixed up with a guy like Theo Whitlock." His back was to the bar, one elbow resting on top, the other arm hooked around me. "That stuff messes with your head."

"What stuff?"

He leaned down, studying me. "You really don't know, do you?"

I sighed, struggling between ripping away from him and settling into his warm hold. I did neither, standing straight, but allowing him to keep his hand on my middle.

"I don't know, no."

"I've been selling your boy dope for over a year."

"Wait, Theo takes H?"

Amir chuckled. "No, no. Your boy Theo juices up with some fancy-ass anabolic steroids. I supply to a couple athletes, but up until a few months ago, he was one of my best customers."

"How...what? Don't they test for that?"

He tapped my nose. "How are you so naive when you come from The Palisades? It's kinda sweet, not gonna lie."

"Amir," I growled. "If you're not going to tell me, then why bring it up?"

His amusement fled, replaced by a dangerous glint. "I told you, Helen, I've always liked you. I see you with a rich boy who uses Daddy's money to cheat the system, I become concerned. Now, tell me, are you still with him?"

I shook my head. "It wasn't like that."

His mouth twitched. "It sounded like that."

"It was sex."

"That isn't a no."

"It is a no. I'm not with him."

"Then you don't give a shit about what I'm telling you."

I placed the drinks going to the Blue Room on my tray, then flicked my eyes to Amir. "It feels good to have the moral high ground for once."

Amir's chuckle sent shivers down my spine, then he moved fast, shoving my hair aside, his lips on my ear. "I understand that more than you can know, Hells Belles."

Then, he walked me back to the Blue Room, reclaimed his seat, and placed Carina back on his dick, like he hadn't just whispered that he'd always liked me and regretted not moving on me back in the day. I wasn't surprised. Amir was a bad guy, and when he did bad-guy things, he was just being himself. It was the truth about Theo, the *good guy* doing really bad things, that threw me for a loop.

And strangely, I was disappointed in him. I didn't know what to do with that, so I shoved it aside and got back to work, avoiding grabby hands and plastering on my brightest, red-lipped smile.

• • • ●• ●• •• •

MY LIFE WAS A study in contrasts, but none more so than tonight.

Saturday night, I'd been in fishnets and booty shorts. Now, only two days later, I was wearing one of Madeline's elegant dresses. It made sense for me to wear it, since I was attending a banquet in honor of her, but I felt more like I was wearing a costume now than I had been slinging drinks at Savage Beauties.

"You look stunning," Zadie said softly.

I spun to face her, smoothing my hands down the front of my fitted dress. "Are you sure I don't look like I'm playing dress-up?"

She shook her head. "I know that was Madeline's dress, but it looks like it was made for you."

Madeline McGarvey was a classic. Her clothes had been simple and expensive. Even when she got too weak to leave the house, she was always dressed to the nines. Her pajamas had been made of silk and always had to be matching sets. And when she changed her will to include me, she bequeathed me her entire wardrobe.

Most of it wasn't me, but I saved all of it, because one day, it might be. This dress was my favorite out of everything. Floor length and long sleeved, with structured shoulders, it wrapped around my middle, cinching in my waist, and flowed loose around my hips. The emerald green wasn't a color I would have chosen, but I liked it so very much.

"I wish I could tuck you in my pocket and take you with me tonight," I said.

Zadie's eyes brightened. "Does that dress have pockets?"

"Yeah, it does." Jutting a hip out, I slipped my hands in my pockets and posed for her. This was a *really* good dress.

I slathered on another layer of lipstick, smoothed my hair, then fluffed it, and Zadie and I walked out to the living room, where I grabbed my phone and tucked it into the tiny evening bag I was carrying.

The door swung open, and Elena came marching in. She threw her backpack on the ground and kicked off her shoes before noticing Zadie and I in the room.

"Hey." Her eyes landed on me. "Oh shit."

Since my breakdown a week and a half ago, Elena hadn't magically become an entirely different person. She was still a caustic, catty bitch, it was just most of that energy was aimed at those outside this suite. Not that we spent time braiding each other's hair, and we definitely hadn't done any more snuggling, but we'd maintained a fragile peace that seemed to become less fragile as the days ticked by.

"Doesn't Helen look beautiful?" Zadie waved her arms up and down like she was a model on *The Price is Right* showing off the fully loaded Winnebago a lucky contestant might have a chance to win.

Elena stalked across the room and got in my face. "You look hot as hell. Now, please tell me you're not going to some arts fundraiser banquet. *Please* tell me."

I took a step back from her. I was not ready for Elena Sanderson, up close and personal like that. "I'm definitely going to an arts fundraiser banquet. Why?"

Her hand went to her mouth at the same time her shoulders slumped. "Shit." She raked her gaze over me. "Well, you look amazing, so you don't have to worry about that."

"I wasn't," I said dryly.

Zadie snapped her fingers. "Spit it out, El."

Elena threw her arms out. "God, fine. I just came from helping Abby get ready for an *arts fundraiser banquet*. She borrowed a dress from me—Prada. When I wear it, I look smoking, but Abby doesn't have enough ass to do it real justice, so you already know you look hotter than her."

My nose scrunched. "There are going to be a lot of people at this thing. I don't really care that she's going to be there too."

Elena hit her forehead, then widened her eyes. "You don't get it. Abby spent the entire time I was with her going on about her little reunion with her ex. Theo is taking her tonight. Abby thinks they're going to be official again ASAP."

Now, that got my attention. It also made me feel like I was on the verge of throwing up seven hundred knives at once.

"We're not together," I rasped.

Elena nodded and grabbed both my hands. "I know. I get it times a thousand. But, babe, as someone who has spent a considerable amount of time with Abby, if Theo chooses to be with her instead of you, that says a shit ton more about his character than yours. Abby is decent, but she's boring and like a walking cliché. She also has a tendency to whine, and the bitch is so literal, half my humor is lost on her, which cuts me to the quick."

"If you're nice to me, I might cry," I whispered.

Elena's eyes narrowed on me. "Your red lipstick makes you look like a whore. God, choose another color already."

My insides untwisted. "That's much better."

She dropped my hands to reach around me and smack my ass. "Get out. I need to shave to prepare for some mediocre sex later."

Zadie lifted a hand. "Thank you for the warning. I'll go find my headphones now." Then she gave me a quick hug. "You'll be great. Just ignore them. You're going for Madeline—no one else."

Taking a deep breath, I nodded. This was for Madeline. Theo could take a long fucking hike in the desert without a drop of water, as far as I was concerned.

BY THE TIME I arrived at the event hall, my bravado had slipped. When I had been asked by the arts philanthropy chair of the Savage U alumni committee to speak tonight, I'd said yes immediately. That was months ago, when Madeline's loss was fresh and I would have done *anything* for her, including standing in front of a richie rich crowd and speak publicly.

What the fuck, past-Helen? We do not engage in public speaking. Much less when our ex...whatever he is...will be present and waiting for us to slip up. Girl, what were you thinking?

One foot in front of the other. That was all I could do. Luckily, I saw a familiar face at check-in. Miranda Wellstein was a well-kept brunette of an indeterminate age, though I was pretty sure she hovered somewhere around fifty. She was the kind of wealthy that could afford to be nice to everyone, and she was.

She came straight for me with a huge, white smile, enveloping me in a warm hug.

"Helen." She pressed her cheek to mine. "Oh, honey, I'm so pleased to see you again."

With my hands in hers, she stepped back and scanned me from my toes to my face. Her smile had grown tight when her eyes arrived on mine.

"I remember this dress." She sniffled and batted at her cheek. "Madeline wore it when we saw *La Boheme* in L.A. Oh, we had such a night, the two of us. We stayed over and had brunch celebrity style the following day. It was lovely, so very lovely. And you, Helen...look at you. She'd be so happy to see you in this dress."

My throat went tight. All I could offer was a choked thank you. Miranda and Madeline had been good friends. During my time with Mads, she hadn't allowed many visitors. She wouldn't say it, but I knew it was down to pride. She didn't want her friends and colleagues to see her near the end, when she was frail, with blue-tinged skin and next to no energy. Miranda had been one of the exceptions, but not for long, and not often. Toward the end, Mads would only talk to her by phone. I'd talked to Miranda almost daily, keeping her updated on her dear friend's condition and spirits. We hadn't grown close, but I guess we shared a bond since we both missed Mads something fierce.

Her hands slid to my shoulders, and she gave them a squeeze. "Now that I'm an emotional wreck, let's go inside. I'll introduce you to a couple people and we'll find our table. You're sitting with me tonight, by the way."

"Oh, thank god," I breathed with relief.

Miranda laughed. "I would never invite you here, then abandon you."

She hooked her arm through mine, then we strode into the banquet hall. There were dozens of smartly dressed people milling about, many with champagne or cocktails in hand. The men were in suits, the women in fine dresses. And I realized I fit, at least on the outside. If no one spoke to me, they'd never know I didn't belong. But shit, I was going to have to get on stage and speak to all of them.

Miranda walked me around the room, introducing me to more than a couple people while never leaving my side, as promised. Once we'd made the rounds, she walked me toward a round table big enough to seat ten. A few people had already sat down.

Miranda steered me to the two open seats between an older man and a younger one.

"Here, darling." She rotated me toward the young man. "Let me introduce you to my stepson and his...friend. This is Theo Whitlock and Abby Fitzgerald."

The world rocked under my feet, and I grabbed onto the back of the chair to steady myself. Theo rose with a practiced smile, one I'd never seen on him but recognized for what it was. In that moment, I was glad Elena had warned me Theo would be here tonight. Otherwise, I might have toppled over at the sight of him.

Theo Whitlock, in a finely tailored suit with a blue tie that matched his eyes, was a sight to behold. I would have never known he hadn't grown up in this world because he wore it so well.

Miranda leaned around me, clutching Theo's forearm. "Theo, this is Helen Ortega, my special guest."

All of him froze, except for his eyes, which darted to mine in wide-eyed shock. I supposed I was the last person he expected to see tonight when he reunited with his girlfriend. A million thoughts raced around my skull, of what I could say, how I could act. I decided to go with the simplest course of action: the truth.

"Hey, Theo." I twisted my neck to smile at Miranda. "Theo and I are in a Shakespeare class together. We're actually working with another classmate, Lachlan, on a midterm project."

Theo let out something between a bark and a cough. Attention returned to him. "I'm speechless. I had no idea you knew Miranda."

I dipped my chin. "Just as I had no idea Miranda was your stepmom."

Miranda clapped her hands. "Oh my, what a small world. Well, obviously it's small here, since you both attend Savage, but it truly never occurred to me you might share a class. This is just perfect."

The beautiful blonde at Theo's side stood from her seat and draped herself on his shoulder. "Hi, I'm Abby."

Theo was stiff, but Abby took no notice. She rested her chin on his shoulder and pressed herself into his arm. My skin felt bathed in acid. He could move on, he didn't owe me anything, but seeing it up close and personal really wasn't fair. But that was life. Shit hurt.

I tilted my head. "We've met...at the T." I looked her up and down. "Elena is my roommate too. The Prada looks great on you."

"Thanks." She smoothed a hand over her hip. "I remember now. You were with a little kid, weren't you?"

"Mmhmm. That was my sister, Luciana. I would have introduced you, but you were all about The that day." I used her stupid-ass nickname, which did not escape her, based on the way she curled her pretty pink lip at me.

Miranda pressed her hand on my back, turning me the other way. "This is my husband, Andrew." The older man, who was unmistakably Theo's father, got to his feet and offered me his hand.

"Helen, Miranda hasn't stopped talking about you for a solid year. It's a pleasure to meet you." His handshake was warm, firm, and sincere. His smile too. His eyes didn't twinkle as much as Theo's did, but I saw where he got it.

"It's nice to meet you, sir."

He waved me off. "None of that formal stuff. Andrew is fine. Are you sitting with us tonight?"

"Yeah. I mean...yes. I think I am."

He pulled out the empty chair beside his. "Come, sit by me. Miranda and I see each other all the time. I haven't had the chance to get to know you."

Miranda patted my shoulder. "You'll sit between us so we don't have to fight over you, darling. This way I can talk to my darling Theo too."

My eyes flicked to Theo, who had been watching my interaction with his dad carefully.

"Lucky you."

I took my seat beside Andrew Whitlock and tipped my head back to make eye contact with Theo one more time. He grimaced like he was vastly uncomfortable with my presence. I wasn't having the time of my life either.

But he'd made his choice.

He'd put us here, and I had zero desire to make tonight any easier for him.

Twenty

THEO

I HAD NO IDEA what Helen was doing here, but Jesus, she took my breath away. She looked like one of *them*, Miranda's people, only sexier and so much more real.

I'd walked into this banquet hall knowing tonight would be nothing but suffering, but I'd been ready for it. Or so I thought. *Nothing* could have prepared me for this. Helen, two seats away, making nice with Andrew. She was clearly already great friends with my stepmom. And that dress, her body, red lips, sad eyes— all of it was a recipe to make me regret every decision I ever made. What really rattled around in my skull and down to my gut, though, was how completely taken with her my father was.

I couldn't hear what Helen was saying with Abby and Miranda speaking to each other around me, but I watched. Helen was twisted in her seat to face my father, her hands moving expressively as she explained something to him. Andrew Whitlock was riveted, nodding and throwing in a word or two, but otherwise listening to all Helen had to say.

Eventually, dinner was served. Instead of eating, I stared as Helen worked her water glass between her hands, spinning it in tight circles over and over. Finally, she must have sensed my gaze. Her eyes slid to mine, one brow arching. I opened my hands. I was at a loss about everything.

Every. Fucking. Thing.

Abby poked at my arm, dragging my attention from Helen. "Isn't this salad good?" She held up her fork like she might feed me if I wasn't careful.

I glanced down at my untouched plate, then back to her. "Great."

Her bottom lip poked out. "You haven't been paying attention to me, The."

"That's because I don't want to be here."

Her mouth fell open, but only for a moment, then she composed herself in all her Abigail Fitzgerald glory. "Then we should go. Although, I'm certain your father wouldn't appreciate you disappearing."

I had nothing to say to that. She was right. Someone brushed by my chair, and my eyes flicked up in time to see Helen striding toward the restrooms, her round hips swaying in that sultry way that came naturally to her.

"Excuse me." I threw my napkin down on the table, not even bothering to hide the fact that I was following her. Like a moth to a flame and all that. There was no resisting.

I waited in the empty hall outside the women's restroom. After a minute or two, Helen emerged, her face impassive, not seeming the least bit surprised to find me there. She started to march by me. Before she could take more than a couple steps, I had my fingers wrapped around her bicep and I shoved her into a shadowed alcove.

She yanked her arm away. "No."

"Yes." I crowded her space, backing her into the wall. "What are you doing here?"

Her gaze was unflinching. "I was invited."

"By my stepmom?"

"Yes."

"Are you here because of me?"

Helen sputtered with laughter. "Holy Christ, dude. How conceited are you? I didn't know you'd be here until Elena informed me you and your girlfriend were coming. And I found out your connection to Miranda at the same time you found out mine."

"I'm with her as a favor to my dad."

She crossed her arms over her chest. "Tell me, Theo, when did you know you'd be escorting your girlfriend to this banquet?"

I stilled as her bullet hit its target. "A few weeks." My hole had been dug. Why not be honest now?

Her laugh was so bitter, I could taste it. "You were going to bring her here tonight and never tell me, right? I bet you would have shown up at my door ready to fuck after rubbing up against your pretty blonde girlfriend all night."

"He didn't give me a choice, Helen."

"Okay."

I slapped the wall next to her head. "Fuck, I hate when you do that. Why won't you call me a piece of shit? Argue with me? Tell me to go to hell?"

She lifted her chin. "I don't need to. You already know."

Looking away from her wasn't an option, even though it bruised all the way to the bone. She was so fucking gorgeous and defiant. And somehow, *somehow*, after the lie she told and truth she omitted, she had the upper hand.

I guess I'd given it to her. No, I knew I had. How could I be angry at her for keeping something from me when I hadn't even considered telling her about escorting Abby tonight?

"You're right. I wasn't going to tell you."

Her head turned, showing me the tight curve of her jaw. "That would have hurt me. Luckily, I don't care anymore."

My hand balled into a fist on the wall. "Helen…"

She cared.

She absolutely fucking cared. Seeing the slightest hint of vulnerability was like bamboo under my fingernails—torture I would have kept on taking if it meant seeing beyond her walls.

"You should get back to your girlfriend." She tipped her face up to meet my gaze. Even in the shadows, her pain was evident. "She looks lovely tonight, Theo. You must be proud."

Then she slipped under my arm, hurrying down the hall, leaving me reeling, like she always did. Only, this time, it was worse than ever. This wasn't the beginning of something wild and crazy, but the period at the end of the biggest rush of my life.

When I got back to the table, Helen was once again rising from her seat and walking toward the stage with note cards in her hand.

"What's she doing?" I asked Miranda.

Her head jerked toward me. "Helen is here to give a speech about Madeline McGarvey's legacy, honey."

"What?"

What?

Miranda patted my arm. "If you'll turn on your ears and listen, I think you'll understand."

A spotlight shone down on Helen's sleek, chocolate waves as she took her spot behind the podium, center stage. It was subtle, but I saw her nerves in the slight tremble of her hands, the press of her ruby lips, the bunching of her shoulders.

"Hi." Feedback from the microphone squealed through the room. Helen laughed softly and adjusted it with her shaking hands. "Hi, I'm Helen Ortega." She smiled, her lashes brushing her cheeks as she looked down at her note cards.

"I'm not an artist or an art major. I'm planning on becoming a nurse, actually. So, you might wonder what I'm doing here, standing on stage, speaking at a fundraiser for the art and design school. It's simple, really. I'm here for Madeline."

Abby looped her arm through mine and tried to lean into me. I shrugged her off and shot her a hard look that had her slumping back in her seat. This wasn't her time. That had come and gone.

Helen shuffled her note cards, then looked up with shining eyes. "I grew up in a trailer park. I never intended on going to college, because, quite frankly, I couldn't afford it and it wasn't important to me. Then, I met Madeline. She saw me chasing three idiot guys out of a skate shop with a baseball bat and said, *'That's the girl I want by my side for the rest of my days.'* She offered me a job right then and there, and I couldn't turn her down."

I'm an idiot. I've been one since the day we met.

Miranda laid her hand over mine as she released a wet laugh. I'd only met Madeline a couple times, but I knew my stepmom had been devastated when she passed. Seeing Helen on stage, it was clear Miranda wasn't the only one.

"Imagine knowing from the time you're a kid that you won't live past forty. That was Mads's reality. She chose not to walk herself into an early grave, though. Instead, she lived as fully as she could. Mads grabbed hold of her life with both hands. Even when the ride was rough and it hurt—and god, did it hurt her—she kept going and going. She saw me with my trusty bat and recognized a kindred spirit. I don't have CF, but the hand I was dealt since birth was—excuse my language—really shitty. I never once considered packing it in or burying my head in drugs or alcohol, though, just as Mads didn't slow down until her body forced her to. But I don't want you to think she stopped. She never, ever stopped."

Helen swiped at her cheek and gave the audience another brave, wobbly smile as she shuffled her notes.

"If you knew Madeline McGarvey, no doubt you knew how important education was to her. Teaching at Savage U, her alma mater, was one of her greatest joys. Introducing art to those who'd previously found it inaccessible was her passion. The art and design school was her second home. So, you can imagine when Mads got her hands on me, a girl who'd never set foot in a museum, had no intention of seeking a higher education, and had never seen a foreign film in my life, she was giddy. I was signed up for online college courses before I knew what hit me. We took trips to every museum within driving distance. I picked up enough Italian and French from all the movies we watched, I could hold a conversation now."

The room filled with soft, sad laughter, but I was filled with something else. Wonder, maybe. It buzzed low in my gut, impossible to ignore. How had I missed this? How had I spent every spare second with Helen and never known any of this? How had I not even come close to seeing her grief, which was lying so close to her surface, it was coming off her in waves?

Helen wiped her cheek again. "Madeline hired me to be her companion when it became clear her body couldn't withstand another transplant or experimental treatment. Don't take that as her giving up, though. Mads had accepted what was happening to her and filled every single day with art, beauty, adventure, and experiences. Because life is short, and it's so damn unfair I could scream, but it can also be beautiful. Madeline McGarvey found that, and it was her living *and* dying wish to spread that lesson."

Helen sucked in a jagged breath. Miranda's hand tightened over mine. I leaned forward, needing every single word and secret she was spilling from her red, red lips.

"I'm here tonight because of Madeline. My Mads. She couldn't convince me to become an art major, but she did instill in me the importance of learning. I'm here, standing before you tonight, because of Madeline McGarvey. Because she saw something in me, believed in me, wanted more for me so fervently, I started to want more for myself. I know I'm only one person, but I bet you could ask any of Madeline's students and they would have a story about the moment a flip switched in them because of her. She's gone, but her legacy will live on. She made sure of that, through me, her past students, and the ones to come. The Madeline McGarvey scholarship will keep her passion going for years to come. She died knowing her legacy would be beauty and hope. Mads passed fully at peace."

Helen choked out a sob, but she swallowed hard, holding back any more tears. Miranda had leaned into my father, whose arm was curled around her shoulders as she quietly cried.

"If I could have one last conversation with Madeline, I'd tell her I saw my first Shakespeare play within my first month at Savage U. It was *Taming of the Shrew*. I'd tell her I really liked it. It even made me laugh. And though I said it a lot during the too-short time we spent together, I would say thank you. Thank you, Madeline, for showing me beauty. Thank you for believing in me and making me want more. Thank you, Mads, for being my friend. And thank you, Madeline McGarvey, for coming from a world of privilege, recognizing it, and using it to help those who don't. I'll do you proud, Mads. Promise."

Helen returned to the table under a roar of applause. If the audience understood she was telling them to use their privilege for good instead of evil, it wasn't apparent, but one could only hope. Miranda enveloped her into a hug, then my father took them both in his arms.

Sitting next to my ex-girlfriend—who was still pouting—watching this, knowing I had no business wanting to take care of Helen, but *needing* to more than I needed to breathe, I'd never felt more wrong in my life.

I hung through ten more minutes of every single person in the banquet hall coming up to Helen to try to grab a piece of her. They kept coming, asking her about her time with Madeline, touching her hair, her arms, invading her grief. She kept smiling, but her eyes were darting to the side. I recognized that look—trapped, panicked, hungry to escape—and I couldn't stop myself from surging to my feet.

Helen shook her head when she saw me move, then she shifted to give me her back. and I remembered I'd put myself here —right where I'd wanted to be.

· • • ● • ● • • ·

WHILE I IGNORED HER, Abby got wasted. By the time I drove her home, her head was lolling on her rest and I had to help her out of the car. She clung to me as I walked her into her dorm. This wasn't where I wanted to be, but I couldn't leave her to fend for herself.

I propped her next to her door and held out my hand. "Give me your key."

"Why don't you love me, The?" Her back was to the wall, her head tipped up.

"Give me your key, Abby."

"Answer me and I will."

Exhaling, I rubbed the space between my brows. "We're done, Abby. We've had this conversation. There's nothing new to say. I need you to let this go. No more showing up where I am. No more shoving our fathers in the middle. I don't know how to be more clear with you."

Her sigh sounded more like a hiss. "It's her, isn't it? That...*girl* with the red lips?"

"You know her name." My patience had just about run out, but now that she'd brought up Helen, it was paper thin.

"You're obviously not with her. She wouldn't even look at you."

"It doesn't matter who I'm with or not with. You and I are not together, and we won't be getting back together. I'd like to be able to look back on what we had and feel good about it, but you're going out of your way to ruin our history."

She straightened, moving into me to press her hands on my chest. "We were so good. I just wanted more. I didn't know how to get it from you. I thought...I thought you'd see how serious I was if I broke up with you and you'd open up to me."

I shook my head. "It was never going to happen, Abbs. I gave you all I could. I'm sorry it wasn't enough. I'm sorry you were hurt, and maybe you're still hurting. But that doesn't mean we have a chance. You need to let go."

Her brow crinkled. It looked like she was trying to work her thoughts out in her alcohol-soaked mind.

"Are you going to give her more?" She'd lost her cutting edge. Now, she just sounded sad. Her hands slid up to my neck, eyes imploring for a different answer than the one she knew I'd be giving.

"This isn't about anyone else. You asked about me and you— that's what I'm answering."

"We were so good, The." She rose on her toes, and before I could stop her, her mouth pressed against mine. I wrenched my head to the side, breaking the connection as soon as it started. "I'm sorry. I'm sorry," she cried.

I took her hands off me and pounded my fist on her door to let her roommates know she needed to be let in. Then I backed away, out of her reach.

"Go inside. I'm done."

The door opened behind her, and I didn't wait to see what happened next. I had a wrong I needed to right, and it couldn't wait any longer.

Twenty-One

Helen

IN MY BEAUTIFUL DRESS, I sat down beside Theo on the steps in front of my dorm. I had expected him to be waiting there for me when my Uber dropped me off, and he hadn't let me down.

He was quiet for a while, and I felt no need to fill the space between us. Tonight had worn me out. Thinking about Mads, talking about her, reliving what it meant to know her, all took a toll. Doing that in front of Theo made it ten times harder.

"You're grieving."

I slowly turned my head, letting my eyes travel over his face. My stomach churned.

"Yeah." I pointed to his mouth. "You didn't wipe off all the lip gloss."

His hand flew to his mouth, scrubbing the shiny pink stuff away from the very corner. "Fucking Abby. She doesn't know when to quit."

"It might be the mixed messages. Taking her on a date then making out with her after would be a little confusing."

He took my jaw in his hand, pulling me into him so our noses nearly brushed. "That isn't what happened. I dropped my drunk ex-girlfriend off and she threw herself at me. That lasted less

than a second before I left her with the unambiguous message
that we were never going to be together."

I shrugged like I didn't care. I wished seeing lip gloss on his
mouth hadn't been a blow to the solar plexus, but considering I
was still breathless, it had been. The hits just kept coming.

"Okay, Theo. You don't owe me any explanations."

His hold on my jaw softened, but he didn't let go. "I owe you
an apology. I realize how I spoke to you was probably
unforgivable, but I need you to know I'm sorry."

I nodded. "That's something."

"I should have asked you more questions."

"You didn't want a girlfriend. I didn't want a boyfriend. What
we had was what we both wanted."

His nostrils flared. "Enough lying, Helen. Jesus."

My hands were still shaking slightly, and I hurt so deep, it felt
like my soul was bruised. He kept pushing me, saying he was
sorry, then pushing some more. I was getting really tired of
being pushed around and made into the bad guy. He wanted to
show up here with another girl's kiss on his lips, offer a little
apology, and expect that to be it? Maybe it was because I was so
raw from spending the evening talking about Mads, but I was
done. Absolutely done.

"Okay, here's the god's honest truth, Theo. I'll lay it all out for
you. Madeline left me a lot of money in a trust. But she knew me
well enough to know I wouldn't finish school if she was gone
and I could cash in the trust, so I'm required to graduate from
Savage U before I can access the money. It's a lot of money,
Theo. *A lot.* She left a separate fund for my tuition, so that's
covered. But neither of us knew my darling mother was taking a
loan from a gangster at the same time Mads was living her final
days. Neither of us had any idea I'd be over a barrel, forced to pay
back the loan while attending school. Mads would have paid it
off. She wouldn't have left me in this situation. But here I am,
stuck. In a couple years, I know I'll have the trust, I'll have Luc,

and I'll be okay. I'll be more than okay. For now, though, I have to do what I have to do to survive."

Theo murmured my name painfully and reached for my hand, but I yanked it away. If he gave me soft, I'd scream.

"Deacon sold weed for me until he screwed me over. That was one of the times I had to strip for the cash I owed Amir. There were a handful of other times I took off my clothes when I came up short. I hated every second of it, but I'd do it a thousand times over to keep Luc safe."

He tried to touch me again, but I slapped him away. I needed to keep going, to level him with my truth so he could see, so he could understand.

"Before you, it had been nearly two years since I had sex with anyone. The last person to touch me decided no meant yes, slammed my face into the hood of a car, and had my pants halfway down my ass before Penelope saved me. So, when I let you inside me, it meant something. I might not have given you everything you thought I should have, but what I gave you was a lot."

He exhaled, his head dropping forward, hands clasped between his knees.

"I'm an asshole," he gritted out.

"Yeah, you are. And the thing is, I felt like trash when you told me we were done. But I've thought about it, I've watched you, I've learned a few things about you, and I came to a conclusion."

He lifted his head to peer at me, his eyes narrowed. "What's that?"

"I'm really too good for you." He flinched, but he didn't deny it, so I went on. "You may have grown up having to be hard, but you've gotten soft, Theo. You let your dad push you around. You let your ex push you around. You didn't stand up for me. Your feelings were hurt, so you tried to get out of our group project, and when you couldn't, you showed up unprepared and threw out accusations at Lock. Your grades are slipping. You're closed off. You live off your dad's money all while saying you hate him. And—"

"Enough," he whispered. "I hear you."

"No, wait. I didn't get to the best part. How do you know Amir, Theo?"

He stilled, studying me so hard, it seemed like he was trying to see inside my mind. Then his head bobbed loosely when he got it.

"He talked?"

"Mmhmm. He told me what he sold you. I don't know how you got away with doping for so long, but I think your moral high ground was actually a deck of cards, and it's completely collapsed."

He stared at me for a long time. Every second that passed, sadness seeped into my bones. Not just for Mads, but for Theo. For who I thought he was—who he could've been if he'd just wake up.

He nodded. "You're right. Nothing you said was untrue. I'm not good enough for you. Not even close." He climbed to his feet and held his hands out to help me stand. He was giving up, just like that.

Theo walked me the rest of the way up the steps to the door. There, he reeled me in to his body, his arms circling my shoulders, gently pressing me to his chest.

It took me a second to understand he was hugging me. It took another second for it to sink in how badly I'd needed this. I'd been embraced many times tonight, but when it came from Theo, my twisted insides unfurled, and I sank into him.

He held me until I let him go.

"I need to go to sleep." I dug in my clutch, finding my key card. "I'll see you in class."

Theo's fingers curled around my arm. "Two things before you go in."

"Okay."

"First, you're so fucking beautiful, it's hard to look at you right now. And you were magnificent tonight when you were talking about Madeline. If people didn't love her before that, you made them fall."

I had to bite on my bottom lip to stifle a sob. Theo touched my trembling chin, telling me without words that he noticed.

"Second is I know I'm not good enough, Helen. That doesn't mean I'm walking away from you. It means I have work to do to get myself there. I won't ask you to wait, but I'm telling you right now, you're the only one I want to be with—and that won't change." He brought his hand up to the side of my neck, dipping his head to make sure I was with him. "It's late. You're tired. When you're ready, I'll tell you everything. About Amir, wrestling, steroids, my mom—all of it. Say the word, Tiger, and all my truth is yours."

"I don't know if I want your truth, Theo."

I was sad right then, but when I had more energy and I wasn't so raw from Mads, the anger would return. And man, was I pissed at Theo.

He closed his eyes, nodding as he exhaled. "Then I'll have to work until you do."

He swiped my key card for me, gently shoved me inside, and closed the door between us. Another nod, and Theo walked off into the night, and I went upstairs to my room, my heart aching and promises yet to be fulfilled.

Twenty-Two

THEO

"LOCK."

The garage bay was almost empty. Lock was the only one working, his head under the hood of a truck. Hearing his name, he looked around, found me approaching, and straightened, wiping his hands on a rag.

"Theo." He was wary already.

"Hey."

He continued wiping his hands, giving me nothing. Made sense. If there were lines in the sand, Lock was firmly on Helen's side. Really fucking deservedly so.

"I'm hoping you can help me out."

Lock's expression turned thunderous. "Are you really?"

"Yeah." I shoved my fingers through my hair. "I messed up. I keep messing up. It's high time I turned things around. I'm asking for your help with that."

Rag clutched in one hand, his fists went to his hips. "Tell me what you're looking for. I'll consider it."

"I know engines. I worked in a garage, my pops' shop, from the time I was a kid."

Again, nothing. Lock was a solid wall. He was going to make me work for every inch I needed, which was fair. I hadn't worked in a long, long time.

"I'm looking for a job, Lock. I have experience in a garage, but I'm willing to work anywhere there's a need for a body. My pops taught me a lot, but I'm a fast learner and willing to get dirty if I need to."

He threw down the rag, his jaw tight. "What makes you think I'd want to help you, even if I could? Besides your nonexistent work ethic, you fucked my friend over."

I decided to lay it all on the line. That was all I could do. He was right. I'd been showing my ass all semester, and I had a hell of a lot to prove now.

"I know I screwed up in a massive way with Helen. I'm working to make it right. To do that, I need to be able to stand apart from my father. The start of that is not being reliant on his money."

"Good start," Lock rumbled.

I tipped my chin in acknowledgment and went on. "For that, I need a job. I was hoping for one on campus. It'd be an insurance policy, in case Andrew doesn't agree with my choices and revokes my tuition. If I work here, I'll get a deep discount so I'll be able to take care of my own tuition."

"You did your research."

I shrugged. "It didn't take much. But I'm not bullshitting around. I need this."

"I don't make the hiring decisions."

"I didn't think you did. But I figured, you being Lock, you could put in a word for me and ease the way into me working here."

"You figured that. Hmph." His head cocked. "Are you serious?"

"Never been more serious."

"And I'm not going to have to hold your dick the whole time?"

My mouth quirked. "I'd rather you didn't."

His expression didn't budge whatsoever. "I need an answer."

My hand went to the back of my neck, rubbing it hard. "No, man. I know a lot, and what I don't know, I'll learn fast. I'm committed. I need this."

"You said that."

"Yeah...well, it bears repeating."

Lock took a couple steps to the right, bracing his hands on the hood of a campus truck. A few beats passed, then he glanced over his shoulder at me.

"I do this, you screw up, we'll have problems, Theo."

I shook my head. "That won't happen."

"We'll see. We're a man down right now. I'll talk to my boss about you. If you can impress him, I guess you've got a job."

I wasn't going to celebrate. This was one step. A step I should've taken years ago. I let myself go soft because it had been easier that way. I'd given up control to my father in exchange for security. But the security he offered was lined in lead, and it had been poisoning me for years.

"Thanks, man."

Lock hadn't stopped glaring the entire time I'd been in the garage. He closed the space between us, giving my chest a light shove. Light from Lock was like being hit with an anvil. I cracked my spine against the side-view mirror of the truck behind me.

"Don't thank me until you prove yourself. And not to me. Helen's going to be the judge of that. If you put that look on her face again, if you make her afraid or feel unworthy, it won't matter what she says or who your father is, you and I will have words—and they won't be gentle." His nostrils flared as he inhaled. "You feel me?"

"If I make her feel afraid or unworthy, I'll welcome what you bring."

Folding his arms over his wide chest, he rocked back on his heels. "Yeah, you feel me."

One step, that was all it was. But it was something.

· · · ● · ● · · ·

HELEN AND LOCK WALKED into the library study room together. She was laughing, leaning into him. He had a wide grin on his face, obviously liking my girl there, hanging on his arm.

Ugliness sat on the tip of my tongue like poison. I did not like them together. Worse, I had no say in what happened between them. Helen had barely looked at me since our talk on her steps Monday night. And when she did look, her gaze teetered between wary and pissed off. There was no forgiveness there. Then again, I hadn't done jack to prove myself.

They both stopped in their tracks, seeing me already at the table, set up, ready to work. I swallowed the poison down, letting it writhe in my guts.

Helen raised a brow but did not disengage from Lock. "Wow, look who's on time. Is this a new leaf?"

I grinned at her, though I didn't feel it. "I'm trying out the school thing. We'll see how it goes."

She dropped Lock's arm and pulled out the chair diagonal from mine, dropping her backpack with a thump. "Interesting. Is this a part of your five-point plan apology tour?"

Leaning on my elbow, I rubbed my chin. "Actually, it's getting my shit together. It was high time."

Her mouth twisted, but her eyes held mine. "Past time, Theo."

Lock was silent during this exchange, taking his seat and turning on his laptop. Helen followed suit, giving me the cold shoulder. I spent this time tamping down the jealousy burning a hole in my stomach. It would do me no good to stake my claim, not when the last time I came to Helen, I had Abby's lip gloss on my mouth. Helen was mine, but I had to earn the right to call her that out loud, and I wasn't even close to that place yet.

Lock cracked his knuckles and peered at me from behind his screen. "Are you ready to present your section?"

I nodded, glancing at my notes. "As I'll ever be."

• • • ● • ● • • •

AN HOUR LATER, WE walked out of the library. For once, my group members weren't pissed off at me, and that felt really fucking good. Not just because one of them was Helen, but because I'd worked hard this week to catch up and get where I needed to be. This was all on me, no assistance, no hiding behind someone else—my sole accomplishment.

I caught Helen's elbow as she turned to skate off to her dorm. "Helen."

She tugged her arm back. "Theo."

"Can I talk to you for a second?"

Her chin lowered. "That's all you get."

"That's all I have." I stepped into her, cupping the side of her neck, then I walked her backward so we were a few feet from Lock. When she didn't jerk away from me, I took it as a victory. "I want to give you a ride home tonight."

"I don't need it."

"I won't read it as forgiveness. I never should've stopped picking you up. That was an asshole move."

"It's whatever." Her teeth dug into her bottom lip. "Carina's been driving me home."

"Coworker?"

"Yeah. She doesn't mind, so I'm covered. Don't worry your pretty little head about me, Theo."

My brow pinched. "I'm going to worry. If there's a time Carina can't drive you, call me. I'll be there. I don't want you on the bus again."

Her mouth opened, but before she could say whatever she was going to, Lock said my name. I exhaled, taking one last look at Helen. All the soft I'd coaxed out of her was back behind her spiky walls. Still, even with her defenses up and her lips turned down, she was the most beautiful woman I'd ever laid eyes on.

"I gotta go." I pulled her into me and pressed a kiss to her forehead. It might've been stolen, but I needed it, so I took. "Call me, Tiger."

Lock was frowning at me with deep furrows around his mouth when I got to him. I grinned back.

"Let's go," he gritted out.

"Ready when you are," I replied.

We'd gone two steps when Helen called out to us, "Hey, lovebirds, where are you going together?"

I turned around, walking backward beside Lock, whose steps hadn't even stuttered. "Gotta get to work, baby. No time to chat."

"What!" She threw her arms out.

"You call me, I'll tell you all about it." Then I tossed her a wave and spun forward.

Lock glanced over at me, tense. "You're getting cocky. The finish line is too far off for you to be this cocky."

That sobered me somewhat. "Point taken."

After a minute of silence, he added, "She was kinda nice to you, though."

I barked a laugh. "Yeah, she kinda was."

"Don't fuck up the little ground you've gained back, Whitlock."

"I'm not going to."

Whether I was patient enough to wait for Helen to come back to me was another story. But if my first day on the job the previous day had been any indication, Lock was going to keep me so busy with backbreaking labor for the next four hours, I wouldn't have the chance to think about Helen. And that was good, since this was about *me*. Yeah, I wanted the girl, but this was more than that. This was me taking the reins of my life back. This was me standing on my own feet and being able to look at myself in the mirror without disgust. This was me living clear and clean. Then, and only then, would this be me going after my girl.

Twenty-Three

Helen

COMING HOME FROM A night of men groping, leering, and opening their stupid mouths to hear Elena faking yet another orgasm was too much. Knowing who the dude was pounding away at her poor kitty made it even worse.

I'd known that lanky-ass fool was trouble when I saw him last summer. He'd been at Savage Beauties tonight with a handful of other frat bros. It stood to reason he was the one who'd told Theo about me riding the pole, although I'd never noticed him before. He must not have made himself known like he had tonight.

First, he'd heckled a couple girls on stage. Hakim had nearly squashed his head like a peach, and he became more subtle after that, sending me back to the bar multiple times when his drink order was "wrong," tossing tips on the ground so I had to bend to get them, rejecting Carina's lap dance in the middle of it because her minor, silvery stretch marks "disgusted" him, refusing to pay her since she didn't complete her dance.

I threw my shoe at Elena's door when I heard her moan, "Oh, Daniel," with pure boredom. The dude must have been rich, or maybe he was blackmailing her. I couldn't see any other reason she'd continue sleeping with him.

In my bedroom, I tucked my tips in the box I kept in my underwear drawer. It was stuffed full, since my payment to Reno was due tomorrow by five. I'd have some extra left this time, giving me some breathing room for once.

After I took a shower and washed the filth of the club from my skin, I tucked myself in bed, the suite blissfully quiet. Elena had either kicked Daniel out or fucked him to sleep. Either way worked for me. Pulling my covers over my ears, I went to sleep.

It was still pitch black when I slowly came awake. Something was tickling my face. I batted it away, but it came back a second later, dragging up my cheek.

My brain switched on, but my body froze. Someone was sitting on the side of my bed, touching my face. Then my covers were inched down from under my chin to my chest, down, down, down.

I stopped breathing.

Fight, flight, fight, flight.

I could close my eyes and pretend it was a bad dream.

I could scratch and claw and hope I could gain the upper hand.

I could lie here.

I could scream.

The intruder lowered himself over me, his chest pressing down on mine, then something touched my neck, hot and slimy, jerking me out of my stupor.

"Helen..." Daniel crooned in my ear. "Are you awake, beautiful?"

My hands came up, but I couldn't fit them between us. "Get off of me," I hissed, barely more than a whisper. There wasn't enough air in my lungs to make my voice louder. If there had been, I would have screamed until the roof shook and windows rattled.

"There she is." In the dark, his eyes searched mine. "You look like an angel when you're asleep, Helen."

I shuddered in revulsion. From the way he pressed his erection into my hip, he took it as something else. Or maybe he liked me being revolted by him. Maybe he got off on it.

"Get off of me, asshole." I shoved at his shoulders and arched my spine. Daniel was lanky, but he had a lot of power in his limbs and easily held me down.

"Mmm." He continued to stroke my cheek like a sweet lover. "I've been wanting to talk to you for a long time. You fascinate me."

I reached blindly off the side of my mattress, struggling to find my bat, but only hitting empty air. Daniel's mouth curved, like he thought it was funny how panicked I was. He even tsked at me.

Finally, my hand came into contact with something solid, but I only knocked it away. My bat fell against the floor with a clatter, and I whimpered at the loss, which made Daniel chuckle.

"Why are you so scared, Helen? I'm not hurting you. I'm barely even touching you. I just like looking at you. Isn't that what you want? When you get on that stage or walk around in your little shorts serving drinks, don't you want men like me to look?"

"Off," I cried. "Off! Off, off, off!" Each successive cry got louder and louder until I exploded. "Get off me!" My cries echoed around the room, jerking Daniel back an inch or two. He stared down at me, squinting like he didn't understand my protests.

"What's wrong?" Perplexed. The asshole sounded perplexed.

Before I could say another word, my door swung open, and the light was flicked on. Elena stood there in her pink, silk, shorty pajamas, only pausing for a half a beat to take in the scene. Me, disheveled and no doubt red-faced and wild-eyed. Daniel, her boyfriend, pressing down on me. Then she flew into action. My bat was in her hands, poised above his head.

"Get up right now," she hissed.

He sat up, his hands held up in placation. I scrambled to my headboard, pulling my knees to my chest.

"It's no big deal, baby. Helen and I were just talking."

"Unless Helen is suddenly great at talking in her sleep, no, you weren't. Take your pencil dick and leave, Daniel." She feigned a swing at him, making him cower. "I'll be glad to introduce your balls to Batty. She gets lonely sometimes."

Daniel leaped from the bed, covering his dick with both hands. "Crazy fucking bitches. Both of you. Dead lay and a whore, what a combination. Put the two of you together, it might make a good fuck."

Elena pressed the end of my bat to his chest. "I guess you'll never know, will you? Get the fuck out, right now, before I show you exactly how crazy I can be."

Elena followed Daniel out of my room, threatening him all the way to our front door, which she slammed behind him. Then she returned to my room, handed me the bat, and turned off the light.

"Scoot over." She pushed at my shoulders. When I shifted to the side, she climbed into bed, pulling the covers over both of us. "Lie down."

I stretched out in my bed, the bat clutched in my arms like a damn teddy bear.

"You okay? Did he hurt you?"

I blinked up at the ceiling. "I...no. He scared the shit out of me, but he didn't hurt me. I don't even know if he was going to."

"He's a creeper. Ugh."

"Says the girl having regular bad sex with him."

"Make that past tense."

I turned my head, even though I could barely make her out in the dark. "Why were you with him anyway? I mean, I get slumming if the dude had a talented dick, but from the sounds of it..."

Her sigh sounded defeated. "My parents are friendly with his. They thought we would make a lovely match."

"And...?" I didn't get it.

"And that's it. My parents mean the world to me. I don't ever let them down. So, I dated their friends' creepy son. Tomorrow morning, I have to break the news over brunch that it's over. Wee!" She draped her arm over my stomach. "If you try to pity me after I just chased my boyfriend from your room with a bat, I won't be able to stand it. Everyone has family shit they deal with. Mine is mine. Yours is yours."

"Okay." I laid my hand on her arm. "Thanks for—"

"Don't even try it, bitch. You do not thank me for that."

"Okay, but I'm thinking it."

She laughed softly. "That's fine, as long as I don't have to face your unearned gratitude. Gross. By the way, I get the bat thing. I'll be acquiring one of my own ASAP. We should get Zadie one too. She'd look so freaking cute chasing bad boys away, wouldn't she? Penelope should probably also have one for when Gabe gets too comfortable."

I snorted, not even close to processing how I was in bed with Elena Sanderson, kind of snuggling. If I tried to wrap my head around it, my head would undoubtedly explode. I focused on the fact that I felt safe and calm and in control. Then, I went to sleep.

* * * * * * * * * *

"WHERE IS IT? WHERE the fuck is it?" I yanked my entire underwear drawer out of my dresser and dumped the contents on my bed. My lockbox was there, but it was painfully empty. All that work, those late nights, missing sleep, getting my ass groped, filthy old men and entitled young ones—all for nothing. *Nothing.*

Zadie was hovering inside my door, watching me destroy my room. She'd tried to help at first, but when I became more frantic, she'd stood back, probably afraid I'd tip her over in my search.

"I'll call Elena. She might have an idea," Zadie offered, hurrying from the room.

Clothes and papers were strewn on every surface. I'd checked nooks, corners, crannies, trash cans, backpacks, everywhere. The fact was, I distinctly remembered the fat stack of cash being in my lockbox last night, and now, it was gone. I wasn't a naturally trusting person, but when Zadie promised she hadn't taken it, I believed her. I didn't really suspect Elena either.

There was one person who'd been in my room last night. One person creepy enough to go rifling through my underwear drawer. Daniel had had plenty of opportunity to take my money. But what the hell could I do? I had no proof, and since he was probably just as rich as Elena and Theo, he really had no reason to steal from me, other than the fact that he was a complete and total asshole.

Zadie came back, her phone held limply in her hand. "I called."

"No answer?"

She slumped against the doorjamb. "No. I heard her ringtone coming from her room. She must've forgotten her phone when she left for her parents' this morning."

"Shit." I sank down to the floor, defeated. "Shit, shit, shit."

Zadie came to sit beside me. "I have a little I could give you—"

"No." I shook my head. "No. Thank you, though. A little won't be enough. I need all of it, especially because I'm going to be late. Reno really hates when I'm late."

One time last summer, my bus was delayed. I showed up an hour late to make my payment, and Reno added an extra thousand to the next one. Just like that, because he could. Because he knew I understood what he would do if I protested.

I glanced at my clock, already knowing what I'd find. Luciana and I had spent the day together. I'd missed her something fierce, more than normal, so I didn't take her back home until almost four. Then I'd rushed back to my dorm to grab my cash, only to find it gone. I'd spent so much time checking every corner of the suite, it was now the time I should have been at Reno's, and I was empty-handed.

All day, I'd been having fun with my sister, and now, I was fucked.

"Can you ask Theo? He could probably give you the money," Zadie suggested.

The idea of asking Theo for money made me sick, especially after my whole speech about him not being good enough for me. I couldn't bring this to him. We weren't together. We weren't even friends anymore. And I had pride. There was no way I'd tuck tail and beg.

"No. I'm not asking Theo. I'm finding Daniel and getting back what he stole. I'm not allowing him to screw me over." Determined, I hopped up and pulled Zadie with me. "You don't have to come."

She looked at me cockeyed. "Uh, yeah I do. I'm not letting you go alone."

My phone rang, sending my shoulders to my ears. I didn't look. If it was Reno, he really wouldn't like my answer. If it was anyone else...well, I didn't have time.

With my bat in hand, Zadie and I charged across campus. My heart thrashed like a wild beast in my chest. It was probably best Zadie was with me because my vision had gone red with images of my bat crashing into Daniel's head like a walnut.

Crack.

Zadie wouldn't let me be crazy. Having her by my side would remind me where I was, why I was here, how much was on the line.

It was déjà vu, arriving at the frat house, a few guys drinking beers on the porch. One asked if I needed help, I laughed and told him hell yes I did, then I charged right by him with Zadie at my heels, gunning for the stairs.

Of course, I had no idea which room belonged to Daniel, but I knew someone who did. Deacon's door was cracked. I pushed it the rest of the way open with my bat. He was on his bed, laptop propped in front of him, the distinct sounds of porn coming from the speakers.

"Oh, gross. Are you seriously jerking off with the door wide open?"

Deacon slammed his laptop shut and stuffed a pillow in his lap. "Who keeps letting you in?"

I flicked his question away with my fingers. "I'm not here for you. One question, then you can fetch that dirty sock from under your bed and continue enjoying your Saturday night festivities."

He peered over my shoulder at Zadie. "Who's the fatty? She's kind of cute."

Without a moment's hesitation, I brought my bat down on his footboard, sending splinters of wood flying up. Deacon scrambled to his feet, wild-eyed, flailing his arms around. His erection was still going strong, poking out the top of his sweatpants kind of impressively.

"You're crazy, bitch!" he cried. "You're so paying for that."

I pointed to his crotch with the bat. "What kind of universe gives a dick like that to a medium dude with a losing personality? Is this a joke? If so, I want a refund. It's not funny."

"Helen," Zadie whispered. "We don't have time."

I turned to her. "You have all the time in the world, sweet muffin. It's my time that's run out." I swiveled back to Deacon. "All right. Now that I've complimented your dick, tell me which room Daniel's in. He and I need to have a little chat."

Staring at me with wary eyes, Deacon cupped his cock. "I could tell you, but—"

"Oh, I'm sorry." I smacked the bat against my palm. "Did it seem like I was giving you a choice? Tell me where he is."

Deacon licked his lips. "He's out on his parents' yacht all day. Incommunicado. I don't know if he owes you money or whatever, but don't expect to hear from him before tomorrow." He got brave and took a couple steps toward me. "Now, you need to fucking leave. Unless you want to help me with my *nice dick.* Either of you works for me."

"You are a disgusting person." I raised my chin. "I need to get inside Daniel's room."

He leveled me with a hard stare. "Never going to happen. Even if I had a key, I'd never give it to you."

I rested the bat on my shoulder, rethinking my approach. Maybe I should have been nicer. It was just that seeing Deacon's dick was triggering. Actually, Deacon's whole face was triggering, if I was being real.

"Is there someone I can talk to who has a key? Daniel has something of mine and I need it back ASAP."

With a smirk on his stupidly medium face, Deacon shrugged. "No one's letting you in his room, I promise you that."

Zadie tugged on the back of my shirt. "Let's go. We'll think of something else. We'll figure it out."

I let her pull me out into the hall, nearly hauling back when Deacon gave me a smart-ass wave. God, that kid was going to get his ass beaten sooner rather than later, I just hoped I was there to witness the smugness being punched right off his stupid face.

Zadie kept her hand on my back as we retreated out of the house. We almost made it to the front door when I heard my name from behind me. I tried to keep going, but then Theo was there, touching my shoulder, making me look at him. A whimper built in the back of my throat, escaping before I could swallow it down.

Theo's head jerked at the sound. "What's going on? Did you come to see me?"

I shook my head. "I don't have time to talk."

"We have to go," Zadie agreed.

Theo moved in front of me, blocking the door. "Who were you here to see? Deacon?"

"No. And I seriously can't get into this right now." My hands were shaking. If Theo noticed, if he saw how distraught I truly was under my layers of bravado and fight, he'd try to get involved, and I couldn't allow that. Not Theo. Not with this.

"You're upset." Now, he was getting in my face, dipping down to examine me.

"I can't, Theo." Those three words were imploring. Based on the way he stilled and stared hard at me without breathing, he'd heard my plea.

"Let me help. *Please*, Helen."

I shook my head again. "I've got it covered. I always do."

He brought his hands up to my face, cupping my jaw with the barest touch. If I'd been less distracted by what I had in store for me tonight, I would have batted him away. We were definitely not in a place where he had the right to touch me like that. But I didn't bat him away. In fact, I may have leaned into his palm just a little.

"What the hell is going on?" he whispered harshly.

I took a step away from him. "Nothing, really. The same as always."

"Fuck, baby. Can we talk? I need to talk to you."

Zadie steadied me with a hand on the center of my back. She also reminded me we couldn't be here anymore.

"Tomorrow, maybe? I have to work tonight."

Theo's jaw hardened. "I'll pick you up."

"No, we're not doing that. I have Carina. I don't need a ride."

A beat passed, then I was in Theo's arms. He held me firm against his chest, and his mouth hit the side of my head. Batty dangled uselessly from my fingertips.

"Some shit is obviously going down right now." His lips were moving against my temple, murmuring low for only me to hear. "You don't have to like me or forgive me to let me help you out."

I ran my hand down the length of Theo's spine, his muscles flexing under my palm. It would have been easy to give in. To let

Theo handle my problems. But then what? I didn't want him to see me as an endless stream of problems he had to solve. I didn't want to be the girl who beat the shit out of boys and cars and beds when things didn't go her way. Not to Theo.

"If I don't get it sorted tonight, I'll think about it." I pulled back, and Theo's hold loosened. "I really do have to go. Work and all that jazz."

His chin lowered, finding my eyes again. "If I don't hear from you, I'm coming for you."

Maybe I'd let him come for me. I liked the sound of that.

"Okay."

Then Zadie and I were off, her pulling, me pushing. It wasn't that I was in a hurry to do what I had to do, it was just that I'd like to make it through the night with my kneecaps intact and my sister not burned to a crisp.

"Now what?" she asked.

I pushed down my fear, disgust, disappointment at where I was and what I had to do. I'd been doing that my whole life, so I was pretty good at it by now.

"If I strip tonight and do a couple lap dances, I'll be able to make enough."

I'd have to do more than a couple lap dances, but that was okay. As long as I had the money to pay Reno, I'd do almost anything.

"I'm sorry, Hells. I know you hate it."

"I can't think about it, Z. I just have to do it, get the money, and then...I don't know. I'll get over it. I always do."

I'd just add this night to the dark corner where I kept memories that were so vile, they'd drag me into an abyss if I spent more than a second reflecting on them.

It would all be okay. If I kept telling myself that, I might start believing it.

Twenty-Four

Helen

I FOLLOWED ZADIE INTO our suite, my mind a whir of what I needed to grab on my way to work. It was nearing seven. I really needed to be on my bus as soon as I could bust out of here.

I didn't notice Zadie had stopped moving until I ran into her back. She whimpered and reached behind her to grab my hand. That was when I saw him. My heart stopped beating.

"Hello, Helen."

Amir had made himself at home in our living room, sitting comfortably in the armchair, his gun on his lap. His dark eyes were predatory, the mirth from the upturn of his mouth not coming close to reaching his gaze.

I got in front of Zadie, blocking her as much as I could from Amir's attention. "I know I'm late but—"

He waved me off. "I don't need reasons. You can give those to Reno and see if he's feeling forgiving. I'm just here to collect."

A storm lurched the insides of my belly. Swallowing back nausea, I squared my shoulders. "I had it. Someone went into my room and took my money when I was sleeping. I just need tonight to earn it—"

He sat forward, elbows on his knees. "Helen, Helen, Helen, come on. I do not care in the slightest. I don't want to be here, playing my brother's errand boy. Give me the cash, and I'll be on my way."

"I don't have it." I folded my arms over my chest to hide the shaking.

He arched a brow. "You don't have the cash you owe my brother and you're giving me attitude?"

"I'm not giving you attitude." I couldn't help the rise of my chin.

Amir chuckled darkly. "Baby girl, give me something to work with. I really don't want to do what I'll have to do if you don't pay." Amusement fell away, leaving the black hole that occupied Amir's insides. "But I will."

I swallowed hard. "I need a couple hours. I'm dancing tonight. I'll make what I owe Reno by the end of the night and bring it straight to you or him...whatever you want me to do."

It physically hurt me to kowtow to this man, but I was smart enough to know I had no choice. I would kiss ass for Luciana. I'd do anything to protect her sweet.

"Hmmm..." He sat back, rubbing his fingertip along the barrel of his gun. "How do I trust you'll do what you say?"

"I don't have a choice," I rasped.

"That's right, you don't." He stretched to peer around me. "If I let you leave this room, I'll need collateral."

I held my hands out to show him how empty they were. "I don't have anything. If I did, I would have given it to Reno."

He stared at me hard, then let his eyes travel to Zadie. "You'll come back for her."

My spine went ramrod straight. "No."

"Yes. Leave your friend here. I'll trust you to come back for her." He grazed his palm over his crotch. "You'll *want* to come back for her as soon as possible."

"No. I can't—"

Zadie ducked around me to stand beside me. "It's okay, Helen. I'll be fine."

Amir's eyes flared at the sound of Z's sweet voice. The interest I read in him made me want to scream. I'd done this to her. I'd pulled her into my filthy, low-life world, and now here we were, down in the dregs together.

"Yeah, Helen, she'll be fine." He nodded to the couch. "Come over here, little mama. Have a seat."

Zadie moved automatically. If Amir had touched her, I might have lost my mind, but he only watched. He also shoved his gun in the back of his pants. It barely loosened the noose around my throat by a millimeter, but at least I could breathe a little.

"If you hurt her—"

"You'll what? Brain me with your bat?" Amir canted his head, like he was truly interested in my answer.

I'd forgotten Batty completely. At some point, I'd let it drop to the floor.

"I'll ruin you, Amir." I had no idea how, but I knew I meant it all the way to my bones. If Zadie didn't walk away clean from this, none of us would be walking away.

His laugh was dry. "Get out of here. Shake that pretty ass and bring me my money. You don't need to worry about anything else."

"Zadie," I started to go to her, but Amir tsked and shot his arm out to block Zadie from me. "Zadie, I'm so sorry. I'll be back as soon as I can. I promise."

She blinked at me with shiny eyes. "I know you will. I'll be fine."

"That's right. Sweet little Zadie will be just fine with me. Maybe you'll come back and we'll be best friends."

I narrowed my eyes on Amir, who was leaning toward Zadie like he was interested. "Don't even think about it."

His gaze was like a whip on me. "This discussion is over. Get the fuck out."

"Zadie," I rasped.

"Go, Helen. I'm okay." She was holding herself straight, being brave, and it made me want to destroy the furniture. But her bravery gave mine a charge. If Zadie could do this, so could I.

"I'll be back soon," I swore.

Then I grabbed my stuff and ran.

· • • • • • • • • • ·

IT TOOK ME FIVE hours of shaking my tits, grinding on laps, and giving away pieces of myself to earn what I owed Reno. Every time I wanted to go backstage and curl into a ball, I thought of Zadie's brave little face, and it spurred me on.

Carina perched on my dressing table, crossing her long, shiny legs. "You did good tonight, babe."

I looked up from unbuckling my Lucite platforms. "I hate it."

"I know you do, but you're damn good at it." She squeezed my shoulder. "At least there weren't any of those Savage U shits out there tonight. Boys think they're big shots, then give me two dollars for a tip."

I shuddered. "I don't know how you do it every night."

"Life, babe. This is where it took me. It's not forever, but for now, it works. And I don't hate it the same way you do. It's a job for me, not a moral decision."

"I'm not judging you." I placed my borrowed heels on the table, scooting them close to Carina.

She palmed my crown. "Never thought you were. I'm just telling you how I can deal." She let go of me to press her hands together. "Now, are you sure you don't mind catching an Uber?"

Carina still had two more hours on her shift, but I was done. I'd covered my stripper gear with sweats and wiped off some of my lipstick, ready to run out the door. I assured Carina I was perfectly fine, then I booked it, my phone in hand, to order my Uber.

I made it to the other side of the parking lot, almost to the sidewalk, when a group of people started coming toward me.

Assuming they were headed to the club, I stepped out of their way to put in the order for my ride.

"Helen."

My head jerked up, and my stomach bottomed out. Reno, flanked by his goons and two women, had closed in on me while I hadn't been paying attention.

"I have your money. I'm sorry it's late, but something—"

Reno caught my hoodie in his fist, tugging me closer. "I'm not in the mood for your sad story. Payment is due at five p.m. When you don't pay me on time, it tells me you do not respect me."

I couldn't bring myself to lie and say I *did* respect him, so I took the cash from my pocket and shoved it at him. A goon took it from me, opening the envelope to count the bills.

"It's all there."

Reno glanced at the cash, then me. "With added late fee?"

My fists clenched, but I kept myself calm. "Yes, I included that."

The goon informed Reno the money was all there, then tucked the envelope in a hidden pocket inside his jacket.

"Good, good. Very good, Helen." Reno placed a hand on my shoulder, getting way too close. "Here's the thing, baby. This is your second late payment. You know how I feel about that. It makes me think you don't respect me and my business."

"I do. I had the money but someone—"

Head whipping to the side from the force of Reno's backhand, I tasted blood and fire. My hand flew to my burning face, but I had no chance to recover before he struck again, shoving me backward so hard, I skidded onto my ass.

Reno crouched down beside me, grasping my hair in his fist. "I don't give second chances, no matter how sweet of a cunt you have." His other hand went to my throat, squeezing tight enough to mostly cut off my air. I grappled with his hold, clawing at his hand. I couldn't die here. Not with Zadie waiting for me at the dorm and Luc counting on me. This couldn't be my end.

When my vision started to go black, he let me go, and I fell on my back, gasping for air. Reno towered over me, his expression ugly yet bored as he spit on me.

"I own you, Helen. You're lucky I don't hit women, baby, or you'd be hurting a lot worse tomorrow." The two women came forward, one reeling back her leg and connecting to my ribs before I could brace for it. "Jackie and Chantal don't have anything against hitting other bitches, though."

He let them loose on me. I got to my hands and knees, only to be kicked back down. My cheek hit the pavement so hard, I saw stars. One of the women kicked me again and again, and I knew if I didn't get up, they'd kill me. I just knew it.

Wheezing for air, I pushed up, getting my knees under me again. I took a blow to the back of my thigh, another to my hip, but I didn't fall. My vision dotted when another boot struck me in the ribs, but I was determined to stand. I had to get to my feet, or I'd die. I'd die at a strip club and be another sad headline. I'd be reduced to a dead stripper. Luc would have to remember me that way. Zadie...oh, I couldn't even think of what would happen to Zadie. I had to get up. I had to get out of here.

I was on my knees, kneeling in front of Reno. I looked up at him, but he wasn't even paying attention to what was happening to me. He was chatting with his goons like they were out for coffee. I opened my mouth to scream, but it never came.

A pointy-toed boot connected with my jaw, sending me flying back. My vision flashed white, and my brain went hazy. Everything became dull, far away, like I was underwater. The hits stopped, then voices faded. It took me some time to understand it was over. Reno and his crew had left me lying there.

I didn't know if I could stand, but my hands worked. I took my phone from my pocket, hitting the first contact I recognized. He answered on the second ring.

"Helen?"

"Lock...please, I need help."

Twenty-Five

THEO

SHE DIDN'T CALL ME.

That shouldn't have been my first thought when Lock told me my girl needed me, but it was. It didn't come from a place of jealousy, but a realization of how far I needed to climb to get back to her. My tiger had been hurt, left in a parking lot bleeding, and I wasn't her one phone call.

Lock met me at the door of her suite, placing a hand on my chest to hold me back. "I need you to go in calm."

My jaw twitched. "Is it bad?"

"Fucking awful, man." He captured my eyes, ensuring I heard what he said. "But she's awake and being stubborn, so I think she'll be okay."

"Why is she not in the hospital? Where are the cops?"

"Did you not hear the part about her being stubborn? She wouldn't let me take her. She was in more of a panic to get back here to Zadie. Wouldn't tell me why, though."

"Is Zadie okay?"

"She's fine."

I pushed against his hand. "Let me in."

"Are you going to be cool?"

"I'm going to try."

He shook his head. "This isn't about you, man. I see you steaming about not being her phone call. You need to let that go. That was her pride on her mind, not her favoring me over you. You feel me?"

"I feel you, but if you don't move out of my way and let me get to her, I won't be cool anymore."

Lock raised his hand and stepped back from the door, and I flew inside, straight to Helen's room, taking a deep breath before I went in. It would do me no good to barge forward like the feral animal raging under my skin.

I reined it in. Not much, but enough that I could face what I needed to face on the other side of the door.

Helen was sitting up on her bed, bags of peas and a couple ice packs scattered on her bare torso. Zadie was beside her, holding ice to her cheek. Above it, she was bloody and scraped, the skin around her eye already turning black. Her other cheek was bright pink with a cut down the middle. Her throat was shadowed in bruises.

Shit. I wasn't strong enough for this. How could I be calm when I was caught in a hurricane of fury?

But then Helen's hand shot out to reach for me, and I came back. She needed me, so I went to her, kneeling on the floor, taking her hand in mine.

"Baby," I gritted. "What the fuck?"

"Hey. Don't talk to her like that," Zadie protested.

"I'm not." I brought our joined hands to my forehead. "Jesus, Helen. You need to go to the hospital."

"No. Please, Theo," she whispered. "I just need to sleep."

"I had some leftover prescription Tylenol from when I got my wisdom teeth out." Zadie stroked Helen's hair. "She took some a little bit ago. It should kick in soon."

"Thank you." I kissed Helen's knuckles. "You should go rest, Z. I'll take care of her. I'm here now."

Helen needed soft. It was next to impossible to give it to her with the violence boiling in my blood, but I would. Whether she agreed or not, whether I'd even earned it, Helen was *mine*. That meant I would take care of her however she needed. Right now, she needed me to leash it all.

Later, when she was feeling better, less vulnerable, I'd unleash the rage in my veins. I had no choice.

After heavy protest, Zadie left me with Helen. Lock poked his head in, said he was leaving but would be back in the morning to check in. Then, it was just the two of us. I stretched out on the bed beside her, afraid to touch her anywhere. I'd already caused her enough pain. I wouldn't do it again.

Her head lolled to the side. "I guess you've been proven right."

"What?"

She pointed at herself. "Trash. Jumped in a strip club parking lot after I shook my ass for strangers."

"No. I'm not letting you take that on. I never thought you were trash. I said shit I shouldn't have based on a past that has nothing to do with you." I stroked her hair like Zadie had. "Someone hurt you, baby. You don't get to take the blame. That's on them. The way I hurt you is on me. It's not you, Helen. You didn't deserve any of it."

She leaned into my hand, her lids at half-mast. "You just think that because your dad and stepmom like me."

"No. I always knew that. My head got lost for a while, but that was always my problem, never yours." I leaned over, touching my lips to her forehead. "Quite fucking honestly, my dad liking you is in the minus column."

"You say that, but I know you wouldn't stand by me if your dad didn't approve. I know it, Theo."

"You're wrong, baby. It's up to me to prove that to you."

She sighed, scooting down slightly. "I think the drugs are kicking in."

I huffed a quiet laugh. "I think so too."

"I might sleep." She grabbed my hand. "Stay, please."

"Wild horses, baby. They'd have to drag me away, and even then, I'd be back."

"Mmm...okay, Theo. Don't make empty promises to the injured, drugged up girl. Not nice."

"Go to sleep, Helen."

"'Kay."

She laid down, and after some pained moans, drifted off. Her brow pinched every few minutes, but her breathing stayed deep and even. I watched her for hours in the dark, counting her breaths, tucking her close when she whimpered. My baby was hurting, and I'd never felt so helpless.

Go*damn*, I was angry. I only vaguely knew what had happened, no details, but someone was going to answer for this. I was almost glad Helen hadn't called the cops. That left me clear to handle this on my own.

I must've dozed off at some point in the night, although I didn't remember it. I woke to Helen slipping out of bed. Or trying to, at least. I snagged the back of her hoodie.

"Come back. Anything you need, I'll get for you."

She glanced at me over her shoulder, her hair curtaining most of her face. "Bathroom, Theodore. I probably have to do that myself."

We both froze at her use of Theodore. I didn't say a word, though. No way was I spooking her out of calling me that again.

"Want me to carry you?" I offered, sincere as fuck.

She snorted. "I can make it. Thanks, though." Thankfully, she was walking instead of limping, although her movements seemed to be stilted.

A minute passed before the door to the bathroom slowly creaked open, but Helen didn't come out. "You okay?" I asked.

"Yeah." She peaked around the door. "I just need you to know I look a lot worse than I feel. Do you believe me?"

My fingers curled at my knees. "If you say you're telling me the truth, I believe you."

"Okay." She stepped around the door and rushed to the bed, climbing onto my lap and burying her face in my neck. "You're going to freak out."

I held her close, keeping my embrace careful. I had no idea how badly her ribs hurt, or the rest of her. "I saw you last night. I already have an idea, baby."

She hit my shoulder with her chin. "You can't call me baby."

"Helen," I breathed out a low laugh, "you're in my lap. A place you put yourself. I'm calling you baby because that's what you are. You're my baby, my little tiger. I haven't been taking care of you, but that's over. Even if you're not up for forgiving me, I'm still going to be taking care of you."

"I don't know if I'm ready to forgive. All I know is you made me feel safe last night and right now."

I stroked up and down her back while my stomach roiled. "That's a lot. You *are* safe with me, baby. But I need to know what happened. Who did this?"

She shook her head. "You can't go after him. He'll kill you. If I hadn't had his money last night—" A rough tremble took over her entire body. "I think he would have killed me. And then he would have gone after my mom and sister."

"Amir?" I guessed.

"No. I mean, Amir was here, holding Zadie hostage while I was at work. But he isn't in charge of everything. His older brother, Reno, is. He's an absolute psycho." She pulled back, cupping my jaw. "Listen to me, Theo. You cannot go after Reno. He's untouchable to you. I need you to hear me."

I heard her, but I was distracted by her black eye, the crusty cut on her cheek, the other cheek swollen and abraded. Her neck bore finger-shaped bruises that made my blood boil and struck a fear like I'd never known in my heart. She wasn't broken, and she was still beautiful, but fuck, my girl had been banged up. I hadn't even looked at her torso yet.

"I hear you. I need you to hear that I'm not letting this stand. You're not going to owe that man money anymore. Your connection with him is over."

She slumped against my chest. "I owe him a lot of fucking money. With interest...it's going to take me until I graduate and have access to my trust to pay him off. I've got years of this over my head."

"No, Helen." Taking her head in my hands, I tipped it back carefully. "Listen to me. I am going to handle it. You have nothing more to worry about. That part of your life ceases to exist now that I'm here."

Her chin trembled, but she clamped down on her bottom lip to make it stop. "I won't let you do that. I know you're working now, but you don't have the kind of mon—"

I covered her mouth with mine, taking what I needed and giving back to her. Her gasp allowed me to delve my tongue between her lips, sipping her taste and letting it spread through my veins like a shot of pure heroin. Helen was calm, smooth, euphoric. Nothing had been right without her.

"Shut up," I murmured against her lips. "No more."

"We're not kissing, Theo. I'm not there with you."

"I know. I jumped the gun, but I needed you to shut your mouth, baby. This isn't your worry anymore. I'm taking it."

I didn't have the money, but I'd find it. There were myriad paths I could take from here, but none of them involved me standing by while Helen gave more and more of her money, time, or self to the man who'd left her beaten in a parking lot last night.

"I stripped last night. Not only that, I lap danced. My ass was grinding on multiple men. I shook my tits in their faces. My friend Carina is a stripper, and she makes it look good. I admire her. When I do it, I feel like I'm never going to be clean again.

But that's the thing. I'll do it again and again. Your promises are nice, but this is reality."

As soon as she laid out what she saw as facts, she climbed off my lap and went to her dresser. She was digging around, but not taking anything out. I got the clear sense she needed space from me, but I'd already given her a hell of a lot. That was done too.

I crossed the room, bracing my hands on either side of her on the edge of the dresser. My chest was pressed to her back, and I bent down to nuzzle the side of her face.

"I didn't know I wasn't breathing until I met you."

Her shoulders stiffened, but she didn't move otherwise. I brushed her hair to the side, leaving a kiss on the bruise mottling her neck.

"I've been in survival mode since I can remember. My body was my weapon. But the war I was fighting wasn't worthy of the sacrifices I made. The training, the starving, the doping." My fingers skimmed her shoulder, and her head tilted, giving me enough of her to see she was hanging on my every word. These were things I'd never said out loud. Thoughts I'd never allowed to fully form for fear they'd tear down what I'd built.

"I would've done anything to get out of my old life. That meant when I moved here and the coaches my dad hired introduced me to performance-enhancing drugs, I took them without question. When they taught me how to game the system, I followed their rules to a T. The testing was different in college, but I heard of this guy who had access to something new—something the tests didn't pick up."

"Amir," she breathed.

"Right. Amir. I took what he gave me blindly. Injected it straight into my muscles without concern for the consequences. The only consequence I gave a shit about was being shipped back to my old life. I was all wrestling, every hour of my life was focused on the goal of being the best, ensuring my dad had a reason to keep me here. I lost Abby, but I kept going and going until I ended up in the hospital with what I thought was a heart attack. It wasn't, but it was a wake-up call. Because what was the point of turning myself into a weapon if my own blade was being shoved deeper into my chest with every stride I made?"

"Theo, you don't have to tell me this."

Taking her by the shoulders, I spun her to face me. "I need you to understand why I get it. I'm going to make it so you never have to strip again, but I also want you to know I get why you had to."

Her eyes met mine. They were so damn pretty, yet so damn sad. "When Amir told me about the doping, I was disappointed in you."

I nodded, taking the weight of the way I'd let her down onto my shoulders. "That's fair. If I were a better man, I'd send back every trophy I ever won. All my victories are unclean. I'm not going to say I didn't deserve them, because I trained my body like a machine, sacrificed almost everything, and I was damn good, but I'll never know if I would have won without the drugs."

Something hard in her expression fell away. "I'm an asshole for being disappointed. I realize that now. I have no room to judge you for doing what needed to be done to survive. And I guess that includes dumping me—"

"Shut up, Helen. There's no excuse for how I treated you. Don't give me an out. I won't take it, not when I haven't proven to you I'm willing to stand by you and stand up for you. I asked you for soft, but the second I needed to give you strong, I failed. That won't happen a second time."

She shoved at my shoulder. "Hey, Theo, a good way to never get back in my good graces is to continue telling me to shut up."

I swallowed back a laugh. "Normally, I'd kiss you, but you told me we're not kissing yet."

"We're not. And don't say yet like I'm a foregone conclusion. I have a lot going on in my head right now. I can't make any kind of decisions. You're telling me all these things, and I want to believe them, but I don't have it in me to trust pretty promises. So, now I'm thinking about going to work looking like I got hit by a bus wondering if I'll have to get on stage again because Daniel stole the little cushion I had—"

"Whoa, whoa, back up. Daniel? What are you talking about?"

She folded her arms over her chest. "Remember I told you the company you keep says a lot about you? That asshole you call a friend snuck into my room while I was sleeping, felt me up, and stole my stash of cash I needed to pay Reno."

Something came over me. A maelstrom of sizzling violence that made my skin feel ten times too small. Electricity charged through the air, sparking every time I took a breath.

Daniel. Touched. My. Girl.

"He's dead." I tore away from Helen, ripping her door open and storming for the exit. She was on my heels, calling my name, asking me to wait, but I'd waited long enough. She wouldn't let me go after Reno, fine. Daniel was another story. If she truly thought I'd let this stand, she hadn't been paying attention.

Lock was in the hall, poised to knock. "Helen?" he ground out.

"Stop him, Lock." Helen grabbed the back of my shirt like she had a chance of doing more than slowing me down. "Or go with him. He's going to kill him."

I jabbed a finger at Lock. "If you attempt to stop me, we are not going to be cool. Helen just told me a guy I live with touched her and stole her money, which led to," I waved at my battered girl, "this. I can't let that go. I don't have it in me."

Lock's hand came down on my shoulder. "I'm with you." He pointed to Helen. "Go back inside. Lock the door. One of us will be back when we can."

Helen grabbed for me, her eyes wide and shiny. "This isn't worth risking your future over. If you get arrested, I'll never forgive you."

I took her jaw in my hand, throwing every ounce of control I still had in keeping it gentle. "You make it easy to light the match, Tiger. Now watch me make it burn."

Twenty-Six

THEO

AS LOCK DROVE US across campus, his fury at what Helen had gone through, the way she'd been violated over and over, fed into mine. I was barely able to contain it all. My chest felt swollen, near cracking. My throat burned to bellow the rage churning inside me.

Lock's teeth had to be ground to dust by the time he parked half on the lawn, half on the curb in front of the house. A few guys were hanging on the porch, probably still drunk from the night before. I grabbed the first guy who crossed my path. Dick was his name. Or Colin. It didn't matter.

"I need you to get Daniel. Tell him he's wanted outside," I ordered.

Colin shrugged at my demand and sauntered into the house, calling out Daniel's name. Beside me, Lock cracked his knuckles and his neck.

A minute later, Daniel emerged, dressed in boxers, slippers, and a silk robe. He had a joint pinched between two fingers and a glass of orange juice in the other hand.

"Wow, what's the drama, Whitlock?" He practically stumbled down the steps. "Isn't it too early for this kind of thing?" He gestured to Lock with his cup-filled hand, spilling OJ over the top. "And what's with the lumberjack? Is he your hired muscle?"

My hands flexed at my sides. "You know why I'm here." Not a question. He obviously knew.

He leaned an elbow against the bottom rail. "This wouldn't have something to do with the practical joke I played on that stripper, would it? I'm impressed with how much money she earned off her sweet little body. It's all upstairs in my room. Why don't I go grab it and you can stuff it in her G-string? I heard she likes that."

"A joke?" I growled. "Was it a joke when you were feeling her up in her sleep?"

He chugged his orange juice, tossed the glass in the bushes, and sauntered closer. "Perhaps my sense of humor is more refined. I thought it was pretty fucking hilarious that your stripper girl was insulted about me copping a feel. I suppose I should have thrown some ones at her first. Is that what you do? Or do you have to shell out the big bucks for full service?"

Daniel was puffing on his joint when I swung at him, connecting solidly with the side of his head. The joint fell, and he staggered to the side, bouncing off Lock's puffed-out chest.

The guys on the porch took notice of what was going on, some getting up to come closer, others dashing inside, no doubt to alert the house of what was going down on the lawn.

He cupped his cheek, twisting an ugly look at me. "Oh, you're dead, Whitlock. Daddy won't save you now."

"Yeah? Is Daddy gonna save you when it comes out you like to creep into girls' bedrooms?"

He scoffed and spit on the ground. "No one cares about a whore, bro."

Lock's big hand fastened around the back of Daniel's skinny neck, giving it a sharp jerk. "Daddy's teat is going to run dry soon, boy. When his date-rapist son's misdeeds come to light to his board members, they're not going to be too happy."

Daniel's face flushed red, his expression flashing with fear he quickly plastered over with indignation. "Fuck you. I don't even know you. Get your filthy hands off me, you fucking ox. Shouldn't you have farm equipment yoked to your neck?"

Lock tossed him aside like a used cum rag. Daniel stumbled sideways, losing a slipper in the process. He laughed, like this was some big joke. To him, it probably was. People like Daniel could assault and steal from a girl one night, then wake up in the morning to spend the day on their parents' yacht without a second thought. It disgusted me that I'd been fighting tooth and nail to stay in a world filled with Daniels.

"I know you just by looking at you." Lock folded his thick arms, sweeping a look of loathing over Daniel and his silk robe. "Better to be an ox than a snake."

"Oh, please." Daniel threw his arms out to the side. "All this over a girl who's not worth *anything* and never will be, no matter what degree she earns? Once a whore, always a whore."

I took a step toward him, my muscles so taut they were vibrating. "Once a little bitch, always a little bitch."

Daniel smirked, like he was amused, glanced to the side at all the guys from our house watching with bated breath, then he charged. I met him before he could gain speed, sweeping his legs from under him and taking him down to the ground easily. He was high, lanky, lazy, and I was filled with righteous anger.

I was on him in a flash, knees on his arms, landing a blow to his jaw. "You don't deserve to breathe the same air as Helen Ortega." Another punch to his cheek. "She has more integrity in her pinkie than you'll ever have in your life, you spineless piece of shit."

He spat at me, saliva mixed with blood. "Fuck you and your whore. You're finished at this school, man."

"That's what you think?" My palm on his face, I mashed his head into the grass, grinding it back and forth while he screamed from his gut. "That's what you really think? You're nothing, Daniel. You have no power. No say in what happens to me or Helen. You're a sad excuse for a man."

He bucked under me, but he didn't even jar me. He wasn't a challenge. Beating him felt hollow, especially with him pinned down so easily.

"I know what color your girlfriend's nipples are, man. Ask Colin. He knows too."

With wild eyes, I found Colin. He held his hands up, backing away. "I don't know anything. My memory is wiped."

Daniel howled and craned his neck to see who else was around. By now, half the frats at Savage U were gathered to watch the show.

"Ask Duncan! He was there too."

Another guy took a similar stance as Colin, shaking his head. "I have no memories of that night. I must've hit my head or some shit."

"That's the right answer," I growled.

"Motherfucking pussies!" Daniel bellowed. "All of you, pussies!"

Dear god, I couldn't stand looking at his face, so I painted it red with a direct punch to his nose. Blood splattered at the sound of the crack, and it kept coming. My fists kept coming too, hitting soft and hard places alike. I was out of my mind with the need to see Daniel as nothing but pulp.

"Dude, get off him!" Someone grabbed at my shoulders, but I shrugged them off. I wasn't done. Not even close.

"Theo, he's had enough. Come on, man." Another pair of hands gripped my arm, this time with more force. I didn't need two arms to fuck Daniel up, though. I slapped him like a little bitch, sending his head sideways.

"Come on." Strong arms locked around me, hauling me forcibly off Daniel's prone, bloody form. He was alive and groaning, rolling to his side, which was unfortunate.

"I'm not done," I gritted out.

"You're done." Lock had me, dragging me several feet from Daniel. "He got the message. All the other assholes got it too."

No one was helping Daniel, not even Deacon, who'd been one of the voices telling me Daniel had had enough. Everyone was standing around, watching Daniel struggle to his feet. Most bore looks of distaste, aimed directly at Daniel. Not that most of these little shits were any better, they were just a little more discreet.

"He's not ruined."

"No," Lock agreed, "but if I know anything about how you feel for Helen, he will be. Just not like this."

I sagged, some of the fight leaving me. "You can let go of me. I'm not going to kill him."

Daniel was limping into the house anyway, everyone giving him a wide berth. I got the distinct impression it wasn't a show of respect, but more like a shunning. No one liked Daniel anyway, but after his show of indiscretion on our front lawn, I hoped they wouldn't be subtle in their dislike.

Deacon jogged over to me, his arms spread wide. "What the hell was that about?"

I narrowed my eyes on him, fury still burning low in my gut. If he stepped wrong, I'd make him feel it too.

"That was about Daniel disrespecting, touching, and stealing from my girl. You've done all but one of those things to her, so you need to know I'm watching you. If you so much as breathe in Helen's direction, you're dead to me."

He flinched. "Helen? Helen Ortega, the drug dealer, is your girlfriend?"

Lock growled low behind me. Deacon's gaze jerked to him, then back to me. Color leached from his face. "You're serious, aren't you?"

"Deadly. And her name is Helen. All that other shit is in the past. If you ever refer to her, it will be with respect, and it will be by her name."

He blew out a heavy puff of breath. "Does your dad know?"

"No, but I do not give a shit what he thinks."

Deacon gestured to the house. "He's going to find out."

I lifted a shoulder. "Again, I do not care."

He tucked his hands in his pockets, giving me a long look. "I hope you know what you're doing."

"This is the first time in a long time I know exactly what I'm doing."

That was the truest thing I'd ever said. For years, I'd gone along, letting others take the lead. My coaches, my dad, even my friends. In my old life, the one in the lead was the first one to fall. It took meeting Helen and being shaken out of that mindset to see I didn't like the direction I was being taken by the people I'd willingly given the reins to. This was me taking them back. My path had never been more clear.

Twenty-Seven

Helen

AN HOUR AFTER THEO and Lock had left my suite, intent on murder, Lock arrived back. He told me Daniel had received a message, Theo hadn't been arrested, and everyone was still breathing. Call me a barbarian, but knowing Theo beat the hell out of Daniel in my honor sent a shot of pleasure up my spine. That was the only type of justice a girl like me could expect to have—and Theo had given that to me.

You make it easy to light the match, Tiger. Now watch me make it burn.

Of course, that pleasure was tempered with his absence. Lock said Theo had some things to take care of and he'd be in touch with me soon, but still, he wasn't here.

I could admit I wanted him with me. I hadn't forgiven him. I didn't know if I could go down that road with him again. But his presence made me feel safe in a way no one else did. Not even Lock, who I had no doubt would throw down for me in a heartbeat because he was that kind of man. Theo's protectiveness came from a different place, something I'd never experienced and couldn't name, but when he gave it to me, it was like being shrouded in a snug, warm blanket.

Lock bought pizza for Zadie and me, then stayed with us to eat. We watched a couple movies, Lock in the armchair, Zadie and I snuggled on one of the love seats. None of us really talked, but we didn't make a move to leave each other's company either.

Theo texted halfway through the second movie.

Theo: *Hey...I'm taking care of some things. It's taking longer than I thought, but it's getting done. Are you with Lock?*

Me: *I'm fine. I'm with Lock and Zadie. Don't worry about me.*

Theo: *I am worried about you. I don't know if I can make it back there tonight. Are you going to be okay to sleep?*

Me: *I didn't expect you to come back. I'm good. I'll probably take Zadie's meds again and pass out. I'll see you in class tomorrow.*

Theo: *You're safe, baby. Nothing is going to touch you again. I promise you that. I'll see you tomorrow.*

The door burst open just as I shoved my phone in my hoodie pocket. Elena flounced in, threw her weekend bag on the floor, and let out a dramatic sigh. Then her eyes landed on us. First Lock, because he was unmissable, then Zadie, and finally me. Her jaw dropped.

Her finger made a circle in the air as she pointed to my face. "That better be from a car accident."

I shook my head. "My mom's loan shark."

Elena charged at me, took my chin in her hand, and moved my head back and forth to examine me from every angle.

"This is unacceptable. Is this person dead now?"

I shook my head. "No."

"Why not?" Her attention shifted to Lock. "Who are you?"

He barely glanced at her. "Lachlan."

Elena stared at him, then me. "I need a hell of a lot more information. Begin with the massive man occupying my favorite chair and fill in the rest."

Lock abruptly rose to his feet. "I'm going to go." He lowered his chin, capturing my gaze. "I'm five minutes away. Anything you need, you call. Don't hesitate. Even if you want me to sit in your living room while you sleep. Do you hear me?"

I nodded, the backs of my eyes stinging. "I hear you, dude. Thank you."

He left quietly but quickly, closing the door behind him with a gentle snick. Elena rushed over and locked it, then she turned back to me, her hands on her hips.

"Tell me everything so I know how many hit men I have to ask my dad to hire."

It took a surprisingly short amount of time to recount the trauma that had punched me in the gut over the last twenty-four hours. When I ended the tale of events with Daniel having the shit beat out of him, Elena's smile was satisfied.

She waved her hand in front of her. "Back up just a sec. I need to know what went down with the whole hostage situation."

Zadie's cheeks went pink.

When I'd gotten back last night, Amir had been gone. I'd barely been able to stand, but the first thing I did was check over Zadie while she tried to bat me away so she could take care of me. We were both crying messes, but Zadie hadn't been injured, and her tears seemed to be solely over me. Once Lock got us in my bed, me covered in ice packs and drugged up, Zadie promised Amir hadn't hurt her, but that had been all she'd offered.

"It was awkward and kind of scary." Zadie shrugged. "He didn't take his gun out again, so that was good. He used his phone a lot, we talked a little, and um...I don't know. He got a call, I think from his brother, then he rushed out of here really fast. That was right before Helen and Lock got back."

Elena drummed her perfect nails on the arm of her chair. "That's it? Your first time being held hostage, and that's the extent of your story?"

"I'm kind of hoping it's my only hostage experience." Zadie tucked her hair behind her ear. "That would be great."

Elena wagged her finger at Z. "I think something else happened. One day, once we've dismantled the corrupt patriarchy in Savage River and shoved dicks down Daniel and Reno's throats—perhaps each other's, I haven't decided—I'll get the full story from you."

Zadie released a sound that was a cross between a whimper and a laugh. "There's no story."

Elena's eyes narrowed to suspicious-looking slits. "Okay, babe. I'll drop it for now. Now, let's discuss everything I know about Daniel that could positively ruin him."

•••••••••••

WITH ELENA'S GRAPHIC REVENGE plots as bedtime stories and Zadie's meds, I got a full night of dreamless sleep, so by Monday, I was aching, but feeling close to human. My hoodie mostly covered the bruises on my throat. I couldn't do much about my face, but if anyone asked, I'd tell them it came from a rad skateboarding accident.

Thankfully, everyone minded their fucking business because the meds wore off by midday, and I was a grumpy, aching bitch. My head was down on the table when Lock sat down beside me in Shakespeare. I grunted at him in greeting. He laughed back.

Except that low, lovely laugh wasn't Lock's.

I peeked up, finding Theo's gentle smile. "You're not Lock."

He cupped the back of my head and leaned his face closer to mine. "Sorry to disappoint. I bribed him to switch seats with me today. How are you?"

"Bitchy."

He kissed my head. "Does it hurt, baby?"

"It doesn't feel great."

"One more class, then you can go home and take a nap. You can do it, Tiger."

I nodded. "Okay." His hand rested on top of the desk. I knew hands like that. Swollen and scabbed-over knuckles. Maybe it was how I grew up, but I liked it. His fighting hands turned me

on and sent a rush of heat between my legs. I pulled his hand to
my lips, touching his knuckles gently. "Thank you."

"You don't have to thank me." He dragged his thumb across
my lip once. "It was my pleasure. Do you understand me? I loved
every second of delivering that message to Daniel."

Watch me make it burn.

Warmth pooled low in my belly at the savagery of that
statement. "I wish I'd seen it."

His grin was smooth and wicked, and he gave me the kind of
look I never knew he had in him—a look that said he understood
exactly why I wished I'd been there to see him beat the hell out
of Daniel, and it wasn't only about retribution.

Theo helped me sit up and scooted his chair closer so he could
drape his arm around the back of mine. And I let him. I was
feeling all kinds of vulnerable and strange, and having Theo
near muted all that. I barely paid attention to a thing Davis
said, but the hour went by fast anyway.

After class, he walked me back to my dorm and followed me
inside without asking if it was okay. When I told him I needed to
nap, it felt natural when he had lain with me, even though we'd
never just lay in my bed together without it leading somewhere.

We were face to face, barely touching. Our feet were stacked
together, and Theo's fingertips were grazing over my injuries.

"I have the money Daniel stole," he murmured. "You don't
need to worry about working this week, okay?"

An anvil lifted off my chest. "Okay. That's good. I was
wondering if I could play the sympathy card for tips, but dudes
don't really come to strip clubs to hear our life stories."

His exhale was heavy. "You're not working there much longer.
Do you hear me?"

I touched his mouth with my fingers. "Shut it. We're having a
nice moment. If you start trying to act like my daddy, I'll have to
be a brat."

"You just got the shit beat out of you, baby. How can you think I'll let you go back there?"

"The strip club didn't do it. Reno did. And guess what? I'll have to go back to him too. This is me. There's no escaping it. Not yet anyway."

He cupped my cheek. "Soon. This will be over soon."

"Stop it, Theo. Please?"

He kissed my forehead and pulled me close so I was tucked under his chin and cocooned in his arms. "Go to sleep."

• • • ● • ● • • •

BY THURSDAY, THE PAIN had eased enough—thanks in part to daily naps snuggled with Theo—that I was pissed. I wasn't the type of girl who took my hits lying down. If I got knocked on my ass, I came up swinging.

Admittedly, this had been a pretty big hit, but I was done feeling sorry for myself. I wasn't going to be afraid of my shadow just because a guy, who I already knew was scary, acted like a big scary guy. That wasn't a surprise, and I should have expected it. The fact that Reno, and by extension, Amir, had any power over my life, made me mad enough to want to break shit.

I needed to deliver a message to Reno, but there was no way I was doing it firsthand. I may have been pissed, but I wasn't stupid.

Amir lived off campus in a Cape Cod–style house with a big porch running along the front. It was surprisingly...housey for a gun-carrying drug dealer who was quite possibly a little psycho.

Like he knew I was coming, Amir was sitting on the porch, his feet kicked up on the rail. I climbed the steps, somewhat deflated I couldn't pound on the door and demand he come out and speak to me.

"You look like shit, baby girl." His face remained impassive, so I couldn't tell if he actually cared or not.

"No kidding. You should have seen the other guy." I snapped my fingers. "Oh, that's right, you've seen him. It was your brother who backhanded me, strangled me, then let his bitches loose to kick my ass. I almost forgot."

His jaw tightened for a beat, then he went back to being impassive. "My brother is not me."

I shrugged. "You're his little errand boy. Guilty by association, dude."

He dropped his feet, braced his elbows on his knees, and steepled his fingers. "I think you misunderstand, Helen, but I'll explain. I don't necessarily always agree with Reno's actions, but I am not your friend. You will not come to my home and disrespect me. Since you're injured, I'll let it pass, but I won't next time. Be sure there isn't a next time."

"Got it." Amir may have been the lesser of two evils, but this was a helpful reminder that he was still evil. "I wish I'd known you were a woman beater when I had a crush on you in high school. I would have gotten over you a lot faster."

Amir's nose twitched, and his lip curled into a snarl. "Helen…"

"No, no, I heard you. You'll beat me bloody if I get too mouthy. My lips are sealed."

He gave me a long look from beneath a furrowed brow, then kicked the chair beside him. "Sit. Talk. Then leave."

I sat, only because it was easier not to stare down at him and the walk off campus had worn me out more than I would have ever admitted out loud.

I took a filled envelope out of my backpack. "This is for next week. I want it out of my possession so I don't have to worry about it anymore. Then I need to rework my loan payments. I don't think I can keep up the—"

"Keep it." He pushed the envelope back to me. "No more payments."

I clutched the envelope hard, suddenly afraid again. Was Reno calling in the entire loan? Holy Christ, was he actually going to kill me and I'd just served myself up on a silver platter?

"What the hell does that mean?" I couldn't even pretend to keep the shake out of my voice.

Amir pressed his fingertips together, frowning hard at me. "Obviously not what you're thinking. Chill, girl. I got a visit from your boy on Sunday. He inquired how much you owed. I told him. He was back the next day with the cash. I'm surprised he hasn't had you down on your knees to thank him."

My mouth fell open in shock. What the ever-loving fuck? "I owe like thirteen *K*."

Loan shark interest was no joke. I could actually kill my mother for thinking it was a great idea to borrow money from Reno. I would have questioned what had been going through her mind, but I knew her well enough to know the answer: not much.

"Owed, baby. Past tense. He got you out from under that bitch."

"Why?" I breathed out.

Amir canted his head, frown deepening. "Baby..." he cooed, "I know you're smarter than that. That boy came here with bruised knuckles, ready to throw down if he had to, and he wasn't doing it for his health. That was for *you*."

I still didn't understand, so maybe I wasn't so smart. "You're talking about Theo, right?"

He nodded once. "I thought he was a little pussy bitch. It's rare someone changes my mind, but I might be swayed by how he showed up for you. It'd have been better if he'd shown up a few weeks ago but can't change history."

I rubbed the center of my forehead, worried my brain had been more damaged from my beating than I'd thought. "Theo paid it all?"

"All of it." Amir unfolded from his chair and stood over me, his hand out to help me up. "I'm about done with this conversation, Hells Belles. Time for you to go."

I folded my arms around my middle. "Do me a favor."

"I'm not in the business of favors. I like things reciprocal and aboveboard."

I shot him a sharp look. "Considering you held my roommate hostage and terrorized her, you definitely owe me."

The look he gave me was even sharper. "Is that what she told you? I terrorized her?"

"She didn't have to. You had a gun on her, dude. That would terrify anyone, especially a girl like Z. What *did* you do to her for all those hours?"

He shut down in an instant, going back to his earlier impassiveness. "I think you should talk to Zadie about that. Tell me the favor you want, then you need to leave."

Worms squirmed in my stomach. What the hell had gone down while I was out of our suite? Zadie was acting normally, so it couldn't have been anything bad. Then again... I shoved the thoughts of what Amir could have done away. I couldn't deal with that. Not right now.

"If my mom comes around looking for money, tell her no. Pass the message to Reno too. The Ortegas are turnips, and you can't get blood out of us."

Amir raised a brow. "True...but now you've got a rich boyfriend, so—"

My hand was up, shooting through the air toward his face before I even thought about it. Amir intercepted me easily, lowering my arm to my side and holding it there. I hissed at him like a feral cat.

"Don't you even think about Theo. He's not my meal ticket, and he's not going to be yours either. He's off-limits to you and Reno. Remember what I said about ruining you? I'll find a way if you go after him—"

"Baby." A slow smile spread across Amir's face, which was pretty disconcerting. Amir wasn't a smiler. "That boy's got you, doesn't he? Good for you, Helen. I like that for you."

"I don't know—"

He shooed me off, his smile instantly dropping. "All right. I've got shit to do. You can go."

He walked into his house without a backward glance, and I started my long walk back to campus, my mind rushing.

What had Theo done?

What. Had. He. Done?

You make it easy to light the match...

Twenty-Eight

Helen

THEO WHITLOCK WAS HOT. That was a fact. No one could have told me otherwise.

Theo Whitlock doing manual labor? That was on another level. It was even more attractive than his swollen knuckles, and holy Christ, had they done things to me.

Add in coveralls tied at his waist, an oil-stained white undershirt, steel-toed boots, and I almost forgot why I was angry. I nearly threw out my reasons for staying away, keeping my distance, shutting him out behind a thick wall—especially when he came out from under the hood of the truck he'd been working on, wiped the sweat from his forehead with his forearm, and twirled a wrench around in his hand like a seasoned pro.

I was a blue-collar baby to my bones, and no amount of fancy education was going to change that. Theo, the mechanic, could get it. Not from me—I was mad at him for going against my wishes—but from someone.

Of course, I'd cut a bitch before that happened.

Savage U's garage wasn't exactly bustling. Theo was the only one on the floor. When I started toward him, he noticed me right away. He tossed his wrench into a toolbox and wiped his hands on the rag hanging from his hip, keeping his gaze on me.

"You're beautiful when you look like you want to murder me, Tiger," he greeted.

I stopped in front of him, hands on my cocked hips. "You paid my loan."

He instantly sobered, moving into my space. "Did someone come see you? I made it clear they had to leave you alone now. *Fuck.*"

"No, dude—"

"Not your dude. I'm not letting you put me back in that spot. Theodore."

"Theo." My eyes narrowed on him. "No one visited me. I went to Amir. Did you actually think I wouldn't find out?"

"No, I knew you would." He kept wiping his hand on the rag. "I was going to tell you. I was hoping to buy some time before I pissed you off again."

"I think you were hoping to buy me." I stepped into him, tipping my chin up. "Is that what you were hoping to do?"

He shook his head slowly. "If you actually think that, you haven't been paying attention. I don't think you really believe those are my intentions. Not after everything. Though, I get it's easier if I'm the bad guy."

"Why is that easier?"

"Because, baby," he picked up a lock of my hair with his stained fingers, and I almost shuddered, "if I'm not the bad guy, then you have to make a decision about me. Are you going to let me back in so I can prove I'm worthy? Or are you walking away for good?"

I knew without a second thought I didn't want to walk away. Not after he'd set the world aflame for me. Not when his presence was the only thing that made me feel truly safe. Not when he looked so fucking good with his head under a hood.

"I threatened to ruin Amir if he came for you."

Something like a growl emerged from Theo's throat. "Helen, wha—"

I pressed my hand to his chest. "How did you have that kind of money? Is that pocket change for you or did you have to ask your dad?"

It took him a second to answer. It was probably the swift change of topic, but I had a million questions and thoughts, and they were tumbling out.

"I sold my car."

"What?"

He nodded. "That's what I was working on Sunday and Monday. I had to get Miranda to agree to it since her name was on the title."

My teeth dug into my bottom lip. "Did you tell her about me?" I hated the thought of her knowing the trouble I'd gotten myself into. Even if it wasn't really my fault, I didn't want her to know.

"No, baby. I told her I had a friend in need. She offered to give me the money outright, but that didn't feel right, and I knew you wouldn't like it when it came out. Miranda tried to give me all the cash she got from selling the BMW, but I only let her give me enough to pay your loan. Then she bought me a Toyota because she's Miranda and she couldn't allow me not to have a car."

"A Toyota? How normal." I scrunched my nose, which made him release a low laugh.

"Living how the regular people live."

"Thank you," I whispered.

He tipped his chin. "You know you don't have to thank me. Not for looking out for you."

A man who'll burn down the world and rebuild it for you.

Theo was making light of what he'd done, but it didn't feel light to me. He'd gone from holding me all night, to beating Daniel, to selling his car so he could pay my loan. That wasn't light.

"Amir told me you have me, Theo." I sucked in a deep breath, looking him square in the eye. "So, no, I don't think you're the bad guy. I'm incredibly wary of letting you in and ending up in the same place where I'm cracked open and you're sucking up every drop of me while keeping yourself sealed tight. So, you, Theo Whitlock, need to decide, if I give you a chance, are you going to give me one too?"

"Yes." He took my hand from his chest and pressed his mouth to my palm. "If you give me you, I'll give you me. It's a shitty bargain on your part, but I'm hoping you make it anyway."

I almost laughed, but he was being real, so I held it back. "Why is it shitty?"

"Because, baby, I've got to deal with my dad, whether I want to or not. I might get kicked out of school and out of his life if he decides something I've done displeases him. I might be a mechanic for a while, or forever, if that happens. Your future's so bright, and mine is so up in the air, I don't know which way it'll land. That's why I'm a shitty bargain."

"I have to tell you, Theodore, the whole mechanic thing is working for me in a mega big way. If your dad chooses to fulfill his asshole prophecy and you spend the rest of your days in coveralls with stained fingernails, I'll be pleased I get to look at you and smell the oil on your skin." Raising up on my toes, I ran my nose along the collar of his shirt. He was all sweat, oil, and Theo. He'd been delicious before, but this was another level.

Before I could spend another second sniffing him, he took my head in his hands and pulled me away, a fierce expression on his face.

"You called me Theodore."

"I did." I caught my lip in my teeth, suddenly nervous. I'd called him that on purpose, but I'd kind of hoped he'd let me slide it in there without making it into a big deal. Not Theo, though. He noticed everything.

He lowered his head slowly, and I prepared for the crash. It didn't come. His lips found mine with a testing kiss, a caress that was so sweet, I had to squeeze my eyes shut to keep from bursting. I chased his mouth, needing more of what he was giving me. My fingers circled around his wrists, then stroked up his forearms.

There was something different about the way we were touching each other. I didn't remember a time anyone had ever been tender with me, but I recognized that was what was happening here. There weren't words in my vocabulary for how this felt, but I liked it. I liked it so much, I was going to keep chasing this tenderness between us and hover around it to protect it.

He spoke against my lips. "I missed you so fucking much, Tiger. The second you left my car that night, I wanted you back. I'm not going to make the same mistake twice with you."

I nodded, my forehead rolling over his. "I really missed you too. I can't tell you how relieved I am that underneath the bullshit and mistakes, you're who I thought you were."

Something clattered nearby, and voices approached. Theo and I drew apart, holding on to each other until the last possible second. He shot me a twinkly-eyed grin, and I was donezo.

"I have to go before I do illegal things to you in front of your coworkers."

A deep, lovely laugh burst out of him. "Jesus, I would have put on coveralls weeks ago if I knew they were the ticket to your heart."

I arched a brow. "No, dude, not my heart. She's a tougher nut to crack. My pants will absolutely fall apart for a man who works with his hands."

Theo's grin wavered. "A man? Any man?"

"Don't fish, Theodore. You know damn well my pants have only dissolved for you recently." I hitched my bag higher on my shoulder. "I'm going now so you can do sexy things with engines and tools."

That got me another laugh. "I'll call you tonight. I have something else I need to take care of, but it should be resolved by tomorrow. Can you clear your weekend for me? I want to take you somewhere after we hang out with Luc."

"*We're* hanging out with Luc?"

He lowered his chin. "Yeah. I missed her too."

Oh yeah, he was sliding right under the thick, nutty shell around my heart.

"All right. I'm yours, Theodore." I blew him a kiss, then I sauntered out of the garage, giving my hips an extra sway so he'd be extra inspired to keep all his big, beautiful promises.

• • • ● • ● • • •

ELENA JUMPED ON MY bed Friday morning, obviously forgetting about my bruised ribs and aching muscles. And sleep. She definitely forgot about my need to sleep.

"I'm dying, you have to wake up," she cried, jumping all around my prone form.

"You seem incredibly alive and annoying." I cracked an eye and was greeted not with Elena's face, but Pen and Gabe's sweet faces smooshed together on her phone screen. "Hello?"

"What up, boo?" Gabe greeted.

Pen yawned. "Why are we awake this early?"

"Because, darling—" Elena lay down beside me so we could both see the screen. And fuck if our faces weren't smooshed together, just like Gabe and Pen's. "I have the most amazing piece of news I need to share with Helen, but I thought the two of you, being her nearest and dearest, would appreciate it very much as well."

Gabe cleared his throat. "Look, Pen is nice, so she won't say it, but she doesn't actually care that Prada announced the color for next spring is going to be glaucous."

Elena held up a finger. "That's not a color."

"It is." He turned to Pen. "Tell them I pay attention in my color theory class, Lucky. Tell them I'm a good little student, and when I'm not, you take your ruler and—"

Penelope covered his mouth with her hand. "Gabriel is a good student, and glaucous is the color of the skin of grapes and plums. Can we get back to why you called, El? I need to go back to sleep."

Gabe winked at the screen. "That's because *someone* wouldn't stop riding my dick all night. I'm not naming names, but it rhymes with Schmelope."

Elena rolled her eyes violently. "Wow, I'm disgusted while also proud of my gorgeous cousin for getting it."

I elbowed her side. "Did you or did you not have something you wanted to tell us?"

"Yes, god, it would be nice if Gabe stopped distracting everyone."

He flipped her off for a second before Pen shoved his hand down. Elena wasn't fazed in any way, plowing on with her news.

"So, as we all know, Helen got dumped by Theo a few weeks ago. He's been trying to win her back, but this badass bitch has held strong, as she should have. You two probably don't know about the asshole I was fucking who stole Helen's money, do you? Or Reno beating the shit out of her because of it?"

Elena's eyes slid to mine, and when I looked closely enough, I swore I could see the devil dancing around inside her, all wobbly dicked and spitting vinegar and fireballs. She knew damn well I hadn't told them about the attack and Daniel. She'd disagreed with my decision not to tell them, so this was clearly her taking matters into her own hands.

I spent five minutes begging Gabe not to drop everything and come to Savage River to "burn some shit down." I spent the next five minutes apologizing to Penelope for keeping her in the dark when all she wanted to do was be there for me.

Elena clicked her fingers. "Okay, that's sufficient. Now, the news. As I said, Theo has been working his way back to Helen. Part of that is righting all the wrongs done to her. He dealt out a dose of physical violence to Daniel last weekend, but that wasn't enough for our Theo. He asked me if I knew anything damning about my ex, and wouldn't you know it, I knew *so* much. Theo knew some things too—and had access to Daniel's computer."

"What happened?" My pulse fluttered wildly in my throat.

"Oh, what didn't happen? Theo found all the goods. Daniel has not only been not writing his own papers for the last two years, he's also been running a cheating ring that spans not just this campus, but several others throughout California. *All* that evidence was forwarded to his teachers, the dean of the business school and, of course, President Whitlock. Daniel is done at Savage U. He'll be lucky to be admitted to *any* university anywhere."

"Oh shit." Gabe cackled. "That's brilliant."

"Elena, were you dating a villain?" Penelope asked.

Elena rolled her eyes. "Dating is pushing it. I was being the good little daughter and spending time with Mom and Dad's friends' son of ill repute."

"Is he really gone?" I asked.

"Well, not yet. These things have proper channels they have to go through. But I have a feeling, since this is such a massive scandal, Daniel will be gone before the weekend is out."

"And Theo did this?"

Elena nodded. "An eensy bit of help from me, but yeah, Theo did it all. For you."

A man who'll burn down the world and rebuild it for you.

"Wow," breathed Pen. "I'm impressed."

Gabe clucked his tongue. "One good deed does not erase this dude dumping my Hells."

Pen smacked him gently. "You, of all people, should be a little more forgiving."

His mouth fell into an O. "Are we really bringing up the past? Because I could talk about the time last week when you were incredibly mean to me. But I won't, because I'm so nice."

Pen turned to stare at him. "You mean the time you decided we should drive to Vegas to get married in the middle of the night and I had to say no because I want a proper wedding with our family and friends there? Was it that time?"

Gabe grinned. "Yeah. That time."

Pen grinned back. "I love you."

Elena groaned over Gabe's response, hanging up on them as soon as they stopped cooing at each other long enough for us to say goodbye. I sat up when she tossed the phone aside, and she stretched out like a cat on my comforter.

"I'm stuck with him for life, aren't I?" she asked.

"Yep. Those two are definitely lifers. Gabe's your fam."

She sighed. "It could be worse, I suppose, but not much." Then she sat up and swung her legs around to the side. "Now, are you going to forgive Theo yet?"

"I've forgiven him. I'm working on the trust part. That's hard as hell to repair once it's broken, and it's not like I give trust out like candy in the first place."

"Mmm...yeah, that would be difficult. Once people cross me, they're dead to me."

I snorted. "Dude, I remember you in high school. You don't have to tell me that. You're a savage."

"Thank you." She flipped her silky blonde hair behind her shoulder and went to my door, where she paused. "To be honest, high school wasn't my best look. I'm not saying I'm no longer a savage, but I have a modicum of self-awareness now, and a small dose of chill."

Cocking my head, I gave her a nod. "I see that."

She finger gunned me. "Go get the boy."

I rubbed the center of my chest. This strange feeling was my heart aching and stretching. How did I handle someone doing what Theo had done for me when he was also the source of one of my biggest heartbreaks?

Mads and I didn't talk about boys or love. She'd been sick her whole life, so her experience on that front had been somewhat limited. But we did talk about heartbreak and living with the scars each fracture wrought.

"Get over it, Helen."

"That's your advice?"

"Yes, it is. Life is unfair and it can be painful. If you choose to stop instead of swimming on, you'll sink. Do you know what happens when you sink?"

"You drown?"

"No. In this scenario, you're a fish with gills. Sinking doesn't inhibit your ability to breathe."

"This is a complicated metaphor. Just tell me what happens when you sink, Mads."

"You spend your time in the dark, looking up at those who kept swimming. And you resent that they can swim while all you do is wallow. The trick is, you could have been up there in the light, but you made a choice to fall down and stay there. Do you understand, my darling Helen?"

At the time, I'd told her I'd gotten it, and she'd been relieved. It wasn't until this moment that I truly understood what she'd meant. I could let my hurt make me miss out on something that could be great. Or I could try again with Theo and risk being hurt again.

Hadn't I been hurt enough? Why the hell would I sign up for the chance of more pain?

But I knew the answer to my own questions. This was Theo, the boy with twinkly eyes who cared for my sister, protected me when I broke his car, and spent night after night waiting for me in a strip club parking lot because he couldn't stand the thought of me on a bus.

This was either going to hurt like hell or be the greatest chance I'd ever taken—and I was definitely taking it.

• • ● ● • ● • ● • ••

I HELD MY TONGUE through an hour of Shakespeare. Theo seemed to have permanently stolen Lock's seat, and I was okay with that. If Lock had a problem with it, he hadn't expressed it, so I took that to mean he didn't.

Theo took notes and paid attention to Professor Davis, but he kept some part of him touching me throughout the whole class. His leg pressed to mine, his arm around my chair, the brush of his thumb over my knuckle. By the time class ended, I was overheated and ready to burst.

I slipped my hand in his as we started for the stairs. He paused and stared at our joined hands. This might have been the first time I'd held his hand first. It certainly felt brand new for me, and my stomach was flippy with nerves.

Then he tightened his fingers around mine and led me down the steps and outside.

"I heard what you did."

He stopped walking. "What did you hear?"

I flattened my free hand to his stomach. "Elena told me about Daniel."

Theo grimaced. "She shouldn't have. I wanted to wait until he was officially expelled to tell you. I wanted to be able to tell you he was gone for good."

"I don't even care what happens to him, it's the fact you would go to that length...for me." I whispered the last part. It was hard enough for me to believe, let alone say.

"That's *nothing*." His brows pinched into a fierce, jagged line. "Daniel called what he did to you a joke. Him stealing from you is almost worse than Reno hurting you. At least in Reno's fucked-up head, he was justified. Daniel had no reason to do what he did other than he could. It's past time for him to feel the consequences of his actions. He will never breathe the same air as you again. Do you hear me? He won't be on campus much longer. You won't have to see him or fear him. He's done."

I bit my lip, unsure if I was going to cry, smile, or scream at the top of my lungs. I felt like a swollen pipe, leaking all over the place, at the very edge of bursting.

"He's really going to be gone? Elena said he had some massive cheating ring."

"Yeah." He shoved his fingers through his hair. "The thing about Daniel is he's a narcissist. He had this scam going, and it was successful, but he needed people to know he was behind it, so he dropped hints about his access to test codes and essays to the guys in the frat. With Elena, he out and out told her what he was doing. Going hand in hand with his narcissism was his feeling of indestructibility. His computer password is his birthday, and he rarely locks his door. It was so easy, it almost wasn't satisfying."

I raised my brows, a wide smile spreading across my face. I loved hearing how stupid Daniel was. Pride goeth before the fall and all that. "But it was."

He stared down at me, nostrils flaring, then some of the twinkle came back to his eyes. "Yeah, it was. It'll be even more satisfying watching all his stuff get tossed out of his room. That's coming soon."

"You ruined him." Just like I'd said, and sincerely meant, I would ruin Amir, Theo had done this for me.

"I will ruin anyone who even thinks of harming you." He took my face in his hands, tipping it back gently, his expression fierce. "And not because I'm trying to win you back. This is for always. I will always fight with you and for you."

...the kind of man who'll be shoulder to shoulder with you in battle, and when push comes to shove, they'll step in front of you and take the brunt of it.

I cleared my throat, at a loss for what to say or think. "Well…"
I sighed and stepped into him, my front flush with his. "I think I
should buy you some mozzarella sticks as a thank you."

Theo's expression broke, and a grin tugged at the corner of
his mouth. "I have to go to work in an hour."

"That's enough time for a heap of mozzarella sticks." I tipped
my chin up. "And since you've been so nice, I'll even buy you a
cookie."

"I'm not going to say no to an offer like that from my girl."

Every time he called me his girl, my heart thumped so hard I
could almost hear it.

"You just get to decide I'm your girl?"

"No." He tucked a lock of hair behind my ear. "It wasn't a
decision. You've been my girl since you smashed my car. That
was a fact, even when I was being stupid. You were always mine,
and I've been unequivocally yours."

I was beginning to think maybe he truly was mine.

Twenty-Nine

THEO

WE WERE DRIVING THROUGH the desert, Helen had her window down, her feet propped on the dash of my new economy sedan. Every once in a while, she'd shift, and the tiny bell on her ankle had a subtle jingle.

We'd been talking for the last two hours since we dropped off Luciana at her friend's apartment to spend the rest of the day and night.

That kid was perceptive. The minute she saw me with her sister this morning, she let us both have it, but especially me.

"It's really about time you guys got a clue."

That was how she greeted us when she'd spotted us waiting for her in The Palisades parking lot. Side by side, not touching.

Helen barked a laugh. "What's that supposed to mean, kid?"

She propped her hands on her hips. "You guys are so obviously in love. I could be blind and still see it. And where's Theo been for the past few weeks while you were all sad and grumpy?"

I turned to Helen. "Were you sad and grumpy?"

She folded her arms. "I'm always grumpy."

"No, you're not." I stared at her hard, trying to read her. "What about sad?"

She pushed my shoulder, but there was no force to it. She let me catch her hand and thread our fingers together.

"Shut up, Theo."

I tugged her to my side and murmured into her hair, "Dog days are over, Tiger."

Luc sighed, her hands clasped at her cheek. "I knew it, I knew it, I knew it!"

Helen's sigh was filled with a lot more annoyance, but her fingers tightened around mine, letting me know she didn't mean a second of it.

"Fine. Theo's back," Helen agreed.

Luc poked her finger at me. "And you're not going anywhere again."

I pressed our joined hands to my chest. "And I'm not going anywhere again."

Now, we were driving. I'd told Helen to pack an overnight bag, and she did, without asking any questions. Pretty sure I was still riding high in her esteem because of my work attire. Setting up Daniel's fall had also been a big part of it. I'd never desired to be any kind of hero, and by all accounts, I'd never lived like one, but when Helen smiled at me the way she had when I told her what I'd done, I got a little bit of a high. It made me think while I might not be a hero, I'd always work my ass off to be Helen's champion if she kept giving me those smiles and that blanket of heat in my gut.

Three hours into the trip, we stopped for gas and snacks. Helen came out of the convenience store with gold Elvis sunglasses and a Twizzler hanging out of her mouth. When she got to me by the gas pump, she traced the Twizzler along my mouth, then quickly replaced it with her lips.

"We're going to Vegas, aren't we?" She pushed her sunglasses to the top of her head. "You're showing me where you grew up?"

I tapped her nose. "Yep. I thought maybe you'd like to see the bright lights too."

"I hate to tell you this, but I'm underage. No gambling."

I cupped her butt and pulled her into me. "I hate to tell you this, but even if you were twenty-one, I'm broke. Sightseeing is free, baby."

"You're not going to try to marry me, are you?"

The thought didn't freak me out, but it wasn't on the agenda for this trip. "Not today."

She bit her bottom lip, but she couldn't hold back her grin. Then she reached into her bag and pulled out another pair of Elvis glasses. "Here. These are for kicking Daniel's ass since I'm not allowed to say thank you."

Laughing, I slid the sunglasses on my face, knowing then just as solidly as I'd known for weeks, or maybe since the first time I saw her, this woman was going to turn my life upside down, and I was going to love every second of it. Because I was in love with her, and when it came down to it, I couldn't think of much I wouldn't do for her.

"I need some red on my lips, baby. It's been too long." Hooking her around the waist, I pressed her against my car. Reaching up, she took my sunglasses off, then she ran her nose along mine and grazed her fingertips across my jaw and cheekbone and tipped her head back, inviting me in. I came readily, taking her mouth with mine in a slow, deep kiss. It wasn't wild, but it was passionate. It wasn't desperate, rather seeking. I asked, and she answered in soft sighs and the wet slide of her tongue.

"You're mine, you know," I murmured against her lips.

"Mmhmm. And you're mine?"

"Yes. I've given you every reason to doubt that, but I'm telling you right here, I won't again."

She patted my cheek. "You better not. I bought you Elvis glasses, Theodore."

I gave her butt a squeeze. "They're officially a family heirloom. Now, get in the car."

The drive had started easy, but as we drew closer and closer to my hometown, my chest filled like a balloon with dread. As if she sensed it, Helen laid her hand on my leg, stroking up and down every once in a while, but mostly leaving it in place. And that was something. That was a lot. We grew up the same. There was no one there to offer us comfort when we needed it. But here she was, offering it to me as easy as breathing.

I put my hand on top of hers when I didn't need it on the wheel. She never tried to take it back once I made it obvious I wanted and needed it there.

When I'd decided to bring her here, I didn't have a plan in place. Not where to take her first, or how to explain myself when I'd spent years hiding and denying the truth. But once I passed the city limits, I knew where I wanted to go first.

Helen stiffened and tried to take her hand back when I parked in the lot of a strip club that had never once seen better days. All its days had resembled the pits of hell.

"Why are we here, Theo? What...?"

"This is where my mom worked when Andrew Whitlock walked in, bought a private lap dance, paid her a little extra, and knocked her up with me."

Helen yanked her hand away and hugged herself with her arms. "Wha—? How could you have not told me this?"

I shook my head. "I haven't been back to this city since my father took me out of here when I was sixteen. Even before that, I tried not to think about my mom." I stared at the gritty, run-down stucco building that housed a den of iniquity. It wasn't anything like Savage Beauties, but every time I picked up Helen there, this was what I saw.

"So, am I like your mom? Is that what you're saying?"

Startled, I twisted to face her. "Fuck no, I don't think that. I'm showing you this hellhole to explain my hang ups about your job and why I reacted the way I did. It wasn't you. It's never been because of you."

"I should have told you," she interjected, "about the times I stripped. I should have told you, but I didn't want you looking at me the way you did when you found out. And I knew you would."

My exhale was heavy. I studied her folded arms, wanting the closeness we had on the drive here back.

"Not for the reasons you thought, but yeah, I did exactly what you feared."

I looked out the windshield again. Something inside me popped, like a rusty lock springing open, and I wanted to tell her everything.

"She was sick. My pops—her dad—told me she had never been mentally well. This place, the things she had to do while she worked here...it only got worse. When I was little, before Pops knew I existed, she'd bring me to work with her. Some of my first memories are of hiding in the dressing room and sleeping in piles of clothes. I can still feel the sequins digging into my skin." I scoffed, rubbing my arm at the phantom fabric digging into my flesh. "I have no doubt I saw things a little kid should never see, but I thank all that is holy my mind chose to protect me from those memories. The things I *do* remember are bad enough."

I pounded my fist on the steering wheel. My chest was tight, throat clogged. I thought I'd come here, show Helen around, open up to her, and not feel it. But it was all hitting me. Every scary night. The sounds, the smells, the desperation for my mom to be safe and happy when she never, ever was. I'd pushed it down and pushed it down, but it was always there. And sitting here with my girl, the one who'd broke the dam with a bat in her hand, a smile on her ruby lips, I was feeling it all.

Helen brushed her fingers through the hair at my nape and murmured my name, but she didn't try to interrupt. She let me give her what I needed to.

"I should hate her. I *do* hate her. But she was my mom, you know?" I had to stop, suck in a breath, push out the long forgotten rush of pain that came along with having Shannon O'Reilly as a mother. "She was my mom, and she was sick, and she never had a fucking chance. My pops did what he could when she was younger, but he didn't know jack about mental health, and she was good at masking. And then it was just too late. Too much bad had happened. This place, the despair in the walls, she soaked it up. It broke her body, then her fragile mind. She contracted hep C somewhere along the line. Probably a slew of other things too, I don't know. It's a blur because I was a kid. Ten years old, and I was helping my mom out of bed because she was too out of it to do it herself."

"Theo…" Helen pushed to her knees on her seat and leaned across the console to shove her face in my throat and wrap me in her arms. "I hear you."

Letting go of the wheel, I held the warm, solid, powerful girl in my arms who would never end up like my mom, who gave up fighting long before her fragmented mind and illness claimed her. Helen would come out of that world clean, not because of anything I did or didn't do, but because she was a warrior. She would fight until the end.

Fisting the back of her hair, I brought my mouth to her ear, and whispered fiercely, "You're not like that."

Her lips moved against my throat. "I know I'm not. I know, Theodore. You don't know how relieved I am that you know too."

"I was protecting myself." I flung my hand out in the direction of the club. "From sliding back into this. It doesn't make sense, right? But logic doesn't touch the fear leftover from when I was that little kid hiding in the dressing room. That's on me. All that's *my* baggage."

She dragged her mouth along the taut tendons in my neck. "I promise you, I understand now. I get it completely."

"I was an idiot to think I didn't still carry that."

She pressed a soft kiss to the corner of my jaw. "Wishful thinking. I understand that too."

The door of the club opened, and a couple guys in suits that stretched across their massive frames strode out. They pointed to my car, and I hadn't gotten so soft, I didn't recognize the potential for trouble when I saw it. I pushed Helen back to her seat and tore out of the parking lot before they could get close to us.

"They didn't look like upstanding gentlemen," Helen said.

"Nope. Not if they work at a place like that."

I drove to another part of town that was even worse. I used to think the cracks in the sidewalks and road were places where the fire from hell had broken through. That wasn't whimsy either. People who lived here didn't go outside after dark unless they were gang affiliated and packing. Daytime was iffy at best too. And if truth was to be told, being inside was only halfway safer.

I pointed to the gutted, blackened remains of a building. "That was my pops's garage before the bank reclaimed it. He'd owned it since he was in his twenties, but never really got his head above water in all that time. Probably because he was terrible at business, but also because he had break-ins at least once a year and had to replace half his tools each time."

"Were you close to him?"

I shook my head. "Not really. He wasn't that kind of man." I pulled into the parking lot of my old apartment building. "I lived here with him and my mom from the time I was five until I moved in with Andrew."

I tried to keep to facts, but these facts were what made me. I'd always have the imprints of sequins in my skin, a tinge of despair in my blood, the shadow of violence and poverty following me. If I wanted to stop fighting and start living—and I sure as hell did—I had to accept that. I was made here, but this wasn't the end of me. It was barely the beginning.

The apartment was yellow stucco, cracked and crumbling—it was pretty much the neighborhood aesthetic—with an outside staircase that was rusted, and from memory, piss filled. Two stories tall, it looked slumped and haggard, as though it was as tired of existing in this violent place as much as the residents.

"Is your pops still here?"

"No." I took her hand and rolled it against my cheek. "He died right before I started college."

Her fingers tensed. "So, when you came into Savage Wheelz...?"

"Mmm. Deacon got it into his head that weed would help me work through my grief. He didn't really get that you don't grieve for a man like my pops because he never allowed anyone to love him. He was just there, taciturn and detached. He taught me about engines, how to change oil and rotate tires, but everything else...I don't think I even knew him. He was more like that random roommate you find on Craigslist than a grandpa."

"Is your mom still here?" she asked carefully.

"Nope. She's probably dead, but I don't know. She took off when I was ten, left me here with Pops. After a year, I stopped expecting her to come back." I inhaled deep, one final taste of this poisoned air. "I'm never coming back here again."

"You didn't have to bring me here."

"I haven't been here since I moved away, but I wanted to see it one last time. This is a needed reminder, Tiger. I don't have to live like Andrew Whitlock. I don't *want* to. But I don't want to live like this either."

"There's an in-between."

I looked at her, finding her peering back at me in the softest, most open way she ever had. She was watchful, taking me in, but also the surroundings. Helen got what it meant to come from a place like this. No matter how deep our conversation was, we both knew not to forget where we were, to stay on edge and ready to roll. This was one of the many reasons she was the only person I could have shared this with.

We weren't exactly the same, my girl and me. We were more like warped reflections in the same mirror. When she said she understood me, she meant it on a bone-deep level. Once I got my head out of my ass, I understood her the same way.

Holding her gaze, I pressed my lips to her palm. "I get that now. I'm finding it."

"Can I come along?"

"Baby, there's no way I'm taking another step without you beside me."

I drove away from my old home for the final time and didn't look back. I'd never forget where I came from, but that was just it: where I came from wasn't where I was going. There was nothing there for me, and there never had been.

"To the lights?" Helen asked. "Are we going to see the lights?"

"Yeah, baby. That's where we're going."

What I didn't say was I'd already seen the light, and she was a red-lipped, bat-carrying, badass beauty.

Thirty

HELEN

I'D BEEN TO EMBARRASSINGLY few places, and nowhere outside California except a couple quick trips into Mexico when my mom dragged me to her favorite *special* pharmacy to pick up her *special* medicine. Theo didn't make fun of me for absolutely gawking at the bright lights and massive hotels on the Strip. He held my hand and indulged my every whim, ducking in and out of hotel after hotel.

After the intensity of his revelations, I thought he needed this, the easiness of being tourists without much care in the world, as much as I did. We ate dinner and walked around until midnight, then we left the Strip to check in to our room at a nondescript hotel. When the clerk asked if we wanted a room with two double beds or one queen, Theo deferred to me. I answered "queen" without missing a beat. I had missed this man badly in every way. I wasn't sleeping without him.

Theo had given me everything. More than anyone ever had. He'd shown me his ugly, an ugly I never would have guessed by looking at him, by knowing him, by falling for him. I saw his ugly, and it made who he was that much more beautiful.

By the time we walked into our hotel room, I was nervous. I wasn't the kind of girl who got nervous, not about sex, or really anything besides my sister's safety. This was new, the things I was feeling for Theo. It wasn't like how we were before. Now, we were stripped down and raw. Two people who'd revealed themselves and dared each other not to look away. I would never look away from him. It was Theo seeing me in the same way that made me want to hide.

I wouldn't. I had a feeling if I wanted to, he wouldn't let me anyway. But the urge was there.

I threw my bag down. "I need a shower."

Theo made sure the door was locked, then sat on the corner of the bed to toe his shoes off. "I probably do too."

My stomach swirled. God, he was hot, even with his Elvis glasses on the top of his head. Maybe him being willing to wear them made him even hotter. Those glasses on his head and the blooming warmth in my chest chased away some of my nerves, leaving room for blatant desire.

"We're in the desert, Theodore."

His brow furrowed, but he gave a little laugh. "I know that, Tiger."

I slanted my head in the direction of the bathroom. "So, shouldn't we conserve water?"

Theo didn't need more of an invitation. We were undressed and under the hot spray of the shower within minutes, washing each other, embracing and touching like it was our hundred-year reunion instead of weeks.

I'd said I had missed him, and that was true. I missed all of him, including *this*. The way he touched me, like he'd never get enough, like he'd never had anything better, like I was both precious and sensuous.

We dried off hastily, then we were on the bed, kissing, stroking, sucking. Theo rolled me to my back, moving slowly down my body. He stopped at my breasts, cupping them to his mouth to suck the beaded tips. His tongue swirled around my nipple, then his lips closed over it, pulling it deep into his mouth. My back arched and knees tried to press together, but Theo was between them, keeping them open.

"Theo," I sighed. "Please."

"Mmm. No. Let me have you, Helen. Give me you."

I glided my fingers through his wet hair, opening my eyes to watch him travel down my body. "You have me."

He met my eyes from between my legs, and the look he gave me made me stop breathing. It was fierce and possessive, with kiss-swollen lips and fire in his eyes.

"You *have* me, Theodore. I'm here with you." I nodded at him. "I'm here just as much as you are."

That was enough for him. He lowered his mouth to my flesh and kissed those lips like he did the ones on my face. Licking, tasting, savoring. He took his time with me, drawing out my pleasure, giving me tenderness mixed with carnal bliss. It was different than before, and better, not because he was going slow, but because neither of us were holding back.

When I cracked, there was an almost audible boom of thunder. My orgasm rode me like an electric storm, sizzling on my skin, pulling me taut with each spark. Theo cupped my ass and rode the flowing energy crackling in the air with me.

I needed him. Over me. Inside me. So, I told him, and he gave it to me, climbing up my body until we were aligned. His eyes were locked with mine as he pushed into me. I would have said he was trying to torture me with how slowly he entered, if not for the way he was looking at me, like he truly adored me.

It was a lot. Almost too much. But this was Theo. And he was safe. I let it happen, let him see the way I adored him right back, then I wrapped my legs around him, curled my arms around his shoulders, and touched my lips to his to *show* him.

He palmed my breast, brow pinching as he stroked me from the inside. "You're so soft, baby. So, so soft."

I nodded, meeting his strokes with the ride of my hips. "For you, I am. Only for you."

"I'm so fucking lucky to have you like this." He nipped at my chin and bottom lip. "All for me. I'm the only one who gets to have this."

I chased his mouth, and he gave it to me, kissing and kissing me as he slid into me so deep, I felt him in my belly. And when he retreated, he dragged along every single one of my live-wire nerves. It had been so long since we were together, but now that he was inside me, there was no rush.

"I never thought I'd have you again. Never thought I'd get to experience your perfect, sweet pussy or touch your smooth skin or taste your pretty lips." He gave me gentle, sipping kisses while the weight of his pelvis pushed on mine, hitting my swollen clit exactly how I needed. His sensual praise only added to the budding sweep of pleasure gathering between my thighs.

"I missed you," I breathed. "Don't fuck up again."

He smiled into the next kiss and pulled his hips back to fuck me a little harder. My body rocked with the force of his thrusts, so I clung to him tighter, taking the ride Theo wanted to give me. Because I knew he'd make it good and right. He'd give me exactly what I needed.

"I never stopped thinking about you. Not just your sweet pussy. All of you." He slid his hand under my head to fist my hair and tip it back. "I am so gone for you, Helen."

My heart didn't thrash. It calmed and soothed, and I melted, every ounce of fight leaving me until I was nothing more than Theo's. He must have felt it, because he groaned into my mouth, and his pace picked up, hinting at a desperation to soak up what I was giving him.

Me. I was giving him me.

We were coiled around each other like snakes, squeezing, sliding, getting closer, closer, both moaning, breathing faster. Theo drove into me with more purpose, and he reached between us to circle my clit.

If he hadn't been crushing me into the mattress, I would have arched with pleasure. But he owned my body and its movements. All I could do was take the mounting pressure in my belly until it became too big to contain, then I dragged my nails along Theo's shoulders and cried out his name.

He shoved his face into my throat and drove straight through my quivering pussy. Catching my hands in his, he wove our fingers together and raised them above our heads. Tears welled in my eyes from the sweetness of it all.

"Nothing like you, baby. Nothing better. Never, ever," he declared against my skin. "Need you, need you, need you. Always, Helen. Always needing you."

I nodded, barely able to move my head. "I love you, Theo." It was out before I knew it was coming, but I didn't have a second to regret it. Theo roared my name. His head jerked back to stare down at me in wonder, then he was pulsing inside me, filling me with hot, liquid pleasure that seemed to be endless.

As soon as he was done, he rolled us, taking me on top of his chest. His hands wove through the sides of my wet hair, tilting my head from side to side like he was inspecting me. Then he pressed a kiss to my forehead, my eyelids, my nose, and finally, my lips.

"I love you too, Helen."

My eyelids fluttered, threatening to take me away from this bare moment, but I didn't let them close. I stared back at Theo, into his twinkly eyes that were somehow brighter than ever.

"I didn't mean to say that."

His lips tipped. "But you meant it."

I couldn't help the smile I gave him back. "I meant it." I knocked my forehead against his chin. "Just...you know, be careful with me. If you decide to dump me again, can you let me down a little easier?"

Theo gripped my chin. "Helen, I just told you I love you and you're talking about me dumping you? Jesus, baby."

My shoulder shrugged slightly. "I'm kind of damaged, Theodore."

His exhale was ragged. "I am too. And I fucked up with you but know this: I have *never* shared with anyone what I shared with you today. Even Andrew doesn't know most of it. When I say I love you, it's not like anything I've experienced. I wish there were different words to describe what I feel for you. It's something so deep, it pierces my bones."

He didn't say her name, but I knew he was telling me this was a whole new ballgame to what he felt for Abby. Because he was Theo, he recognized that I needed that reassurance and he gave it to me. He gave me more than I could have asked for.

"Okay," I whispered. "I believe you."

He swatted my butt lightly. "If you try to dump me, you're going to have to fake your own death or change identities. I'm not going to let you go otherwise. We tried that, and it was no good. It did not work for me."

I snorted a laugh and patted his cheek. "It really didn't work for me, and faking my own death sounds like a lot of work, dude. I'm not down for that."

He was grinning again, running his hands up and down my spine. "You're dude-ing me again?"

"Yeah." I pressed on his bottom lip with my index finger. "I told you I love you, so I think you can handle an occasional dude. You're not going to get the skater out of me just because you're my man."

With a growl, he rolled us again, then he sat back on his knees and flipped me to my front. His hand slid under my belly, raising my hips off the bed, ass in the air. His other hand came down on my butt cheek with a loud smack.

"You're going to get it." He smacked me again. "You're a bad girl, Tiger."

I grinned at him over my shoulder. "I thought I was your good girl."

His eyes met mine, and the slow, sensual grin he gave me set me aflame all over again. "You're so good, you're bad, baby. Now, it's time we go over what it means for me to be your man."

"Dude," I whispered, giving him hell.

"Tiger." He outlined the curve of my hips with his hands. "What me being your man means is I would never want to take the skater out of you. What it means is I'm going to take care of you in all the ways you need and that I see fit. It means sometimes I'm going to make love to you, and sometimes I'm going to spank your ass and fuck you dirty." He leaned over my back, brushing my hair over my shoulder. I shivered from his touch and the things he was saying. "It means *everyone* is going to know you're with me and I'm all about you. As your man, if anyone fucks with you, I will *end* them. I love you."

"I love you too, Theodore." I was panting from the seductive promises he'd whispered and almost swooning from the sweet. God, this man did it for me.

Theo's erection slotted between my cheeks, and I groaned, my toes already curling. Then he smacked me between my legs, and I almost shot through the ceiling.

"My baby wants to play," he crooned.

"I want my man to play with me."

"Gladly."

My eyes rolled back in my head when he started his version of playtime. Yeah, this whole being in love and having a boyfriend thing was going to work for me. It was going to work for me in every way.

Thirty-One

THEO

WE HAD A WEEK before we were summoned to the Wellstein-Whitlock manor. I was almost relieved when I'd gotten the text from Miranda. I'd known it was coming. Too much had gone down for me not to have to answer for it, including making it official with Helen, which Miranda somehow knew about. Then again, she had her finger on the pulse of campus, and I'd very publicly claimed my girl against every brick wall I could find. Word had gotten around.

The week had been fucking fantastic, though, even with the inevitable summons hanging over my head. I'd spent almost all my time I wasn't working or in class with Helen. She was good for me, and I liked to think I was good for her too. She made it easy to want to try and keep trying until I got it right.

I had told her I could breathe for the first time when I met her, but since we got back from Vegas, it was like I had new lungs. The breaths I took were full and clean, and my chest was no longer weighed down by the past I'd been unable to face.

"Holy shit, Theo."

I laughed. "I told you it was a mansion in Malibu. Did you not believe me?"

Helen peered up at the glass house Miranda's money had bought when she and Andrew got married. It wasn't quite on the beach, but it was on the right side of the highway and had ocean views from the roof deck.

"I did, but still, holy shit."

I walked around to her side of the car and helped her out. Helen was wearing a dress. I'd seen her in a gown, and she'd been absolutely stunning, but this was the first time she'd worn a casual dress around me. This was...almost sweet, if she hadn't made it sexy with her curves. Short and red with little white flowers, there was a ruffle at the hem, and a tie at the side I planned on tugging when I took her home as soon as possible.

Like the green gown at the banquet, she'd inherited this one from Mads too.

"You saw where I grew up. Imagine moving in here at sixteen after living in a dump my whole life."

She elbowed my side. "Okay, I see why you leaned in hard to the whole laissez-faire, rich-boy lifestyle. If I'd lived in a place like this when I was sixteen, I wouldn't have known what to do with myself."

I peered down at her with narrowed eyes. "You wouldn't have changed."

She lifted a shoulder. "We'll never know."

Stopping her at the front door, I pulled her into my chest. "We can still make a break for it."

"Nope. Let's get this over with. I'm actually looking forward to speaking to Miranda again anyway. Your dad, you can handle."

"That isn't very encouraging, Tiger."

She curled her fingers on the sides of my neck. "I'll be your buffer, okay? If your dad gets to be too much, I'll bring up my dead friend—that always stops people in their tracks."

Even with as much as I was dreading walking through the door, she still made me laugh. "This is why I love you. You're always coming up with brilliant ideas."

Once I stole a quick kiss and Helen wiped the red off my lips, we went inside. Miranda greeted us first, pulling us both into tight hugs. Andrew followed, shaking my hand like we were acquaintances instead of father and son, then gave Helen a warm peck on the cheek.

Miranda stole Helen almost immediately, offering her a tour. I tried to follow, but my father held me back with a clawed hand on my shoulder.

"I've heard your grades are improving."

I nodded, not even a little surprised he'd been checking. "Yeah. I have Helen to thank for that."

He folded his arms. "In what way?"

"She was as unimpressed as you with my commitment to school, and she let me know."

"I suppose that's admirable for a girl like that."

I slanted my head. "What does that mean?"

He flicked his wrist. "I think you know. She comes from nothing, barely graduated high school. If not for Madeline McGarvey's influence, and let's face it, her money, who knows where she would be?" He clucked his tongue. "I'd be careful with that one. She already sucked Madeline dry. She might think she found another target in you."

Heat suffused my skin as boiling blood surged through my veins. He'd been so interested in her at the banquet. Either he'd looked into her background afterward, or he'd been putting on a good show. With him, it could've gone either way. It wasn't a surprise he'd turned on her. I'd been expecting it. I was just relieved Helen hadn't been around to hear it.

"That's my girlfriend, Andrew. Never say anything like that about her again. I won't go into all the ways what you just said is untrue, but you have no idea what you're talking about. None at all."

"Girlfriend? Hmph."

The doorbell rang before either of us could say anything else, which was for the best. If I had to spend another minute with him, one of us would end up bloody, and I highly doubted it would be me.

While Andrew was getting the door, I poured myself a Bloody Mary from the pitcher Miranda had set out in the kitchen, adding my own extra dose of vodka. I'd need it to get through brunch with my father and whoever else they'd invited to join us.

A hand lay between my bunched shoulders. I spun, expecting Helen, and was severely disappointed. "Abby, what the hell are you doing here?"

She kept her hand on me, sliding to my bicep. "That's some greeting, The. Wow."

"It wasn't a greeting, it was a question. Why are you here?"

She didn't drop her hand, but a fraction of the spark in her eyes faded. "Andrew and Miranda invited my parents and me for brunch. I didn't think it would be a problem since we've both moved on."

I gave her hand a pointed look. "Have you moved on? Really?"

A slow smile spread across her pink lips, and all I could think about was the kiss she stole the last time we were in close vicinity and the sickness I felt when Helen had to see Abby's gloss on my mouth.

"Of course I have. Did you really think I'd be pining after you forever?"

"Good. I'm glad for you." I said the words, but there was something I didn't like behind her smile. It read false to me.

"Are you?" She stepped closer, tilting her head back to peer into my eyes. "There isn't some small part of you twisting into knots when you hear I'm with someone else?"

Shrugging her off, I backed away. "Absolutely no part. Like you said, I've moved on."

I strode from the kitchen, finding Helen with Miranda and Abby's mom, Jill. They were talking about Helen's dress when I joined them, hooking my arm around Helen's waist. Jill gave pause at the sight of me with someone other than her daughter, but she kept her opinions to herself, thankfully.

"We were shopping in this little boutique Madeline found online." Miranda bit her bottom lip, but it didn't stop her chin from quivering. "She was always finding little places like that, taking me on adventures. I miss so much about her, but our adventures might be the thing that tops the list."

Jill's gaze swept over Helen. "It's lovely that Madeline's treasures are getting the chance to live another life. That dress looks so pretty on you, Helen. Madeline would undoubtedly approve."

"Thank you for telling me the story behind the dress, Miranda." Helen squeezed my hand at her hip. "And, Jill, I hope she would approve. She was always teasing me for wearing cutoffs and holey Vans."

Miranda swiped a knuckle under her made-up eye. "Oh, please. Mads would have been wearing Vans and skateboarding with you if she'd been up to it. That sounds exactly like her."

Helen laughed. "She made me take her to the skate park so she could watch, so I have no doubt that's true. Her Vans wouldn't have been holey, though."

Miranda released a watery laugh. "Oh, that's very accurate."

Abby approached our group, holding out a Bloody Mary to her mother. "I ran into The in the kitchen, and he had the best idea." She raised her drink, then took a sip. "Mmm...this is delicious, Mir."

Miranda sobered, her eyes bouncing between Abby and me. "Thanks, sweetheart. Why don't we all go outside to the patio? I have some absolutely delicious fresh fruit set up."

The three of them were on their way, but I held Helen back. "I had no idea she'd be here," I murmured.

"Would you not have invited me?" she asked.

"No. I would have disinvited myself."

Helen snorted a short laugh. "It's no biggie, The."

I groaned at the terrible nickname. It was like nails on a chalkboard to me. "You're sure? We can leave if you're uncomfortable."

"I'm sure. She doesn't bother me. I know you're with me." Helen flipped her hair, spilling soft waves of chocolate behind her back. "Was your father awful?"

"Entirely, but I'm used to it."

She hooked her arm in mine, and we headed to the patio. "How did he land Miranda?"

"He's on his best behavior around her. Wait and see. He's like a lovesick puppy with his wife, though I haven't figured out if it's her money or her he's more crazy over."

"He's really dumb if the answer isn't his wife. She's cool as hell."

"That she is."

Brunch went by in fits of awkwardness, followed by fits of eye-rolling boredom. Abby's dad, Bob, liked to golf, and Andrew liked to talk about it, so that dominated much of the conversation. I was grilled by both Bob and Andrew about my classes, and Abby took it upon herself to talk about hers. All the while, Helen ate her fruit and waffles and periodically held my hand under the table.

Toward the end, I had started to relax, probably due to the extra vodka in my two Bloody Marys, but a lot came down to sitting beside Helen, who was so unbothered by it all, it was impossible not to take that in. She really didn't give a fuck what any of these people thought about her, but she'd also made an effort with her dress, her smiles, her answers, to make a good impression—and that was all for me.

Leaning close, so my mouth brushed her ear, I whispered, "I love you."

She smiled without turning her head and squeezed my fingers with hers. The words didn't need to be spoken back for me to hear them.

"Theo, son," Bob wiped his mouth with his cloth napkin, "I didn't see the i8 in the drive. Is it in the shop?"

Abby giggled. "Daddy, Theo doesn't have the i8 anymore."

"Oh, really?" Bob sat forward, resting his arms on the table. "What are you driving these days?"

I cleared my throat. "The Toyota in the driveway is mine. I wanted something less flashy."

Andrew scoffed. "He sold the i8 without saying a single word to me and came home driving that piece of shit parked out front. Let's just say I was not pleased."

Miranda laid her manicured hand on his arm. "I explained to Andrew what happened. Theo had a friend in an emergency situation that required money to solve. Theo didn't want to ask me for a handout, so he proposed selling the i8. You know me, I can't say no to helping a friend, and I am well aware Theo never liked my old car, so I helped."

Helen's ease had disappeared, leaving her stiff and shifting uncomfortably in her seat. I took her hand in mine, stroking her knuckles to let her know I was right there with her.

Andrew sent me a hard glare from across the table. "I've yet to hear who this friend is and exactly *why* they needed the money."

"It's private," I gritted. "All of this is private."

Abby giggled again, and her eyes landed on me. "Well, it can't be Helen. She has a job I've heard is *very* lucrative."

I stood so fast, my chair scraped on the patio stones. "Enough, Abby."

Abby's eyes rounded. "What? It's not like it's a secret Helen's a stripper. Everyone knows. All the frat boys like to go watch her dance on the weekends."

Bracing a hand on the table, I leaned across, jabbing a finger in her face. "What happened to you? Are you so fucking jealous and spiteful you have to go after a girl who never did a single thing to you? Or is this who you've always been, and I was too stupid to see it?" I shook my head when her mouth fell open. "I don't give a shit what your answer is. Anything good we ever had is erased. I don't know your name anymore. I don't recognize your face. You do not exist."

Abby gasped, and she wasn't the only one, but I didn't care. She could be jealous and rude and get her little digs in. I'd swallow it down. It didn't matter what she said to me. But this? No, this would not stand. She'd gone way too far.

Helen's warm fingers wrapped around my wrist. "Theo, come on. It's okay."

"Is this true?" Andrew boomed, his face bright red and throat mottled.

I started to respond, but Helen got there first. "Not entirely, but it's also not untrue."

Enough was enough. I wouldn't allow Helen to be subjected to any more of this. Unwrapping her fingers from my wrist, I caught her hand, tugged her to her feet, and started striding for the door. My father barking my name stopped me.

He spoke to my back. "Wait in my office, Theo. We need to talk."

Without turning around, I nodded and continued inside. Once I'd gotten Helen well away from the patio doors, I backed her into a wall and bracketed her head with my arms.

"Are you okay?"

She stared back at me, earnestness in her expression. "Are you? You must be so embarrassed."

"No." I captured her jaw, tipping her head back. "I'm not embarrassed. I'm seething. I don't know how Abby found out, but she had no right to spill your personal business to everyone. She's just a jealous little cunt. God, I'm so sorry."

"Theo." She stroked my cheek with her fingertips. "You have nothing to be sorry for. I made choices, and I have to own them. Abby might be jealous, but it's not like she lied."

My fist came down heavily, making Helen flinch. "She got one detail right, the rest was a pack of bullshit—and we both know it."

The sound of heels clicking hurriedly on the marble floor froze us both. Abby came to a halt three feet from where I had Helen pinned to the wall, her eyes welled with tears.

"I shouldn't have done that," she rasped. "I wasn't going to. It's just...Daniel told me about her when he found out I was coming here today. I guess I let my mouth get ahead of me. I told them I was mistaken on the details, but your dad wasn't really listening. I didn't mean—"

"Shut up," I hissed. "Get out of here. We. Are. Through."

Abby glanced helplessly between Helen and me, then quickly spun on her toes and fled, a quiet sob following in her wake.

With a sharp shake of my head, I pulled Helen from the wall and into my arms, her front flush with my side. Her arms looped around my middle, and her head tucked under my chin.

"I guess we know why Daniel's been quiet." Helen smoothed her hand along my side. "He was waiting for an opportunity like this."

"Fuck Daniel," I gritted out.

He'd been officially expelled, just as I knew he would be. The evidence had been too damning, even for his father's fat pockets. Added to that, the school's newspaper had gotten their hands on the same evidence sent to the president and deans, and Savage U couldn't afford not to rule with an iron fist.

He'd left the frat house the day of our fight and never returned, not even to pack up his room. One day, movers arrived and carried all his belongings out, and I'd hoped that would be the end of it. I guessed he'd needed to get one last jab in. Since he couldn't fight worth shit, he'd sent in a ringer.

I planted a kiss to Helen's temple. "Let's get out of here."

"That's an excellent idea. I'm done with all the richie riches. No offense, Theodore."

Even though I was pissed, she made me chuckle. "Absolutely none taken."

We headed toward the front door, but luck wasn't on our side today. My father met us in the hall outside his office, blocking our path.

"Will you two step into my office? We need to have a quick conversation." His voice was calm. Scarily so. The last thing I wanted was to have any length of conversation with him, but this was inevitable. We might as well get it over with.

Helen squeezed my side. "It's fine. I'm fine."

I swept my gaze over her. She truly didn't seem any worse for wear. I felt like I was going to climb out of my skin, but my cool girl was a cucumber. That reminded me she'd dealt with far worse than Andrew Whitlock. I wanted to punch a hole in the sky so I could give her the fucking moon and stars to make up for it.

I met my father's eyes. "You have five minutes, and if you say anything I don't like to Helen, we're out."

He swiveled, striding to his desk. Helen and I waited on the other side of it, neither of us moving to sit. Andrew opened a side drawer and withdrew a leather-bound ledger. My stomach revolted at the sight of it.

Bracing both hands on his desk, he directed his gaze to my girl. "I'm going to be blunt. I do not want a stripper in my family. Having a woman like you by his side will only hurt him. It's clear from her behavior Abigail Fitzgerald isn't fit for Theo, but neither are you."

"That ship sailed when you fucked my mom, Andrew." My ears were ringing from the blood rushing through my veins. "This is bullshit."

Helen put her hand on my arm. "No, let's hear what he has to say. I'm curious."

Andrew gave her a wan smile. "You're smart, I'll give you that." He opened the ledger, revealing rows of checks he tapped with a pen. "Do you know what these are?"

Helen furrowed her brow. "Um...aren't they checks?"

"That's right. Now, you're going to tell me your price for walking away from Theo and leaving our family alone. Is it five thousand? Seven?"

I almost laughed at the audacity of this man. He clearly didn't know anything about Helen if he thought for a second she'd entertain this offer.

Helen sucked in a breath and peered at the checks. She glanced at me, then back to Andrew. "Ten thousand."

No.

Two words. That was all it took to stab me in the fucking gut.

Thirty-Two

Helen

ANDREW'S SALT-AND-PEPPER EYEBROWS SHOT up in surprise. "I would have gone as high as fifteen." He chuckled like he was so damn clever, then started writing my check. "But ten sounds just fine."

My nails dug into the palms of my hands. "It's Helen Ortega. O-r-t-e-g-a."

"Helen, Jesus Christ," came Theo's tortured protest. "What are you doing?"

I raised a brow, but I couldn't look at him. I could not bear to see his expression. "I'm being smart."

Something choked and tormented clawed up his throat, and I felt it slide down mine. Hurting Theo hurt me right back, but it was a necessary evil. I didn't know what else to do.

Andrew tore the check out with a flourish and handed it to me. My hands were steady as I accepted it. I sat down to inspect it and whipped out my phone.

"Checks are so funny." I scrunched my nose as I held my phone over the piece of paper. "Isn't it crazy how I can just scan it with my phone—and boom, the money is deposited in my account? I don't even have to go to the bank."

Theo sank down in the chair beside mine, covering his eyes with his hand. I could feel his confusion and anger bubbling up, and I had to put an end to it. This was too much on top of too much.

"Hey, Theodore, can you send me your account info?"

His head slowly turned in my direction. His eyes were bleary and wet, barely focusing on me. "What?" he croaked.

Oh, my heart. I hated doing this to him, but it would be over soon. "Send me your account info and I'll transfer the ten *K* as soon as it clears."

"Baby?" Theo squeezed his eyes as if to clear them. "What did you say?"

Andrew slammed his ledger down on his desk. "What is the meaning of this? You will do no such thing."

I rose to my feet and braced my hand on his desk, just like he had. "I can, and I will. I'm not for sale, Mr. Whitlock, and I'm not leaving Theo. If you decide you can't support a son who has a former stripper for a girlfriend, then that cash you so kindly gifted me will come in handy to him. But this is the last time you use me as leverage over your son. I hope we understand each other. There is no amount you could give me that would make me walk. If you want to try, I'll be happy to keep transferring it over to Theo each and every time. Are we clear?"

Theo rose behind me, pressing his front to my back. "Angel of vengeance, you're going to pay for taking a hundred years off my life," he murmured.

"I love you," I told him.

Andrew had turned puce. If his coloring was any indication, he had to be in danger of stroking out at any moment.

"I don't know what kind of game you're playing, young lady, but you do not want to test me. You won't win. Remember who the president of your university is. I can very easily find a reason to have your enrollment revoked."

That struck true fear in my heart, but I wouldn't be bullied. If I never graduated from Savage U and collected the money Mads left me, it would be a massive let down, but it wouldn't break me. So, I squared my shoulders and didn't even blink.

"Try me, old man. I don't know if you noticed, but I'm really fucking scrappy. I won't back down."

"Enough." Theo squeezed my nape. "You won't threaten Helen."

"What makes you think it's a threat? I have her academic future in the palm of my hand, and right now, I'm not feeling very altruistic. If you care about this girl, get rid of her, Theo."

Theo released my neck and claimed my hip, pulling me into his side. "That's never going to happen. And let me tell you why. What do you think people will say if they find out you personally approved my wrestling coaches administering performance-enhancing drugs to me when I was a minor? Do you think that will go over well with the alumni?"

Andrew chuffed, and somehow turned an even deeper red, bordering on purple. "No one would believe that. And even if they did, you would ruin your own reputation in the process."

"That might be true. Or the public might feel sympathetic toward a kid you abandoned as a baby being thrust into an unknown world of privilege and doing anything he could to gain his father's approval." Theo played with the bow on the side of my dress as he spoke. "As for them believing me...well, the emails I have saved should do the trick. I don't *want* to release any of it, but I will. If you threaten Helen's academic future or bother her in any way, all the evidence I've saved will come to light. I think I have more of a leg to stand on than you do, but if I go down, at least I'll take you down too."

Andrew was struck speechless, and honestly, so was I. I would never let Theo go down, but the fact that he was willing to, that he would ruin himself to save me, struck me so deep in my heart, I'd never lose it. This was love, real love, and it was mine.

"That's enough, Andrew."

The three of us whipped around to find a stony-faced Miranda in the doorway.

She turned her attention to Theo and me. "You two should go. Andrew and I have a lot to discuss."

Theo didn't hesitate. He took my hand and pulled me along, away from his father. At the doorway, Miranda stepped to the side, but she touched Theo's arm to stop him.

"You will never have anything to worry about. Both of you. I'll take care of this." She gave me a fast hug, then patted my shoulders. "Madeline would want that. She would adore the two of you together. So, go, be in love, and don't worry for even a second."

"Thank you," I whispered, my throat tight with emotion. Mads *would* definitely adore Theo.

Taking Miranda at her word, we ran to the front door, and kept running, past Theo's car, down the driveway, and through a narrow passage between houses to a set of wooden steps that led down to the beach.

We didn't stop until we hit wet sand, then Theo fell on his butt, pulling me down on top of him to straddle his thighs. This stretch of beach was private and deserted, so it was just the two of us and the roar of the ocean.

He held my face in his hands. "Never, ever scare me like that again. Find another way."

I nodded as much as I could with him holding me. "I'm sorry, so sorry. I had to think on the fly, and that was the best I came up with. I couldn't let him do that to us. I just couldn't."

He dropped his forehead to mine and exhaled. "Jesus, baby, I love you so much. You went to battle for me. For us."

"Of course I did. You're mine, Theo. I'll always protect you and what we have. No one gets to decide our future except for you and me." I touched my mouth to his and sighed. "Do you think he's done?"

"I think Miranda will make sure he is."

I thought he was very right. I was almost certain Andrew Whitlock was being flayed alive by his wife, and he deserved every second of it.

Scooting closer, I wrapped my arms and legs around him, hugging him with all the fierceness I possessed. "I really am sorry I hurt you, Theodore. I couldn't look at you when I was doing it or I would have broken. I just...I love you. I never want you to doubt that."

"Love you too, Tiger. Believe me, after that, I'll never doubt you again. *Never.*"

He held me with the same ferocity edged with his Theo tenderness that settled my soul against his. We stayed like that, two wounded, world-weary people who had taken down our walls for each other, baring all our soft places, knowing we'd be safe.

To think, I could have missed this if I hadn't had my Mads's words in my head. I would have still been sinking under the weight of my pain instead of swimming with Theo in the light.

Life hurt. It took and took. I'd learned that way too young. It took me longer to see the flip side. Sometimes life offered up something so big, it didn't erase the past, but it overshadowed it. It made the hard, painful past seem a lot less important than the soft, safe present.

That was Theo and me.

He was the good, necessary kind of trouble I could keep getting into for a long, long time.

He nipped at my jaw and pressed a sweet kiss to my cheek. "Love you, Tiger."

"Love you too, Theodore."

Mmm...yeah. This just might be forever.

Epilogue

Theo

Five Years Later

I WAS ON MY ass, skateboard rolling in the opposite direction, being pointed and laughed at. Not for the first time, I wondered how I'd gotten into this position. Then a hand reached for me, helping me off the ground, checking me over for breaks, and I remembered.

Helen.

"Are you broken?" She tried to hold back her laugh, but Luciana was egging her on, snorting out little giggles, so it was no good. Helen burst out laughing again. "How can a person be so incredibly athletic and have no sense of balance?"

I threw my arms out. "Baby, I think I'm done trying to be a skater for you. It's hopeless."

She tucked herself against me, petting my chest. "I think you're right. I don't want you broken. You'll be no good to me then. I need you at full power."

"Gross." Luciana covered her ears and started humming at top volume. "I can't hear you. I'm going inside to barf."

She ran up our long driveway and into the house we'd bought and moved into a year ago, slamming the door on us. Helen and

I weren't her parents, but we were close enough to that role that when we kissed, we grossed her out and she always left the room. At this point, we sometimes did it to drive her crazy. Other times, because we couldn't help ourselves.

The truth was, Luc was seventeen and still as sweet as she was when I met her at twelve. I was pretty proud to say the worst part of her life was having to witness her sister and brother-in-law kissing every once in a while.

I picked up my skateboard and touched my lips to Helen's forehead. "Are you disappointed I'm putting this thing into retirement?"

"Nope." We started up the drive, our arms around each other. "Truthfully, I'd be jealous of you skating while I'm sitting on the bench for the next few months."

I patted her side and the swell of her belly. "You'll be the one teaching her to skate. You and Luc. I'll teach her to ride a bike."

She gently elbowed my ribs. "You can ride a bike? You don't fall?"

Tossing the skateboard into the garage, I rounded on my wife and took her in my arms, nuzzling her neck until she was giggling. *That's right.* I made Helen Ortega fucking giggle. I did it on the regular too. We'd built the kind of life together that made it easy to relax, breathe, and enjoy every second.

"I seem to remember balancing you on my face last night and no one fell."

She cupped my jaw and brought my mouth down to hers, giving me a long, slow kiss, her tongue sliding and mingling with mine. Her little belly, round with our daughter, pressed into me. It was a new feeling, but Christ, it was so sexy and sweet at the same time, I found myself constantly taking her into my arms so I could have more of it.

"That was me doing the balancing, Theodore," she murmured. "Don't try to take credit for that. I've got a baby on board and I managed to take a ride."

"Really, baby? Trash talk after all the times I made you come?"

She melted into me, head on my shoulder. "Fine. You're very good at a *lot* of things, you're just terrible at skateboarding."

I ran my nose along her crown and grinned to myself. "I'll take it."

After a minute or two, we walked around the side of the house to the back patio, collapsing onto one of our double loungers beside our pool.

Helen and I had gotten married when I graduated from Savage U, but it only took me a year after our showdown with Andrew to get her to agree to wear my ring. Gabe had been pissed Helen and I were engaged before he'd locked down Penelope, but he made it happen, then eventually forgave me and stood beside me as my best man at my wedding.

Helen graduated from Savage U a year early, just like she had planned, got a job as a nurse, and entered her master's program. Now, she worked as a labor and delivery nurse and she absolutely loved it. I didn't know a lot of people who were eager to go to work, but Helen was one of them. The hours were long, and she was on her feet sometimes her whole shift, but there was never a time she dragged ass out the door.

She didn't have to work. Honestly, neither of us did. Madeline McGarvey had left Helen a lot of money. Hells called it "fuck-you money." In other words, my baby was a millionaire. But she didn't take having that kind of change for granted. For her, it was room to breathe, and it had made it easy for us to take permanent custody of Luciana as soon as Hells had the money in the bank.

Helen wove her legs with mine and rested her hand on my stomach, sighing. "Tell me again what we have to do."

I covered her hand with mine, moving her wedding band back and forth with my thumb. "You know what we have to do. You made the list."

"I know, but I need you to tell me out loud so I'm not overwhelmed by all the words in my notes app. If you tell me in your lovely voice, it won't sound like so damn much work."

"Baby," I chuckled, "remember volunteering our backyard for Asher and Bex's wedding shower? That was all you. If it's too much, we'll figure—"

She covered my mouth with her hand. "Don't you dare. It's not too much. It's the perfectly right amount. We bought this house to hold parties, so we're going to hold parties, dammit."

I laughed behind her hand, then I licked it. She snatched it back and tried to snarl, but I kissed it off her.

"We have had parties, and we'll have more parties, but this one—"

"Shut it, Theodore." She knocked her head against my shoulder and gave me one of my favorite red-lipped smiles. "I still have four more months of this pregnancy. You can't treat me like an invalid."

"But, baby," bending forward, I lifted her shirt to kiss her belly, "you're a hot invalid."

She shoved my forehead. "Stop it and help me plan this party."

"I thought Grace was planning it."

"She is, obviously, but it's at our house, so I have to do things. Plus, you know, she's busy with Bash and the baby."

For the first two years of our marriage and a year before that, we'd lived in a rental house halfway between campus and Luciana's school. We'd been hunting for something perfect, something comfortable, private, roomy, but not a mansion. When we found this place, we knew. It was the first big purchase Helen made with her inheritance—and it'd been a-fucking-lot—but we were both pretty certain we'd be living in this house forever.

Our backyard was what had sold me on the place. It was like an oasis away from everything, with a covered patio, pool with attached hot tub, and a wide, but not overly big, expanse of grass, all surrounded by trees to give us privacy. I wasn't any kind of landscaper or anything, but I liked to be outdoors, and within a couple days of living here, this patio with my girl snug in my arms had become my favorite place on earth.

We'd had a lot of parties back here. First a housewarming, then birthdays, Grace's baby shower, our anniversary, and now Asher and Bex's coed wedding shower. Her friends—who had become mine over the years—were really her family. There wasn't a lot she wouldn't do for the people she loved, because that was my little tiger—fierce and protective, with a massive heart.

Luc stuck her head out the patio door. "There's a party a bunch of people I know are going to tonight. Can I go?"

Helen raised a brow. "Where is it?"

Luc checked her phone. "This guy's house. His name is Javi? I don't know him, but I heard his kickbacks are really—"

Helen threw her flip-flop in Luc's direction. "No, ma'am. *I* went to Javi's parties when I was your age. I know exactly what happens at Javi's parties. There is no way in hell you're going to a party at Javi's."

Luc glanced at me, but I shook my head. I'd been to one Javi party, and that was enough for me to know our girl was not going there unless she walked over our dead bodies. And even then, Helen would probably reanimate just to stop her.

Luciana groaned, but she didn't stomp off or curse us out. "Jeez, fine. I didn't really want to go anyway. I'm going to see if some of the girls want to come over and practice makeup tonight. I just got that new palette and I've barely used it." She walked away, typing messages on her phone.

Helen's eyes were wide, then she poked her belly. "Okay, we got lucky with one kid. This one is going to be a hell-raiser, I know it."

Madeline. Helen was surprisingly superstitious, so she didn't like to refer to the baby by her name, but we both knew she'd be Madeline the second we found out we were having a girl.

"I hope she is. She'll be just like her mom, and I happen to like her mom a whole lot." Lifting her shirt, I traced the faint dark line that ran up the center of her. Before Helen got pregnant, I'd never looked twice at another pregnant woman, but her...God, I felt like a teenager again, walking around with a perpetual hard-on. My tiger was sexy always, but the added curves and knowing she was carrying our child sent my attraction to her into overdrive. She even smelled different, and I was constantly sniffing her.

Helen palmed the bulge in my shorts. "Maybe we should let her go to the party so we can have the house to ourselves tonight."

I moved her hand away. I knew this wasn't going anywhere. Not until later, when I could get her alone.

"Wow, you're hard up, aren't you? Willing to sacrifice your sister for some action?"

Helen nodded enthusiastically. "She'll be fine at Javi's."

"Okay," I started to get up, "I'll go tell her."

"No you won't!"

Helen tugged on the back of my shirt until I flopped down and rolled her on top of me. She shifted so her belly wasn't pressed against me, then snuggled under my chin.

We didn't have a lot of this, just sitting and doing nothing, or reading to each other in our favorite chair. We made time to be together—pretty sure it was impossible for us to be apart for longer than one of Helen's shifts—but we were busy. With the house, friends, Luc, her job, and mine...

Working with Lock in maintenance at Savage U had opened up an unexpected career avenue for me. I got back into my love of fixing cars, and it took on a life of its own from there. One of the mechanics there knew a guy who owned a custom shop in

Savage River. I started apprenticing there my junior year of college, learning *everything* there was to know about making cars run. When I graduated with a business degree, I stayed on at Savage Customs as an assistant manager. Two years ago, I'd used most of my savings to buy in as a co-owner.

Andrew hated it, but he wasn't a big part of my life anymore, so his opinions were background noise. A few years ago, Miranda basically gave him an ultimatum: get with it or get out. He didn't pull his head out of his ass, so she divorced him, but she didn't walk away from Helen and me. She became the steady support system I'd never had, and she actually got a kick out of me going my own way and not following Andrew's path. She wholeheartedly approved, in fact.

It was strange, really. I never thought I'd have that, even when I was bending over backward to seek it out from Andrew. I didn't need Miranda's approval, but it felt really good to have it.

Helen and I spent a little more time relaxing and talking about the things we had to do to the house to prepare for the party next weekend. Then it was time to go inside to make dinner.

Luciana liked to help Helen cook. Sometimes, they let me chop. Other times, I was relegated to being their fan club. Tonight was the latter. I sat on one of the stools at the island in the center of our kitchen, going over some paperwork for Savage Customs while they prepared fish tacos and fresh pico de gallo.

Helen and Luciana kept bumping into each other, then they gave each other little shoves, laughing every time. I put my phone down to watch. Luciana didn't see the way her sister looked at her, but I did. Helen loved her like she was her kid, and it was there, written all over the way she watched Luciana cut tomatoes, in the soft curve of her lips, the warmth in her eyes at the small, everyday acts they did together.

I used to think I had to tell Helen to be soft. That was before I really got it. Helen didn't need to be told to be soft. She had always been that way. Not for a jackass kid in his stepmom's luxury car who'd told her he didn't want to be responsible for her feelings. No, the kid I used to be hadn't deserved Helen's kind of soft. The man I was now got to see it and revel in it every day. I didn't have to ask. That was just who she was when she was well loved and she loved well.

Helen was a rolling storm. She was the spark in the air, the scent of rain right before it fell. Helen was lightning touching down in an open field and the gentle breeze that carried the clouds. She was the steady mist that fell on thirsty ground and made it thrive.

Helen Ortega-Whitlock was soft.

Soft like thunder.

BRIGHT LIKE MIDNIGHT

Are you dying to find out what happened in that dorm room between Zadie and Amir? Find your answers in Bright Like Midnight, coming in April 2022!

Pre-order now: mybook.to/BrightLikeMidnight

Make no mistake, Zadie Night, I am the bad guy here.

The first time I laid eyes on Amir Vasquez, he held me hostage in my dorm.

You made me a promise.

I swore to myself my second year at Savage U would be different from the last. No more hiding from things that go bump in the night. I'm dating now. Making friends. Living my life.

But then someone starts leaving me notes and whispering my name in the dark, scaring me right back into my shell.

Are you my pet?

I'm shy and soft. Amir is dominant and hard. He stole a kiss once, and then he left me.

I should stay far away from him. But you know what they say about the devil you know...

Do I own you?

Amir will protect me, but not without cost.

I'm his, to do with as he pleases.

He thinks it's a punishment.

But what he doesn't know is I haven't stopped thinking about him since he was my captor.

No one's going to hurt you.

I'm safe from harm if I'm with him, because he's the biggest bad on campus.

Show me your whole universe.

And somewhere along the way, he became my haven, too.

You should be scared of me.

I can't believe I've fallen for the villain.

PLAYLIST

Skater Shawty-Crisaunt
Maneater-Hall and Oates
Pretending-Anthony Amorim
Stay Away-MOD SUN, Machine Gun Kelly
Hollow-Belle Mt.
Landfill-Daughter
I'm a Mess-Bebe Rehxa
brutal-Olivia Rodrigo
She Tastes Like Summer-Spilt Milk Society
Crush-Tessa Violet
Hands To Myself-Selena Gomez
Toxic-Melanie Martinez
Hurt Again-Julia Michaeals
Panic Room-Au/Ra
I've Had Enough-Melina KB
Alcatraz-Oliver Riot
The broken hearts club-Garret Nash
Oblivion-Grimes
Sweetest Thing-Allman Brown
Adore You-Harry Styles

https://open.spotify.com/playlist/1qh7ASzGcxoCpJcidt8zux?si=bf45d28c4c4740e8

Stay in Touch

Come join me in my reader group!
  Julia Wolf's Sublime Readers
  Follow me on TikTok!
  https://www.tiktok.com/@authorjuliawolf

Acknowledgements

Welcome back to Savage River!

How did you enjoy your visit?

When I tell you I was absolutely giddy to write this book and explore who Helen really is under her pretty red lipstick...I loved every second of discovering her. Helen is my book girlfriend. I couldn't have written this book without the enthusiasm of my readers. You were begging for Helen's story and you made me excited to add another series on to my Savage River universe.

Thank you to my author soulmates, Alley Ciz and Laura Lee, and my extended chat group/sanity keepers/sound boards (you know who you are!).

Thank you to my beta readers, Jenny and Jen, and the other Jen in my life, my PA. So many high quality Jens!

To my sweet, sweet Kate Farlow, thank you for my beautiful cover *and* the wonderful alternate paperback cover. I love them so much. Did I mention I'm in love? I really do love them.

Thank you to Monica and Rosa for polishing my words. This is my twenty-something book and I still have no idea how to use a comma or the correct use of lay/lie/laid/lying/laying. Luckily you're nice to me and pet my head.

About the Author

Julia Wolf is a bestselling contemporary romance author. She writes bad boys with big hearts and strong, independent heroines. Julia enjoys reading romance just as much as she loves writing it. Whether reading or writing, she likes the emotions to run high and the heat to be scorching.

Julia lives in Maryland with her three crazy, beautiful kids and her patient husband who she's slowly converting to a romance reader, one book at a time.

Visit my website:

http://www.juliawolfwrites.com

Also By

The Seasons Change

Falling in Reverse

Stone Cold Notes

The Savage Crew

Start a Fire

Through the Ashes

Burn it Down

Standalones

Built to Fall

Rocked

The Unrequited Series

Unrequited

Misconception

Dissonance

Blue is the Color

Times Like These

Watch Me Unravel

Such Great Heights

Under the Bridge

The Never Blue Duet

Never Lasting

Never Again

The Sublime

One Day Guy

The Very Worst

Want You Bad

Fix Her Up

Eight Cozy Nights